"Sil Evareen—Ibex's myth. Some three thousand years ago there was a widespread high tech civilization here, and they were on the verge of leaving the planet. Then came war. And the pestilence and famine that followed. They pounded their cities into rubble. Killed off all but a remnant—they did it to themselves—rid themselves of their technology. Used up all the metals, hydrocarbons, whatever . . . And they're still fighting each other out there. I don't think the Ibex wars will be over until every indigene is dead.

"Sil Evareen is supposed to be the single city that survived from the ancient time of glory. The few here who bother to interest themselves think it's just a golden age myth."

It was strictly illegal to investigate Ibex beyond the electrified walls of the shut-in spaceport—but Aleytys had to do just that. For a thirty-years-old message from the mother she had never known pointed the Star Hunter toward that mythical city . . . and a world of implacable hostiles.

JO CLAYTON
has also written:

MOONGATHER   *(Duel of Sorcery #1)*
MOONSCATTER   *(Duel of Sorcery #2)*
DIADEM FROM THE STARS
LAMARCHOS   *(Diadem #2)*
IRSUD   *(Diadem #3)*
MAEVE   *(Diadem #4)*
STAR HUNTERS   *(Diadem #5)*
THE NOWHERE HUNT   *(Diadem #6)*
GHOSTHUNT   *(Diadem #7)*

THE
SNARES
OF IBEX

JO CLAYTON

DAW BOOKS, INC.
DONALD A. WOLLHEIM, PUBLISHER

1633 Broadway, New York, NY 10019

DAW Collectors' Book No. 602

First Printing, November 1984

1 2 3 4 5 6 7 8 9

PRINTED IN U.S.A.

I

HANA

I, Hana Esgard, was in my eighth year when the she-Vryhh came. My hip was hurting and I couldn't sleep so I was up in the tower garden watching the storm clouds rumble-tumble across the plain to be shunted aside by the deflector screens over the Yastroo Enclave. The noise they made was muted by the glass that shut me in and by the forcefield but was still loud enough to excite me, a feeling I liked and courted as often as I could. It was late, past midnight and the streets around Esgard house were empty, the whole area was deserted. I don't know why I turned away from the lightning and the boiling clouds but I did look down and I saw her coming toward the House, striding along with that predatory grace they all had, those secretive wide-faring Vrya.

She-Vryhh. An ugly locution. Esgard doesn't like me to say it and frowns at me, so I don't say it aloud. But I think it. I've heard them called worse before and since, but they're Esgard's bread and butter so he grovels at their feet—not that they seem to care about that, they ignore courtesy and rudeness alike. They need nothing urgently, as far as I can see, so they can walk away from anything that might irritate them.

She came down the street, her long cloak blown by the wind the screen let through. Coming here. I knew it. Why else would a Vryhh be in Yastroo? Father always sent everyone away when he met his Vryhh clients. He's a secretive man. Perhaps I should say *was*—but I don't know that for sure, not now. I won't know before Aleytys gets back. Aleytys the famous Wolff Hunter. Easy to fool as the stupidest

Worm. Half-Vryhh, as arrogant and ruthless as the worst of them. If she gets back. She—ah, that's confusing. The first she I was talking about was no half-breed. That she came— what?—more than a quarter of a century ago. Funny. How much longer a quarter of a century sounds than a mere twenty-five years. I was eight then. I said that. My mother left the next year. She got tired, she said, of having only a fraction of a man since that was all Esgard would afford her. She didn't like him spending so much time with that she-Vryhh. And she was irritated beyond enduring because he barred her from helping with the business and bored beyond enduring with the idleness that filled her life. There was nothing for her to do but gossip with other women or take lovers and she didn't care to do either. She didn't like women much and found an occasional lover no more satisfying than the occasional attention she got from her husband. She left with a free-trader, saying she might go hungry now and then or get killed but at least she wouldn't die of boredom. Left me too, but she never liked me much and would always shy away from my left side. Esgard was a lot older than her when he married her. He should have known better, old fool. So should she. His ways were set and he wasn't about to change them.

He usually brought his Vryhh clients up to the tower garden. Funny. They spend years zipping about in those fancy ships of theirs, shut inside tight walls like nutmeats, but let them hit ground they had to have open space, lots of it. And green things and Nature with a capital N. Force fields don't count if they're far enough away so they can be ignored.

When I saw her swinging down the street I knew she was coming here even though it was far after business hours. The Vrya never took thought about discommoding others. There was always a market for what they had to sell so they cared nothing for anyone's feelings or inconvenience. Esgard would bring her up here, I was sure of that, and I looked about for a place to hide so I could see what was going to happen. In the tower garden our trees had their growing points lopped off, so they spread out wider than they were tall, becoming more like tall bushes than real trees, but they were big enough, any one of them, to hold a runty eight-year-old girl. I chose an ancient chanda, the tree nearest the furniture, three armchairs about a pedestal table. The chanda's bark was smooth and hard, with small spreading cracks and runnels of hardened sap like black glass that had a sweet-tart smell and a sweet-tart taste. I settled myself close under the flat, broad crown, my cheek against the bark, my eyes on breaks in the lacy foilage where I could see the chairs and table and a little space around them.

He brought her up to the garden as I thought he would. She looked like any Vryhh, no older, no younger, an indeterminate age somewhere between nineteen and thirty. How old she really was I hadn't the faintest notion. I'd seen her before, I thought, though I couldn't be sure, they all looked much alike; put a woman's clothing on some of the men and they'd be dainty enough to be taken for women. She had that thin pale skin that flushed so readily with anger or lust, the bright green eyes, the red hair. That night she wore her hair braided tightly and wound close about her head. She looked tight all over like she was doing something against her inclination, driven by a need she didn't want to admit. Esgard had on his trading face so there wasn't much to see in it, but I could tell he was tired. The she-Vryhh didn't know that or didn't care. She settled into the chair Esgard indicated but as soon as he'd seated himself, she popped up again and began pacing about the tiles, glancing out the curved windows at the storm breaking over the Enclave, touching the plants as she moved past them. She walked right under me, I could have spit on her and thought of doing it, but I knew Esgard would be furious and punish me so I didn't.

She moved behind Esgard, smoothed down the tuft of gray hair at the back of his head, a quick almost tender gesture. "I need a favor, Ken-ti," she said. She brushed her fingertips down the side of his face. Her hard-edged tautness was suddenly gone, she was as soft as a new-opened silkflower and, oh, promising. Yes, that was it, promising things an eight-year-old didn't understand and didn't want to understand. I burned. I wanted to jump out of the tree and attack her, but my hip was throbbing and I knew I'd fall on my face and make a fool of myself so I stayed where I was.

Esgard caught hold of the hand, kissed the palm, then pulled

it away from him. He chuckled and I was comforted. He
wasn't fooled by her. "Favor, Shareem?" he said.

Up in my tree I was fuming. He was using her personal
name without any honorific and there was a teasing in his
voice that spoke of other intimacies.

She pulled away from him, the nervousness creeping back,
banishing the softness, and went to stand by the glass. The
lightning had stopped for the moment and the rain was coming
down in sheets; though it was shunted aside by the forcefield,
it made things very dark in the Enclave in spite of the efforts
of the street lights, turning the glass into an obsidian mirror.
Her reflection looked embarrassed and uncertain, a little uneasy.
The fingers of her left hand tapped an edgy rhythm on the
glass. "I played the fool on Elderwinnesh."

"The Revel?"

"Ummm. There was a man."

"When is there not? That's never bothered you before."

"None of them ever gave me a fever before. I feel such a
fool. I knew I shouldn't have let him take me away from the
Temple." She shrugged, turned to face Esgard, leaned against
the glass, her shoulders pressed flat against it, her hands
pressed flat beside her hips. "Some kind of swamprot, I
suppose. With a long incubation period so I didn't suspect
anything. Caught me hopping the worst possible minute,
when I was halfway through the white-water suns. You know
that shiptrap. I can't even remember now why I was there. A
little crazy in my head already, I suppose. White-water spat
me out like a prune pit. I crashed. Like a lot before me. On
Jaydugar. Lucky to live through it, I suppose. But sick, eeh,
sick enough to forget who and what I was." She pushed
away from the glass and began walking about again, not quite
so agitated as before "The swamprot, or whatever it was,
cancelled out my antifertility shot. I was close to the edge
anyway. Hadn't crashed, I'd have renewed, but no use regret-
ting what can't be changed. I was too sick to remember
anyway. Or defend myself from . . . well, it's done. I've
got a daughter, Ken-ti. I left her there when I came away."
Her fingers twitched, her movements turned abrupt, almost
awkward. She came and stood behind her chair, her hands
closing tight over its soft padded back. After a moment's

strained silence, she said, "I couldn't bring her with me." She wasn't trying to convince Esgard, he wouldn't need convincing, more likely need explaining why she was making such a fuss. He said nothing. Trying to convince herself. Hah.

"There was danger and difficulty ahead of me. And I couldn't know how much she might have inherited from me and how much from him. If she was all his, I didn't want to see. . . . I left her a letter. I left her your name. Left her the names Ibex and Yastroo and where to find Ibex, the coordinates. And I've set things up with our Tetrad. That was a mess. Had to worm about for days before they'd agree, but it's sealed now and no one. . . ." Her lips snapped together and she scowled over Esgard's head. "No one can change that. Or get around it. When she gets here—if she gets here—send the message down the pipe and she'll be picked up. If she wants to come. I suppose if she gets this far she'll want to finish it. I would. I think I would. A lot of things might happen. She probably won't come. But I gave her a chance." She fell silent and stood kneading the chair's padded back, her bright head bent.

She ran off, I thought. Ran off and abandoned her child. I felt vindicated. That arrogant graceful careless Vryhh whose slightest word meant more to Esgard than . . . she ran off and left the cub she'd dropped. She's fussing now, but she doesn't really care what happens to it, not if she wouldn't bring it with her. She creates this fuss to make herself look prettier, not like what she really is. I pressed my cheek hard against the satin bark and sneered at her.

Esgard waited without speaking. He saw through her, oh yes he did. Finally he said, "Twenty, maybe thirty years. A long time to wait. What's the profit for me?"

She looked up, the unease smoothed from her as if the storm outside had sneaked in and washed it away. She stepped around the chair, settled herself in it, crossed her legs and rested one narrow shapely hand on her knees. "My services," she said crisply. "For a specified number of projects within a specified length of time. It's no big thing what I'm asking you—to record what I say and send a message if circumstances require."

"Ah, but there's trust. Trust with the knowledge of a half-Vryhh daughter, her location, the fact that you care to some degree what happens to her. That's worth rather a lot."

She tapped the nail of her forefinger on the polished wood of the table top. "Ah, but think what the loss of that trust would cost you. You've served the Vrya well, Kenton Esgard—and served yourself equally well." She chuckled, a low musical sound with none of the harshness that had vibrated in her voice such a little time before.

"I'm not a young man, Shareem." Esgard's voice had a tight, held-in quality. "Sixty years I've known you. And I wasn't that young when we first met."

She blinked several times, staring at him as if she had difficulty comprehending what he was trying to say to her. "So?"

"In thirty years I might be dead."

Her eyes widened, then narrowed to slits as she shook her head. "Nonsense. You're barely middle-aged for your kind. Well?"

He contemplated her a long minute. "Time specified?"

"One year standard."

"Three."

She shook her head, smiled slightly. "Two years standard. Max." She waved a long forefinger gently back and forth. "Max, my friend."

He tipped a hand in a lazy gesture that both accepted and deprecated the limitation. "Ten projects."

"You're pushing, my friend." Her smile tightened. "Three."

"Seven. Otherwise this isn't worth my while."

"Nonsense. Five. Max."

"Guaranteed?"

"Guaranteed."

"Double my usual commission."

"Missions reduced to three or no doubling."

"Agreed."

"Done." The she-Vryhh leaned back in her chair with a long sigh as if she really cared about getting this thing done. Esgard relaxed also, smiling a little, his cream-licking smile. He was entirely satisfied with his bargain. She made a face at him, acknowledging her recognition of this, then turned her

head and stared out the window at the storm that was beginning to pass on into the east. The moon's glow was breaking
through the western edge of the clouds, a patchy light that
only heightened the darkness elsewhere. "She was just beginning to talk when I left. She'd be three, maybe four standard
now," she said after a while. "She had hair like mine, a little
lighter perhaps, but that could change with time. Her eyes
were a much bluer green than mine. I suppose that too could
change with the passage of time. I named her Aleytys—the
homeless one, the one without a place to lay her head. I don't
think I was quite sane even though I'd recovered from the
fever, stuck on a mudball with only half a chance of getting
off. She might change even her name if she wants no part of
me, though it's harder than one thinks to change a name, it's
like cutting away a bit of yourself somehow, but she might
want to rid herself of anything that reminded her of me. Hard
to say, I don't know her well enough. She was born on the
ship-trap monster Jaydugar in a mountain valley that the folk
who live there call a vadi. A river named the Raqsidan cuts
through it. She'll know my full name and sept, might even
have the letter though she'll have passed through several hells
getting this far, I'm sure of that, all too sure, and probably
lost the book along the way. What else? Never mind, I'm
babbling. You don't have to remember all that." She dipped
into a pouch on her belt, pulled out a disc. "All I can think of
to identify her is on here. Dates. People. Events. What she'll
be like, well I don't know, Ken-ti. We're a vindictive lot, the
Vrya, I mean. Almost all of us, as if it's in the genes. Be wary
of her but don't worry about me. Whatever she is, I can
handle that. And will." She touched the back of her hand to
her forehead, sat with eyes shaded, closed, for several minutes,
then she stood, stepped away from the table. "That's it, my
friend. Send a call when you have the first project set up. My
two years start the moment I step back into this room, right?
Right."

They left, Esgard thumbing off the lights as he went through
the door. In the new darkness, the clouds that crossed the
moon's face made the moonglow inside the room dance with
shadow. I watched them play, moonlight with cloudshadow,
and nearly fell asleep in the tree. A cramping muscle in my

buttock woke me. I almost couldn't move I was so stiff from
staying still so long. I couldn't feel my hip at all and that
made me afraid. I half-fell down the tree and lurched to my
room with just enough sense left not to call the serviteur that
looked after me before I washed off the traces of sap and
changed into a clean nightrobe.

Thirty years later the half-breed Vryhh Aleytys came to the
House of Esgard looking for that message. Whether she had
the book or not, the one with Shareem's letter in it, I don't
know, nor does it really matter; who she was, that was plain
enough.

But I lied to her by implication and omission. I played her
like a puppet, making her dance to my pulling. It was and is a
good feeling. The day may come when I have to answer for
what I've done, but regret it I never will.

II

ALEYTYS IN YASTROO

1

Aleytys sauntered down the tree-lined Promenade that cut through the center of the free-trade sector of the Yastroo Enclave—sauntered because she was in no hurry to come to terms with her future, something she'd have to do once she had the information Kenton Esgard was holding for her.

She strolled along, thinking:

I took a long, time getting here. I wish I could put this off. I wonder what Esgard is like. Swartheld described him but that doesn't help. His hair's gone gray, his face lined, an old man, testy with folk that waste his time. Tall with a slight stoop, a jumping muscle beside his left eye. The Vrya trust him—at least, my mother did. My mother. . . .

She winced, closed her hands into fists.

Shareem Atennanthan di Vrithian clan Tennath who crashed on Jaydugar and came to the Vadi Raqsidan late one autumn night.

Vajd (who loved me a little once, but no more, no more) told me this while he still loved me:

The night she came, Aab and Zeb rose early, kissing, and the clouds that were piled high about Dandan were whipped to rags by dry winds so the night rains never came. On the Common the bonfires leaped red and gold

13

into the sky, painting warm highlights on the tawdry fair
booths and the posturing slave women and the drovers
selling the slaves' services. A woman dressed in black and
white sat on the steps of a caravan. Her hair was long and
straight, curling only at the ends, shining like avrishum
fiber in the light of the small silver lantern that hung over
her head. She was a glowing woman with greenstone eyes
that glittered with fever. Her hair was redder than the fires,
red as Horli when she rises alone. There is a beauty that
catches the beholder in the throat and robs him of the will
to turn away. She had that. She sat very still, looking at
nothing, her hands resting in her lap. The Azdar came. He
stared at her, the pale tip of his tongue moving around and
around his lips. She looked him over coolly then lowered
her eyes. He reached out and wrapped his hand about her
hair at the nape of her neck. "What is your name, woman?"
His voice was a beast's growl. "You come with me, I pay
well."

She hardly seemed to see him, even when he forced her
head up and back.

A caravanner came into the circle of light cast by the
silver lantern, a short dark man with hard black eyes. He
was muscled like a bull gav and had a fleshy mouth that
was small and tight and greedy. He smiled as he stepped in
front of the woman. From his belt he pulled a sharag.
Dangling the jagged strands in front of her, he said softly,
"Speak, woman, tell this fine gentleman your name."

The indifference left her face and the fever glitter in her
eyes fired hotter. The change that animation made in her
was startling. Suddenly, instead of a marble and copper
goddess, she was a vital passionate creature. Magnificent.
"Shareem Atennanthan di Vrithian." She spat the words
at him. Azdar pushed past the man, picked the woman up
and slung her over his shoulder. "I'll send the price
tomorrow. Azdar's bond."

And so me, Aleytys thought. How ancient and unreal it
seems.

She wore gray from toe to crown, trim gray shipsuit, long
loose gray wool mantle edged with silvercoat fur, gray suede

boots, gray suede gloves, a gray chiffon turban, twisted round and round her head, one end caught up in the twist on the far side, hiding her hair, veiling her face from the middle of her nose to her chin. Veiling her face, hiding her hair, because face and hair were becoming just a bit too well known. It was one thing to confront Kenton Esgard, another to proclaim herself Wolff's most notorious Hunter to the Enclave where there was more than one who might have strong reservations about her presence.

Merchants walked with sober dignity along the promenade, alone or in groups gravely conversing. The whole street was discretion made visible, with a suppressed vitality like a smell hidden away inside walls, hints of which kept trickling out. The goods passed by overhead, never descending into the gravity well of the world (that would be foolishly expensive), transferred hold to hold or stored a time in the circling warehouses, but the trading was done on the ground where being could sit with being around small tables over a drink of this or that and chat about possibilities never quite defined but fully understood nonetheless. Where they could tap the planetary core for power to run computers the more boastful swore could reconstitute the universe on the basis of a single atom.

Aleytys sauntered along the Promenade, the fur trim on her coat whipping about her booted ankles, her arms swinging free with her movements, gloved fingers brushing against the soft coarse cloth of the long coat. Yastroo Enclave. She clicked her tongue in the double taps. Yas-troo En-clave. An irregular circle, sliced into six reasonably equal parts radiating from the central dome where the descendants of Memephexis dwelt and collected rents and oversaw the running of the Enclave. Six sectors: Free Traders, touchy, suspicious, reacting constantly to snubs never offered; Cavaltis Hegemony, belligerently insular, no outsiders need apply; Singarit Empire, dangerous, powerful, better left alone, tending to avenge insults with extravagant violence, a nuclear bomb to obliterate a pesky mosquito; Chwereva Company, Wei-Chu-Hsien Company, Ffynch Company, hold onto your back teeth and read the fine print and have your food shipped in from outside, in other words no different from any other Company sphere.

Her bootheels clicked down, her toes lifted in time with the names beating in her head. Kenton Esgard. Ken-ton Es-gard. Yas-troo En-clave, heel-toe, heel-toe, don't think, no, don't think or you won't go on. Don't think, let the clicking of your feet, the names in your head drown out your fears, your uncertainties, your reluctance. She was pushing herself forward, fueled by will alone, like pushing upstream against a flood. She wasn't ready to face her mother, wasn't ready now, perhaps never would be, was frightened of what she might find out. But she knew she should confront this fear—confront it and put it behind her. Should. A marching word. Should-should. She was confortable enough on Wolff. She had a place she fitted rather well, a life she enjoyed no matter how she might complain about its constraints. But *should* was driving her. So she listened to the click-scrape of her feet, listened to the names slipping through her head and tried to ignore the fears that crawled beneath them.

Small greenspaces broke the monotony of the muted stone façades, the row of manicured conifers. Men and women sat talking over streaming cups of cha or kaffeh, now and then speaking into witness circuit black boxes as they finalized deals in the cool sunny morning.

Cool morning, fresh with promise. It felt strange to be out and away from Wolff without the strictures of time and act enforced by a formal Hunt. She felt as if she'd been tied in fetal position an eon or two, then cut suddenly loose so that she was only now working the cramps out of her body.

She read the nameplates as she moved past. Free traders, a litany of famous and not-so-famous names of families, clans, partnerships, line kin. No Companies here—or perhaps only Companies in embryo, without the reach of the sphere holders, the world owners, the power wielders that wore worlds like charms on a watchchain. Traders and agents whose ships went anywhere, carried anything. Mashoupan Brothers, Zenosy Lines, Xortuhakh and Lees, Malinq and Daughters, tre-Jatell Consortium. And on and on.

She tugged the veil out from her mouth, tired of tasting the gauze. Funny to think of Swartheld marching along here like a prowling tars or a bit of Starstreet thrust into this decorum. Swartheld . . . ah, Madar. Gray coming in on us . . . furious

. . . shouting . . . cold . . . throwing ultimatums at me. . . .
"No," she whispered. "I won't think of that." Ken-ton
Es-gard. Heel-toe, click-clack. Breathe in. Breathe out. I
don't have to think about that. Think about here. Think about
the years getting here. How many years? Count them. Right.
She spread out her hands, folded a finger or thumb down as
she ticked off the stages of her convoluted journey to this
placid street.

(Thumb) Raqsidan to Romanchi, off of Jaydugar, one;
(forefinger) Lamarchos to !Ikwasset slave pens, one; (second
finger) Incubating on Irsud, one. Maybe; (ring finger) Drifting with the smuggler Arel along the spiral arm to Maeve,
one. Maybe—she passed hastily over this, it was painful
remembering her first meeting with Grey; (little finger, thumb,
forefinger) University, three years; (second finger) Kell and
the hares of Sunguralingu and parading myself before the
escrow board on Helvetia, the gaping faces, the speculative
eyes, the disbelief, the interminable questions—ah, but that's
over, no need to bother about that any more, one year; (ring
finger) Rest, settling into my house on Wolff, one year; (little
finger) Haestavaada and the escrow board again, more gapers,
an endless string of them, but I got my ship in the end so
perhaps it was worth it this time, one year; (thumb) trying the
ship, tentative forays into life on Wolff, riding with Grey,
buying a stallion and some mares of my own, oh what delight
to watch them running in a pasture and know they're mine
and the pasture is mine, the last payment on the house and
land and that's all mine now, one year at that; (forefinger)
The Cazarit Hunt, Stavver and my son who hates me so much
he wouldn't even keep the name I gave him, ah damn,
escrow board again. Not so much trouble this time but Madar!
the hassle from people wanting to talk to me. Home to Wolff
and more problems, more than I dare think about, most of
them, yes, most of them I created for myself. Never mind.
How long? About a year.

So how much is that?

Roughly—very roughly—twelve years-standard.

Twelve years from ignorant mountain girl about to be
burned for a witch to notorious Hunter who a lot of folk
would pay to see burned as a witch or whatever.

She sighed and began watching the name plates again, looking for Esgard House. Backed up against the curtain wall, that's what Swartheld said. An old man with a restless shift to him, Swartheld said. Shrewd old devil, dealing in art objects as well as serving as intermediary between the Vrya and the folk who want their services. Talk about irony—he could have been the one to set up the link between my great, etc. grandfather, the murdering malicious bastard Kell, and that cabal on Sunguralingu. He'd sneered gently at the facism samples Swartheld showed him, dismissed him without interest and without any suspicion about his motives, or so Swartheld said.

Aleytys took a deep breath of the silky air and sighed with pleasure. It was, in spite of all uncertainties, very good to be alive. She laughed aloud, grinned at the stares from those around her.

Kenton Esgard. Esgard House. An elegant bronze nameplate. Words engraved in the pared-down grace of interlingue symbols. The façade was warm brown stone laid in intricate interlacing, no windows, nothing to break the race and weave of the narrow stone slabs. The door was unadorned, tight-grained wood hand-rubbed to a deep umber glow. She ran her tongue a last time across her upper lip, tasting the dry acridness of the veil, the salinity of the line of sweat drops dotting her lip. Then she tapped her forefinger below the symbols.

High overhead a soaring bird gave a harsh wild cry and the vines on the curtain wall rustled, distantly, peasantly. The breeze drifting along the street brought the perfumes of flowers from the greenspaces, the savory smell of roasted nuts and the deep brown bite of kaffeh, the tang of the conifers, the soft mutter of voices, the click of glasses, of metal against metal, footsteps, coughs. These sounds surrounding her, she watched the door slide with a rich elegance of silence into the wall, straightened her shoulders and stepped into the entrance hall. The door behind her closed and the door at the far end opened with the same perfection of speed and silence.

Beyond that door there was a pleasant, low-ceiled room, irregularly shaped, filled with green and blooming plants, with subtly lighted art objects, most of them relatively primitive in style and material. A relaxing room. A welcoming room with its nooks and chairs and glowing tapestries and fingerstones and a thousand small delights. A subtly disarming room. An empty room.

Aleytys looked around, grimaced as she sensed the fine prickles of probes tasting at her and a very good almost unnoticeable psi-damper hovering like the moon shadows that one never quite sees when one turns to look directly at them. Search all you want, she thought. I carry no weapons of the sort your sort of senses can find.

Beginning to be irritated by the lack of response to her intrusion (the probes were automatic and couldn't count as response), she moved to the middle of the room and called, "Kenton Esgard."

"He's not here."

Aleytys swung around. "What?"

A young woman stood in a sudden opening. Fine pale hair fluttered about a longish thin face, blue-tinted lids dropped over almost colorless gray-blue eyes as Aleytys faced her. She came into the room, her left foot dragging a little, her left arm thinner and stringier and stiffer than the right. Neither obvious nor off-putting, these small disabilities enhanced the air of fragility hanging about her. She moved to a table that slanted into the room, cutting off the corner of the nook nearest the door by which she'd entered, settled herself in the chair behind it, picked up a pad of paper in her thin pale fingers. She gazed at the white rectangle for a long moment, then looked suddenly up sideways, past the fall of ash blonde hair, quickly turned her head to stare directly at Aleytys for half a heartbeat, her ice-colored eyes opened wide. An instant later she was looking away, her eyes set once more on the pad she was holding. "What is your reason for wanting Kenton Esgard?" Her voice was so soft and unassertive Aleytys had to strain to hear her.

Aleytys tugged the veil loose, let the gray gauze drop to hang in soft folds beside her face. Talking through it made her uncomfortable; she felt that at any moment she would suck the cloth into her mouth and the thought set her teeth on edge. "That's for his ears only," she said. "If he's not here now, when will he be back?"

A three-part sideways dart of pale eyes exactly as before.
The young woman's skin was silky, her face delicately carved
with high cheekbones, thin straight nose, wide, thin-lipped
mouth. The tip of her tongue touched the shallow fold in her
upper lip, a flicker of pale pink immediately withdrawn.
"You didn't know, Despina?"

"Know what?"

"Esgard retired at the beginning of this year. Six months
ago. I'm Hana Esgard, his daughter."

Aleytys rubbed at her nose. "It's a very old matter," she
said slowly. "Information he's been holding for me until I
could come to claim it."

Hana Esgard's fingers tightened briefly on the pad then she
set it on the table with slow, deliberate movements. "If you
could explain a bit more."

Aleytys scanned the shuttered face, frustrated by her inability to judge all she sensed; she simply knew too little about
the woman. Behind that pale mask churned anger, wariness,
resentment and sly excitement, far too charged for the
circumstances. She didn't understand why it should be so and
it made her doubly disinclined to trust Esgard's daughter—
but then, what other option had she? "My name is Aléytys,"
she said, blinked as she noted a jerking of the long fingers, a
faint tic at the corner of the long mouth. *Is she recognizing
the Hunter or does she know something about my mother's
message?* Aleytys chewed on her lip. There was no way of
telling.

Hana pushed the pad across the table to Aleytys, fished
beneath the table top and added a slim black stylus. "If
you would write a few details about the matter, Despin'
Aleytys."

Aleytys took up the stylus and tapped the end against her
cheek, then bent over the pad. She had strong reservations
about this, but could see see no way around being more
forthcoming if she wanted an answer. She shrugged off her
uncertainty and began writing.

Kenton Esgard:
About thirty years-standard ago, a person left a message

with you for her daughter to pick up later. I have come to claim from you my mother's message.

> *Aleytys,*
> *Jaydugar and Wolff*

Aleytys tore off the top two sheets, read what she had written, wondering if it was too much or too little. She shrugged again, crumpled the second sheet, handed the top sheet across the table to Hana Esgard, not bothering to fold it; the woman would certainly read it before passing it on to her father—if she did pass it on. "This is important to me, Despina Hana," she said quietly. "And might prove important to your father." She turned and started walking toward the entrance hall.

"Wait!" Hana cleared her throat, went on hoarsely. "Aleytys of Wolff. The Hunter?"

Aleytys swung around. The sudden urgency in the woman's voice startled her and roused expectations smothered a moment before. "You know of me?"

"I've heard. . . ." Hana didn't bother going on. She was staring down at the paper, twisting it in her fingers. She lifted her head and for the first time looked full on and for several moments into Aleytys's face, scanning her features as if trying to find something there. A resemblance? Did she know Shareem? Possibly. Or was it a question as to the reliability of whatever rumors had reached her ears?

Aleytys smiled grimly. "Good or bad?"

"What? Oh. Good, I suppose." Hana's mouth trembled into a smile. "Depending on what side one favored." She dropped a thin cold hand on Aleytys's arm. "I'd like to talk to you. Perhaps a cup of cha? Or kaffeh, whichever you prefer. There are things I need to tell you about Esgard. Do you mind?" Hana tugged at her arm. "Please. There's a courtyard in the back that's very pleasant now."

2

Hana stopped talking as a serviteur brought them hot cha and small sandwiches. The court was larger than seemed possible from the narrow façade of Esgard House, filled with flowers

and trees, a wide stretch of lawn and a spare elegant fountain
that added quiet water music to the muted sounds of the wind
playing through the grass and leaves.

Aleytys sipped at the cha then held the cup between her
palms, savoring the warmth, staring into the brown-amber
liquid. "Sil Evareen?"

Hana nodded. "Avalon. The Isles of the Blessed. Nadori-
madana. Kahlak-laksmin." A smile tugged at the corners of
her mouth. "Vrithian."

Aleytys chuckled. "Sometimes I wonder."

"Dreams. Myths." Hana clicked her nails against the side
of the cup. "Sensible persons don't take them for anything
else. Myself, I've heard a Vryhh tell Esgard that the Vrithian
men talk about never has existed."

They sat together at a small table of polished wood in
chairs that were like sawn-off barrels whose stubby backs
were just high enough to hit the sitter in the middle of the
spine.

"Sil Evareen," Hana said. "Ibex's myth. This world isn't
much now." she moved her shoulders impatiently. "When I
was a lot younger, Esgard used to talk to me about it. Showed
me photos from the satellite cameras. You know." She began
speaking in a quick impersonal voice, the words pouring out
in a soft patter as if she'd learned to mouth them but didn't
understand what she was saying, or at least understood it only
intellectually, not in her blood and bones. "Some three to
five thousand years ago there was a widespread high tech
civilization here with a population in the billions. And they
were on the verge of leaving the planet. There are signs they
reached their moon. But that was the end of it."

Aleytys bent forward and touched the back of Hana's hand.
"What happened?"

"According to Esgard, it was war. And the pestilence and
famine that followed. They pounded their cities into rubble.
Killed off all but a remnant—poisons, diseases, missiles,
bombs, hand-to hand weapons, you name it, they did it to
themselves. Rid themselves of their technology. Used up the
metals, hydrocarbons, whatever. They destroyed themselves,
bankrupted the world millennia ago. And they're still fighting
each other out there. I don't think the Ibex wars will be over

until every indigene is dead." She drew in a deep breath, sighed it out. "Sil Evareen is supposed to be the single city that survived from the ancient time of glory. The few here who bother to interest themselves in the indigenes of Ibex think it's just that, a golden age myth. Oh yes." She brushed the back of her hand across her mouth. "It's illegal to have contact with the indigenes, enough to get you barred from the Enclave if anyone is forced to take notice. In spite of that there's some contact beyond the Wall. A bit of trade. Poisons mostly, some drugs, an art object or two. They do know their poisons out there." She shivered delicately. "Esgard got along with the indigenes as well as most, even had his pets." She pinched her lips together, distaste twisting her face. "One time . . . Phah! He brought this filthy savage into the Enclave. Brought it here. If Center had found out, he'd have been skinned. The business confiscated, yes, but that's not what I mean. Hung from the scaffolding outside Center and his skin peeled off, that's what I mean. And me sold." She turned her head away so that Aleytys could see only the soft shining waves of pale blonde hair. A shudder passed along her thin body. "The last ten years especially, he sucked up every whisper he could get about Sil Evareen. He had a stroke, you see, a minor thing, but he was incapacitated for a few days and it reminded him of his mortality." Her head came round, her eyes darted at Aleytys and away again in that shifting glance that was like a nervous tic. It was beginning to irritate Aleytys.

"So," Hana murmured, "Esgard started sending out men and women to dig up what they could. Many of them never got back; still, there was always some idiot willing to chance it for the money he offered. He certainly spent enough on them." Her mouth thinned, her hands wound together, resentment and disapproval blasted out of her. "Finally he left off when he wasn't getting anything new."

"Then he has gone out himself this time?" Aleytys sighed as Hana nodded. "Dead, do you think?"

"Do you have any idea what it's like out there?" Hana unlaced her fingers and lifted her cup. Her hands were shaking. "Unless you know what you're doing, you take two steps past the agri-fence and you're skewered. Well, possibly not you, if your reputation has any truth in it. You'd think grinding themselves back to stoneculture would teach them something, but they keep killing each other." She twisted the cup round and round, staring pensively at the turgid liquid. "No." It was a breath, no more. "Not dead," she said more firmly. "I don't think so. The ones from here they kill, doesn't matter where they kill them, they always bring the heads back and catapult them over the wall. And Center sends its Peacers to collect them. They know Esgard well enough. They'd call me if they picked up his head." She gulped down the cold cha, nearly choked, coughed, set the cup back on the table. "For questioning, you see? What was he doing outside? Why shouldn't we confiscate his business, give us some good reasons, huh? His head hasn't come over. For what that's worth."

"Well, what is it worth?"

"God knows."

"So. Since he took himself into that mess, he must have some idea where he's going. What did he tell you?"

"Nothing." She tilted the cup, stared at the dregs, set it back. "He left piles and piles of notes. On paper, in the computer. He didn't block access to those, not like he did to his Vryhh-data." She cut off the last word as if she regretted saying it. "No one dies in Sil Evareen, that's what the stories say. No one dies." She scratched at the table top, shivering now and then at the harsh sounds she made. "No one dies," she repeated very softly. "He was dealing with Vrya all the time, the same people over and over, year after year, decade after decade and no change in them. It got to him, especially after the stroke. He went slyer than before, more secretive, and that's saying something. And he spent money faster than ever as if it was . . . oh, I don't know . . . as if it was leaves off that bush." She jabbed a thumb at a squat bush not far from the table. "Ancient artifacts, there's a big market in ancient artifacts. I could understand if . . . but that's not why . . . no . . . immortality . . . my god, Hunter, every culture has such stories. If it isn't in the genes . . . he spends . . . spent . . . he . . ." Again she struggled for calm. Her hands squeaked from the pressure as she twisted them together. "Old fool," she burst out. She jerked her hands apart and slapped them flat on the table. "What did you want from Esgard? What do you really want?"

"You read the note." Aleytys made an impatient gesture as if she brushed at cobwebs. "It's not difficult to understand, no hidden meanings. My mother was . . . is . . . Vryhh, she left a message for me with Esgard. It's no secret I'm half Vryhh, that's probably the only true part of the stories about my making the rounds. I want that message. That's all."

Hana reached into a slit in her belt, brought up a crumpled sheet of paper, smoothed it out on the table and gazed down at it. The note. "I'll need more than this to run a search." She drew a forefinger across the paper. "Vryhh. Umm. Esgard kept his Vryhh records apart from the rest of the business, guarded in layers from snoopers, never let anyone know what he was doing. And when he left. . . ." She stopped talking and stared past Aleytys as if she saw something she wanted there.

"When he left?"

"The day he left he changed the access code, sealed it so no one could get at it. I don't have access, I'm sorry. Unless something you know—dates, names, whatever—might let me sidestep the Seal?"

"I know my mother's full name and clan, some dates." She scowled at the backs of her hands, closed them into fists. "Another name. I'll have to think. . . ."

Pale eyes darted up, away, down; shaking hands smoothed across the paper. Hana fought to conceal her eagerness. "The more data I have, the more avenues I can explore, the bigger the chance I can find a path around the Seal. I'm very good at that, you see, I do know computers, even Esgard had to admit that. So he was extra careful. I've tried. . . ." She passed the note across to Aleytys. "This isn't enough."

Aleytys took the paper, reread the scrawled words. She was reluctant to give out more information because she didn't trust Hana any more now than she had when she wrote the note. She could read the mess of emotions working in the woman—anger, resentment, fear, greed, loneliness, ambivalence, doubt, sly amusement, self-pity—so much emotion she could miss even an outright lie and half-lies were possible.

"Your father isn't likely to get discouraged and come back on his own?"

"No."

Aleytys began tearing the thin tough paper into small bits. "My mother—I don't remember her at all, even in dreams." She gathered up the shreds, held her hand at eye-level and let them cascade down. "She crashed, lost her ship, but made it off Jaydugar anyway, it's a long story, and she made it back to Vrithian. I think she did." She closed her eyes, digging into memory, calling back scraps of her conversations with Kell when she was his prisoner on Sunguralingu. She shook her head. "I think she did." She licked a finger, pressed it onto one of the paper bits, turned it over and contemplated the loop of black ink cutting across the dirty white. "Shareem Atennanthan di Vrithian clan Tennath." She scraped her thumbnail across her fingertip, sent the wisp of paper into a soggy arc. "That's about it."

"Thirty years-standard. A long time."

"Getting here wasn't easy."

"Interesting, though, the little I've heard."

Aleytys shrugged.

Hana stirred the bits of paper with her forefinger, pushed them aimlessly around. "If you'd write down all you can remember?" She slanted one of her twitchy glances at Aleytys. "I'll run the information through and see what I can come up with." Aleytys had to strain to hear the soft voice over the sound of wind and water. Hana straightened in her chair, then leaned forward, her body taut. "Hunter." Her voice was louder, almost harsh. "I can't afford your fees. Couldn't come close. But I want you to find him. I want access to the data he sealed from me. I can't get at it on my own; I've tried, oh god, have I tried. I'll try again, but I don't have much hope, he's a cunning old . . . so you better find him."

Aleytys lifted a hand, let it fall. "Damn," she said with quiet fervor.

"Huh?"

"I put my foot down firmly against just this kind of coercion less than a year ago."

"I'm not trying to force . . . you're the one came to me . . . would you at least take a look at Esgard's notes?"

Aleytys sighed. "I suppose I must." She slid round in her chair and sat gazing at the water playing in the fountain, too irritated to look at Hana any longer. So many difficulties. Every time things seemed about to smooth out in front of her, another snag turned up. She was tempted to let the search slide and try again some other time. It would be so easy to go back to Wolff and settle into life there. So easy to say hell with it, I don't need to know. But she did need to know, the need had eaten at her so long there was no way she could escape it. And if she backed away now, the time would never be right again. There'd never be enough time free, never the right circumstances. She passed her hand across her face, straightened her shoulders and faced Hana once more. "When will you finish the run?"

"Can't say until I make some preliminary checks." Hana's anxious body angles were slowly softening. "After you give me your data. If you wish. . . ." She got to her feet, stood with her hand resting lightly on the back of the chair. "If you wish, you may move from the Inn to a guestroom in this House. There'll be rumors already, you must know that. You're too . . . striking . . . to much like the Vrya that used to come to Esgard House not so long ago. Even if you're not recognized, Hunter, there'll be noses sniffing round you. Rumors . . . you see?"

"I see." Aleytys pushed her chair back and stood. "Thanks, Hana. I'll come."

3

Three days pass in a confusion of papers and computer printouts, of searches and tentative sorting out of data. Hana hovers about on the fringes. Aleytys tears at her hair, she is not really good at this kind of activity but slowly she manages to bring a kind of order into the chaos.

4

Aleytys sat in the sunny courtyard, poring over sheets of paper, maps, computer printouts. She looked up when she heard a light tapping against the door. Hana stood in the doorway, a squat serviteur beside her.

Aleytys brushed hair out of her face, rubbed at her eyes. "Noon already?" She blinked up at the sun, surprised to see it hanging directly overhead. "Unnh. Lost track of time." She rubbed at her back, then gathered the maps and other papers and piled them on the chair beside her. "I'm hungry." She shook her head. "Did I forget breakfast again?"

Hana smiled, nodded, then stepped aside to let the serviteur roll past.

As the serviteur slid the dishes from the cavity in his body and set them with delicate precision on the table, Aleytys leaned back in her chair, letting the gentle sounds of water, birdsong and rustling leaves wash away some of her weariness and frustration. "Any results yet from the search?"

Hana seated herself, her eyes a grayish flicker in the habit that made Aleytys want to take hold of her head and set it up straight on her shoulders. She lifted the cha pot and filled a cup. "Nothing so far." She passed the cup across the table to Aleytys. "I keep slamming up against Esgard's Seal. He was lamentably thorough." She filled a second cup. "He knows me far too well. Nothing I've tried—even with your new information. . . ." A hand wave, angularly graceful, acknowledging the Hunter's contribution. "Nothing seems to pierce that seal."

"Perhaps you can't get at the data because Esgard erased it all. Ever think of that?"

"No." The word came out quickly, a gasp of negation. "No," Hana said more slowly. "Esgard, he's not a man to blow away his pods. One way or another he's figuring on coming back, whether he finds Sil Evareen or not, there's not the slightest doubt of that in my mind. Or in his, I think. And he wouldn't even consider having to start from nothing again. That's not his way." There was little overt emotion now in the soft voice, but a stew of resentment behind the quiet mask. "And you," she said, "Aleytys. . . ." She hesitated over the name as if to emphasize her diffidence. More games, Aleytys thought. "Have you found out anything you could use?"

"Mainly that your father was a meticulous note taker." Aleytys took up a sandwich, lifted the top slice of dark bread to inspect the filling. "A few hints. If Sil Evareen exists anywhere, it's across the western ocean on the smaller continent. There should be maps, more than this." She dropped her hand on the paper pile. "I've found mention of several I haven't seen yet. You say he's a cautious man. Would he expect you to organize rescue if he takes overlong to return?"

Hana surprised Aleytys with a chuckle of appreciation, a warm bubbly sound. There were these rare and startling moments when the woman behind the construct Hana showed the world glinted out of the eyes of the mask. "He knows me, Hunter. If I have to go after him, I certainly will. But it'll cost him."

"The Vryhh data."

"That and a few other things."

"So there'll be maps logged into the computer, not conspiciously but available if you hunt for them. This too, Despina Hana—he must have left more comprehensive notes as to his intentions. All this is research, nothing about the route he planned. Check for me, will you? Maps, route, perhaps some journals." She began eating. The whispering silence settled once more on the court.

When the meal was finished, Aleytys laced her hands behind her head and frowned at the leaping water. "One thing puzzles me."

"Only one?" Hana brushed a hand across her mouth, hiding a small smile.

"The satellites can select out and photograph a leaf in a forest of leaves. How could a city exist and escape that kind of surveillance?" Then she laughed, answered herself. "Camouflage, underground, whatever. Still, there would be traces. Good planning and a year's work with a flitter—given a competent surveyor-pilot—would answer all the questions he's left dangling here." She tilted her head, raised a brow.

"There are no flitters on Ibex."

"What?" When Hana said nothing, only stared at her plate. Aleytys sighed and brought her hands down flat on the table. "You didn't mention I'd have to walk if I took this on. All right, tell me."

Hana settled herself in the chair as she went from chat to lecture. "This is what Esgard said. When Memephexis built the Enclave, he had to hurry up the wall because the indigenes objected. Not that they were that dangerous, it was just the constant interruptions, the need to stop work and slap them down. They wouldn't stop, no matter how futile their attacks—and those attacks weren't that futile, really, those poisons, remember? and they had some sort of trained gnats whose bites were regrettably fatal." Hana wound a strand of pale hair about a pale finger, watched as it loosened and fell away. "The Wall stopped that. But . . . not long after the sectors were starting to be settled—with Memephexis sitting in the Center Dome like a spider at the heart of his web—not long after they were moved in, a Singarit Empire merchant sent out a heavily armed trade mission to the indigenes. Those poisons." She giggled. "A fatal attraction." She slanted a glance at Aleytys, then shook herself back into the bland, uninflected speech. "As soon as the Chwereva, Ffynch and Wei-Chu-Hsien Companies heard about that, they cursed a blue streak. . . ." She blinked. "Blue streak? Well, they cursed and assembled their own missions and sent them out. Armed, of course, and with flitter escorts. The satellites weren't in place yet. Free Traders watched and gloomed. They didn't have the resources to match the Companies." Hana leaned back in the chair and closed her eyes. "The Singarit mission vanished. No trace. Not a hair." A small smile lifted her lips for a moment but she didn't bother to open her eyes. "Not till later. Um. Of the Company missions, the Ffynch mission vanished at night. The flitter was down. There were guards out, a sentry circuit up, a man was even talking to the Ffynch rep in the Enclave. He broke off in the middle of a word. Nothing more, not a squeak. The other two were hit in daylight. There was an incoherent call from a pilot as his flitter went out of control, something about swarms, things crawling over him. There was a steadier report from a camp—indigenes rushing them, getting past the energy weapons somehow, past the outriders and the guard shields. Then nothing. Like before, nothing. Five days later indigenes from half the settlements about the Plain were sitting in hostile groups outside the Enclave, catapulting things over the Wall. When Memephexis sent Peacers out to examine the objects, they found the decaying heads of all the folk in the four missions. All. Even those of the flitter pilots. As if they were purging their world of the souls of the invaders. The Companies, they wrote off the loss. The Singarits—well, they're Singarits. They sent a punitive force to blow to ash whatever indigenes they could find. No one knows exactly what happened though a few reports did come back. Center tapped in on these, that's how we know the little we do, the Singarits never opened their mouths; these reports were about equipment not working, creeping fungus, bugs, gases, stinks. Then nothing. Three months later Yastroo was under siege, battered by Singarit and Company weapons, Company flitters in the hands of indigenes. Well, it survived—barely. Since then, the only weapons allowed down here are personal side-arms and taking those outside the Wall means death on the spot. And no flitters. Absolutely non-allowed past orbit. And the folk that smuggle you out, you can't fool them. High tech that could be twisted into weapons stays inwall, you agree or you don't go. And you're skinned if you try it on your own. Skinned. Not a metaphor. Remember?'' She slanted a glance at Aleytys. ''Esgard's agents went out on foot with bows and knives, you know. Those that got back, well—sometimes I helped Esgard when one of them crawled back, nibbled at, you know, or wingling on some drug an indigene fed him.'' She gazed down at gently twitching fingers. ''Enough of that. I've found something, oh no, not in the computer, in one of Esgard's hideyholes, one I missed before. Journals. In a sort of code; at least, I can't read them. Maybe you can. I suppose they train you for that sort of thing.'' She turned a palm up, sighed; her three-part glance flickered. ''Maybe he's got some clue in there to the new access code, a way past the Seal. I don't really expect it's there, but maybe there's something useful to you, you did ask me to look for journals.''

''I didn't expect you to come up with them quite so quickly, even before I asked.''

''I thought you might be going to ask, so I looked around.'' She beckoned to the serviteur standing patiently by the door, snapped open a cavity in its side and pulled out four soft-bound books. She pushed her plate aside and put the journals on the table before her. The serviteur began collecting the dishes and stowing them in its body. ''You know how to program a translator? That's silly, of course you do. As a favor to me, if you can break the code, will you set up a program so I can read them?''

''Mmm.'' Aleytys rubbed at her nose, trying to ignore a twinge of distaste. ''Pay my docking fees while I'm gone.''

The pale eyes opened wide.

''No.'' Aleytys frowned, turning cautious as she caught a whiff of greed behind the seraphic gaze. ''On second thought, put a sum in escrow equal to the cost of . . . mmm . . . say six months' docking, to be released to me when I turn over the program for the translation.''

''Escrow?'' Hana's pale pink lips worked over the word and it came out slow, stupid.

''Play your games with someone else, Hana Esgard,'' Aleytys said briskly. ''I'm tired of them. Listen. One of the things I am is empath. You hear? So forget the posing.'' She snorted. ''Listen, my girl, if there's one lesson I've learned the past several years, it's that I don't give my skills away.'' She hefted one of the soft-bound journals and waggled it before Hana's nose, dropped it on the table. ''Make up your mind, Hana Esgard; if you want to use me, you pay for the privilege.''

''Oh. . . .'' Hana let the word trail off, making an effort to look crushed. She dropped her gaze to her hands. ''I can't deal with people,'' she murmured. ''Esgard despised me, you know: he wanted a son and all he got was a deformed daughter.'' She turned her stiff hand over and half-closed it, making it evident that she could not close the fingers farther.

''Empath,'' Aleytys said and grinned at her. ''Save it for the susceptible.''

Hana's tongue flicked out to touch the fold in her lip. She seemed to shake herself, then said calmly, ''There's nothing about your Shareem in any memory I can get at. So far. I'll keep looking, there's a few more things I can try.'' For the thousandth time, the three-part flicker of her eyes. ''I know a smuggler who can get you beyond the Wall.'' She pressed her lips together hard, then stretched them into a weak smile. ''I've no choice, have I? Six months docking fees in escrow. Agreed. When will you start out?''

Aleytys rubbed at her nose, scowled. ''Depends how fast you can equip me. Tomorrow or the next day at the latest. I hope.''

III

GOING OUT

1

Spread out on the floor about the smuggler:

Maps—computer drawn from data contributed by the imaging satellites, printed on tough fine tissue and folded flat to take up as little room as possible.

A digest of Esgard's notes on his projected route.

A compass, a folding sextant, a telescope of sorts (little more than a collapsed case and matched lenses), a chronometer set in a thumbring (wafer thin and not much larger than her thumbnail).

Long knife (blade the length of her forearm), three throwing knives, much smaller, a hone.

Staff—two meters of tough hardwood, steel-shod at one end, armed at the other with a hollowground, three-sided spike, each edge honed sharp enough to split a bug in flight.

Laminate, recurve bowstave, extra bowstrings, two dozen arrows, extra points, a shoulderstrap with quiver and a spring clip to hold the bow when she was on march, packet of glue bits with a coil of fine wire for fletching (in a pocket on the quiver).

Coil of rope, coil of monofilament line (very fine) useful for various purposes including fishline; assorted fishhooks.

Soft leather belt, wide with many pockets. In these: salt, spices, assorted herbs, soap, needles, pins, thread, wax, flint and steel, burning glass, matches, folding knife with assorted blades and gadgets, split lead shot for fishing, assorted small supplies.

Packframe, packsack. Canteen. Solar powered still.

Flour, dried eggs, dried meat, dried fruit.

Spare underwear, soft leather moccasins, spare soft-sided boots, second set of trousers and tunic.

Cookware, assorted utensils, superlightweight, some of it collapsed.

Blankets, ground sheet with grommeted corners, plastic sheeting.

Shortrange, pre-set com.

He took up each item, turned it over in delicate six-fingered hands, set it down.

He was a small blue-gray humanoid, a nocturnal with large liquid eyes, large mobile ears set high on a small round head, the short hair on that head like blue-gray plush. He was nervous beneath his outer calm; a muscle jerked beside an orange eye.

He took up the packsack, his fingers passing over every surface, feeling, pinching, prodding, even the nested light-weight stiffening rods. Finished with that, he ran a small buzzing detector over the sides of the pack, his tongue click-ing as it continued to register negative. Without comment he refilled the pack with quick precise movements that left it neater than he'd found it. He wiped his fingertips delicately along his shorts, rose to his feet with a smooth flow of muscle. He looked her over from head to the scuffed toes of her gray suede boots, held out his hand, snapped thumb against finger.

Aleytys unwrapped the gray gauze turban, let the length of webbing flutter from her hands. He watched it fall, stood waiting. She shrugged out of the coat and handed it to him. He turned it inside out, ran his fingers over the clipped-fur lining, then passed the detector over every inch of it. He dropped the coat. "Boots," he said, his voice a grumbling burr.

Sighing, she dropped to the floor, tugged the boots off and tossed them to him. He pinched and probed them, ran the detector over them, examining with greatest care the soles and heels, grunting as he found nothing.

Aleytys sniffed. "I'm not trying anything, Ha'chtman." She bent to pull on the boots.

He stopped her. "Strip," he said.

"What?" she shook her head. "Run that thing over me, that's enough."

His mouth pursed with distaste. "You no treat to me, 'spina." He snapped his fingers. "You choice."

"Strip or forget it?" She got to her feet. "Ah-hai, I wonder if it's worth it." She jerked loose the neck laces of her tunic, pulled it over her head, threw it at him, snapped loose her trousers and kicked out of them. She sniffed, held out her arms. Her underwear was flimsy, translucent, more a protection of her skin from the material of her outer clothing than anything meant to conceal. He ignored her irritation, passed the detector over her body, then began running the soft gray material of the tunic through his fingers

Aleytys sighed and began to rewind the gray gauze, tucking in stray wisps of hair escaping from the braids pinned close to her head. "You're really serious about this." She stepped into the trousers as he handed them to her, slapped the closure shut, reached for the tunic.

"I like my skin where it be." He held the coat for her, then helped her on with the pack. His wiry body was stronger than it looked; he handled the pack's weight with ease. "You got any notion what you walking into?"

"Some. I'm no tender flower." She followed him from the room into a narrow noisome tunnel. Bundles of lightfibers and fingerwide conduits snaked like tangled roots along the top of the burrow. Short sections of light strips cast a pale blue glow that turned her skin into something maggots might love and made little impression on the murky shadow she was wading through. Though the floor was dry enough, moisture slipped in greasy runnels down the metacrete walls and slid into drainslots. The air was chill, with a moldy musty smell. The occasional scrape from their feet, their respirations, these small sounds traveled far ahead and behind them until it was impossible to tell new from old noises.

The smuggler went quickly from one tunnel to another, winding in a complex pattern of twists and turns. She suspected that he'd be coming back by a far more direct route, that he only wanted to confuse her so she wouldn't be able to return alone when the time came for her to return. Protecting

his income, she thought, made a face at his narrow back and
set herself to memorizing the way though she certainly
didn't plan to make a habit of this.

They met no one in the subterranean maze but slogged
along in unrelieved tedium.

Her guide halted without warning, took a sudden step to
one side when she almost stumbled into him. "Wait here,"
he muttered and darted around a turn a few paces ahead, the
words lingering behind him, broken by echoes. Aleytys mopped
at her face with her sleeve and considered taking the coat off,
but decided against this; having her hands free seemed more
important at the moment than getting rid of a little discomfort.
She touched the coarse gray material of the sleeve, thought of
the small grayish nocturnal ahead somewhere. "There are
mice in your walls, Memephexis," she murmured and chuckled at her feeble joke.

Ha'chtman the smuggler returned. "Come."

Melodrama, Aleytys thought, tried not to grin. She followed him around the bend and stopped with him in front of a
neat opening in the side of the tunnel. A plug lay on the floor
beside him, a spider on its back, long thin clamps like legs
lifted into the air. Ha'chtman jabbed a thumb at the hole.
"Go down that," he said. "If you be planning to get back in,
you'd best note that the door here and on the other end, they
open from inside. There's no coming back without someone
opening for you. Best not lose the com or you'll need a deal
of luck and more to cross the Wall." He was cool, remote,
uninterested in her or in her motives for venturing outside,
doing the job he was hired for without fuss or effusion.

Aleytys shrugged the pack to a slightly more comfortable
alignment, chagrined and amused at that chagrin. She was not
accustomed to indifference, found it a salutary dash of cold
water that settled her to the task ahead. She frowned at the
unlit and uninviting hole, sighed and bent unstably to ease
herself and pack into the passage. As soon as she was clear,
the light behind her vanished; the smuggler had swung the
plug up and into place. She heard a series of thuds as he
snapped home the toggles. The blackness around her was
thick enough to taste.

She reached out, touched metacrete, smiled. A secret pas-

sage lined with metacrete. How practical and how absurd.
She groped her way along the tunnel, hoping there were no
branches to confuse her. The thought of wandering for hours
or days or forever in this claustrophobic blackness made her
itchy, but she forced down the distracting uneasiness and
went on, one hand dragging along the wall, the other probing
the darkness before her.

Her outstretched fingers stabbed painfully into something
blocking the tunnel ahead of her. For the first time she
thought of the matches in one of the belt pockets; she sighed
at her idiocy but didn't bother getting them out now. She
explored the surface of the plug, discovered a stubby lever
that jutted upward from a narrow slot and shoved it down
until it clanked against the bottom of the slot.

The door slid open. She could make out the fronds of a
fern drifting beyond the edge. As soon as she pushed past the
lacy growth, breath coming fast and shallow with anticipation,
the door snapped shut behind her. "Well," she murmured,
"good thing I don't want to change my mind."

She glanced up. The moon had set and the air had the cool
stillness of predawn about it. The sky was thick with stars,
lusher than other skies she knew, even University's. And
night on Wolff was starker by far. She pulled at the lapels of
her coat, smiled as she remembered Head's daughter who
kept tugging her tunic down when she was nervous. Aleytys
shifted the straps on her shoulders, sighed. Tamris was on her
first solo Hunt. She'll do fine, her mother over again, though
she wouldn't thank me for saying it. She thumped the blunt
end of the staff against the dampish earth in the bottom of the
wash she found herself standing in. "Move your feet, Lee,
time to get on with it." She started walking away from the
Wall.

The banks on either side of her did not quite reach her
chin. Visualizing her gray-wound head sliding along like
some odd-shaped badger sniffing after mice, she chuckled,
then began looking about her as she strolled along the wash
bottom. Stubby brush grew here and there on the tops of the
banks, rows of old dried weeds leaned against these or fell
over into gray piles, making way for new weeds pushing up
around them and where there were no weeds or brush, matted

grass grew, winter-dried and limp, pale in the blaze of starlight.
Spreading as far as she could see to her left or to her right
were plowed and planted fields, a haze of early growth
beginning to mask pale brown earth; robo-cultivators like
small stilty goats ambling down the rows. In a few of the
fields sprays of water from sprinklers glistened like silver
mist. Over all the fields hung a profound silence where the
whisper of the wind was like a shout, the hiss of the sprinklers penetrating. The cultivators moved in eerie silence with
the fluid grace of flesh rather than the metal stiffness and
clatter Aleytys expected. The cultivators she knew were the
women of client families attached to the Houses of the Raqsidan
and they had never labored in such silence. No, there were
groans and grunts and sneezes, laughter, gossip, shouts, all
done to protest or palliate the crushing labor demanded of
them.

She walked along the winding wash, the staff thumping in
the increasingly sodden bottom. When that bottom began to
ooze and hollows in it had a skim of water in them, she
moved up onto the bank, the heavy pack threatening to
overbalance her until, catching herself with the staff, she
worked out a way to walk that wouldn't strain her too much.
She shrugged and wriggled the pack to a new angle and in the
end was able to settle into a steady three-point rhythm. Now
and then she glanced back at the looming Wall, feeling
absurdly conspicuous, wondering what it was that kept
someone, anyone, from seeing her, coming after her. If anyone at all bothered to look she had to stand out from the
landscape as if she yelled and waved a flag in their faces
saying here I am. But she went on, unchallenged, marching
away from that great pile whose shadow still weighed on her,
would press down on her even when she crawled beneath that
outer fence that was no defense but only something to keep
wild ruminants out of the fields. A shadow that weighed
heavier on her than the backpack though that was heavy
enough. I've gone soft, she thought. Too much sitting. Flitters.
Flying. She shrugged the backpack about again, shifted the
webbing straps. Haven't settled to the work yet, she thought.
She smiled suddenly. In an odd sort of way this was like the
night she ran from the vadi Raqsidan out into a world she

knew nothing about, hunting then—as she was hunting now—something that more than likely did not exist.

She walked on, half-expecting to hear yells of outrage from the Wall, to feel the shock of a stunner in the middle of her back, set to react, almost disappointed when the night remained so very tranquil, her strengths untested. The mush in the bottom of the wash grew deeper and slushier, the stiff round reeds thicker; a stagnant musty smell wafted from the skim of water and a hum of glassy insects filled the air a handsbreadth above the bottom. A few minutes later the agri-fence was before her

It was metal mesh for the first meter then electrified barbed wire stretched between the metal fenceposts on white ceramic insulators. Where it jumped the wash it left a gap that someone had attempted to fill with a half-moon of mesh. Aleytys glanced over her shoulder at the Enclave, saw the tip of the center dome showing above the Wall. She saluted it, grinned at herself then began examining the gap.

The mesh patch was broken, twisted, rolled aside, part of it buried in the mud, the rest covered with rust and scaly lichen. She looked from the soupy mud to the rusty, snaggled wire, grimaced, then shrugged out of the pack, laid it on the bank, drove the spiked end of the staff into the dirt to hold it out of the muck, settled herself beside it and pulled off her boots. She scraped them on the wiry grass, folded them inside her coat, thrust that bundle through the shoulder straps, rolled her trousers above her knees, squatted in the ooze and used the staff to muscle the pack through the jagged opening. Her feet kept sliding in the slime, but the tough roots of the reeds gave her a precarious purchase as she struggled with the awkward burden; with a grunting heave she managed to land it on the far side of the fence mostly out of the muck. Breathing heavily, still squatting, the reeds combing through her toes as she moved, she inched forward and wriggled through the gap. She straightened, joints creaking, waded a few steps more, threw out her arms in an explosion of triumph and freedom—though the Wall's shadow still held her, not too far ahead she could see starlight frosting the grass. She stretched her senses out as far as she could, searching for the indigenes in ambush Hana had led her to

expect, but either it was the off-season or she was simply
riding a belated bit of luck. Kicking her feet through the limp
dew-spangled grass until most of the mud was washed away,
she ambled along the bank, yawning and stretching, until she
was back beside the pack. Ruefully aware that an hour's
walking was nothing compared to what lay ahead of her, she
rubbed at her shoulders where the webbing straps had reddened the flesh, then she eased down on the damp grass. The
creaks and strains of all beginnings, she thought. She yawned
again, pulled her coat from the packstraps and dabbed at the
last of the mud. She slid her feet several times over the grass,
enjoying the feel of the cool wiry stems as they passed
beneath her soles. It felt so good she was reluctant to put her
boots back on, but the pack was too heavy and the going was
too ragged to allow her the luxury of barefooting it. She
worked the boots back on, hesitated over the coat; the air held
intimations of warmth to come, so she tied it on the pack,
then muscled the pack around, worked her arms into the
straps and used the staff to heave herself onto her feet. She
stamped her feet to settle them into the boots, wriggled and
humped the pack about until it felt comfortable and stable
enough, shook her head as another sweep confirmed the
tranquility and uninterrupted solitude of the night, then started
walking south.

2

ESGARD'S NOTES:
Notes on the planned route with warnings about what to
watch for on the way, located by Hana in a guarded loop;
she used a key found in the journals once they were translated.
The notes were computer printed and bound into a small
black book.

It would seem easier to follow the river westward, but I
have been advised this is too certainly dangerous. War bands
from both sides of the Plain travel the river upstream and
down to raid villages on the other side. Therefore, I shall
leave the Enclave on foot, but Fasstang my best hunter will
meet me with his troupe outside the agri-fence and we will

*head south to the NewCity ruins and thence west along the
remnants of one of the ancient roads. Fasstang reports and the
satellites confirm that there is plenty of water, a series of
springs and several small creeks at comfortable stages along
the road. This route has its dangers, but it's better than the
river way.*

*You who read this—if you plan to follow me, watch for
my sign:* ✕ε *I'll try to leave it at reasonable intervals.*

Beyond the irrigated land the wash bottom began to drain.
Soon the bottom was hard and dry, strewn with brittle-
thorned dead brush and smooth pebbles that were treacherous
footing in the deceptive brilliance of the starlight. She followed the wash until the grim grey wall of the Enclave had
sunk behind the rolling hills, followed it south until the sun
was clear of the horizon. The wash finally faded away,
leaving her in prairieland with small hillocks packed as thick
as horripilation on a wind-chilled skin. She glanced at the
sun, unsnapped a belt pocket and consulted the compass,
glanced at the chronometer on her thumb. "Lot left in the
day," she murmured and started moving at a slow trot up the
side of the hillock before her. Now that her body was loosening up and she had grown accustomed to the shift in balance
required by the pack, she intended to run as long as she could
without tiring herself too much, then continue walking. Her
body was in good condition, but exercise was one thing, eight
hours of travel (or more, depending) on foot was something
entirely other. Still, there was no help for it, not until she
could buy or steal herself a mount, and from all she'd learned
there was little chance of either before she got close to the
hills.

Her body on automatic, she fished about for something to
take her mind off the residual aches and pains, finally went
back to Sil Evareen, wondering if it even existed, deciding
soon that it did not matter to her whether it existed or not, it
only mattered that she be able to follow Esgard's signs and
find a way to cut into the six-month lead he had on her,
deciding too that catching up with him was more a matter of
luck than planning.

It was early summer on the Plain. Dry scrubby broom

shook dust on her as she loped past the spindly clumps. Squat
and thorny brush snagged at the soft suede of her boots. At
the periphery of her senses she could feel an intricate web of
busy small lives eating, mating, fighting, birthing. A breeze
began to stir the weeds and blow into her face, a soft and
silky breeze, heavy with the pungent odors of brush and
broom, noisy with the blended hum of insects and the tooth
clicks and chatter of small rodents in the grass.

At first she felt frustrated as the ground passed with painful
slowness under her feet. She had to fight her urgency to keep
from running herself out too soon. Accustomed for too long a
time to great gulps of space taken so easily by flitters,
skimmers, even skis during Wolff's winter, her pace seemed
like that of a figure in a nightmare running and running and
getting nowhere. And the unchanging landscape reinforced
this sense of effort spent to no result; one hillock looked
much like the last or the next, brush, broom, grass, even
outcroppings of rock, but as the morning wore on, she began
to adjust to this slower rhythm and feel more relaxed, more
comfortable with that slowing.

About mid-morning she stopped for a short rest. The fitful
breeze tugging at the turban ends felt cool and welcome when
she took the turban off and let the air play against her neck.
She dropped the pack on a patch of grass, pulled loose the
thongs of the neck opening, swabbed at the sweat trickling
down her throat with the bundled-up turban, rolled her sleeves
up past her elbows. She stretched her hands high over her
head, rising onto her toes, twisting about, working every
muscle she could. With a groan she stretched out on the grass
beside the pack and eyed her feet. They were hot and sweaty
but she decided not to pull off her boots, having doubts about
her ability to get them back on. She drank sparingly from the
canteen, checked the compass, decided it would suit her
better to sling it around her neck with a bit of leather thong
than to leave it in the belt pocket where she'd have to fish for
it when she wanted it. She thought of checking her position
on the map but at best it would be little more than stabbing a
finger at random, there were no landmarks, only the swells
and dips that stretched identically away to the horizon on all
sides now. With a sigh she cut off a bit of thong, tied the

compass about her neck, consulted the chronometer and got to her feet. Maybe make the ruins close to sundown. Maybe. She took another drink from the canteen and clipped it to the belt, hefted the pack and worked her arms through the straps, then forced her stiffening body into a downhill lope.

Planning's only guessing, she thought. *I'll have to go from sign to sign, hope I can come up with something to cut the lead.* In her head, words and phrases came to echo the shift and slide of her body. *Don't know nothing, don't know nothing 'bout this blasted world.* She nearly tripped over a clump of grass giggling at the pun that had slipped into her stream of thought. *Blasted world. That it was, oh yes it was. Wonder if there's slaving here. Hai-ah, kill the last hope I have of finding friendly souls. Esgard, damn you, why not wait a few months more? Slavers, no ah no, don't think so. Not logical. Not reasonable. Kill themselves, kill anyone come near them—except, oh yes, those who've tamed themselves to value profit over precept. Not worth the trouble, no, I think. Esgard knew things he couldn't possibly, things they wouldn't tell their cousins, never an outsider. Bribery? Weapons would untie their tongues. That's out, I think. He was too wary a man to put his hide in hock like that; skinned, Hana said, hanged from a scaffold outside the Center Dome. No end for him, too wary a man. I think he was. What do I know about him? Something, I think, from the notes, a thing or two from Hana. Locked the Vryhh data away from her. I wonder why, oh yes I wonder. Is it that he wanted his business tight in his own hands? Or has he promised to protect his Vrya? Has he a thousand, thousand reasons I couldn't even guess? Oh Madar, it's a pain not knowing. And no way of finding out, now now, not without finding him and who knows, maybe not even then.*

Her feet moving automatically over the dry earth, she loped up and down those hillocks, her arms swinging free at her sides—the staff was tied out of her way now, riding the pack—and she had no way of knowing which hillock she was climbing or running down the backside of and no reason for trying to know, they slipped behind her unnoted as the sun slid farther along its day arc. The sky was a pale, pale blue.

Cloudless. A bird was a dark speck off to her left, the only thing moving across that blue.

Sil Evareen and Kenton Esgard. Like Vrithian. A little like Vrithian is for me. A place I look for. A place to be. A place to explain what I am now and what I might become. A place to fit myself into. Not have to worry about jealousy, about hostility, about the thousand pains of living a long life in the midst of shortlives. (And even as she thought this, she knew it wasn't true; she'd met Vryhh Kell. The Vrithian that had formed him was certainly no paradise.) *Is there a slot for me on Vrithian? Madar knows. Does it matter? Madar knows. Haven't I been making a place for myself on Wolff? But what happens fifty years ahead? Time. There's still time for Grey, I think. If I can patch things up again. Again. How many times have we* . . . Grey and Swartheld glaring at each other like two silvercoats over a hunk of meat. *Miserable coincidence.* The two of them getting back the same time, the same day almost. She shied away from the memory of that volcanic encounter.

Sil Evareen, she thought. *A dream of immortality. Harskari and Shadith and Swartheld, they all had a kind of immortality and all of them seem eager enough to quit it. Esgard swallowed those tales. A shrewd man, both Hana and Swartheld say that, but the shrewdest of men will swallow whales if their desire is great enough. I'm as bad*, she thought suddenly. *What am I doing, running like a fool through this beat-out world chasing a ghost chasing a dream? Ghost? Could be. An old man. Still—a canny old man. Hana said he went alone on foot like me, but that's all she saw. I wonder if she watched me leave? He left alone but he didn't stay alone long. Oh no, he knew better than that. Old man. Spent the last ninety years-standard inside Enclave walls. Even with daily workouts and other training he wouldn't be ready for this, no, he simply wouldn't be attuned to life in the wild. Book knowledge isn't enough, it just isn't enough, takes too long to react in emergencies, has to go through the intellect; still, he seemed aware of that, provided himself with men who wouldn't need to think before they acted.* She chuckled. *How many angels can dance on the head of a pin? All this is speculation, word play with no data, useless. Still, he did manage to survive the cutthroat world of the free-traders for nearly a century. Chasing a dream . . . ah, Aschla's hells . . . what else am I chasing . . . a dream I'm not even sure I want . . . at least he knows what he wants. . . .*

The sun sank low in the east, the shadows lengthened, pooled about her feet as she dipped into hollows and miniature washes between hillocks. In spite of several rests and a lengthy lunch break, she was tired, her feet hurt, her legs were heavy, her head ached, but she refused to stop. She intended to reach the NewCity ruins before halting for the night even if that meant she kept moving long after sunset.

She trudged up the side of a hillock and stopped at the summit. One of the ancient roadways she'd read about came slashing out of the east, a littered black surface here and there twisted and distorted by ancient and recent earth movements but remarkably intact and shockingly incongruous in this primitive scene. She went wearily down the slope and stepped onto the road. Up close the surface was not quite so unmarred as it seemed from a distance; a webbing of small cracks like lines on an ancient's face cut through the resilent topping, and scattered spots had gone hard and gray and were beginning to flake away like cancers eating into the substance of the road. She began walking along the pavement, feeling as ancient as it was, all the more tired since its presence was a sign that her day's effort was nearly done. It was hard, hard to keep her feet moving.

As she started to circle around a spill of glittering white dirt where the face of a cut had been torn away by a shifting of the earth in the not too distant past, she kicked against a pale round object that went clunking off. With some surprise she saw it was a bit of skull, humanoid from the size and shape. She blinked at it a moment, then turned to stare at the denuded earth. Not even grass grew on the steep slope though she could see a whitish-green fuzz of roots reaching over the rim of the cut. By the end of the summer the grass would have claimed much of the slope as it had claimed and lost and claimed again the rest of the Plain. She went closer.

A curious conglomerate, that newly bared earth. Fragments of glass fused into irregular iridescent lumps, redbrown lines of corrosion from metal lodged among and around the glass lumps arranged in a pattern she couldn't quite make out, fragments of bone, the most clearly recognizable being teeth and the ball joints of thigh bones. The matrix was hard alkali soil, a yellowish white, brittle, chalky, paler than the pallor of the bones. Bits of plastic that even the centuries had not melted away. Straggles of cloth that had survived the ages locked in the soil, fluttering now in the wind, fraying against bone and slivers of plastic. Mostly bones. Humanoid skulls, beast skulls, large and small, jaw fragments and teeth and temple bones, the curve of ribs, a finger bone pointing at her from inside an eye socket. Bones. She walked over land that was the flesh of men and beasts, layered with the bones of men and beasts.

She shivered and turned away, overwhelmed suddenly by the weight of the dead, happy to have her bootsoles insulated from them by the pavement. Hana had mouthed the words telling of the wars without any real understanding of what they meant. And Aleytys had, half-unconsciously, blamed her for this, thinking she herself understood the pain of what had happened, but now she knew she'd been as ignorant as Hana, the reality of death here was beyond the understanding of anyone, even those who had lived with that reality. She walked on the dead, layer on layer of them, numberless and nameless as the stars that filled the night sky. Numberless and nameless, covered in the end by that grass, sanitized by eons of sunlight, leached of their poison by ages of rain, the dead, the ancient untimely dead.

The wind whispered through the carpeting grass, rustled through newly green brush. A small brown rodent with front teeth comically protruding from a blunt black muzzle sat erect on the top of a hillock, holding in black forepaws a bit of debris that caught the sun and gave back a blinding glitter. Clutching its prize to the puff of reddish fur on its chest, it watched Aleytys gravely as she plodded closer, then with a flirt of a plumy tail, it vanished down the far side of the hillock. Aleytys smiled, her dark mood lightened. She walked on along the road, tired, sore, but more contented than she'd been, moving slowly but steadily toward the setting sun.

The road curved in a long arc about a rash of hillocks. Above them she saw the top of a wall, a pale flat dash against.

the sky. As she got closer, she saw the dark green of trees that hugged the curves of a small creek she couldn't see but knew from the map. *NewCity ruins*, she thought, then started as the sky ahead filled with noisy black apostrophes, small birds, heading for their nests as night approached.

She rounded the curve. The road straightened and she was walking into the glare of the sunset, the NewCity walls a black silhouette against the crimson sky. At that moment, as she walked toward the city, she saw it as a child's replica in modeling clay of the darkly massive Enclave, a fleeting notion, instantly banished as she came close enough to touch the wall and stepped into the alcove formed by the set-back gate.

The gate was made of massive planks, mottled blue-brown and gray, changed by time and rain and chemical action to something close to stone. She pushed on them but there was not the slightest give—as far as she could tell—the ages had cemented them into place. White dust rose in drifts in the corners and against the planks; except for her own footprints, the dust was unmarked though the wind had carved ripples into the surface. She backed out and began following the wall, one hand slipping along its surface.

Around the curve some distance from the gate, the wall was breached for at least three meters, the opening spreading wider near the top. She stepped into the gap, touched the dust of the crumbled bricks. The wall was made of sun-dried alkali mud dug out of the Plain and mixed with some substance that kept the bricks impervious to water as long as the outer skin was intact. The broken bricks had melted out of their transparent shells, leaving these behind, and the shells had been battered and shattered by wind and weather. Aleytys crossed the width of the wall, nearly three meters and twice that many steps. There were shards of brick shell in the thick dust piled against the inside of the wall, glinting red out of the shadow as they reflected the dying sunset. The buildings inside the wall were thrown up in a bewildering maze, broken down and roofless, gradually melting to meet the dust rising against the walls as time, man, beast and bird destroyed the integrity of the shells. Keeping close to the inside of the great wall, she moved back toward the gate. It seemed to her that there, if anywhere, was the place to find Esgard's sign—if he'd left any, if he'd actually come here.

The main gate was much the same inside as out, drifts of floury dust rising against it here too, no wind ripples but pocks from drips and miniature coulees eaten into the slopes, running into the stream which came into the ruins though a broad low arch quite close to the gate, an arch that spring floods kept flushed clear of most debris, though mosses and slimes thrived there. She kicked aside a drift of dust, walked close to the inner side of the gate, ran her fingers over the new mark chiseled into the ancient stone-hard wood— $\mathcal{X}_{\epsilon}$. She sat down suddenly as her legs melted under her, the dust whooshing up in billowing puffs, falling back on her as she bowed her head to her knees. For a moment she could only sit in that slowly settling white fog, could neither think nor move. Then she lifted her head and stared at the mark, bewildered by the excess of her reaction. "I don't understand," she said. Her voice croaked, broke over the words. "It's too much. It's a game, isn't it? Why. . . . What's happening?" She rubbed at her thighs, her hands trembling. *Need,* she thought. *I must, no, it can't be my choice any more, I never felt like this, never before, never. . . . I didn't realize . . .* She got shakily to her feet and started to turn, not sure what she wanted to do, where she wanted to go, not really thinking of anything at all, trying to feel her way through the confusion she'd created for herself.

A blow. In her back. Low. Beside the backpack. At first there was no pain, only a vast unfocused surprise. Her knees trembled, her head swam, but she managed to finish the turn; she stared at the creature with the bow standing between two of the shattered houses, waiting with predator's patience for her to fall down. She sensed his eagerness, his—or hers? or its?—utter confidence in the efficacy of the shot. The pack shifted a little, bumped against the shaft. She went to her knees, heat flashing through her, then sudden intense pain piercing the shock. She set her teeth on a whimper and *reached* for her river. And faltered as poisonheat followed painheat and brought weakness and fuzziness of will with it. Poisons, Hana Esgard said, they know their poisons. She struggled with the weakness, a weaknesss that grew paradoxically stronger with time; the longer she fought the more surely the battle was lost. The ground boiled around her, the dead boiled up from the ground, blue-white and rotten, stinking and maggot-filled, staring at her out of white bulging eyes, so many dead—men, women, children—heads hanging by strings, arms flopping about loose on the ground, hands crawling for her, she screamed as a soft soapy hand touched her, screamed again as the dead converged on her, packing together, multilated, hideous, the stench drowning her. She struggled against nausea, struggled for focus, tried to *reach* again. . . .

Then Harskari was with her. It seemed to her the ancient sorceress stood beside her and scolded her, though dimly, distantly, she knew this could not be so. Harskari's deep contralto beat at her though she couldn't understand the words. She lifted a hand and it seemed to her Harskari took it. She felt strength pouring into her and for the third time *reached* for her symbolic river. And the power came roaring into her, the black water was flushing through her, driving out the poison. She sat up, blinking, and with much relief saw only the spreading white dust, lit by a moon already high as the sunset faded. She eased her arms out of the pack straps, let the pack fall with a dull thud she gave no part of her attention. With Harskari blocking the pain and Shadith whispering encouragement, she reached around behind and caught hold of the shaft

And forced the tanged head through her unfeeling flesh till it poked out through the skin at the front of her body. She lifted the tunic and stared gravely at the shining white point streaked with her blood, faintly surprised to find it a substance resembling porcelain rather than the metal she was familiar with, faintly surprised too when she heard an undulant shrill cry from the creature. She paid it no attention as she slipped the long knife from its sheath and began sawing at the shaft close behind the point.

Shadith's wordless cry of warning brought her head up. The creature—she couldn't call it man or woman—the creature had its bow raised once again. Harskari was wholly occupied with the wounded flesh, but Shadith melded with her as she'd done before on Maeve and elsewhere and in an instant had sought, found, and struck against the weapon's weakest point. The frayed bowstring snapped at the very moment the creature had it at full stretch, about to release a second shaft at her. The arrow tottered, fell at its feet. Its arms jerked, it gained its balance, stood gaping at the arrow half-buried in the dust beside a misshapen foot. With a cry of rage it tossed the broken bow aside and charged at her.

Trusting Harskari to hold her body together, Aleytys lifted onto her feet; brandishing the long knife and roaring a challenge at the charging monster, she dropped into a crouch, the blade angling up to meet it. With another howl, this time a screech of fear, it back-pedaled frantically, kicking up clouds of dust, reversed direction and fled into the maze of broken buildings.

Floating detached, ignoring the not-now-existing pain, standing with her feet spread, her knees locked, Aleytys finished cutting the point away, noting absently as it fell from the shaft that bits of it were missing. She watched it plop into the dust then reached around and pulled the shaft from the wound. It came away easily enough. She flung it aside and fumbled at her back, touched a warm wetness. She brought her fingers around, stared at the slather of blood on them, felt a touch of anxiety, which she ignored as she would ignore an undemanding itch, and *reached* for the energy she'd need to reknit the flesh.

Harskari slapped her down quickly, glacially. "Clear the wound first," she said, her contralto booming painfully inside Aleytys's head. "You've got garbage left in there, girl. Wood fragments and the tips of the tangs."

Oh, Aleytys thought. Obediently she began to probe in the lacerated flesh with mindfingers that were clumsy and uncertain, a result of her uncertain training. Even at university, though they acknowledged the existence of the psi-skills, they tended to focus on more predictable and controllable events—at least in the schools where she'd got the greater part of her education. All she had to guide her was the haphazard instruction Harskari and Shadith had provided, instruction by example rather than exposition, instruction centered about chance events rather structured lessoning.

When Harskari was satisfied, Aleytys stimulated the growth

of her flesh and healed the long wound, working from the inside out in both directions until she finally sealed off the skin, a task so easy now from much practice she hardly needed to think what she was doing. Shadith sighed with relief; Harskari let go her hold on the pain center. "That should not have happened," she said sternly. "You were careless."

"Yes, a little careless," Shadith said with reluctance and a taste of wariness—Harskari had been distant and snappish for the past few months as if she were trying to work out some problems of her own.

Aleytys turned slowly, her eyes moving over the melted houses. "Yes. I suppose I was." She nodded at the gate. "The bones we saw out there, they showed me the past clearer than I wanted to see it. I forgot about the present." She kicked at the pointless shaft, sent it flying in clouds of floury dust. "That was a painful reminder." She swung her arm in a long swooping arc. "Look at this place. It's too ancient, too . . . oh, what can I say . . . too dead." She shivered as she remembered the putrid flesh of the dead in her poison dream. "Who would think of anything living here now?" The creature was not that far from those lunatic images, but at least it was alive. Piebald, crook-backed, scaly like a lizard with a lizard's crest fringing the misshapen head, short torso as if there was only a single pair of ribs and organs shoved high and tight, frail spidery legs, feet more like crude hands with their long knobby toes. It wore clothing of a sort, rags, bits of animal hide. She looked at the bow half-covered by the dust, walked over to it, touched it with her boot-toe, picked it up and examined it. Good work, she thought. If that hideous thing made it, then the thing was a man—or a woman, she reminded herself and felt sick at the thought. She walked to the remnant of a house wall and laid the bow on it, looked around again. With starlight and moonlight glowing on the pale dust, the pale brick, all that lifeless pallor and all those shattered empty shells about her made her feel more as if she walked in a surrealistic dream. Ruins, yes, but as much the ghosts of ruins. And the creature was the ghost of a man, well, not exactly a ghost but a battered remnant of his ancestral type. She shivered again.

Shadith was jittery. Aleytys felt her like an itch inside her head. "I don't like this place. Let's get out of here. What if that thing comes back and brings its friends along?"

Aleytys felt a sudden wave of sadness. "I don't think it can have any friends."

"What difference does that make?" Shadith blinked rapidly. "You've found Esgard's mark, that's all you wanted. Let's go."

Aleytys nodded though she knew Shadith could not see the nod. It was satisfying to speak with her body; anyway, what Shadith couldn't see, she could feel. Harskari had retreated to that remoteness that was her private place and was unavailable for comment or converse. Aleytys hefted the pack, worked her arms into the straps and trotted back out the breach in the wall to look for a spot along the creek where she could set up a reasonably safe night camp.

3

The first day had been tentativeness, excitement, urgency, fear, confusion—most of all confusion.

The second day began in pain and stiffness and depression and ended in a weary euphoria

She ran along the road until her feet began to hurt then walked on the dirt and grass beside the road. She saw no one, nothing except a few birds and startled rodents; there was nothing to break into the tedious sameness of the landscape, the road thrust westward unchanged without even a shifting of the earth to mar the straight black line. At sunset she reached one of the springs marked on the map, surprising herself because she'd covered more ground than she'd thought possible. She almost passed the clump of trees off to the right; only the tops were visible over the swells of the hillocks, dark green domes, near black in the crimson glow of the setting sun, but a noisy flock of small birds came swooping over her head, twittering, wingfeathers whiffling as they passed her, breaking the trance of weariness she moved along within. As the birds settled in the trees, she stared after them thoughtfully, waking to a sudden awareness that she was hungry enough to eat a dozen of them, feathers and all.

Later, beside a glowing heap of coals in the firehole, replete with cha and roasted fowl and fried bread, she spread the map across her knees and found the next water. "Noon here, I think." She raised her brows as she saw another of the ancient roads crossing the one she followed, folded the map and tucked it away. She took off the belt and draped it beside her on the groundsheet, stretched, yawned and looked lazily about the small hollow. The fire painted the leaves and branches over her bright red, dark red, changing, continually changing, bright and dark with the shift of the wandering wind that crept about the hollow. Out beyond the roof of leaves the moonlight was a spread of ice on the bubbling spring. Dark fliers the size of her fist dipped low over the uneasy surface, clawing up small fish as they came to feed on the skater bugs darting here and there over the moonlight, starlight sparkles. "No sign of his sign." She yawned again. "But he'd travel faster mounted than I did on foot. Maybe the noon stop, probably the crossroads. That sounds likely. Crossroads."

After she drowned the fire, she stretched out on the groundsheet, folded her coat for a pillow and rolled herself into her blanket. She lay staring up at the interlacing branches and the layers of leaves and felt every ache in her body. For what seemed an eternity she lay there, all the interminable internal arguments running on tracks around her head—Grey and Swartheld, Vrithian, her own reluctance to dig into what she thought of as the cesspool of her inheritance from her mother, her violent and unexpected emotional investment in this search, and Grey again—and a sudden urgent need for him that built and built and sent her writhing out of her blanket her breasts aching—until finally, wearily, she used her breathing exercises to shut off her mind and drifted off to the twittering of birds in the trees, the buzzing burring chirps of cicadoids, the lazy bubbling of the spring, the squeaky papery insistence of the stiff round leaves as they rubbed against each other.

4

The third day she woke filled with energy and general well-being. Her feet had stopped aching and her body felt comfortable again. She tore a strip of cloth from the end of the turban and used it to tie her hair into a long red tail flopping clear of her neck so the air could get to the skin.

Again the quiet of the day was undisturbed by any threat from predators—either human or animal.

That night she sat dreaming over the fire and the map—her face warm, the wandering night breeze cool against her back and ears—sat staring into the coals, not-thinking, drifting, relaxed, content, in a semi-trance, smiling a little, rubbing the fingertips of one hand over the tough slick film the map was printed on; decisions to be made, but nothing urgent, another dozen days at least, nothing threatening, all the time in the world available to her; Shadith and Harskari were with her, sharing her contentment, saying nothing, just there in her head as companions and friends. She could feel their presence and it made her happy. If she closed her eyes and looked within she could see their eyes shining in the dark, she could see the ghost images of their faces sketched about those eyes. She watched red and yellow play across the shining black charcoal. She felt like laughing but was too comfortable and too weary to make the effort.

After drowning the fire, Aleytys stretched out on the ground-sheet without bothering to pull the blanket over her. The moon was a ragged half round of milky white rocking across a starfield whose blaze almost killed her light. She blinked up at the display, yawned and slid with an ease that startled her in the morning into a deep and mostly dreamless sleep.

The days passed, slow golden days. She stopped thinking—as if the running became more important than the goal she was running to reach. Day on day, picking up some of Esgard's signs as their halts coincided, missing others, unworried by their absence, stopping early some days to hunt her dinner, other days to fish for it in creek or spring. Dry golden days, warm and filled with a peace she could only compare to the misty white days, the ice time, when she ran with Grey into the wild, that wild trek so long, so very long ago.

Her placid dream lasted until mid-afternoon on the seventeenth day out.

5

A short time after her lunch-break she began to feel edgy. It was rather like the oppression before a storm breaks, but the sky was a shimmering blue dome without a wisp of cloud in the great round visible as she stood atop one of the innumerable hillocks. She kicked fretfully at a clump of grass, swore as her toe scratched up a bit of ancient bone. She booted it away, depressed by this reminder of all she'd worked to forget about this blasted world. This time the phrase didn't make her smile. She scanned the sky for the hundredth time, the edginess building within her. South and west of where she stood, near the horizon at first then soaring closer, she saw a small dark speck, a hawklike bird riding the rising thermals, moving in lazy spirals not quite toward her, more north than west.

Moving slowly, with great care, nothing sudden to catch the eye, she lowered herself until she was crouching beside the clump of dried-out broom growing like a topknot out of the crest of the hillock. Prickling all over as if she'd brushed inadvertently against the rim of a tingler probe, she glanced repeatedly but briefly at the flier, amused (briefly) by her sudden likeness to Hana Esgard, then sent out a wary probe to touch the bird.

And snatched it away, cut it off, clamped her shields tight. Awareness. In the bird. Someone—something—searching for her. Her? Well, searching for something. The bird glided toward her. She stiffened. It curved back on its northern course. Aleytys flattened herself against the brown-gray stems of the broom, hoping her matte gray clothing would blend with the broom and the ground, at least blend sufficiently to mask her from the flier's sharp eyes. Hoping too that the snap-back of her probe and the snap-up of her shields were quick enough that the mindrider had not had time to locate her. The mottled shadow and the overhang of the dusty prickly brush were scanty cover at best but she could find no sign she'd been discovered. She held her breath as the hawk wavered back and forth, swooping east toward her, curving back almost immediately to the north line.

Moving as slowly and easily as she could, careful about fluttering the broom above her, she slipped her arms from her pack and pulled out the gray gauze. Awkwardly, her nose in the dust, she wound the gauze about the bright hair that was the thing most apt to betray her presence. She was clumsy with the need to avoid brushing against the strands of broom, finally tied the ends in a knot, hoping she'd done sufficient; the winding felt loose and unsteady.

She lay very still for some time after that as the hawk dwindled into the blue haze on the northern horizon, waited until the prickles running over her skin faded to nothing, waited several heartbeats longer, than eased up onto her knees. She glanced at the sky, then froze.

The hawk was coming back, no more elegant curves, darting like an arrow south and west. As she watched, it plummeted behind the horizon, going to earth somewhere beyond her range of vision. She got to her feet and stood staring into the unresponsive blue, chewing on her lip.

Harskari's amber eyes were bright glows in her head. "Mind rider," she said. "Interesting. Explains some things Hana Esgard said."

"So it does." Aleytys brushed twigs and crumbs of dirt off her clothing. She untied the gauze strip and began winding it into a neater turban, sighing as she tucked in the last wisps of hair. "Scout," she said. "I wonder what it was looking for." She swung the pack up, settled it in place, looked about, then started down the slope, the contentment of the past days shattered. She felt disgruntled, angry at the breaking of her mood. "Back to work, I suppose. Damn."

Aleytys left the road, cutting into the hillocks until she'd moved almost a kilometer south of it. Her senses out at widest stretch, she kept to a slow but steady walk, thinking this less likely to attract searching eyes. Several times more she saw the hawk and froze, but it showed no interest in her; each time it spiraled northward, each time it came darting back dropping to the earth somewhere roughly west of her. She could see the mountains, a faint blue line low on the horizon, a gently undulating line like the worn-out teeth of an ancient ruminant; they were still several days away; according to Esgard's notes the indigenes when not on a raid kept close to their settlements so she should have had at least another two days of peace. She frowned, trying to visualize the map, then nodded. There was a Blight ahead, not half a day's journey south from the road. That could explain the presence of an indigene band this far from the hills.

ESGARD'S NOTES:

Like cancers the ancient cities are dotted about the Plain. Pockmarks in the grass. Slathers of glass, slag, twisted shells of rotting steel, a few snagtooth ruins, not many, the greater part of each city is melted level with the ground. Dangerous radiation still, though the wars that flattened the cities are millennia in the past. Don't know precisely what they used, but it was dirty and uncontrolled; they were most thorough in their intent to destroy. Blights. Filled with mutated plants and animals (Fasstang says people too, but I find that rather hard to believe), most of these poisonous, plant and animal alike, some useful, many equipped with psychogenic defenses along with the poisons built into glands, spores, darts, symbiotic insects. The Ecology of a Blight would be a fascinating study if one could survive the circumstances. The indigenes prospect the Blights much as men on other worlds hunt precious metals and gemstones. Mark the Blights STAY AWAY.

The hawk was up and cycling close as Aleytys broke a dry and hungry camp, swung into the packstraps and settled the pack comfortably against her spine. She watched the hawk a few minutes, frowning, then cautiously climbed a hillock and stood on the crest looking about, wondering how she should proceed. In the south, some distance from the point the hawk was circling, she saw a clump of trees poking like black fingers high above the rest of the Plain. "Harskari," she murmured, "Shadith, tell me. What do you think about a jog south for a look around? It's not too far off-line."

There was no sign of Harskari but Shadith's eyes opened. A sketch of the delicate pointed face formed about the purple eyes, the red-gold curls were bouncing with energy. She grinned. "Why not."

Senses outreaching, watching the hawk with wary, quick
glances, ready for any change in him, Aleytys started moving
south toward the trees. A look across the land, that was what
she needed. A look to help her avoid the mind rider and
whoever was with him, someone had to be—no one but me
would be fool enough to come out here alone. She slowed her
walk, glanced nervously at the hawk. It was, she thought,
hovering over the mind rider and his band—if there really
was a band with the mindrider—and it was working slowly
south and east, angling to intercept her path not far beyond
that clump of trees. That was only an estimate, perhaps she
was wrong, but even the possibility bothered her. She didn't
want to come anywhere near that mind rider. She almost
turned aside and headed back to the road, but she couldn't
forget the scouting flights of the bird. Something was coming out of the north. Something. That high tree looked better
and better the more she thought of the difficulties ahead.

An hour later she was standing on a hump of ground beside
tangled underbrush spilling out from among the trees, looking
over a lowland slough spreading across sunken bits of ancient
road, muddy scummy water filled with tules and purple-
flowered pad plants and a thousand, thousand other sorts of
vegetation, ugly bulbous plants trailing across bubbling pools
of muck. No two plants seemed alike and few of them even
this far from the Blight were without dead and decaying
patches. Here and there small shadowy beasts fled from
clump to clump of vegetation, attacking and being attacked
by the vegetation and other beasts. The slough wasn't quite a
Blight, but close enough for her. She shivered and turned
away.

Struggling not to breathe—the rank smell from the rotting
mess was thick enough to chew—she began forcing her way
through the tangled undergrowth. The bark of the smaller
trees was filled with an oozing fluid whose baleful smell was
strong enough to mask the stench from the slough. She tried
very hard not not to touch these. The great tree in the middle
stood atop a naked rise; not even grass grew under it. This
made her nervous but she wasn't going to be around long, so
she ignored the pinch in her stomach, hung the pack from a
warty branch and started climbing. It was a parasite, that tree,

a strangler; a seed blew into a crotch of another tree, rooted there, then dropped tendrils to the earth some distance below, tendrils that swelled and swelled until they choked the life out of their host. She could still see that other tree's rotting fragments inside. At least the bark on the strangler's multiple trunks was dry, though brittle and crusty like a fossilized sponge.

The brittleness of the bark made climbing treacherous, drops of acid sap clung to her hands, but it was easy enough, especially when the first limbs began spiraling up around the trunk. The branches grew shorter as they wound higher and the concealing crust of foliage drew in closer. The tree began to sway a little. She went up more cautiously, intent on getting as high as she could, and when the trunk split, pulled herself into the crotch and settled herself straddling the fork, heels braced on smaller, lower limbs. She broke off a few of the leaf-bearing spikes to give her a window on the world, then she dug out the collapsed telescope and began fitting the parts together, looking out across the Plain as she worked. A group of riders was huddled in a hollow between two of the swells. There was a tautness in the small wiry forms that caught her eye. Ambush? She polished the lenses, set them in the expanded tube, attached the eyepiece and brought the scope to her eye, fiddled with it until she had a clear image.

The head of a hawk, feral golden eyes, cruelly hooked green-brown beak, shaggy gold-brown feathers, black-tipped russet feathers in a crest swooping up above the black-rimmed eyes.

She slid the telescope down the hawk. The field of view was so limited she could only get small bits of the scene.

Slim brown hand resting, trembling, on leather leggings. Slim bare brown arm.

Girl's face, not pretty, but handsome, a brilliantly colored, brilliantly drawn hawk's head painted on a flat brown cheek. Aleytys moved the lens around rapidly, until she was dizzy from the jitter of the images.

Jump face to face to face, twenty women, young to middle-aged, pale tan the color of sundried grass to a rich red brown like oiled mahogany.

Some with bi-colored hair (large patches of blond, or white, or red among browns and blacks), others brindled brown and black and white like the back of a darshee hound, one among them with hair as pale as moonlight and skin like polished walnut. Hair twisted into tiny braids threaded through wooden beads that shifted with every movement.

They all wore leather, tunics laced close to the bodies, stained in complex floral and faunal designs, leggings, sandals. Each rider held a short bow, a quiver of arrows jutted past small heads, a short green vine as thick as her thumb wound around left arms of most, right arms of two, a loop of vine heavy with shiny blue-purple gourds was tied to saddle pads beside leather-clad knees.

Aleytys lowered the telescope, held it on her thigh while she scrubbed at streaming eyes

Down in the hollow the women were talking, gesturing, excited, exuberant, waiting for something. Waiting for what's coming out of the north, she thought. She shivered. This miserable bloody world. She turned away from the women; the riding beasts weren't waiting to kill—or if they were, it wasn't out of malice but merely their natures and their need for food.

The beasts were tall limber-necked creatures with short shiny black horns growing in graceful curves between leaf-shaped ears, a small tail flap, black around the edges with a white underside that flashed bright as a mirror signal each time a tail flipped over. Their coats were a short sleek dappled gray like slightly tarnished silver.

The moon-haired woman rode over to the hawk rider, swung an arm up and jabbed a flat-held hand north. The girl nodded. She smoothed a brown forefinger delicately down the hawk's neck, let it rub its beak along that finger, then put her leather-wound right arm beside the perch. The hawk danced on the perch, sidled onto her arm, spread its wings and powered itself into the air. It spiraled a few times above the rider, then darted away toward the north. In her tree, Aleytys nodded at this confirmation of her fears, sighed.

While the hawk rider was dispatching her bird, the moon-haired woman was spreading out the other riders, using crisp abbreviated gestures. A number of them rode across a dip in the hillocks—Aleytys had taken it at first glance to be a long shallow wash, but a look through the telescope changed her mind. It was another of the ancient roads, this one in much worse condition than the others she'd seen, more a series of fragments sketchily lined up than a continuous paving. The women slid off their mounts, tapped them on their hindquarters to send them dancing away a short distance, then knelt behind topknots of broom or crouched low enough on the offslopes that the slant of the hillock and fringes of new grass concealed from anyone riding along the road.

The leader and three of the riders were still mounted, waiting in the hollow. One of them was the hawkrider. The leader was holding her in the saddle, her slight form limp, slumped. Aleytys scowled, wishing she knew more, the telescope wasn't much help in interpreting cultures. The other two women were focused on the girl, their lips moving. Chanting? What did that mean? Something to do with that hawk? Something to do with what was coming along the road?

The hawk sailed in tight loops above the broken road, coming gradually closer to the ambushed women. The fragmentary glimpses she got through the telescope were confusing, made her head ache; she set the scope on her knee and leaned forward, frowning at the scene. A second group of riders came in view, the hawk soaring above them, fifteen of them, broader in the shoulder, stockier with thicker arms. With a sigh she lifted the scope. Men. Armed with staffs like the one Aleytys carried with no metal sheathing and no spike, short-shafted spears and spear throwers lashed beside the staffs. Saddlebags bobbed like gray egg sacs against their thighs. They wore heavy cuirasses of stiff leather, stamped and carved with bold angular designs, flared helmets of the same leather, carved with the same designs. The points of the spears shone milky white through the haze of dust stirred up by the hooves of the beasts, reminding her of the arrow point the creature in the NewCity ruins nailed her with.

The women in ambush crouched on their toes, taut with anticipation, arrows nocked, bows ready, waiting for that moment when they'd surge up and loose those shafts.

The riders came steadily on. She frowned at them, disturbed by their unjustified confidence. They hadn't even bothered to send scouts ahead to check the route, but rode as if they knew, absolutely knew, the way was clear. *What about the hawk?* she thought. *They must have seen the hawk, they must know what it could mean. Are they so isolated, then, these groups, that they know nothing about the folk they kill? Do they refuse to know? One of the men did ride out front, alone, but he was only a beast-length ahead of the others.* She turned the scope on him, gave a soft startled exclamation. Blind. He had to be blind. Under warty wrinkled lids his eyes were a chalky white without a sign of pupil or iris. His gaudily painted face was slack, idiotic; he swayed on the saddle pad, clinging, it seemed to her, by instinct alone. *Drugged,* she thought. *Why? Are the others?* Ignoring the strain that made her eyes water, she jumped the scope from face to face. *No,* she thought. *Not pretty, some of them, but certainly not drugged.* She rubbed at running eyes. *What's he doing?* She scowled at the tiny figure. *He's something special. Shaman? Psi-man? Whatever he is, he's not warning them about the ambush.* She leaned against the forward branch of the fork and gazed from the women to the men and back. They seemed human enough, more than that thing in the ruins. Offshoot of the cousin races from that first diaspora back in mythic time? Impossible to tell.

The riding beasts moved at a brisk walk, rapidly closing the gap between them and the ambushers, the men relaxed on the saddle pads, talking lazily, scratching, yawning. A wizened little man with patchy white hair and a nervous twitching face kicked his mount into a shambling trot and went to ride beside the painted man. After a few moments of scowling silence, he leaned close and asked him something with overtones of urgency, got back a wobbly shake of the blind idiot's head.

The ambushers waited, their presence unsuspected.

Aleytys began taking the scope apart. Time to go if she wanted to snatch a mount while the indigenes were occupied with each other. She slipped the lenses into their suede pouches, tucked them away in her belt, collapsed the tube and put it with the lenses, took a final look at the road. The lead riders came even with the first of the women; she didn't move but drew in on herself, quivering with eagerness. "I don't want to watch this," Aleytys whispered, but she didn't look away.

Like a striking storm the women uncoiled, painted arrows with creamy ceramic points whistling eerily as they sped toward the men.

At the first sound several of the men dived off their mounts, but slower reactors had no chance. Three fell screaming, no death wounds, but the poison on fiber bundles tied behind the points worked fast and the screams cut off as they hit the ground. Two swayed on the pads, scratched on face and arm by glancing shafts, weakened by the poison but far from dying. The leather armor and the speed of the rest of the men kept them clear.

The painted man was untouched. Deliberately so, Aleytys thought. He sat without taking notice of what was happening about him; when his mount started to wander off the road, away from the chaos around him, he let it go on without attempting in any way to guide it.

Almost before their feet hit the ground, the surviving men grabbed spears and sent them whistling a deeper song at the attackers.

As soon as they loosed the shafts, the women dropped. Like the men, several were too slow. Two died, spearheads slicing through them and bursting out their backs, another caught a spear in the throat and tumbled down the hillock side away from the road, spraying blood everywhere until her body was emptied, the fourth was slashed across the shoulder, the spear thrown with such force it cut through the short leather sleeve of her tunic; she fell writhing to the ground, foam spattering from her working mouth.

The men who were still on their feet dragged staffs from the nearest riding beasts and went charging up the hillocks. Two more fell to the few arrows the women had time to get off, several nearly reached the crests only to begin a hasty retreat as the women snatched up purple gourds from vine loops ready at their feet and hurled these as fast as they could. Some hit the ground, shattering, splattering, releasing small dust clouds. The men twisted frantically to avoid these, flinched and ducked away from the gourds still flying at them. Those that were hit began clawing at themselves as the red-purple juice bubbled, fumed, and the clouds settled on them, bits of the clouds crawling into the crevices of their armor and their bodies. The remaining men came weaving up the slopes again, swinging their staffs at the purple gourds, trying to pop them while the women still held them.

A woman snatched the short green vine from around her arm and snapped it at the man charging her. It whipped through the air, touched his shoulder, writhed, slapped around his neck and began strangling him. He sawed at it with a stone knife, but the tough, fibrous skin of the vine turned the blade. In seconds he was on the ground twitching feebly; in seconds he was still.

The riding beasts were scattering, shying away from the popping gourds, away from the curses and shrieks of both sets of fighters. By mutual consent neither side injured the beasts—as if the combat was an act so familiar and formalized that it more nearly resembled an elaborately choreographed dance than the happenstance of war. The history of this world, she thought, this blasted world. She swung out of the fork and dropped swiftly down the tree. No more time for looking on; if the care with which they avoided hurting the beasts meant anything, the victor of that battle would expect to claim them once the fighting was done and and she had no desire at all to face either of those bloody bands of fighters.

She hooked the pack off the warty limb, slipped her arms through the straps though she didn't like the bulk it added to her body when she needed to stay inconspicuous, but she didn't want to have to come back for it and there was more than a fair chance she wouldn't be able to come back.

Keeping to the shattered road, she loped toward the fighting, slowing to a walk and fading into the brushy hillocks when she got near enough to hear the noise of the conflict. She moved forward more cautiously, hesitated, then eased out of the pack and stowed it under a drooping clump of brush. Dropping to her stomach, she crawled to the summit of the next hillock, dust and pollen sharp in her nostrils, cries and cracks sharp in her ears. Concealed by a squat bush, she found herself watching two women and a man so intent on what they were doing, she could have walked around them without attracting any notice.

Aleytys bit her lip as the translator in her head slammed into action with the usual blinding pain, triggered by the curses the fighters were hurling at each other. She lay carefully still, eyes screwed tight, watering, head throbbing. When the throbbing finally stopped, she opened her eyes and found nothing much had changed.

A woman with a white flower and three heart-shaped leaves painted on her cheek was throwing small white discs with razor edges at the man, one after the other. The other woman—she had a branch with berries on her cheek—held one of the green vines lightly looped between her hands as she circled him, searching for an opening.

He was remarkably quick, attacking with the staff, keeping the women off balance, flicking one end up to deflect the knife discs, holding off Berry and her vine with darting stabs of the staff.

Abruptly he slipped on a tuft of grass. With a triumphant cry Berry whirled her vine at him. He rolled up, grinning, snapped the end of the staff around, knocked the vine into the grass where it lay coiling and uncoiling though there was nothing for it to close on. With a smooth continuation of the motion he cracked the staff's end hard against Berry's skull. Without waiting for her to go down, he went after White Flower, plunging recklessly at her, howling his hate, matching her hate, red-eyed with fury.

An instant before the butt of the staff crushed her throat, she flung a dart at him. It cut his face, a shallow scratch but that was all she needed for her vengeance. He fell in agony on the dead woman, his body arching backward into a half-circle, the bones of his face and frame looking for a hideous moment as if they would burst through his skin.

Enough of this, Aleytys thought. She scooted down the slope on hands and knees and crouched in the hollow, probing for the feel of the beasts. Gyori, her mind told her. Ahead. Yes. A little to the right, farther away from the road. She moved quickly toward them, keeping low, her outreach set to warn her if she got too close to one of the indigenes. The warm placid furry feel of the gyori came more strongly to her. She dropped to her stomach and wriggled as quietly as she could over the grass, turning the swell of a hillock with great caution, froze as an alarm rang in her head. She crept to a weedy pile of rocks and eased around it until she could see what was alarming her.

A slender form came plunging over the crest of a swell ahead, dug her heels in, wobbled around to face the way she'd come. A girl. The hawk rider. In her left hand she had one of the short spears, in her right hand a glass knife. This glittered in the sunlight, host to small rainbows, deadly and lovely. She backed down the slope, waited taut and alert in the hollow.

A battered, ugly man with a knobby staff appeared on the crest of the hillock. One eyelid drooped over an empty socket, his ears were enormously enlarged, the lobes flopping as he moved; palps of soft flesh dangled past the corners of his mouth. The hands that held the staff shook a little. Age or infirmity, Aleytys thought, certainly not fear. His dark brown eyes were greedy on the girl child's slight form but he was wary of the knife. After a moment's hesitation he came down the slope toward her. She backed away slowly, began to circle round him, darting in to use the knife whenever she saw a chance but never quite touching him because he was too quick with the staff and she had to twist away. Sometimes the jabs she made with the knife were feints. When he reacted to these she cut at him with the point of the spear. She was very quick but she was tiring, her face flushed and dripping with sweat, her breathing harsh. The man was tiring too, but grimly intent on defeating her. There were small cuts on his face and legs from the spear point, one on his neck very close to the large artery. Either the spear point was not poisoned or the poison had been rubbed off. A hair closer, though, and he would be lying in a pool of his own blood.

Hidden behind the weeds, Aleytys cursed under her breath. She couldn't leave without being seen and she wouldn't bet anything against them declaring a temporary truce and setting after her. And there were no beasts close enough to justify breaking cover, though she could see a small herd beyond the circling man and girl, not twenty meters away, browsing placidly at the soft green tips of new growth on the brush.

What bothered her most was the quieting of battle noise beyond the hillocks. She could hear triumph growing in the shriller voices of the women, felt anger and fear blasting out from the remaining men. She waited, hands clenched into fists, while the contest played out before her.

The man slammed the end of his staff suddenly against the spear, the crack of wood against wood painfully loud; the spear flew out of the girl's hand and she let it go, lunging at him, knife seeking flesh, any flesh, to unload its poison. He flipped the staff around and drove the butt into her diaphragm just under the join of her ribs, a brutal blow that drove her into a backward sprawl. Before she could catch herself and roll up, he slammed the staff against her head. From where she lay Aleytys could hear the crack of bone along with the dull thud of the blow.

The man straightened, glanced over his shoulder toward the unseen fighting, his large ears flapping. Muttering a curse, he shouldered the staff and loped toward the gyori.

As soon as his back was to her, she was on her feet and racing after him, careless of sound, intent only on speed. He started to swing around but she was too close. She slapped her open hand across his face, activating the stunner implants as she did so, jerked her hand away as she felt the hard muscles under her fingers go soft. He fell at her feet. She knelt beside him, felt the strong pulse in this neck, stood again. At least she wouldn't have to explain a dead indigene, though from what she'd just seen, the indigenes would understand her far better if she simply slit his throat.

She started for the gyori. Shadith's eyes popped open. "Lee." The singer's shout throbbed in her head. She stopped walking and rubbed her temples. "My head's already tender, take it easy, Shadi." She sighed. "What is it? Be quick. I want to get out of here."

"A body," Shadith cried; the face forming about the purple eyes was twisted with anguish. "The girl, Lee. Dead. Just dead. Look at her. See if you think I can . . . see if it's possible. Please."

Aleytys pulled her hand across her face. "What a time to choose." She moved quickly to kneel beside the small broken body. "She's certainly dead." She closed her eyes and moved her hands over the girl's head then down the body. "Brain damage, cracked skull, internal injuries, broken ribs. You sure you want to try this?"

"You can fix that, you know you can. Once I'm in, anyway. Please, Lee, I want to try it."

"Harskari, what about you, what do you think?"

The amber eyes opened. "If Shadith is determined—we can be ready to snatch her back. I am ready. Quickly then or the chance is gone."

Feeling unduly rushed and precarious with the victorious women—Centai-zel, she noted—about to come pouring over that hill to collect their spoils, Aleytys closed her eyes, *reached* and drew power into herself, filled herself until she felt the symbolic black water overflowing, rippling about her. She shaped a funnel and poured the power into the body, gathered the forces that were Shadith like a ball balanced on her fingertips; helped and held steady by Harskari, she flung Shadith into the dead girl's brain and body. When what was empty was filled, what was on hold an instant before began to change; stirred by the touch of Aleytys, the lapping power, the small burry fields of Shadith, the bones began to knit together as Aleytys held the bits in place, the torn flesh began to repair itself. She flooded the body with more energy to keep it going, to kick it over again from death into life. Time passed, Aleytys never knew how much, so intently was she focused on the constant struggle to support Shadith as she fought to fit herself into the body.

Finally Shadith could blink the girl's eyes, move the girl's hand. She opened the hand flat, closed it into a fist. She swallowed, worked the mouth. The heart was beating steadily, the body was breathing not so steadily, but it did keep breathing. She moved one foot, then the other, bent one leg then the other, licked the lips; then the eyes, bright with new life, shifted from Aleytys's face to the sky beyond Aleytys's head. The mouth opened. The tongue ran over dry lips. A croaking sound came from the mouth. Once again the tongue moved along the top lip, back along the bottom. "I am in . . . I'm in. . . ." The words were blurred, hard to make out.

"Wait, let me finish," Aleytys said. She put her hand on the girl's forehead and began searching through the brain.

The grosser injuries had already been repaired, now she began work on the finest structure, cleaning away dead cells, mending the most delicate of the nerve cells, replenishing the trace chemicals, so intent on the work she once again lost track of time, saw nothing at all but the near abstract images in her mind, leaving all her own defenses to Harskari, trusting the sorceress to protect them from attack. Now that she'd started this thing, she had to finish it thoroughly, Shadith's life and happiness depended on her care. Time passed in a gray haze.

But the task was finally done and as well done as she could contrive. She let go of the breath she seemed to have been holding forever

Shadith blinked, her eyes beginning to glow, the girl's masklike face warming into a crude likeness of the lively image Aleytys had seen so often in her mind. Rather clumsily, but much less so than before, Shadith reached across her body and touched Aleytys's arm. "Let me up."

Aleytys closed her eyes, let the power snap back into her symbolic river and lifted her hands away from the warm and vital body.

Shadith fumbled at the grass, pushed herself up until she was sitting. She held her hands out, palm down, turned them palm up, threw her head back and laughed with delight. She tried to stand, tumbled back on her buttocks, giggled, pushed away Aleytys's hands when she tried to help. "Let me do it," she said. "Been a long time." Her voice was burred and thick, but the words were coming clearer each time she spoke. Shifting her weight more carefully, she got to her feet, took a step, swayed uncertainly, caught her balance, blinked at a sudden wild shout from beyond the hillocks. "We better get out of here."

Aleytys chuckled. "Who's holding us up? I ask you." She rose to her feet, surprised at how tired and stiff she was. She moved her shoulders, stretched cautiously, twisted herself about until the worst of the stiffness was gone. "Catch us a couple mounts, I've got to fetch my pack."

IV

MOUNTAIN PASSAGE

1

Aleytys swung up onto the gyr, shifted about to settle herself as comfortably as she could on the thick rather lumpy pad, wiggled her boots in the woven-rope stirrups until they took her weight properly. The gyr pranced about whooshing and hoomping and shaking his head. Aleytys bent forward and patted his rolling shoulders, scratched vigorously along the curve of his neck as high as she could reach, down again between the shoulders. The gyr vibrated with a deep rumbling purr, stopped his fidgeting and stood nosing at the grass, calm and contented. She smiled, stroked his shoulder a last time, then glanced anxiously at Shadith who was sitting her own mount a little awkwardly and gazing blankly at the blue waver of the mountains. "You all right?"

"Stop fussing. I'm fine." Shadith moved restlessly on the saddle pad; her voice was still a little rough but her articulation was much improved. "Where we going now?"

"North. Back to the road." She looked over her shoulder, shivered as she heard a few shouts and more muttered conversation. "Back on Esgard's trail."

They left behind the dead, the living, the dying confusion, and cut into the rolling land, heading directly north, back to the ancient road. Now and then Aleytys scanned the Plain slipping behind her, worried about possible pursuit by the remnant of the Centai-zel band; each time she saw only the

70

heat haze gilding the brush on the swells; the afternoon was filled with a profound silence—even the small lives in the bush, the rodents, reptiles and insects, seemed to have retired for the duration of the fight and perhaps for the duration of the heat. High overhead the hawk was circling tentatively after them, slipping up to them as if he expected something and when that didn't happen, sailing away, dipping back toward what was left of the women's band, returning to renewed disappointment, faithful in the end to the body even if the mind was changed.

Shadith's new body was short and slight, fine-boned with long narrow hands and feet. There was an unfinished look to her face, her breasts were shallow curves; she seemed very young, barely past puberty. Her skin was baby smooth, fresh, a warm pale brown, her long thin braids a golden-brown, threaded through beads carved from at least a dozen different woods. The fine short hairs that escaped the discipline of the braids curled about her face, caught the thick light of the lowering sun and glowed a bright gold in a feathery halo. Her eyes were a brown so dark it was almost black; they slanted down at the outer corners, nearly rectangular in outline, giving her a look at once quizzical and deeply serious. On her left cheek she had a hawk's head painted with exquisite detail and brilliant color; the leather tunic she wore was stained in imitation of a hawk's feathers, done with the same fineness of detail as the head.

When they rode away from the ambush place, her face was in repose, almost no expression; only the restless shifting of those dark eyes showed the presence of the life settling into the body. During the first hour of the ride she said nothing, concentrated instead on the double task of keeping her balance in the body and on the gyr.

Aleytys watched her anxiously, ready to catch her in a hammock of power if she should falter, relaxed when she saw the slow return of easy natural movement to the body, saw the face slowly light to life to match the eyes. Shadith was beginning to delight in her new body, Aletytys could smell the perfume of that delight spreading out from her.

With watching Shadith and checking the backtrail for followers Aleytys had enough to contend with, but she was all too soon aware that she had another problem. Harskari. The amber eyes flicked in and out of her mind; Harskari was there and not there, waiting to help if Shadith's body tried to reject its new owner, fighting at the same time a desperate new loneliness, a loneliness that seethed and boiled over, inundating Aleytys as well. Aleytys knew a little of what the sorceress had passed through in the first centuries after she succumbed to the trap of the diadem—trapped alone and aware, seeing, hearing, knowing without eyes or ears. Centuries of madness and hate and despair until the old disciplines of her learning reasserted themselves and she moved beyond madness to a slow gathering of memory and purpose and applied herself to expanding the claustrophobic circumstances of her existance. Finally, in the ruins of an ancient world, a wandering poet and singer found the diadem. Shadith. And Harskari found a companion to share her prison with her.

For a short lifetime they roamed from world to world, Shadith wandering as she wished, unconcerned with roots or family, using her hunt for songs and tales as an excuse for that wandering, many of her finds merely serendipitous. Wandering was her hunger; she was restless, easily bored by the familiar. She thieved where she had to, worked when she must and always the goal was a new place, a new people to dip into. Something of this Aleytys knew from the years at University when she retreated from the difficulties of dealing with others as arrogantly shy and manipulative as she was and didn't want to be.

Now Harskari was alone again, trapped alone and feeling it. No matter how she gathered her emotions to herself, she'd had no time to prepare for being so abruptly bereft of her last companion; loneliness, fear, envy, shame and regret escaped her and Aleytys felt them all. Felt them and was herself disturbed by the chaotic whirl, disturbed too by her own inability to comfort Harskari or even speak of these things to her. In spite of their intimate connection, Harskari held herself intensely private. There were moments when she relaxed and spoke of her world before the diadem entered her life— snatches, disjointed vignettes—but Aleytys learned more of her from Shadith's rambles and from the friendly sparring between the two of them.

The hawk gave a plaintive questioning cry as it dipped low over them on one of its hesitating returns. Aleytys frowned, then *reached* for him. Once before, a long time ago when she ran from the Raqsidan and was lost and was out of water and was desiccated from thirst, she had mindridden a highflying predator, driven by her desperation to master a skill she'd only touched on before. She felt the hawk's fear and uncertainty, its need; she risked a brief projection of warmth. The flier twisted, lost the wind a moment, re-oriented itself and climbed with a few quick strokes of broad wings. Carefully Aleytys eased onto the brain and after a few moments gazed with the bird at the unreeling Plain. She hooked her hands under the saddle pad, a little disoriented herself as she looked through two sets of eyes at radically differing views—not simultaneously, of course, but switching rapidly between them, so rapidly she rapidly grew dizzy. She closed her eyes and willed the hawk back along the broken road until it hovered over the ambush place

The zel had rounded up the stray gyori; some were stripping the corpses of the males, slitting throats if they showed the least sign of life, others were packing the spare beasts with what their sisters gleaned. She found the man she'd left stunned and saw without too much surprise or even regret that he was stripped, his body tumbled on the grass, his throat cut. There was no sign of the painted man. He wasn't among the dead or anywhere the hawk could see.

Though she kept the bird high, one of the women looked up and saw him, pointed him out to the others. With a soft annoyed exclamation Aleytys sent the bird darting eastward and down until it was out of the women's range of vision, then brought it back to hover near her. She opened her eyes and saw Shadith watching her. "Wanting to fly, hawkrider?" she said, smiling into the eager face.

Shadith drew her hand slowly down the front of the tunic, stared down at the hawkfeathers stained into the leather, "Think I could?"

"Better not try it yet. Wait till you're settled in a while longer." She grinned suddenly. "I don't think you'd much like spending the rest of your life as a hawk."

"Hunh!" Shadith fingered the soft leather of the tunic. "I

wonder if she made this herself; I like to think so." She rubbed her nose, her brows pulled together, a short vertical line between them. "I wish I knew more about her."

They rode in a comfortable silence for several moments, then Shadith began humming. She hummed a moment, listened to herself, hummed some more, listened again. When she had enough of that, she began some vocal exercises, doing them slowly, carefully, listening intently with a gradually increasing glow as she discovered the flexibility and rather astonishing range of what was as yet an immature voice. She laughed, tried out a few snatches of song, then began singing softly to herself.

2

It was dim and cool under the overhanging branches of the pungent riveroak. Aleytys sat with her back slumped into the curve of a thick ancient trunk, watching Shadith pace about in and out of shadow, finally sink onto a flat rock jutting out into the river. Shadith threw her head back, shook it, listening to the wooden beads knocking musically against each other; she sniffed with delight at the mix of odors—the damp earth, the dry tart smell of the trees, the lingering salty warmth on the wind blowing west across the Plain, teasing up shallow ridges on the smooth surface of the water. Rising onto her hands and knees, she tried to see herself in the water, but the wind and the current and the glitter of sunlight defeated her. She laughed again, her giggle as liquidly rippling as the water moving past her. She reached down, swished her fingers through the water, caught up a handful of it, let it fall in a cascade of silver, snatched up more, let it fall, wiped her hand on her leggings, lifted the tunic's bottom, raised her brows at the neatly pleated loincloth, the points of the leggings tied with flat smooth knots to the leather belt that held the loincloth. She folded the tunic back down, crooked her right leg, inspected the sandal, fingered the lacing that tied the straps together. She stretched her leg out again, scratched a fingernail through the thin layer of moss on the rock, sniffed at the finger, pulled up a stem of grass and cleaned the green muck from behind the nail. She smiled. Threw back her head again. Laughed at the clatter of the beads. Shook her head until the thin braids danced wildly and the wooden beads clacked like rain on a rooftop, her chuckling diminishing to small triads of gurgles. She swung around, drew her legs up and wrapped thin arms about them. "Oh, I'm drunk with this, Lee. Drunk. So drunk. Drunk on smells and sounds and feels and oh—everything. It's a great body, it's a marvelous body, it's a splendid body. It sings." She shook her head again and laughed with the noise of the beads. Then she lifted her hands and pressed their backs against her eyes. "I'm tired."

"Busy day. How are you fitting now?"

Shadith yawned, looked startled. "I'm hungry."

Aleytys pushed away from the tree. "Haven't done any hunting, you know that. We'll have to catch some fish. You want to do the catching while I get the fire started?"

Shadith yawned, nodded.

Aleytys busied herself with the pack. "I think I'll distribute these things among the saddlebags. We can dump out the weapons or whatever else we can't use. That later, though." She drew out the sections of fishing pole, dug deeper for the coil of line and the packet of hooks. "Anything at all left of that girl?"

"You asked Swartheld that. Something like that. I remember." Shadith sounded drowsy. Her voice dragged a little, the words were slurred. Aleytys glanced anxiously at her, frowning. She had her arms crossed on her knees, her cheek rested on her forearm, her eyes blinked slowly as she stared at the lacing of light and shadow drawn around the trunks of the grove. "Some habits . . . I think . . . don't know . . . got the language . . . from you . . . before you transferred me . . . I think . . . no . . . memories . . . no. . . ."

"Shadith?" Aleytys dropped the rod and ran toward her as she began slumping over. "Harskari, help me." As the amber eyes came open, Aleytys lifted Shadith's head, her palms firm against the delicate hollows of Shadith's temples. She felt the uneasy flutter of life in the shell beneath her hands and *reached* frantically for the power to shore up that life. With Harskari supporting and helping shape the force, she shook

Shadith into a sort of alertness and funneled that energy into
the body.

Gradually the Shadith entity woke from lethargy and began to seize control again. The body seemed to fight them all,
to try rejecting the new indweller. At times the body trembled
with sudden flashes of intense pain, at times the young flesh
glowed with a fever that burned Aleytys's hands, at times the
body convulsed and though she was by far the stronger, she
had much difficulty keeping it from doing injury to itself. The
night deepened about them. The wind fell. The intervals
between spasms lengthened as the fragile fluttering of life
within the body settled toward a low but steady burning.

3

Aleytys dipped the rag into the pot of riverwater and drew it
once again across the still, small face, noting that the colors
and fine black detailing of the hawk's head had worn away
with the sweat and tears and the passing of the rag as she
sought to cool away a little of the fever. Though the colors
and the finelining were gone, the outline of the head remained,
a medium brown line not too much darker than the skin,
tattooed or set there with some other process that permanently
melded pigment with flesh. She dipped the cloth in the pot
again, wrung out excess water and draped it across Shadith's
forehead, scowling as she did so, staring down into the face
that was no longer the face she knew so well. She moved her
shoulders impatiently.

Shadith made a small sound, nothing like the animal noises
of the fit where her voice had turned harsh, shapeless, ugly.
Aleytys lifted the rag, looked anxiously down. The girl's
eyelids fluttered and opened. Dark, dark, chocolate dark
eyes—a shock like a small jab of electricity to see brown
where she unconsciously anticipated lavender. It was the
same with Swartheld, the face she knew from the inside of
her head; both faces now, Swartheld's and Shadith's, different,
the eyes different—she had to will herself to recognize them
each time she looked at them.

Aleytys shook herself out of her depression and touched

the girl's cheek just below the hawk's image. "In the saddle again?"

Shadith blinked. Her lips worked like a baby's mouth hunting for the nipple, then spread in a weary but triumphant grin. "Almost thrown," she whispered. She moved her hands, tried to push up, shook her head when Aleytys sought to persuade her into staying stretched out on the grass.

With Aleytys's help she sat up. "Ah. That's better." She lifted her hands, held them out, watched them tremble, then smoothed them over the multitude of tiny braids with their noisy wooden beads. She smiled, rubbed her stomach. "I'm hungry."

4

Aleytys woke to rustling darkness, not knowing what it was that roused her. She sat up, her extra senses sweeping in a circle scan and finding nothing to justify her sudden wakefulness. She smiled, shrugged, brushed tangles from her eyes and looked about. Only starlight played with shadow under the trees. Shadith lay beside her, wrapped in the blankets she found tied behind the saddle pad of the mount she'd adopted. Beyond Shadith the river glimmered black and silver in the icy light. Aleytys ran her fingers through her hair, scrubbed at her eyes. I ought to go back to sleep, she thought. Madar knows what we'll have to face tomorrow.

But she didn't lie back and pull the blankets about her. She got to her feet and went to sit on Shadith's rock where she could watch the endless changes of the water flowing past. Unthinking, lost in the sinking of the starlight, deep, deep into the water, her breathing slowing with her pulse, she felt unmixed the weariness of the ancient land, its weariness and its patience. Having endured the millennia of assaults, having been bombed and burned and raped and poisoned to near sterility, it had outlasted finally the malevolence of its parasite humanoids; slow and slow and slow the grass grew over the sores though the healing wasn't finished, no not yet, oozing ulcers still pocked its surface. But the grass had time now. The metals were gone, corroding slowly back into the soil, the last of the tanks and bombers and other lethal machines had used up their fuel and were crumbling away, most of the ancient deadly skills were lost. Time to heal.

Aleytys shifted on the rock. She probed for Harskari but the sorceress had retreated somewhere deep within the diadem and was answering no calls. It felt very strange to see the old one so uncertain about her wants and needs, so moody, so withdrawn, radiating an itch that reinforced the painful uncertainties already troubling Aleytys. She gazed into the water, floating as if she hung half-in, half-out of her body.

I don't know, I don't know, why struggle anymore? I don't have to like my mother, I just have to find her. I certainly despised my father. She watched silver lines curl and slide away across the black water. *My people. I wonder. Vryhh Kell called me mud. Half-breed. Hate in his voice. What does it matter anyway? No. It does matter. My body thinks so anyway. Body? Madar knows, I certainly don't. Kell. Ancestor of some sort. Great—how many greats?—grandfather.* He'd more than hinted he'd been her mother's lover, Kell whom she'd fought and defeated on Sunguralingu, then cured of the disease that was withering him, Kell who'd gone from Sunguralingu to destroy her son, who had somehow driven her son from his home and into the arms of Stavver, the thief who had brought her the curse of the diadem. She stared into the water and saw again Stavver's face in the viewscreen, pity in his milky blue eyes—pity, somehow, a greater insult than hate or indifference ever could be—as he'd told her that her son refused to talk with her, refused even to let her look at him. She felt again the pain of that moment and shied away from considering it. Wriggling uneasily on the stone, she stared up through the fringe of stiff leaves at the spray of stars. Wolff's sun wasn't visible from here; she wouldn't have been able to find it in that blaze anyway. Wolff. She rubbed at her nose.

The timing of Swartheld's return couldn't have been worse—the day before Grey returned from his Hunt, weary and troubled, needing her more than ever, quietly furious, then bitterly vocal about his pain when he found Swartheld with her. She shivered. Bad. Other dangers, other agonies, even other quarrels, they all had the virtue of being relatively cut and rapidly cleared up, one way or another. Here nothing was clear, she didn't know what she wanted most—no, not true, she wanted Grey, she loved him, needed him, needed the need he had for her; he validated her, gave her direction, restrained her excesses. The prospect of leaving him was such a pain she didn't want to think about it. Grey was nearing the end of his Hunt years, wanted to stand for Council, said Head needed some support for a change. Aleytys gazed into the water without seeing it any longer, wondering whether she would be an asset or a liability in this. There was a group, a fairly small group, but a vocal one, virulently opposed to her presence. Vicious about it. And he wants a child. Wants to tie me to him. He knows I couldn't leave another baby and keep my sanity. She slipped her fingers through the water, let a rain of crystal drops fall back, listening absently to the music this made as she did it over and over. Her first experience of motherhood had been a disaster, though she couldn't be sorry her son existed—and there had been happy times, times she didn't dare think much about even now because the loss was still too sore. She was tempted, she had to admit that, she would like Grey's child, problem was it would be hers too with all that entailed. I have to see my mother, she thought. I have to know her so I can know myself better, so I can know more about what my child might be. Another reason for finishing this, she thought. Balanced against her growing desire for that child, she was also beginning to feel a net tightening about her. Sometimes she actually liked that net, it gave her a feeling of security, of belonging; sometimes she felt so stifled she wanted to scream.

And there was Swartheld. She twisted her mouth as she remembered her old bear and Grey facing each other, stiff, polite, hostile. How could she bear to part with him, so long, so very long a part of her? Who made her lose control of herself, who, like no other man or woman or child—even Grey, jarred her outside the shell of defenses she'd reared about herself. She loved him as friend, father, lover, her other self, a feeling natural to her as breathing. She had to work hard at her relationship with Grey. With Swartheld there were no points to make, no confusion, no awkward maneuvering. *I want both. I want Grey and Swartheld both.* She closed her eyes a moment, passed her hand across her mouth. *We'll work it out,* she thought a little desperately, trying to prop up a feeble hope it might be so.

But that hope soon washed away, drowned by too many other anxieties. Vryhh. Half-breed Vryhh. She gazed at the water, remembering the night before she left to come here. Remembering waking, slipping from the bed and standing beside Grey who was sunk deep into a sleep that nothing could breach, his face still showing some of the weariness and the bitterness of the day. She watched him a moment, sadness and tenderness so mixed in her she didn't know where one stopped and the other began.

Abruptly she turned away and padded to the wall mirror, touched on a hooded light and began examining her face and body. No scars. That was the first thing. All the beatings and burnings and wounds and mischances that had happened to her hide—there was no sign of any of that, all the marks vanished into the quicksand of time and the self-healing of that hide. Not even stretch marks. She smoothed her hand up over her stomach and felt like weeping, no sign at all she'd ever borne a child; this seemed somehow to wipe her son out of existence, at least for her. She tried laughing at her foolishness, but the sadness remained.

She leaned closer to the mirror, pulled at the skin around her eyes, drew her fingertips down her cheek past the corner of her mouth, rubbed at the firm flesh beneath her chin. The skin was soft and fresh and unlined as it had been the day she'd run from the vadi Raqsidan. She stepped back and gazed at herself. *I look older,* she thought. *No lines, but there's an assurance I didn't have a dozen years ago.* There was a knowledge of life that altered her expression, the way she stood and moved, a knowledge of pain and grief, a knowledge that one survives and goes on, no matter what the pain. She turned slowly, swiveling her head to watch herself. *Longlife? Shortlife? I can't tell.*

She shook her head, touched off the light and padded back to the bed. Grey was still sleeping heavily, muttering now, the words unintelligible. *Dreaming,* she thought. *I wonder what. Not pleasant, whatever it is.* She sighed and turned away, circled round the foot of the bed and settled herself beside him. She touched him with her fingertips, carefully, so she wouldn't wake him, stroked them across his forehead, brushing sweat-damp strands of hair off his face, smiled at the softness and fineness of the gray-streaked black strands, drew her fingertips down the side of his face, feeling the taut muscles as she heard the grinding of his teeth. There was a new scar close to his eye, a nick in his jawline. She hadn't noticed those before and felt a sinking coldness as she saw how close death had brushed by him. She touched the nick. An inch from the artery. She closed her eyes. Ay-Madar, so close. She sat very still for several minutes, then sighed, relaxed and began smoothing her fingers across his forehead, letting the healing flow gently into him. He relaxed under her touch and was soon sleeping more easily.

She sat crosslegged staring into the darkness of the bedroom, going over one more time the quarrel so precariously made up this night because of the physical need between them. Old hurts and new. Sores skinned over and picked open and worried at. She'd come close to telling him who Swartheld was but she didn't, a complex knot of loyalties tangling her tongue.

Aleytys leaned down to the river, flicked her fingers through the cold swift water; she was beginning to shiver, beginning to get sleepy. *He's a little afraid of me, I think. He doesn't know it yet. Hasn't put all he knows together, no, not yet. When he does . . . ah-Madar, I've got some time left me. A little.* She stood, grunted at the stiffness the riding had left her with, that and the cold. She stretched, yawned, glanced at the sky. A little time. She smiled. For sleeping. She went back to the groundsheet and stood looking down at Shadith— curled on her side, a fist pressed against her mouth. Shaking her head at the complications knotting up her life, she wound herself back in her blanket, closed her eyes and hoped determinedly for sleep.

5

The hawk circled high over the Centai-zel—the eight of them left from the band of twenty—sliding in and out of the gathering clouds, riding the thermals above the Blight. The women were scattered and on foot, searching through the vegetation on the fringes of the Blight, wading out into the noxious liquid with an insouciance that startled Aleytys (watching them through the eyes of the hawk). Esgard had written: they prospect the Blights much as men on other worlds hunt precious metals and gemstones.

Aleytys coaxed the hawk back above her and left him to follow as he would. She watched Shadith awhile. The girl was riding easily, her face far more animated than yesterday; the chocolate eyes scanned the road ahead and now and then turned wistfully to the hawk. Aleytys sighed, hoped she'd have the patience to refrain from trying out her newly acquired talents, at least until night camp. She examined the eager young face and doubted that the girl did have the patience. *Young,* she thought. *How very young she seems.* She smiled. Young and ancient at the same time. It was hard to think of her being centuries—no, millennia—old. She groaned. *I don't really know her,* she thought, *even after all these years. The body makes a difference, ay-Madar, it does.* She sighed again, rubbed at the crease between her brows as she contemplated the mountains ahead, gaining definition as they drew nearer.

The road ran more or less parallel to the general course of the river, cutting across the twists and turns without coming within half a kilometer of it. Her gyr moved along at an elastic canter, his hooves dancing over the hard surface of the road as easily as they had over the variety of footing on the plain—dirt, grass, gravel, brush and rock. She chuckled as she felt the soft nose of her gyr nudging at her knee. Mild affectionate creatures, these beasts. She leaned forward, dug her fingers into the fleece growing thickly on the limber neck, chuckled again at his soft lowing grumble of pleasure.

Shadith broke into her musing. "You're not taking this very seriously."

"Not at the moment," she said after a moment's consideration. "Why not relax, there's no world-shaking urgency about this. Nothing much riding on what happens."

"Nothing much?" Shadith raised both brows.

"All right, all right, you know better, I know better. I still say I could go quite happily through life if I could forget all about Vrithian and my mother and all that.''

Shadith looked at her and looked away, skepticism printed on her face.

Aleytys smiled, but the smile quickly faded. The jar against expectation that Shadith's new body and her increasing independence kept delivering to her was showing her things about herself she didn't want to see. Control. She'd fought any way she could others having control over her mind and body and she'd struggled with the temptation of controlling others. But the distress she was feeling at Shadith's independence made her failure in that fight distressingly clear. Having lost control of Shadith by freeing her from the prison on the diadem, she was now having trouble coping with that freedom, an ugliness that appalled her.

She shook herself from her developing depression and frowned at the mountains ahead—still a few days' ride off. It was time to make up her mind about what she wanted to do. She slipped the map from her belt, unfolded it and spread it out on her mount's shoulders. After locating the Blight, she moved her finger north, found the road and followed it until it met the river close to their last camp, then skipped along it until she thought she'd located them. Not too far ahead a bridge crossed the river. A part of the broken road. *Where the men came from,* she thought. She traced the road and the river with her thumb, following them into the hills until the road disappeared for a space, covered by half of the river as it split around an almond-shaped island at least half a kilometer long. There was something written beside the island, tiny letters, black ink in the finest of points. DANGER, they said. CENTAI-ZEL. LEAVE ALONE OR I'M DEAD. That little note to himself brought her a vivid image of the old man bending over the map, scratching a reminder to himself with his fine-nibbed stylus. Centai-zel, she thought, so that's where they were coming from. Almond-shaped island with a deep swift moat around it. She tapped a thumbnail against the pass above the island, then drew her hand back down to the bridge, followed the broken road north cutting across the arc of the foothills until she found another valley, a deep bite out of the mountain chain, dotted with small blotches that might be houses. A

thick dark line blocked off the front of the valley. *A wall?* she
thought. She shivered. Whatever it was, it blocked access to
the pass she saw higher in the mountains. She ran her fingers
up and down the mountains. The next pass either north or
south was at least two months' ride away. She frowned at the
map. There was no real time limit, but supplies were getting
low, the attrition worse now that Shadith was with her. Soon
she'd have to live completely off the land and that could be a
hard scrabbling existence, especially if the rest of the indigenes proved to be as hostile as those she'd already seen. It
was one thing to listen to Hana speak of the vehement
animosity of the indigenes, another to see them fighting to the
death with such vicious determination that they smeared poison on all edged weapons. Riding too close to folk with that
mindset made her very nervous. She began refolding the
map.

Shadith cleared her throat with an annoyed peremptory
scrape. "Could I have a look?"

"Sorry." Aleytys kneed the gyr closer and passed the map
to Shadith. "I forgot." She waited until the girl had the map
open in front of her. "I was thinking we'd do best keeping to
the road, well, not exactly the road, that's probably too
dangerous. We'd better cross over the bridge ahead and circle
round the Centai-zel." She glanced at Shadith's intent face.
"You see what Esgard says?"

"Ummm, right. Wonder how he planned to get past them?"

"Maybe he didn't. Maybe he's moldering bones fertiliz-
ing the grass."

"If they caught him, he sure is—from what we saw back
there." She nodded toward the south, slapped the map back
into its folds and tossed it to Aleytys. "Not much point in
speculating."

"Not much." Aleytys tucked the map back into her belt.
"It would have been a bit more helpful if he'd marked the
route on the map he planned to use when he slipped past
them. There'd have been snow on the ground when he passed.
Did that make it easier or harder? His guide knew. Local
knowledge—which we don't have."

"Right." Shadith tilted her head back, searched the sky
until she found the hawk, then watched him skimming in and

out of the clouds. "A map's well enough, but the data is a bit old. I'd feel happier with a look at what's there now." Her face determined and rather defiant, she snuck a glance at Aleytys.

"Not you," Aleytys said firmly. "Keep an eye out." She slumped on the saddle pad, settled herself comfortably, closed her eyes and reached for the hawk, then sent him winging north along the broken road, wanting to see for herself that thing that might be a wall, wanting to take a good look at the possible alternate route across the mountains. For some time the prairie land and the foothills reeled past unchanging, then she saw a large herd of ruminants eating its way over the hills like a many-mouthed worm. She took the hawk lower. Several smallish indigenes—boys or prepubescent girls—rode lazily about the herd. As she watched, one small figure kicked its gyr into a trot and went chasing after a lollopping youngster hot-footing it away from the rest. As she sent the hawk winging on, the rider turned the calf and chased it back.

A little to the north of the herd she saw a few scattered stone structures—then the wall itself. She sent the hawk higher, soaring through wispy clouds. Blocking the mouth of a broad chunky valley she saw a massive stone wall with crumbling cliffs of rotten rock on either side. There had to be rockfalls often, especially in the spring after the wear of winter ice. It was hard to estimate the wall's height, looking directly down on it as she was. The only break in it was a complicated double gate, a stone maze between inner and outer. Inside—squat one-story houses built of dressed stone or brick with thatched roofs, fields enclosed in stone walls, a green blush of vegetation in some, animals grazing in others. Small figures walked in the rambling lanes between the houses or worked in the fields. It seemed a placid peaceful sort of life, but the hawk didn't like it there and began to rebel against her control. She let him circle back toward her, soothing him with small friendly touches. Gradually he grew calm again; when he was easy once more, she teased him south toward the main flow of the river, let him ride the thermals above the water and stroke himself against her hold until he and she had shared the pleasure of such soaring.

Aleytys shook herself out of her absorption, left the hawk

on a long lead, opened her eyes, stretched, twisted her head about to get the stiffness out of her neck. "Just as well I got a look north. Confirms what the map shows and Esgard said. No way across there. Wall." She rubbed at her eyes. "Lot of rotten rock, liable to break the neck of anyone trying to climb it."

Shadith shifted impatiently on the saddle pad. "Let me look ahead."

"No." Aleytys yawned, patted the yawn. "Not yet."

"Why not?" Shadith frowned at the sky. The hawk wasn't visible, but she ignored that and yearned toward him; she could feel him, that was obvious. With a soft curse, Aleytys slapped her back and slipped into the hawk before she had time to recover. Once she was sure Shadith was simmering but settled where she belonged, Aleytys touched the hawk south and west, along the river to the moated settlement.

The long sinuous valley was not blocked by a wall, there was no need of a wall. The fields in the valley proper were lush with growth of all kinds—row crops in some, graze in others with small furry beasts cropping busily at it. The varied areas were separated by prickly hedges—or it might have been thorn-vines growing thickly over posts and connecting threads.

The island, a pointed oval, had a curtain wall of prickly vine thrice the height of a tall woman woven between trees growing around the rim. A laughing, shouting crowd of women and girls knelt at the riverside scrubbing clothing and sticking the pieces they rinsed on the thorns of the great hedge. Inside this green wall the island was thickly wooded with many small clearings where beasts grazed in pole corrals, where pole fences outlined miniature garden plots, where more groups of women and girls worked, spinning, weaving, twisting rope, staining, cutting, sewing leather, learning chants, a thousand things.

As the hawk drifted across the island and circled back, Aleytys found no exit in the hedge and no sign of boats, small or large, no bridges of any kind—and the women certainly didn't wade across, both branches ran deep and swift, so deep even the hawk's keen eyesight couldn't see the bottom though the water was clean, clear. Yet there were more women and girls working in the fields, stooping to pull weeds, pick bugs and worms off plants, collect ripe pods or fruits. She frowned, sent the hawk circling round again. No housing visible anywhere. Did they live underground? In the trees? She thought of sending the hawk lower, but there were several of his brothers loose in the clouds with him and she didn't want to stir up interest and have it waiting for them when they tried to slip past. She tried to call the hawk away. He fought her hold. She clamped that hold tighter and wrenched him away from the settlement. He struggled against her, his flying erratic, until he left the valley behind, then began to calm as she petted and soothed him. Finally he calmed enough to let her withdraw without fear of losing him. With a slight shiver she left him and opened her eyes.

Shadith was scowling. "When are you going to let me try him? How can I know if I can unless you do?"

"Give him a rest, Shadi. I ran him hard."

The girl pouted. "You're always putting me off. Worse than Harskari when she goes maternal."

Aleytys snorted. "You say that after last night? Try acting your real age, not your body's age and I'll try not interfering."

"Last night." Shadith fluttered her fingers, airily dismissing last night. "That's all over. I'm in solid now."

"Why take a chance?"

"Why not?" Shadith moved restlessly on the saddle pad. "You can catch me easy enough if I start wobbling. Come on, I've got to try some time. It's no big deal."

"Big deal?" Aleytys grinned, firmed her mouth into sobriety. "That body of yours has overactive glands."

"Hunh. Well?"

Aleytys shook her head. "I knew you wouldn't wait." She closed her eyes, swept a probe around them as far as she could, used the hawk's eyes for a double check. Nothing moving, nothing threatening, not yet anyway. She glanced at Shadith; the eager reckless young face was not at all reassuring. She sighed. "Listen, Shadi."

"Well?" The word was like a stone flung at her. Shadith had no patience left.

"We don't have time for playing. . . ."

Shadith made a small spitting sound, like an angry cat.

"No," Aleytys said, impatience making her louder than she liked. "No. Stop fussing and listen. I need your help. I got chased from the settlement before I had time to search the mountains. We need to find a way round, Shadi, you know that. While you're trying out your flying, keep well away from the valley floor, find us a way. Can you do that?"

Shadith's eyes sparked with enthusiasm. "Sure."

"Go ahead. But take it easy. You know what I mean."

"Yes, mama. Of course, mama. I'm not a fool."

Aleytys smiled. "Remember, ancient sage, you're in a young body and it's affecting you. You're acting fourteen, not the fourteen thousand you claim. Cool the mix or you're asking for trouble."

"You didn't dig at Swartheld like this." Shadith squeezed her face into an exaggerated pout, then she giggled. "All right, mama. All right. I'll be good."

"Hah. I'll believe that when I see it."

Shadith grinned, then wriggled about, settling herself onto the saddle pad, her feet into the stirrups. She took a deep breath and closed her eyes.

Aleytys watched over the entry. In moments she felt immaterial tendrils extruding tentatively from Shadith. It was very strange seeing this happen from the outside. The tendrils moved more swiftly, more surely; then the hawk gave a series of short sharp cries, lost the wind a moment, caught it again and began turning tighter circles. He had accepted Aleytys passively enough, but this seemed both joy and pain for him; he almost recognized the touch, though the mind behind that touch had changed—enough residue of the last owner left to disturb him.

She smiled at Shadith's brimming pleasure and excitement as she mounted the hawk's brain and eased within until she was looking through the bird's eyes. She watched the girl a moment longer, then relaxed, satisfied, and left her on her own.

Aleytys lifted her head to the morning breeze, pulled off the turban and let the air play along her face and neck, enjoying the fugitive coolness; it was early but already there was more than a hint of the heat to come. Dust and pollen lay in a golden haze about the hocks of the gyori, kicked up by their

hooves as they paced along the thick-strewn road between
deepening swells that were reaching for the stature of hills.
The two of them were yet a day's ride from the mountains,
but already she could feel them drawing her. She pulled the
gyr to a slower walk, the other gyr slowing with him, pace
for pace; she was reluctant to reach those mountains, as if
they were a kind of trap, as if they meant a commitment to
something she was not willing to face—though she had to
wonder about the outcome of the tug between what she
wanted and what something deep and primitive demanded of
her. Mountains. They marked a change. Once past them, this
light-hearted journey would turn to serious labor.

Brooding over these discomforts, Aleytys forgot about
Shadith—until a nip from Harskari recalled her. She swung
round and stared at the girl.

Shadith was riding easily but her face had gone dull and
empty, her eyes had a glaze that grayed their rich chocolate.
Aleytys *reached* out to her . The girl had an attenuated feel
that startled a curse out of her. "Shadith," she called, her
voice sharp with anxiety. "That's enough. Get back."

Shadith ignored her. Or didn't hear her.

Aleytys reined her gyr closer until she was riding knee to
knee with Shadith. She set the flat of her hand against the
clean curve of the girl's cheek, poured a jolt of energy into
her and called again, "Shadith!"

A look of strain twisted the young face, then the dark eyes
were open, blinking. Shadith drew a deep breath, held it
while she rubbed her face, then exploded it out. "Wild trip,"
she said on the tail of the breath. Her voice was hoarse with a
tremble in it.

"I wouldn't try that again. Not for a while." Aleytys
nudged her gyr until she rode at a comfortable distance. "Did
you find a way?"

"Hard to be sure." Shadith frowned. "In a skimmer I
know how to find my way about; funny, though, to have to
walk over ground I've flown over, it gives a different perspec-
tive somehow even if nothing else changes. I've found a way,
I think, if the gyori can walk it, on the north side of the
valley. You're right, we'll have to cross over the bridge,
leave the road behind. I'd like to take the hawk into the

mountains again once night comes, see how the way looks by starlight. It's too exposed for daylight crossing but maybe when they're all asleep. . . ." She shrugged.

They rode on through the golden morning. The heat rose with the day and the dust and muted the invisible noises of insects and small rodents as if the soft pungent touches of the lazy wind sucked away the energy from them.

❻

"I'm tired," Shadith said suddenly. "And hungry."

"You and the hawk." Aleytys pointed. The bird plummeted into the dust and heat haze, high now as the sun was swinging low. He rose again with something limp and furry in his talons and flew down to the dark line of trees hugging the river.

"You think it's him working on me?"

"Or you on him." Aleytys rubbed her nose. "Mmmh. It's a bit early."

"Hah. I told you. You're in no hurry."

Aleytys chuckled. "Well, you're right." She pushed the nudging nose of the gyr away from her knee, scratched absently at its neck. "Besides we need to do something for supper. Bird, beast or fish?"

"Fish, I think." Shadith yawned. She wiped sweat from her face, pulled her hand down and grimaced at the smears on it. "I'd forgot about sweat." She eased herself on the saddle pad. "Or the aches and pains a body can feel. At least you fish sitting."

Aleytys raised her brows, turned her gyr toward the river. "I've sweated enough on occasion."

"It's not the same." Shadith wriggled once again on the saddle, reached down to touch the small area of bare flesh between the top of the leggings and the edge of her loincloth. "Ooh! You're going to have to do some healing, Lee. You'd think this body would be used to riding. Maybe it's just I've got a different way of doing it." She reached inside the tunic and scratched thoughtfully. "Eh—Lee, there's a drawback or two having a body of your own."

Aleytys chuckled. "It'll all come back to you, ancient child."

"You're a big help. Hunh!"

7

"What you think of this?" Shadith twisted the hook from the fish's mouth, held up the flapping body, her mouth compressed into a disdainful pout. The fish was long and skinny, gnarled, warty, with many scars and open suppurating wounds. She held it a moment longer then tossed it back into the river. "Enough to kill a goat's appetite." She frowned over her shoulder at the fish piled on a swatch of grass. "You think any of those are fit to eat?"

Aleytys yawned, watched her own float bob energetically, decided it was only the tug of the current. "I'll take a look at them later." She twitched the pole, watched the float hop about, looked lazily at the heap of fish. "Think that's enough for the two of us?"

"Um. Who cleans them?"

"Flip you for it."

"Hah." Shadith began looping the fishline into a small neat coil. "I might as well get busy."

Aleytys grinned. "You saying I'd cheat?" She started pulling in her line.

Shadith sniffed and settled herself by the heap of fish. "When you can make things dance like their feet which they don't have are on fire?"

"That's supposed to make sense?"

"Yes." Shadith picked up a fish that was limber and snakelike with hard and very sharp fin spines. "Ugly bastard."

"But edible, one hopes." Aleytys fitted the hatchet head onto the handle and began lopping limbs off a down tree, the dead wood brittle as glass with orange crystals of solidified resin spiraling through its dull cream. She gathered the light fragments and brought them back to the hole she'd dug into the bank and lined with water-polished stones from the river. She knelt, glanced at Shadith as she began arranging the wood in the hole. "No need to hurry," she said finally, swallowing her urge to protest more vigorously as Shadith's knife slashed recklessly at the fish, snicking off the dangerous fins, stabbing at the belly to empty out the entrails.

"Yes, mama." Shadith didn't bother looking up or changing the way she was working.

"I'm talking to myself." Aleytys went back for more wood.

8

"What are you going to do?" Aleytys finished the cha in her mug, picked a leaf off her tongue.

"Do?"

"Once we get off this world?"

"Haven't thought much about that." Shadith searched among the bones for the last flakes of delicate white fish, then set the plate on the grass beside her. "Hook on with Swartheld for a while, I suppose. What about you? After Vrithian, I mean. Going to stay on Wolff?"

Aleytys lifted a hand, let it drop. "I don't know."

Shadith snorted. "Playing games." She got to her feet, brushing her greasy hands together. "Where's the soap? Never mind, I see it. Setting up paper targets because you won't face what's really eating at you." Towel over her shoulder, she half-ran, half-slid down the bank, landed on a chunk of sodden wood at the edge of the water. "You're not going to leave Grey until you have to. Unless he kicks you out over Swartheld or something dumb you do. That was one blazing row you had, the two of you after Swartheld took off." She knelt and began scrubbing her hands.

"You shouldn't be fouling the water with that soap." The words were flat, tight, her body felt flat, tight. She was suddenly and furiously angry, so angry she could barely talk. So angry she frightened herself. She clamped her teeth on her tongue lest she say things that would drive Shadith irrevocably away from her, things she knew she would neither feel nor believe in a quieter state. Like the collapse in the NewCity ruins, there was too much fury, a fury so far beyond anything called for that it had to be coming from some source beyond the irritation of the present moment. She pressed the heels of her hands against her eyes and tried to stop shaking.

Shadith chuckled, wilfully unaware of the struggle behind her. "Pollute this?" She splashed water about. "I shudder to think what it's doing to my skin."

Aleytys ground her teeth together. The fire crackled and hissed, overhead waxy leaves rattled, an unseen bird chirped a few times and fell silent, night bugs flitted over the water, between the trees, whirring and chirrupping with mindless persistence, and under all these varied sounds, the brushing roar of the river. Aleytys shuddered, sighed, pulled her hands down as Shadith came up the bank, her face glowing from its scrubbing, her voice rippling energetically through what sounded more like vocal exercises than any formal song, to Aleytys at least.

Aleytys checked the cha-pot, split the last cha between her mug and Shadith's. She felt deeply tired, lassitude like chains on her body—a reaction to the rage that had burned to ash moments before. She handed Shadith her mug without speaking to her, then sat sipping at the lukewarm liquid while Shadith settled with a sigh of contentment and a boneless grace against the trunk of an aged gnarled tree. Aleytys hesitated, the silence between them was comfortable enough now, but she spoke anyway, embarrassing herself but unable to help it. "Grey wants a child."

"I heard." Shadith crooked an arm behind her head, leaned against it, turning her face toward Aleytys. Her lips curled into a quick smile that quickly faded. "What about you?" The smile again. "You're the one who'll face the fuss."

"I don't know," Aleytys mumbled into the mug. "Look what happened with my son. Why bring forth another freak like me?"

Shadith stretched, dropped her arm into her lap. "Well, I never regretted being alive and look what happened to me. You figure out what you really want then to hell with what might happen." She drew her leg up, tapped her fingers on the knee. "How far would you say that valley is? We should aim for a couple hours before dawn, I think. Reaching it, I mean. People generally sleep hardest about then. Those women scare hell out of me. Poison, gahh. Nasty. Bugs. Strangle vines. God knows what else they've got on home ground. Remember what Hana said. Them and others like them, they wiped out a Singarit attack force armed with weapons that could blow away the world. Armored fighters breathing their own air. Armed and armored fliers. Think about it."

Aleytys shifted uneasily. "I am. I'd rather not." She drew a hand across her eyes. "Couple hours' ride, I'd say. Make it three to be safe. Madar, I'm tired." She slapped at a gnat on her arm. "It's been easy so far. Easy enough." She brushed impatiently at gnats looping about her face. "Bugs. The plain is empty except for ghosts." She shivered. "Ghosts. And bones." Twisting round, reaching, she found a length of twig. With a grunt at the effort she straightened and sat breaking the twig into small pieces. She looked at the bits in her hand, flung them at the fire. "Toss me that bag by your feet."

ESGARD'S NOTES:

The settlements that ring the Plain are fragments broken off the old society, each fragment considering itself the only whole and true representation of the genius of that society. Sil Evareen to them seems, from what I could gather, either heaven or hell, the representation of all that is desired, the reward for achieving perfection—or it is the repository of demons for the torment of those who fall from grace. Due to their self-enforced isolation along with external and internal pressures, these—call them tribes—these tribes have petrified to an extent I would not have thought possible in any except the most moribund societies—and one must admit, these folk are far from moribund in spite of their determined attempts to exterminate each other—or perhaps because of them. How's that, fond reader, for fence sitting?

The road and the river meet close by one of the odder fragments. The Centai-zel sit like a minefield across our best route to the sea, the ancient road and the most manageable of the passes. If I could start later in the year, we would have a broader choice of passes, but too many things have to lock into place for me. I have played with the pieces and shifted them about, and the answer is always the same—for me, the optimum time to leave is late autumn or early winter. Fasstang also prefers crossing the mountains around the first snow. Says it's safer. The Centai-zel are less apt to be roaming the hillsides.

CENTAI-ZEL Daughters of the Green. All-female society. Nothing especially odd about that, there are several such represented here in the Free Trade Sector. Use parthogenesis and sex-determination for continuance. A little strange sometimes, but not impossible to deal with. Too busy and too self-confident to bother with hostility toward those of other persuasions. Not the case with the Centai-zel. No indeed.

The Zel have several means of maintaining their numbers. Adoption of adult females is possible but rare. Natural birth is much more common. Raiding parties capture selected males, who survive a few months or until a sufficient number of pregnancies is confirmed, then are ritually slain. Male offspring are kept until weaned, then returned to the father's tribe. Female children are mothered by the whole adult population, suckled in turn by all lactating females. They also raid for special children who are mixed with the born members and the distinction between them is deliberately and thoroughly wiped from the collective mind so that in a few years the born and the snatched are indistinguishable to themselves and to the adults. In both cases—raiding for breeding males, raiding for chosen infants—the head witches or whatever they are send someone along to dowse for exceptional talent (both conventional and psi) and exceptional intelligence. Though how they combine giftedness and intelligence with such a rigidly structured and stifling existence, well, that's beyond me. You who read this, watch out for them, believe me.

A smuggler's group managed to cut out a zel from a raiding party crossing close by Yastroo. They brought her inside under heavy sedation and interrogated her with a probe. Looking for some way to get to the Zel, wanting to acquire one of their plant-herds or at least samples of the semi-sentient plants they use to guard their settlement. The stories some of my collectors told about those, well! The

zel played them like she'd been a stinger all her life, gave
them a little general information (I bought it cheap from
the survivors), lulled them into thinking she was safe to
handle, then mushed the psi-damper, near wrecked the lab,
fried some brains, came near getting away. Would have
except one had gone out to fetch something and came back
in time to get off a lucky shot.

You who read this, be warned. Pass the Centai-zel with
fear and trepidation and at the greatest distance feasible—
and you just might survive.

Aleytys closed the book. "You're satisfied with that way
you found?"
Shadith frowned at the dying fire. "I don't know. Fear and
trepidation, he said. I suppose we take a chance and go on
tiptoe, well . . ." She grinned. "Not exactly on tiptoe.
What about our other? What does she think? She's been very
quiet the past few days unless you've been forgetting to tell
me."
Aleytys set the notebook aside. "You're right. The word is
quiet. Harskari?"
The amber eyes came open reluctantly. "Do what you
want. What do I know about this world? Don't bother me
with nonsense, Aleytys, I thought you were over that
dependence. You know your gifts, you read what the man
said, make up your own mind." The eyes snapped shut.
Aleytys felt as if she were a waterweed whose roots had
been jerked loose leaving her bobbing uncertainly in a flood
whose direction and force were incalculable. Rootless and
uncertain and shapeless. She ran her fingers through her
tangled hair.
Shadith's beads clattered. "What did she say?"
"She declined to say anything." Aleytys frowned. "She's
acting . . . well, odd."
Shadith shrugged. "She gets these moods now and then.
All you can do is let her work it out. Stir her up and she
bites." She grinned, winced. "Swartheld provoked her once.
Let me tell you, I folded in tight on myself until they
finished scratching. We were locked up in the RMoahl trea-

sure vault then. Nothing to do. She was getting antsy. About the Centai-zel. Comes the push, you can handle them. You and Harskari. And me, I suppose I can do a bit of scratching too. Still, prudence is better than rashness.'' She grinned at Aleytys, mischief glinting in the chocolate eyes. ''I know, the way I've been, it's a laugh for me to be talking about prudence. Umm.'' She rubbed at her nose. ''Listen. Let me tell you what I saw. Can we both look through the hawk's eyes, that would be useful, no? Too bad, well, there's this long slope that leads. . . .'' Her gestures as she spoke were sinuously expressive. Her face was never still, changing expression with each flitting thought like cloudshadows shifting with the wind.

Listening absently as Shadith described in rapid detail her planned route, Aleytys watched her and felt once again how little she understood of this woman who knew her so intimately. The new body was a distraction and a complication, but she was trying to look behind that and what frightened her was the strangeness of the spirit inhabiting that body. She rubbed her hands along her thighs as Shadith finished and waited expectantly for her comment. ''Sounds possible. I'd better have a look.'' She straightened her back, patted a yawn. ''Dammit, I don't feel like moving.''

Harskari's eyes snapped open suddenly. ''Tell young Shadith that a few second thoughts and a lot less babble about things she doesn't understand would improve her immensely.'' The eyes shut again. Aleytys raised her brows. ''Well,'' she said. ''What?''

''Harskari.'' Aleytys picked up the notebook and slipped it into the saddlebag, repeating Harskari's words as she worked.

Shadith grimaced. ''I'm just as pleased she can't pin my ears back personally.''

''And me in between the two of you.'' Aleytys shook her head. ''Time to fly the hawk and forget all the rest of this.'' She smiled, leaned against the trunk of the tree behind her, closed her eyes and felt about for the bird.

9

The waning night was cool with dew thick on drooping grass,
dripping disconsolately from the stiff waxy leaves of the
trees. They rode through the gray halflight, the night blackness thinned by the blaze of the stars. The split gyori hooves
whispered through the grasses and the squat wiry brush. The
land was rising, its alternate dips and climbs were each a little
higher than the ones behind. The mountains were close enough
to tower over them, dark and silent and vaguely threatening.

"Psi-pool," Shadith said. She was talking to both of them,
to herself and Aleytys, but more to herself as if by her words
she thought to probe into the oddities of the body she was
now tied into. "There's nothing of her left, at least nothing I
can find, that I can reach now. Except echoes. Echoes.
Ghosts, I suppose. Psi-pool has that kind of echo. All the zel
are in it, I think. That sounds right. Lee. . . ."

"What?"

"A chill just walked my spine."

"Wrap that blanket around you."

"Not that kind of chill."

"Oh. Well?"

"Maybe that's a talent this brain has that's mine now—
precognition, hunch, whatever. Maybe we should wait till
tomorrow night. Maybe next year."

"Fear and trepidation?"

"Definitely." She shivered. "There's always the joker in
the grass who never shows up until you step on him and it's
too late for second thoughts. Talking about second thoughts,
what was Harskari going on about? Never mind, I suppose I
know, she was listening when I was talking about her snits."
She fell silent again and they rode past the dripping trees,
around them the smell of riveroak and resinous woods, of
wetness and dark earth, of rot and life. Around them soft
whispers of water and wind, plops of fish feeding, hum of
insects, sleepy twitters of birds.

Aleytys pulled her gyr to a stop. She looked at the mountains looming ahead, twisted around to gaze back for a long

moment at the black and silver serenity of the Plain. "I tell you, Shadi, half of me wants to listen to your chill, turn back and spend the next six months drifting." She swung back around. "Other half says let's get going or the sun will find us still on the mountain."

Angling away from the river they started up the long slope for the fold in the mountainside Shadith had spotted, finding the going more difficult than either of them had anticipated; it was one thing to plot a route over the convolutions of the landscape through the eyes of a hawk soaring on even winds, it was another to crawl over those convolutions. Again and again the creases and conformation of the mountain tried to nudge them down toward the river and the settlement, as if the land itself had been shaped by the women for their defense.

Below, on the relatively flat floor of the valley, the river began its division. The light from the stars caught drifts of vine out from the hedge and sparked off what had to be drops of dew although even the hawk's eyesight wasn't keen enough to pick out the individual drops. The hawk flew in long spirals over them, a day-bird forced from his natural cycle and unhappy about it. Aleytys had to keep calling him back from the island. He was unhappy about that too, inclined to be noisy about it so Aleytys had to keep soothing him and choking off his cries. The wind blew the smell of damp earth and new green into her face, blew also snatches of bird song and the sleepy muttering of animal life. It was very quiet, very peaceful—

Until Aleytys saw a second hawk climbing in slow circles above the island's trees. She pressed her lips together, sank herself more deeply into the hawk and sent him edging closer to the isle. Uncertain whether they'd been seen or not, uncertain about what she should do, she temporized by seeking more information—telling herself that if they were already exposed a little more wouldn't hurt, all she was venturing was the hawk, if the Zel hadn't spotted them, again all she was venturing was the hawk.

Clusters of trees with small open spaces, grazing beasts, garden plots, she'd seen those before. Recklessly she sent the hawk swooping low. Great swollen trunks, holes in them dark against the pale smooth tree-skin. *That answers one question*, she thought, *they live in the trees*. Several small zel were busy in the pole corrals, driving the squat blocky beasts into a long lane that led to a thatched shelter. *Milkers? Probably.* Aleytys dipped into dim memory, called up an image of herd-girls bringing in brimming pans of milk not long after sunrise. For several minutes she saw no more zel, then she stiffened. There was a movement high in one of the boundary trees, a scraggly giant considerably taller than the rest. As the hawk spiraled higher, she examined the tree each time he came round facing it, snatching quick looks that showed her a watcher, perched high, straddling a limb, leaning out away from the trunk, face turned toward the rising bird.

She fought the hawk away from the island, swooping him out and around in a wide arc, bringing him in low and coaxing him onto the crude perch they'd fixed on Shadith's saddlepad, soothing his protests until he sat still and sullen on the perch. She withdrew from him, leaving only a tenuous thread to hold him where he was, opened her eyes and looked around. They were in a steep-sided coulee, going downhill. She frowned. Out of sight, but once again being pushed toward the river. In a stillness broken only by the scuffling hooves of the gyori, she heard a distant warbling whistle. Then another, an answer to the first. Then a third. She rubbed at her neck; it was stiff and sore from being held without moving for the long search with the hawk. She glanced at Shadith. "Hear that?"

"Whistles."

Aleytys smiled. "Uh-huh. There was a watcher. Perched in a tree. She spotted the hawk. I think she knew it was ridden, maybe she spotted us. Any sign of that?"

Shadith screwed up her face, scowled at the gyr's twitching ears, the hawk's hunched shoulders, then she gazed over her shoulder at the left bank of the coulee up where it merged with the bulge of the mountain. "Nothing I saw, but when we came over that bump, if she's got good eyes. . . ."

"You don't set up a near-sighted watch." Aleytys sighed. "Damn."

"Well, there was always the chance." Shadith shivered suddenly, looked startled.

"More chill?"

"Spiders walking up my spine." She fidgeted on the saddle pad, glanced at Aleytys, chocolate eyes sparking with excitement. "What now?"

"We better get out of this, it's taking us straight to the river." She heard a harsh challenging cry, felt her hawk tugging at her hold. She looked up, saw the village hawk circling overhead. "No use trying to hide now."

Shadith laughed, her eyes bright with excitement, then set her gyr at the slope. There was a frission of fear in the excitement but that seemed only a spice in the mix. Aleytys was dismayed as she followed her up the bank. This reckless buoyant creature was no one she knew. She forced the thought away.

More whistling, almost constant now. They topped the bank. The island was closer, alarmingly closer. A long sustained warble. Aleytys clutched at her head as the translator there slammed on, pain blinding her an instant as it always did, knocking her loose from the hawk. She shuddered, distantly aware that Shadith had taken hold in her place. As they dipped into the next coulee, into the next wrinkle on the mountain's face, she shook herself back into order. "Whistle talk, that last blast did it." She nodded at the bird. "Thanks."

"Recognized the symptoms. Better you than me, though it comes in handy I suppose. What they saying?"

They climbed the bank and dipped again. "They don't understand what they're seeing." Aleytys frowned. "They've recognized the body. Hawk rider did and passed it on. Me, I'm enemy. Stranger. Though they find it puzzling I'm female and alone. They're very worked up about a stranger in the valley. Not much love your enemy here. We're confusing them, you riding free beside me. Doesn't follow the rules. You should be trying to kill me, not riding along with me. They're sending out more hawks to look for ambushers set to take them while we distract them. The hawk rider has reported that you're not bound or anything, there's more about that going the rounds, sounds like the lot of them are in those trees now.'' Aleytys shook her head. "Not much use going on, just more of the same."

Shadith laid her finger against the hawk's head, let him take it in his beak; he held it a moment as if he tasted the familiar flesh and took comfort in it, then turned his head forward and sat more comfortably on the perch, swaying easily with the swing of the gyr's back. Shadith frowned at him. "He's upset," she said. "He feels the hostility coming from the island and it's confusing him."

"Let him go if it gets too bad."

"Maybe," Shadith said grudgingly. There was a stubborn, almost angry look on her face.

They were cutting across the wrinkles as expeditiously as possible, trying to get as much distance as they could between them and the island, again and again turning uphill only to be driven down again by some gnarl or twist or crack in the mountainside. Up. Over. Down. Around. Hunt the easier slopes to spare the strength of the gyori. And always the mountain turned them away, pressed them down toward the river.

More whistle talk. An aviary inside the hedge.

Anger and aggression building. Bubble about to burst. Hornets disturbed.

Hawk riders: they are alone, there are no ambushers.

Half the population in the treetops. If the island were a boat their weight would capsize it. Armed. Bows. Madar knows what else. They're worried about Shadith—clothes, hair, gear, hawk, it's all theirs but what is one of theirs doing riding so docilely with Centai's enemy?

Aleytys smiled suddenly, tugged the leather thong from about her hair and let the long mass flutter loose behind her. The wind caught it and whipped it off her face, blowing it back like a tattered banner, a flaunting challenge to the watchers. Holding her hair off her face, she glanced behind as they topped another of the rises. There was a touch of red in the east—dawn down on them before she was ready for it, though when she thought about that, it made little difference since the night hadn't hidden them all that well. She snatched a quick glance at the island before dipping once more down the side of a coulee. They were even with the western end of it, right opposite its pointed prow. She shook her head, leaned back to balance the gyr as he scrambled down the crumbling bank.

The village bird dipped lower. Aleytys tossed her head, fluffing her fiery hair, laughing as the whistle talk increased again. Woman. Witch. Daughter of fire. Much consternation. Test her. Test her. Test-test-test-test. The echo bounced round the mountain, round the island. She turned to Shadith. "How's your hawk now?"

"Better," Shadith said. "It's easier for him when he doesn't look. He's dozing."

"The Zel are getting antsy about us, working themselves up to an attack, I think. Maybe I can make them think again. I'm going to see if I can take that hawk from its rider."

Shadith frowned at her, loosing her recklessness abruptly, absurdly in maternal anxiety. "Waving a flag in their faces. Think you should?"

"Yes."

" 'Ware the joker, then."

"Here." Aleytys tossed her the braided rein. "See us clear while I'm busy." She locked her hands on the front edge of the saddle pad, wriggled about a moment until she felt steady, then slowly, warily, began insinuating herself into the hawk.

The rider was immediately aware of her. She struck at Aleytys with shocking speed and power. A little shaken, Aleytys countered.

More minds, bubbling up, merging with the first.

More minds, psi-pool. The Zel whole.

Stepping up the rider's power.

A wave looming over her about to break over her.

Aleytys countered.

Wave dissipating, melting into mist.

The bewildered and beleaguered hawk lost hold of the wind and tumbled, shrieking its distress.

The Zel are chanting.

Can't hear the words.

Ta-thun, ta-thunn ta-thunnnnn, ta-thun, ta-thun, ta-thunn.

Beating into her blood.

Beating with the throb of her heart.

Web spun around her.

Silver strands shimmering in her mind, in the darkness of her mind.

Caught. I'm caught.

Yellow glows in the darkenss in the dullness of her mind.

Harskari.

Help me.

Harskari holding her, like a babe in arms, holding her.

Harskari chanting, the sound a silver knife slicing through the silver threads.

One by one, two by two, the threads fall away from her.

Free. I'm free.

And she calls on the black water the river of power and the water roars into her and fills her and takes hold of Harskari's chant and thunders it back at the Zel-pool.

And the pool is a maelstrom.

And they are caught, they are caught, they are caught.

In their own trap they are caught.

Frantically they counter.

The maelstrom dissipates, melts into a mist.

And they are away.

The hawk gave a great hoarse cry and died, tumbling into the swift current of the river-moat, carried away by the current.

And there was a sudden terrible silence in the valley.

And Aleytys snapped back into herself.

Shadith was holding her in the saddle, her chocolate eyes dark with worry. "What happened?"

"Sky fell on me. Let's get out of here. Esgard was right. Swing wide around the Centai-zel if you want to live." She straightened, drew her hand across her face. The hand was shaking. She was trembling all over. She swallowed, drew a deep breath, exploded it out again. "Harskari?"

"Yes?" The amber eyes opened. The sketched face forming around them had a measure of complacency in its smile.

"Thanks, Mother."

"Mmph." The nose of the image twitched—or that might have been imagination, a trick of Aleytys's tired brain. "It's time I began teaching you. . . ." Harskari's voice trailed off. "That's for later. We've stirred them out of their nest, daughter.

And they learned entirely too much about us from that encounter.''

They set the gyori at the coulee bank, hesitated on the mounded top, looking back, as Aleytys sketched to Shadith what had happened. She stopped talking abruptly and stared, then pointed.

Shadith bit her lip, glanced at Aleytys and away.

The thorn hedge was coming apart at the west end of the island, spreading by itself it seemed into a broad arch wide enough for three to ride abreast. Over the northside branch of the river-moat a mist was forming and thickening, incorporating in its ghostly white a touch of rose reflected from the burgeoning dawn.

"That answers that question," Aleytys murmured. "Semi-sentient plants. What Esgard wrote. Remember?"

A band of riders came three by three through the arch. The first three wore long white robes bunched up awkwardly because they rode astride; their heads were shaved bare and painted. Those who followed were like the warriors of the zel band that had ambushed the men. They all came at a fast trot through the arch and raced improbably across the mist bridge, urged on by the hoots, howls and whistles of the watchers perched in the trees.

Aleytys swung around and frowned at the green corrugations stretching ahead. "We might as well give in and head for the valley floor. No speed over these humps." She looked gravely at Shadith. "Even with Harskari's help, Shadi, I don't think I can handle them." She scowled at the shallow coulee, turned to Shadith with raised brows. Shadith nodded and set her mount at the slope.

They went at a quick lope along the narrow bottom of the wash. They were in between deepening green walls, riding in stillish air and a growing grayness as the night's dark fled before the rising sun, the only sounds the slashing of gyori hooves through the grass, the grunts from them as they ran downhill. Shadith rode ahead, her beaded braids bouncing and clicking in a buoyant small rhythm half the time lost in the noise of their progress. She was riding easily now, having settled into her body far more completely. The old muscle memories no longer had to fight the mind.

Aleytys rode behind her, alarms ringing in head and body. She'd stowed most of the supplies from her backpack in the saddle bags on both beasts, but the wide belt still rode her hips. Driven by an impulse she didn't seek to understand, she unbuckled the belt, slung it across the pad in front of her and held it there as the coulee sides spread and flattened and they plunged out onto the valley floor. She swung out and around, prodded her gyr into a faster run until she was riding knee to kness with Shadith. "Shadi," she called. "Catch." She tossed her the belt. Her voice a hoarse scream, she yelled, "Go ahead. The pass."

"Joker's wild," Shadith shouted to her. She'd forgotten her role as anxious mother and was glittering with excitement.

"I don't like the look of the bald-heads," Aleytys screamed back. "We could get burned bad."

They raced along flatter ground, moving past the outermost of the thorn fences. Aleytys glanced back repeatedly at the riders coming after them along the riverbank, the width of the valley floor and its patchwork of thorn-fenced fields between them, glanced back then gazed hopefully at the inner end of the valley where the land rose in a series of lumpy waves toward the pass she still couldn't see. The road, she thought. If we can only reach the road ahead of them, we've got a chance. "Shadi," she yelled, her voice urgent. When the girl turned toward her, she held up the single rein. "Take this. Keep us going while I do some probing." Shadith caught it deftly, nodded, leaned over her mount's neck and urged him faster, knowing that Aleytys's gyr would match his speed without any urging from her.

Aleytys gripped the saddle pad and probed at the riders. They were walled off from her behind a barrier like a sheet of thick glass. A touch or two was enough to convince her she would need quiet and time and concentration to pierce it—none of which she had in great supply at the moment. She scowled at the riding beasts, whose silly complacency annoyed her, scowled a moment later at nothing. As unobtrusively as possible, she tried to insinuate herself through or around the barrier—and stiffened as she caught a taste of hate and furious anger and surging power.

The aura of murderous rage hanging about the pursuers

was directed in large degree against Shadith—or rather, at the body she wore. Their own, as far as they knew. Their own turned against them. She shivered and withdrew her probe. "Go on ahead," she called to Shadith. She snatched at the rein, got it back, scowled at Shadith who was ignoring her and watching her rather anxiously. She urged her mount faster. What those women would do to Shadith if they discovered what she was didn't bear thinking about. "Get away. I can't protect both of us."

Shadith blinked, nodded, slapped the rein against her mount's neck and sent him scampering on ahead.

Aleytys relaxed a little. If one had to fall—and she didn't yet concede that—then better it was her. Even now, even so imminently threatened, even so surrounded by attack as the white-clad elders or whatever they were reached around and through the barrier to slam probes against her shields, she did not really feel endangered; she knew bone-deep she was going to get out of this, that nothing so puny as a bunch of regressed indigenes was going to make her cease to be.

Hawks came at her, stooping to strike with talons she surmised were smeared with poison; they tumbled in helpless flutter as she slapped them away, snatching at the many mind leashes with devastating accuracy and effect. Four, five, six—astonishing herself at her sureness.

Ahead of her grass grew twice its height in minutes, tangling about the gyr's ankles, tendrils from the thorn hedge grew with the same rapidity and slashed at her with their tainted spikes.

She withered the grass, deflected the canes and took her gyr away from the hedges, up onto the more uncertain ground beyond the cultivated land.

The grasses on that uneven ground grew even faster, longer, more tenacious. The air was thick and thrumming with power. It was hard to breathe, it was harder to think. Midges swarmed up from the hedges to attack her, hornets swung nervously around her.

The gyr stumbled, the coarse grass winding about his ankles.

With a blast of exasperation she withered the grass, reaching deep within herself to discover the limits of this new skill, the obverse of her healing gift.

The gyr righted and she fled on, beginning to feel desperate.

The attack slowed her. Shadith was gradually pulling ahead, her slighter body and easier passage making the difference. Now and then Aleytys saw her looking back, her face anxious, her brow furrowed but she didn't slow to wait for Aleytys for which good sense Aleytys was ruefully glad—as she was relieved to be the main target of attack.

Air pummeled her, short sharp blows to her body. She endured them, bent lower over the gyr's neck, comforted his worry with words and touches.

Sound drilled into her head—agonizing shrieks close to the limit of her hearing, screeching irregular rhythms. The gyr moaned and faltered. Harskari laid hold of her speaking parts and sang a countering chant at the beast while Aleytys wove a shield out of air that damped the sound. Between the two of them they took from it its power to hurt.

Wasps long as her little finger dived at her, stung her. She endured. The sudden sharp burning was distracting, the poison loosed in her body turned her light-headed, but she endured. She turned, laughed as she saw how much the distance between her and the zel had increased. We're going to make it, she told herself, and giggled, then got a firm hold on the pad and herself and *reached* for her river, flushed the poisons out of her body.

They were both a good distance beyond the island now, nearing the end of the cultivated land. Shadith was already riding up the tumbled waves at the end of the valley, angling across them toward the road. She was almost out of sight, a flicker of movement and color over the top of each roll of the earth. Aleytys looked back once again as she came round the end of the last field and crooned the weary gyr into a run for that road. The women were spreading out, riding slower, the three elders knee to knee, holding hands, their painted heads bobbing in unison. She wanted to laugh again, instead bent low over the gyr's back and urged him on.

The wasps came again, came in waves, attacking not only her but the beast she rode.

The gyr screamed with pain, screamed and bounded in

convulsive twists as he sought to throw off his tormenters. He fell, jarring to his knees, lurching until he lay, moaning, twitching, his neck stretched out flat against the ground, his large red eyes tearing, his mouth working.

Aleytys was thrown in the first series of bounds but managed to roll up onto her feet as she hit the ground.

Shaken, trembling a little, she stood by the gyr's hindquarters and faced the advancing zel. Triumphant warbles and whoops mixed with the gyr's plaintive moans; rage flamed high in her. Without thinking, she gathered power in her hands, shaped it into glowing spheres and flung one after the other against the shield to claw savagely at it, rebound from it, seek again the targets, mind driven, humming round and over the shield, slamming into two of the warrior women, charring them instantly black and dead. The gyori of the living screamed with pain where the molten light spattered on them, burning holes in hair and flesh. But the shield held. She couldn't break through it. Drained, empty, she stood watching them come.

The gyr surged suddenly to its feet and ran off, head pulled back so it wouldn't trip on the dangling rein, disappearing after Shadith before Aleytys could collect herself enough to remount. "Harskari," she said, her voice breaking over the word. The answer came immediately, but it seemed weak, the eyes and face dimly sketched in the darkness of her mind.

Slowly she got control of her breathing, slowly her trembling stopped. Once again she *reached*. Relief poured into her with the power, both filled her. She lifted her hands again.

The warriors spread in a shallow arc. The three elders stayed close in the center of the arc, facing her. Their shaved heads, their faces, were wildly intricate interweavings of flowers and vines, painted in brilliant color until the features were so obscured she couldn't make them out. Aleytys saw them with an extraordinary clarity as if the air between them had gone perfectly clear and curved itself into a magnifying lens. The grass was blowing with tender delicacy in a slow-motion dance; every movement the women made took an eon to complete. Aleytys gathered hot gold light about her hands, raised them to fling it at the women.

Ropes of air twisted tight about her body, tightening with every breath she took.

She burned the ropes off and began backing away.

The painted heads swayed more vigorously, a throbbing chant beat out from the three.

The ropes whipped around her. Her mind began to grow sluggish as something like an inhibitor field settled round her with them. She whispered to Harskari to hold the attack steady on the women while she fought the double force that sought to bind her in place. As she fought, she continued to back slowly away from the zel. She won perhaps twice her body length, almost to the road on the river-bank, and was beginning to rejoice again as the power of the elders' attack lessened rapidly with the greater distance between them. With Harskari shielding and wielding the power Aleytys pulled in, with Aleytys stripping away the clinging ropes of air, the dulling cap of power, they were winning a slow and painful victory.

The zel came stubbornly after them, stung but not stopped by Harskari's sniping.

Aleytys felt the hard resilient paving under her feet. The road. She smiled. A little more. A little more, blessed Madar. The road was rising, a fair gradient, she could feel it by the ache in her calves. The river's roar was steady and calming. A little more.

Tough fibrous eel-like creatures came whipping from the river, wrapped around her ankles and calves. More of them came—with a speed that shocked her—snapped up and around her body as high as her waist. She fought them, tried to burn them but they wouldn't burn; she stabbed probes into them, searching for centers of volition she could take over as she'd taken over the hawk, but she found nothing and then there was no time, no time at all. She was choking, an eel—or was it a vine—about her throat.

Her mind dulled. Blanks in her percepts came as if the world had winked off an instant then on again. She was exhausted. Her will was leaching away. Her mind retreated from the barrage, she ignored Harskari's urgent demands. The stiff overlaid coils of the vine-eels held her upright or she would have collapsed. She retreated deep into herself, not exactly unconscious, just elsewhere. Her body heat rose a few degrees as the neglected power pool stirred restlessly within her. The vine-eels creaked and shifted, made uncomfortable by the unaccustomed heat inside their coils. She retreated still farther until even Harskari's prodding could not reach her.

10

In the shadow of the forest Shadith heard the zels' triumphant cries as they echoed eerily back from the mountain. She gritted her teeth and turned off the road, threaded through the trees until she spotted a strangler like the one Aleytys had climbed at the edge of the slough. The gyr wouldn't go near it, so she tied him to a resiny conifer, ran across the bare earth surrounding the strangler and threw herself at it, ignoring the crackle and tear of the bark as she pulled herself up, ignoring the wet prickle and burn of the sap she released. She reached the topmost fork and scrambled into it, broke away branch spikes with their scabby foliage until she could see back along the road, could see what was happening.

She saw Aleytys standing beside the gyr, flinging fire at the zel, saw the gyr scramble to his feet, saw Aleytys begin her step-by-step retreat. Her hands closed tight on the forward branch of the fork shaking it as she fought each step with Aleytys, fought too her near overwhelming urge to go racing to Aleytys's defense. If she couldn't defeat them, Shadith certainly couldn't; it would be futile to get both of them captured. "Go, Lee, do it, shrivel the bitches, ah!" Aleytys reached the road and began backing along it, increasing the distance between her and the zel. "That's it, a bit more and I . . . oh god." Long ropy things slithered from the river and lay coiled beside the road as Aleytys backed closer and closer to them. She opened her mouth, closed it again. Shouting was no good, the wind was against her, the river was too loud. She struggled to project warning, chewing her lip in her frustration. "Around," she breathed. "Turn around, Lee. Oh god." She watched, helpless, shaking, as the ropy things whipped up and around Aleytys. "Do something, Lee. Don't just stand there. Do something.'' The things were around her neck now and the zel were swarming up on her. ''If they kill her, if they kill her. . . .'' Tears streamed down her face, she bit her lip until it was bloody, worked her burning hands on the branch. Rage seared through her, a rage that was as much fear for herself as it was anger at the stupid hostility of the women below. She pressed her face against the trunk of the tree, clinging to the trunk as if the life in it could sustain her life. Chills went through her in waves as she thought about her predicament if Aleytys was killed. To the traders of the Enclave she would be an indigene, a zel, since she wore the body of one; even the smugglers would shun her after their experience with the other, the one Esgard wrote about. Getting into the spaceport would be near impossible, getting up to Aleytys's ship worse, getting into it something she didn't want to think about. The possibility that she might be trapped on this hellhole world and be forced to spend the rest of her hard-won new existence here chilled her stomach and roughed her breathing.

She glared down at the zel. *Damn them for putting me in this mess. Damn us for our stupid overconfidence.*

The zel moved about Aleytys, now obscuring, now revealing what was happening to her. Shadith saw one of the white robes stroke a thin hand along a ropy form. The eels or whatever they were unknotted themselves and slithered back into the river. Aleytys crumpled into a heap at the white robe's feet. She stepped back, gestured, the warriors closed in around Aleytys.

Shadith stopped breathing—then went limp with relief. They picked up the body and tossed it over the saddle pad on a gyr, then a zel mounted behind the body and the rest of them remounted and rode at a slow canter toward the island.

She can't be dead, Shadith thought. *Or they'd not bother. Unless they're cannibals. Oh god, let them not be cannibals.* She felt horribly alone, not lonely, not even solitary, just alone, single, only, kin to nothing that existed here or otherwhere. She clutched at the tree and felt like howling. Aleytys had kept off the realization with her presence because she and Harskari within her were kin of a sort—now came her body's reaction, a hard clenching of muscles, everything, a twitch, a jerk that loosed her grip and nearly threw her from the tree. Her kin and kind were dead and gone, dead and gone, lost in the millennia she rested incomplete in the diadem's snare, a concatenation of forces that formed a core of consciousness with abilities to reach around the confines of its point presence to know the lives of the ephemerals who clustered about her repository, the only thing that kept her sane and whole, insofar as she was whole—measuring herself against the lives she shared; she watched her chosen families, saw them hatch, reach adulthood, mate, flourish, die, suffered with their suffering and through all this held on to her self with painful desperation so that she didn't lose the memories and gifts and feelings and reactions that made the sum of her personality, her sense of herself. She'd codified that self, held it rigidly unchanging for all that time because she was afraid—no, more than that, terrified—that if she let anything go, anything at all, let anything change, it all would go and she would forget, be no longer Shadith but only a nameless, purposeless wraith who had not even the promise of death to free her from that futile existence.

And then Aleytys.

And then borrowing Aleytys's body to be herself again, wholly, wonderfully herself. To sing, to feel the physical pleasure of fingers writing, smoothing across paper, seeing the deep black ink looping across the page. Poetry had always been as much a physical as a mental exercise with her. The slide of the stylus across the ivory paper. The tiny vibrations of stop and start and dot in the diacriticals. The feel of the paper under the slip and slide of her hand, even the smell of it very faint, dry, and the smell of the ink, dark and musky. Unnoticeable, but there, there to be noticed and savored, and when not there, to have its absence noticed. The jagged strings of black lines. Peripheral things, but cherished, needed, all the more so since she had them once again after that long, long hiatus. Aleytys had laughed once when she emerged, laughed at the memory of Shadith sniffing and caressing a particularly lovely sheet of paper. The words came when her hands wrought them. When she had no hands, they did not and she suffered for it. She'd laughed herself, sensing though not actually hearing that laughter in her niche within the

diadem's rooted forces. Gradually she'd loosened the hold
she'd put on herself until she finally found her songs again.
Oh, the joy of that loosening, the generosity of the woman, to
let her live again a whole being even if for no more than an
hour or so at a time. Harskari had never asked and had even
refused such loosing when Aleytys offered. Shadith had been
shocked at that refusal; in the subtle secret way they'd developed
over their millennia of bonding, she asked her why. But
Harskari seldom explained her actions, never if she was not
so inclined, and she simply didn't answer, leaving Shadith
astonished and a little appalled.

She shook herself loose from her gloom, scowled at the zel
riding now across the mist bridge. They vanished through the
arch, the hedge writhing closed behind them. She sighed,
leaned against the fork of the trunk behind her and inspected
her hands, rubbing at brown splotches burned in them by the
acid sap. "Need a healer," she murmured. She shook her
head, then swung out of the fork and started down the tree.
There was nothing she could think of now to help Aleytys.
Nothing.

11

Aleytys woke, numbed and claustrophobic. Leaf-dappled
light glanced through irregular shapes on a pimpled wall. The
smell of the earth was rich and loamy, mingling with the
odors of bits of desiccated wood strewn about the pounded
dirt floor. Another smell—one that could only be called
generic greenness. Crumbling hardness under her. Voices
coming from somewhere, she couldn't tell, indistinct and
stripped of meaning, burring into each other like the whine of
mosquitoes. A fist was clamped about her mind, clamped
about her body. She gasped for breath.

And discovered she was stripped and bound, wrist and
ankles.

She lay on her side, curled up, breathing in floor dust and
motes of the rotted wood. She was vaguely aware of two
other people in this odd room with her, but she couldn't focus
on them and they remained indistinct as if they were spun up
from snarls of black thread instead of flesh.

She swung her wrists closer to her face, saw thick green vine wound round and round them. It was alive, seemed to her a distant relative of the vines in the river that had trapped her. An image forced itself up through the haze in her head—*a woman snatched the short green vine from around her arm and snapped it at the man charging her; it whipped through the air, touched his shoulder, writhed, slapped around his neck and began strangling him.* Aleytys felt its stubborn life, green mindless life. It was locked tight about her wrists and she knew without trying that all her strength wouldn't shift it. Her head ached.

With a grunt knocked out of her by the effort she had to put forth to move, by the stepped-up throbbing of her head, she sat up, closed her eyes until her stomach settled and the room stopped blurring and swaying. After an uncomfortable minute or two, she opened her eyes again and looked about. She was in a roughly circular room with grass matting hanging on the wall, an inverted vee of greenish light filtering through the coarse mesh. At one side of this doorway sat an aged woman in a voluminous and very wrinkled white robe. Her head was shaved and painted, the whole waxed to a high gleam so that the mote-filled rays from the holes and the speckles of light pushing through the mesh reflected brightly from it. A much younger zel sat beside her, dressed in the same wrinkled white, painted with the same primitive colors.

The walls of the room had a slick brown surface, a kind of inner bark much like the outer. Aside from the hanging mats, the women, the shifting beams of leaf-filtered dusty light, the room was bare even to the smooth-skinned ceiling, a pointed dome. After a while she became aware that more than light and air was coming in the holes. Smoke. Being fanned in. Now that she listened she could hear the whisper of fans outside the windowholes, a sound just a little louder than the scraping of the leaves. *I'm in one of the bloated trunks*, she thought. Her mind moved sluggishly, it seemed to take enormous energy to form a single thought.

She pushed tentatively at the thing closed tight about her mind.

The old woman made a series of small sounds, a meaningless rhythmic chant that tightened down the net until she was gasping for breath again. She lifted her bound hands and pressed her fists first against one eye then then other, then against her lips as her stomach threatened to revolt. That was the drugged smoke. So many things working against her. If the smoke were absent, she could use time to build strength for defeating the women and breaking free of the damper, if the damper were absent she'd have no trouble dealing with the drug in her system or the vines on her wrists and ankles. The combination was continuing to defeat her, but she had confidence she could defeat it, given time. That was the question, would she be given enough time?

Time passed, the minutes sliding away with the tick-tock of her heart. The leaf-dappled shape of the windowhole on her left crept down the opposite wall and slid toward her feet. She swallowed. The smoke was drying out her mouth and throat. She endured it a while longer, then croaked at the silent women, "Water."

Neither the old zel nor the young one moved a muscle.

"So you plan to torment me," she said, putting all her scorn into her hoarse voice. "Savages. I thought so. Ignorant of civilized custom." Her throat hurt and she fell silent, her eyes on the old woman's impassive face.

The zel's face didn't change expression by so much as a shift of a wrinkle. And she said nothing.

Aleytys felt a surge of rage that stirred up the pool of power trapped within her, heating up her body dangerously. She calmed herself, damped down the pool. She'd forgotten about it, it was something to think about, a powerful weapon against these women—if she could use it properly. One thing at a time, that was all she could think about, one thing at a time, that was all. She stared at the old woman and knew her anger showed but she didn't care. Hunger and thirst, something to add to the draining effect of the smoke and the dulling of the damper powered by what? The chant? The drug? Well, she'd survived hunger and she'd survived thirst. She settled herself to endure.

And grew bored with that in minutes. She began making tiny tentative nibbles at the forces binding her, testing her various skills to see if a possible ignorance of such skills could give her a window to work through.

Each small nibble brought a response from the women; they blocked access to her talents, blocked all attempts at outreach. She had the reserve pool seething in bare control, knew how dangerous the powerpool could be if she held it unused for too long, but it was her greatest chance for survival so she refused to bleed it away.

Her passive receptors worked well enough, although somewhat numbed and slow. She could sense the hostility in the women guarding her, a hostility especially hot in the younger one who watched her with a personal rancor Aleytys couldn't understand. What surprised her more, though, was the lack of curiosity, especially in the elder zel. It seemed to her that curiosity should be a driving force in any intelligent being; the probing of the Blight for new plants and animals and insects had to be the result of some sort of curiosity. Perhaps curiosity wasn't quite the right word. Perhaps that search was so long institutionalized into the culture of the tribe it was in a way instinctive. Wasps, she thought. Complex behavior that looks like intelligence but is only wiring, a program. That doesn't seem to fit what Esgard wrote. Or does it? Don't know enough to judge.

Her Wolff implants were powered up, the sensors drawing in data without disturbing her guardian zel; she located a score of large lifeforms moving past her tree or lingering near it. Three or four more moved about above her, something that would have puzzled her except for her dredged-up memories of Maeve's forest people he slanted a glance at the chanters and smiled, knowing she could stun them if she could just free herself from the vine.

The zel sat cross-legged murmuring a near inaudible series of nonsense syllables. Aleytys knew it as nonsense because her translator didn't manifest itself; even the most effective psi dampers she'd come up against had never managed to suppress its operation. The young one glanced at her, hate in her dark eyes, went back to rubbing her thumb over and over a small shining smoothstone, her chiseled lips moving about the nonsense syllables, tasting them with a sort of triumph.

She edged onto one buttock and swung her tethered ankles around so she could reach the coils of clingvine binding those ankles. She felt it throb and jerk a little as she stroked her fingertips along the uppermost sections, teasing at the vine a little with the tractor function grown into the fingers of her left hand—tiny fibers wound round the stunner fibers (their minute projectors nested flat beneath her nails), reaching up her arm and down her body to the organic power cells implanted in her buttocks. The Wolff surgeons had worked their minor magic mostly on her left hand which was marginally clumsier and weaker than her right. She came close to being ambidextrous but was not quite; there was a measurable difference between her right- and left-hand skills. She stroked her right hand (with its heat and depth sensors) along the coils and sought to probe into the vine by a mixture of active and passive perceiving.

But the zel by the door grew rapidly aware of what she was doing and clamped the net tighter on her brain.

She sighed, stretched her legs in front of her and wondered what she could do to escape a growing boredom almost as numbing as the drugged smoke.

She tried again to reach Harskari. Again there was nothing.

She examined the zel. The painting on their shaven heads was an intricate knotting of vines outlining eyeshapes with flowers, insects or small beasts painted in the openings. The design on the heads of the two zel were similar but not identical. Motifs were the same, but the hands that painted them were manifestly different. On the elder's head there was an infinity of fine, almost finicky detail with delicately shaded colors. On the other the vines had vigor and simplicity, as if drawn with slashing strokes that only a skilled hand kept from disaster. The colors were bold, unshaded, demanding. The robes they wore were crudely made, far more so than the fitted leather tunics of the warrior band. Two rectangles of coarsely woven white cloth, sewn at top and sides, leaving holes for head and arm. There were wrinkles and stains on the white, especially under the knotted belt tied round the waist. Hand loomed, uneven, weaving of the simplest kind, no sort of embroidery. The robes weren't even hemmed; threads straggled out from the ragged edge, bits of yellowed grass were caught by the cloth fibers. It had to be deliberate, this roughness, something to do with their calling, their talent.

But that was speculation. Aleytys smiled. *Angels and pinheads again,* she thought.

The eyes of the younger zel came back to Aleytys again and again, dark eyes, darker even than the chocolate brown of Shadith's new eyes. They had a matte umber flatness that was as opaque as a stretch of obsidian. The elder zel's eyes were a mud color with a bit of yellow in them when the light hit them right.

The younger zel radiated a fierceness barely controlled. *She'd cut my throat in a minute if something weren't stopping her.* The older was not filled with hate so much as with a sheltered, shuttered certainty of rightness. It oozed from her like melted butter from a biscuit. She was gelled, immobile, no feeling in her, no emotion in her to be directed toward Aleytys. As far as Aleytys could read her, she simply refused to admit the outsider to her life. Neither one offered much opportunity for rapprochement, but Aleytys began after a while to think that she preferred the younger one's active malevolence to the utter indifference of the older. She closed her eyes; her head felt thick and drear, scattered haphazard into bits and pieces. She drew in a breath, filled her lungs, drew her shoulders up and back to pull in more air. She held the breath, seeing the lined gentle face of the man who'd taught her how to calm her anger so long ago. Several lifetimes ago, she thought, remembering the sullen lonely child she'd been. She emptied her lungs, scolding herself for inattention, focusing in on the exercises until she was purring along at a slow calm pace, most irritations brushed aside, all of her focused on her breath.

And a yellow glow lit the back of her mind, a glow that wavered then strengthened to become Harskari's bright amber gaze.

"Aye, Mother," Aleytys said aloud, her voice and her body tranquil. The two zel stirred as she spoke, the older settled back without further reaction, though the younger scowled, perhaps because she didn't understand the words and resented that; perhaps because she resented the captive speaking at all.

"Rashness has received its own reward," Harskari said severely.

The young zel stirred as if she'd found an itch she couldn't scratch.

"Don't scold, mother," Aleytys said dreamily. "Are you bound within, my mother?"

"Not exactly." The amber eyes blinked slowly. "If I use your gifts, I am bound—for now, yes, for now; later—we'll see. Shadith is loose and well."

"Good." After her heart speeded in reaction to the relief, Aleytys went back to the exercises and slowed herself into tranquility. "Is there more?"

"She's restless up there. I think she'll come back in the night to prowl about and see if there's any way she can help, to be there if you manage to break loose."

The young zel started a whispered argument with the older, her obsidian eyes flashing now and then at Aleytys.

"Can you get word to her?"

"No."

Aleytys measured her breathing some moments more, then she closed her eyes. "There's more," she murmured.

"Yes. The zel, they are debating what to do about you. Kill or keep; it sits on a balance now, could tilt either way. Be ready to jump."

"Mmmm, hard to jump with my head bound like this."

"Don't speak," the young zel shouted suddenly. "No more, don't speak."

"My god," Harskari said, "I think she senses me. I'd best be quick. Feel the cycles of the chant, Lee, learn to drift with them." She went silent, a far-off look in the dimming eyes.

Aleytys eyed the fidgety zel, subvocalized, "What?"

"Listen." Harskari's eyes blinked, dimmed, grew bright again. "That young one is extraordinarily powerful, if she were as trained as she is talented. . . . I had better take myself off before I tip the balance the wrong way. Listen to the chant, Lee. Listen and fit yourself onto the pulses of the chant. Once you know the beat, you can counter it by disrupting it, or change it by riding it. Think. Go with the beat and let it help you wash the drug from your system." The eyes narrowed to a glimmer as if Harskari frowned with pain. "Quickly," she said and slipped away.

Aleytys sighed. Listen, she thought. What'n Aschla's hells

does she think I've been doing this interminable day? She swallowed, grimaced as her dry mouth hurt, her dry throat hurt. "Listen," she whispered, grinned at the furious young face, then closed her eyes again and went back to her breathing exercises until mind and body were quiet enough to listen. Again and again, she calmed herself when frustration roughened her surfaces as she thought she'd caught the thing Harskari meant, then lost it. Finally, by ignoring the pulse of the sound, by listening/feeling to the pulse of her body, listening/feeling to the pulse of the zel bodies and fitting these together, she found herself riding a rising/falling ocean of whipped cream. She slid along with stately grace and knew with a gleam of triumph that temporarily spoiled the glide (she got it back easily enough) that she could reach out and trap her trappers in their own net. She laughed aloud, opened her eyes and met the venomous glare of the young zel. *Why?* she thought. *Why hate me with such a personal rancor? What have I done to you?*

Her thirst was a torment now. "Water," she said, not asking now, demanding. She touched her fingers to her cracking, caked lips.

The old zel ignored her, the young one smiled.

Aleytys shrugged and turned inward again. It was easy now to ride the beat and twist it round her capacity for self-healing, freeing it for her use, then was surprised to find it little needed. Unbidden, her body had spent the long hours slowly, imperceptibly changing itself, organizing itself to deal with the intrusion of the smoke-drug. She flushed out the stubborn remnants of that drug and felt leaner, easier. "Harskari?" she subvocalized, but wasn't much surprised when she got no answer.

When the light coming in the east hole was greatly diminished and that coming in the western one had a tinge of red, the doormats were pushed aside and another zel came in. She was short and stocky, more muscle than fat wrapped around her sturdy bones. She had a rounded face and pale eyes, bi-colored hair braided through beads larger than the others Aleytys had seen, the end beads stone rather than wood. Heavy lines cut from her nostrils to the corners of a wide, full-lipped mouth. Her chin was only a gesture, a narrow slash of bone apparently there to underline the sensuality of the mouth. She rubbed her thumb across that chin as she gazed at Aleytys. "How long has it been awake?"

The older zel answered. "Since mid-morning."

"Has it tried anything?"

"It's been poking and prying about, testing more than trying. It has no way to escape and it discovered that, so in the past hours it has settled into calm."

The younger zel looked as if she wanted to dispute this. The newcomer frowned at her, bent and whispered in her ear, listened to the answering whisper, eyes sliding now and then to Aleytys. She straightened. "Spokash is ready as it can be in these dangerous times." She stroked her forefinger over the gyr's head painted on her cheek. "Bring it." The door-mats dropped behind her, scratching and bumping against the smooth inner bark.

The old zel came to her feet and crossed to stand by Aleytys's bound ankles. She bent with an awkward ease, touched the vine, crooned at it—all this while continuing the beat of the chant deep within her. She put her hand down beside the vine and waited a moment while it whipped from about the ankles and up around her stringy arm. She straightened and stepped back to the door. "Stand," she said.

Aleytys worked her ankles, drew up one leg and began massaging the foot with her still-bound hands. Ignoring a repetition of the command and waves of irritation from the two zel, she repeated the massage on the other ankle, then got carefully to her feet, stamped each foot hard against the packed earth. She raised an eyebrow, grinned at the young zel. "Well?"

The two women stepped apart, moved away from the door, sidling along the curving wall. The older flicked long bony fingers at the mats. "Go outside," she said.

With a lift of her brows, Aleytys looked from one painted face to the other, then moved slowly to the door, smiled briefly as she felt Harskari grow strong within her. She shoved aside the mats with her bound hands, stepped outside into a lamp-lit gloom. She moved a few steps from the door, glanced up.

Overhead, living vines were woven into a thick matting

that ceiled the entire clearing. Bulbous porcelain lamps hung here and there from the vine mesh, casting a gentle amber glow over the silent seated figures packed into the smallish clearing about her prison tree. The lamps gave off a clean green scent that brought back suddenly a memory from her childhood—the scented candles that burned in the night lamps of her home on holidays—a pleasant perfume that mitigated somewhat the pungent body odor of the assembled zel. She heard the soft slap of the doormats and knew her guards had come out to stand behind her.

There was an aisle left open in front of her, wide enough for five to walk abreast. At the far end of that aisle, seated on high seats beneath the outstretched limbs of another sort of tree were five women. Watching her.

The Center she knew, the chunky woman who'd come to look at her. On her right was a very ancient woman, head shaved and painted, white robe gathered in folds about her skinny body. On that one's right was a woman dressed in the fitted leathers that most zel wore; she held a staff whose apex was carved to represent long thin leaves curled tight about a center stem topped by a head showing three rows of grain. On Center's left sat a long lean woman with glittering eyes, those eyes fixed on Aleytys with fanatical intentness. A short bow lay at her feet and she held an arrow in her right hand, casually, as if it were no different from any other. But even at her distance Aleytys caught the copper sheen of the head, the silver sheen of the flights. Metal—on this world where free metal virtually did not exist. A measure of her importance. Beside this zel, seated at her left, was a quiet withdrawn woman. She was harder to read than the others. There was considerable interest in the gaze she fixed on Aleytys, a sort of measuring. She was simply dressed, leather tunic, the rest of the common gear. A gyrhead was painted on her cheek and the staff she held was a sort of animal compendium with beast heads carved one above the other, a gyr's head topping the whole.

Aleytys waited, wondering if she should move out farther. Since her guards said nothing, she did nothing.

The Center zel took up a small hand drum and drew a rapid rattle from it. Eyes swung from Aleytys to the seated zel. The

Center stood, her hands curling around the drum. "The question," she declaimed. "The question is—what do we do with that?" She jabbed a forefinger at Aleytys. "We caught it this morning. What shall we do with it? Your Miuvit have pondered and asked of the Green and the Green has answered, but the answers have no meeting ground, the Green has answered desire more than need." She swung her torso to her left, held out the drum. "The mielel Medveh of the beasts."

The arrow-holder took the drum and passed it to the quiet woman on her left.

Medveh, Moulder of beasts took the drum, tapped a slow rhythm while she sat with eyes down, contemplating the yellowed parchment drumhead. "Our blood grows thin. Oh Centizeltai, O daughters of the green world, our purpose is strong in us still Ah Hai! (the exclamation is echoed by the seated zel) But we are less each year than we were." She threw up a thin hand to stop the protest. "I do not mean in numbers, though a few days ago we lost two hands, two fingers of our zel. It's easy enough to replace the bodies, though we shall miss their souls and grieve for them. I do not mean in skills, the tranjiti we do have are more skilled than most. I mean we are less in the energy with which we pursue our purpose. We have grown too easy in our lives. I say we are less than we were. I say to the Warleader, our ranjit Sursa: Pardon me if I say what seems to lessen you and those you lead, I do not mean that, but our defense is strong if our tranjiti are strong. Ah Zel, I speak long, my throat is sore with the unhappy words, but they make a truth we must face if we really desire to fulfill the Purpose. We are weaker than we were when I was a zelling crawling through leaf-shadow. There it stands." She lifted the drum, gestured with it toward Aleytys. "Our captive. Look at it. Look at the length and strength of the limbs, ask ranjit Sursa to speak of the strength of those limbs. Ask tranjiti Valah, Vetross, Vetar of the strength within. Ask how it nearly won free even after Vetar Beastherd set the wasps on it. Ask why tranjit Vetar set the wasps on the gyr and not the rider, ask our great three how it fought them. I say we keep it and breed it. The daughters we get from it will be zel, zel of strength and power. Others of your miuvit say it is too dangerous to keep. I say there is

more danger in not keeping it. Hamstring it so it must crawl.
Blind it. Tear out its tongue that it may not curse us, though
the Green and the Lady surely would not hear a stranger's
curse. Drug it so it cannot impose its will on us. Do what we
must to make it safe, but keep it and breed a new line from it.
We need its gifts for the Purpose. I have done.'' She passed
the drum back to the Center.

The leader quelled a rising mutter with a few taps on the
drum. ''The tranjit Maslicha speaks.'' She gave the drum to
the withered ancient on her right.

A rattle of the drum. A breathy old voice raised higher than
usual to send the words to the back of the clearing. The Spirit
Moulder spoke. ''The Purpose. Ah Hai! (she waits impatiently as the seated zel repeat the words). It is too big. It is
too strong. It is too dangerous. It will pervert the Purpose to
its own ends. It will corrupt the Zel. Ay Zel, ask the three
how powerful, how dangerous it is, ask them how close it
came to smashing them. Ask Abella and Cantise—ah, you
cannot, you say? And why? They are burnt and black and
dead!'' She shouts the last word then quells the murmur from
the crowd with a gesture of the drum. ''Ask Tranjiti Milice
and Juli how it keeps twisting and testing and fighting the
things that hold it, the smoke and the green-friend on its
ankles and wrists, the still-chants of the two. Not one tranjit
but two are needed and that when it's hungry, thirsty, weak.
Ask young Juli how it summons an ancient spirit who dwells
within it. Demon-kin it is. Ask the hawk-herd meld who
fought it in the bird and lost. It is too dangerous to keep
among us. We do not want it, I speak for the tranjiti-sve who
must bear the whole of its presence. We do not want this
burden, not for a year, not for a month, not a day. Kill it.
That is my word.'' Without waiting for the Center to receive
the drum, the tranjit Maslicha passed it to the woman at her
right. ''The Veril Savilis speaks with me.''

The plant-herd took the drum, didn't bother to sound it,
just held it and said calmly, ''Kill it. We do not need wild
blood.'' She passed the drum back.

The Center scowled at the tranjit as she took back the
speaker's drum. The tranjit would not look at her, only at the
coarse white cloth she was pleating and unpleating over her

knees. The Center sighed, held the drum in two hands before
her. "The ranjit Sursa speaks."

The Warleader took the drum and made it rattle loudly with
the silver point of her ceremonial arrow, then sat holding the
drum on her knees. "Wild blood, phah! What else do we
search the edges of the Blights for if not for wild blood to
enrich our lore and our stock of green-friends? What do we
dowse for when we raid for breeders and for daughters, if not
for wild blood to bless the Purpose? If we seek it for our
green and for our own, how can we not rejoice that the Lady
and chance have brought us such a blessing? I say to you,
Zel, give me three bred zel like that who stands so calm and
watching and ready, look at it, all of you, look at it! Give me
three zel like that and the Purpose will be gained within my
lifetime. The cursed losigai would be wiped from Centilla's
face, the world would be purified, the greatness of the Zel
spirit would be loosed across the face of the great Mother. I
say breed it. Do what you must to make it safe but get
daughters on its body. If you, Zel, give the word, I would
claim my one from it, one to replace my love, my ranjih
Treainah, so lately slain. Give me my one. Make it ours this
way for the Purpose. For the seeing of the Purpose made true
in the lifetime of us all, not in some distant future when we
are all and finally one with the Green. Let the Purpose be
fulfilled. Ah Hai!"

"The Purpose, Ah Hai," the zel repeated dutifully. Their
eyes kept darting toward Aleytys; in their response she thought
she heard more doubt and more enthusiasm than before.

Aleytys pressed her lips together, little enchanted by either
fate proposed for her. She tilted her head, examined the
basket weaving above her. There were several layers of the
woven vines forming a tight resilient ceiling. Close to the
trunk of her prison tree, though, she saw a section of rot,
withered vines and jagged holes. A bit of good fortune to
lighten the bleak outlook—perhaps less good fortune than the
effect of the fire that produced the smoke used to stupify her
and the smoke itself. The heat and smoke that escaped the
fans had eaten away at the vines and killed enough of them to
give her access to the tree top if she decided to go that way.
They must keep the breeding males in that tree and drug them

too, too much damage for just one day. "You see that?" she murmured, winced as the young Juli pinched her and hissed a warning in her ear.

"Yes." Harskari answered, golden eyes narrowed with thought. "The only way if things get tight."

"I'm going to get ready to stun the vine. Cover me?"

"If I can. That child is astonishingly perceptive. I've never before met a sensitive who could detect my presence." Harskari was silent a moment, brooding. "Take her out first and fast."

"Will."

Aleytys lowered her chin and frowned at the Center, the jidar Zhutra, the Mediator. She had been summarizing the arguments on both sides. What Aleytys heard as she fitted herself onto the beat of the chant was the end of a clear and concise statement of the alternatives. Ready to burst her mind bonds the moment it seemed necessary, Aleytys twisted her left hand round to touch the bindervine.

"I can see no middle ground," the Jidar said. "Kill or breed, that is the choice."

"They could just let me go," Aleytys muttered. "I'm no danger to them no matter now powerful I am."

"They don't see it that way," Harskari murmured dryly.

"This is not a thing to be decided at a single sitting," the jidar said. "The Lady rides full soon, there are things we shall have to do before then whatever you choose to do, Zel. Sisters and Daughters, circle and speak and by morning light, choose. Kill or breed. Each line will speak its choice. If the balance remains, my word will decide. Look at it." She waved the drum at Aleytys. "Remember the words of the Miuvit—the tranjit, the veril, the mielil, the ranjit. Weigh and decide, Zel of the Centai. The Purpose. Ah Hai!"

"The Purpose. Ah Hai!" The voices came back in a subdued roar.

As the crowd beneath the ceiling began to break noisily apart. the tranjit guards took Aleytys's arms and led her back through the doorway. As soon as she was seated again, the older woman stripped the vine from her arm and wrapped it around Aleytys's ankles.

The doormats slapped aside and two new tranjiti came

through into the prison tree. They held palm against palm
with Milice and Juli, touched foreheads for a long moment
until the newcomers had taken up the chant without break or
roughness. Juli followed her companion out but couldn't
resist a last glare at Aleytys.

As the mats slapped shut after her, the new pair of spirit
moulders separated and began strewing round blobs of fungus
about the perimeter of what Aleytys thought of as her jail
cell. The fungus gave off a cold white light that didn't carry
far but was quite bright close to its source. The tranjiti settled
themselves one on the right side of the door, the other on the
left. They looked like twins, identical in voice and gesture,
identical in the careful neutrality of their gazes.

The night passed slowly. At first the tranjiti were as silent
as Aleytys but as the dark thickened outside and in (despite
the glowing of the fungus), they began to talk. Aleytys dozed
and listened now and then.

The tranjit at the left of the door: Like fire that hair.

The tranjit at the right of the door: Fire. Fire-demon.

Left: Maybe. Fassa said it's heavy as a yearling inuk.

Right: Doesn't look it.

Left: No. Skinny I'd say. (She smoothed the coarse white
cloth over plump full breasts with a complacent smile.)

Right: Skinny.

Left got to her feet and crossed to Aleytys, squatted beside
her, took hold of the vine about Aleytys's ankles and with a
grunt of effort heaved at it, lifting feet and legs half a meter
from the floor, dropped them, prodded at Aleytys's thighs
and calves with an exploratory forefinger, then went back to
sit beside the door—all without losing a beat of the chant.

Left: Tight and heavy.

Right: Different flesh. Sterile most like with a Centelli
breeder.

Left: Looks like us, except that hair. It's young enough.

Right: Hot to handle, though.

Left: Quiet enough now.

Right: Biding.

Left. Think so?

Right: Look at it. Listening. Waiting.

Left: Come the sun, no more waiting.

Right: Think so? Don't know. Got a point, the ranjit. Zel off that one and we could go against the Shippua-shen and their Zumar, get our own back for the zel they killed just now.

They continued to debate the question of kill or breed. In the beginning they were on opposite sides, mildly so, but as the hours passed they slowly reached agreement—Aleytys was too different, too dangerous. Nodding gravely in tranquil accord they began talking about something they called ild-libran which Aleytys translated as fire-fête. At first she paid little attention, drifting in and out of a light doze, then she began to understand what they were saying and no longer felt any desire to sleep. On special occasions, when they collected a special breeder or an unusually effective and vigorous enemy, they absorbed its vigor and power by roasting the individual whole and passing out portions to every zel, even the nursing infants who got a fingerful of dripping to suck on. Bones were ground later to feed the green.

Aleytys was not at all charmed by the prospect of serving as honoree at a feast, not when it meant she was the main dish. With a sinking feeling she suspected that the outcome of the debate between the two tranjiti was an accurate foreshadowing of the outcome of the morning's vote.

Later. The tranjiti were showing signs of being at low ebb, mentally and physically, still speaking now and then, short phrases about nothing much, making noise to prod themselves awake. Aleytys began her breathing exercises, no need to calm herself but she had to drive off torpor and pull into focus her drifting mind. She twisted her hands about and got her stun-fingers firm on the binder vine. "All right, mama, ride that chant," she whispered.

Harskari chuckled. "At your command, O daughter." Using a bit of Aleytys's brain she climbed onto the chant and began altering it, not enough to free Aleytys completely, but enough to smother any apprehension or warning from the vine when Aleytys began her attack.

With a breathed plea to fortune, Aleytys rolled onto her side and stung the vine. It contracted painfully until she thought it was going to crush her wrists. Grinding her teeth together to keep from crying out, she stung it again. The ends went limp, the vine loosened enough for her to pull both hands free. Cautiously she brushed it back until it was coiled in a tight miserable knot against the wall. She arched her back and drew her legs around until she could reach the ankle vine. She gave it a larger jolt, used her tractor implants to pull it off her, then pushed it away as she had the other.

She stretched out, groaned with pleasure as she exercised her stiffened muscles. Then she curled up on her side, her back to the dreaming zel, and rested while the stunners recharged.

An hour passed. Harskari withdrew and waited quietly. Aleytys yawned, touched the checkpoint on her wrist. A little longer, she thought, just a little longer. She shifted around so she could watch the zel, listening to the chant, feeling the pulse, amazed at how thoroughly Harskari had fooled them. They're as shuttered as the old one, she thought and spared a moment to bless fortune for sending Juli away. While this pair was certainly adept in shaping their power, that was a weakness as much as it was a strength. When things went along as they expected, they could cope with anything. The unexpected brought panic; it was that as much as general caution that would condemn her, Aleytys thought suddenly. *They can't cope with me, so they'll do their best to kill me*. Juli was different; not that much skill, but raw strength powered by hate and suspicion made her far more dangerous. She checked her charge again. "Time," she whispered.

Harskari's eyes twinkled. "Visit's over."

Aleytys suppressed a chuckle. "We don't want to strain their hospitality," she whispered.

Harskari reached out and rode the chant again, twisting it to tranquilize the women so they wouldn't panic or call for help when they saw Aleytys rise unfettered and come toward them. It would have been simpler, more certain, if Harskari could have imposed the stasis on them, but she was uncertain about the effect of this on the rest of the zel; it was all too likely to act like a warning siren to those sensitives and bring the whole zel psi-pool pouring onto them, so she turned the chant and tranquilized the tranjiti into a state of indifferent euphoria. As she got to her feet Aleytys could feel Harskari's satisfaction. "Yeah, mama, you did good." She grinned at

Harskari's snort. The two zel watched dreamily as she bent over them; she applied fingertips to one temple then the other, stunning one then the other, the clamp finally gone from her head. *Free*, she thought. *Finally*. But she would not let herself rejoice yet in her freedom, kept her shields locked tight. Too many sensitives around for her to let herself expand however deeply she desired that.

She pushed the doormats aside. The lamps were out, the ceiled clearing thickly dark, but to her sensors there was no one about, no auxiliary guard. Tense, apprehensive, she crossed the clearing and began winding through the trees, moving as directly north as she could, heading for the curtain hedge. The night was quiet and cool; down here among the trees the air was still and soft against her. The island might have been deserted.

A sudden explosion of breath, two smallish hands that clamp about her arm, jerk her around. "Demon-kin," Juli screamed at her. "What did you do with her?" While she shouted at Aleytys she was blasting a mind alarm to the rest of the zel. "What did you do with my laska?"

Aleytys wrenched herself free, slapped her left hand hard against Juli's face and emptied the dregs of the stunner into her.

Shouts in the dark, rustlings, snaps, unseen zel moving hastily, a heat gathering around her as the psi-pool presses on her.

She leaps Juli's body and races for the curtain hedge, running full out, the blaze of the stars and the light from the ripening moon coming through the leaves enough to show her the boles of the swollen trees. The ground is clear between them. She weaves recklessly through them, vaults a pole fence, stumbles as an arrow whistles past her shoulder, catches her stride, dodges precariously around a startled hooting beast little more than a shadow shape, more arrows, all missing but not by much, she vaults another fence, races on. There are zel on the ground now, converging on her. The psi-pool thrumms, pressing confusion on her.

The hedge looms ahead. The sentinel trees grow within it. She leaps for the nearest, catches hold of the twisted trunk, with a grunt pulls herself up. Long canes whip out from the

thorn hedge, slapping and clawing at her, trying to dig their
thorns in and drag her off the tree. The tree writhes and
bucks, sending out alarms as it tries to dislodge her. She goes
up it like a frightened cat, crawls out on a whipping limb,
hurls a blast of NEED into the night, screams Shadith's name
after it, leaps out from the bucking branch into the north arc
of the river-moat.

Pain. Arrow in her shoulder, scalding burst of confusion.
Poison. She grinds her teeth, fights her body upright, flashes
the poison away with a touch of hoarded power. Pain again.
And again. Arrow through her side, arrow driving through
her thigh.

She hits the water feet down with a jarring splash, sinks, the
breath knocked out of her. No time for that. The poison is
churning in her. She is disoriented, not knowing up from
down, but can't deal with that now; she uses more of the
power pool, flushes away the poison. Can't do anything
about the points grating in her flesh.

Her lungs are burning, the current of the river is tumbling
her over and over, involuntarily she gasps, swallows too
much water before she can catch herself, flounders desperately until her head almost by accident breaks the surface.
She coughs and chokes, gasps in air and water, fights to keep
her head up. More of the arrows are arching at her but she is
a moving small target and all miss her. The current has its
hands on her. She gasps and tries to ignore the grinding of
the points and the pain as she kicks and reaches out, struggling to fight the current and swim for the northern shore.

12

Shadith twitches in her sleep.
(Aleytys. Naked. Running.
Running between nightmare trees that slap and snap at her.
Fleeing a black wave of fury, the psi-pool rearing up to crash
over her.
Aleytys clawing up a tree that convulses under her.
Aleytys plunging feet first into the river, shafts feathering her
body.)
Shadith sleeping sweats.

(Water closes over flying fine hair.
Minutes passing, passing.
Aleytys floundering up, tumbling away as the current takes her.)
Shadith jerks awake, gasping and dripping sweat.

The dream was vivid, though fading swiftly even as the worst nightmares do once the dreamer wakes. She sat up, drew her arm across her face and considered the dream. "Prognosticator," she murmured, grinned briefly, scowled into the darkness under the trees. "Better take a look, whatever." She got to her feet with a vigorous thrust of her muscles and bustled about repacking the saddlebags and rolling up the blankets. She stopped and frowned down at the pile. "Might be chasing me. Might not. Better to have a stash." With cheerful, slap-dash movements, she flipped the saddlebags and belt over her shoulder and went swinging up a deciduous tree resembling the riveroak of lower elevations. She tucked them in a crotch high enough to be invisible from the ground, returned moments later with the blanket rolls. On the ground again, whistling softly, she kicked a few old leaves about, scratched over the little clearing with a half-rotted branch, leaving it superficially returned to its wild state. It wouldn't fool a tracker but a casual glance would miss her traces.

Minutes later she was riding down the road leading the second gyr, singing a lively song under her breath. Stealth hadn't worked before, now maybe boldness might. Anyway it was a lovely night for a ride and if her dream wasn't just a dream Aleytys would be about ready to take on the zel and hell with them, half a sec and I'm away with her and devil fork the hindmost. The road dipped down from the corrugations at the far end of the valley and flattened out beside the river. She wrinkled her nose at the water flowing close beside the black paving. "Don't you look pretty, you. All shiny in the starlight and worms in your belly." She rubbed absently at her gyr's neck. "I wonder if those things'll be after her. Gahh, what ughs." She grinned. "Creepy-crawlies." She reached the western point of the island unchallenged and rather taken with the soundness of her judgment. Scratching thoughtfully at the hollow between the gyr's shoulders as he ambled along, she murmured, "See, stroll by like you got all

the time and all the right in the world and they bow and
scrape and urge you on.'' Her voice trailed off as noises
drifted to her over the brushing roar of the river. "Or Aleytys
has got them so bothered they got no time to watch the
road.'' In any case the road was leaving her, dipping under
the water to come up on the far side of the river. She urged
the gyr up onto the weedy space between the river and the
fields. "Some timing, if that's what I think it is.'' She bent
over the gyr's neck and urged him into a ground-eating lope,
the other following nose to flank as if he were glued there.
She glanced anxiously and repeatedly at the dark blob of the
island, the thin foliage of the sentinel trees like black lace
against the starfield, galloped past without stopping when she
saw the turmoil in the solid blackness of the hedge and the
silhouette of one of the trees bucking about as if a hurricane
had got hold of it. She shivered under the impact of that shout
of NEED, just made out the pallor of the plunging figure,
heard the splash as Aleytys hit the water, but nonetheless kept
the gyori racing along the riverbank.

When she was past the eastern point of the island, she
swung her gyr about and sat peering anxiously at the dark
water, trying to spot Aleytys when she came up and before
she went whirling past. The current wasn't something to fool
around with.

With an explosion of relief, she saw a white arm slicing
through the water. After dropping the second gyr's rein and
leaving him with a command in his head to stay where he
was, she urged her mount into the water and set him swimming toward the struggling woman. Aleytys slammed into his
side and kept kicking blindly on, fighting to reach the bank.
She didn't seem to see Shadith and the gyr. Coaxing and
encouraging him, Shadith got him turned around and was
back beside her in moments. She bent and caught hold of
Aleytys's unwounded arm, yelled her name as she tried to lift
her onto the gyr. Wet, slippery, too heavy, Aleytys almost
unbalanced the desperately swimming gyr even when she
woke up enough to add her help to Shadith's efforts. Finally,
she shook her head, clung to the saddle pad and let the gyr
drag her ashore.

It was still a fight; the gyr moaned his distress and more than once seemed about to give up and let himself be carried away, but Shadith prodded him and crooned to him and caressed him with hand and mind until his hooves touched bottom and he heaved himself up out of the water to stand panting and gasping on the bank. Aleytys dropped on her face and lay like a log on the straggling grass.

Shadith patted the gyr, then swung down and knelt beside Aleytys. "Come on, Lee." She looked over her shoulder at the island. It had gone quiet, but she didn't find that quiet very reassuring. "Help me; I can't lift you."

"Yaaah . . ." Aleytys sucked in a breath, shuddered. Her arms and legs twitched, drew up. With Shadith helping her, she rose on hands and knees then got her torso erect. She sat on her heels while Shadith led the spare gyr closer. She swallowed, tried to push onto her feet, but her legs were too weak. "Get him to kneel." Her voice was blurred, mushy, she had to repeat the words before Shadith understood her.

Once they were both mounted, Shadith urged her gyr into a lope, heard the other following close behind. There were shouts and whistles from the island, more arrows. A curse from Aleytys; Shadith felt a blast of heat behind her, swung around. Energized by her anger, Aleytys was gathering light about her hands; she saw Shadith watching, smiled grimly. "No more," she said. "I've had enough." The diadem flickered about her wet hair, a ghost image as she summoned everything she could command and compressed it into that light about her hands. With a long ululating scream she flung the fire at the hedge and the sentinel trees.

Shadith grinned as she watched the flames leap along the black, searing the thornvine woven into the hedge, leaping from treetop to treetop. She whooped with glee, then quieted as she saw Aleytys's weary, half-smiling consternation.

No more arrows came at them as they rode past the island. Shadith shivered a little though as she felt the rage and fear and hate that hung with a cloud of black smoke like a pall over the zel settlement. She urged the weary gyr into a faster lope, then bit her lip and turned to Aleytys to ask if she could stand the rougher ride.

Aleytys freed a hand, moving with slow painful care, and

waved her on. "Don't mind. . . ." She didn't try to finish
but hooked her hand once again about the front of the saddle
pad; she leaned tensely forward over the gyr's neck, her face
gaunt, strained, wet hair she was too tired to shift plastered in
strings across it.

An ominous stillness settled over the valley as they fled up
the road—as if the valley and the zel were gathering themselves for one last effort. Even the river ran hushed, or so it
seemed to Shadith. The air weighed down on her.

Wind suddenly pounced on them, howled at their backs,
the gyori went wild with fear and something else, as if the
wind had breathed a demon rage into them. Shadith clutched
at the saddle pad as she fought to control her mount; gradually she managed to pluck rule from the wind and drive him
on along the steepening road; she tore a second loose to look
round at Aleytys, worried about how well she was coping
with the buffeting.

Aleytys rode crouched low over her gyr, not in trouble,
handling him well enough though the strain in her face, the
glaze on her eyes warned Shadith that she was running on the
dregs of energy and will.

The gyori bounded up the stiff grading until they reached
the band of trees embroidered across the crests of the mountain,
a dark green hatching on the lighter green of the grass.

"Aleytys. This way." Shadith waggled an arm at the trees,
slowed her weary gyr and turned him into the darkness under
the trees. The wind pushed unimpeded up the mountainside, a
tidal ram of malevolence. Once they were out of this ram the
gyori settled to their usual amiability with snorting relief and
ambled along nuzzling at each other and at their riders'
knees.

Shadith clucked to her gyr and tried to get him to move
faster but he was too weary to respond. She frowned at
Aleytys, sighed and settled herself to wait until they reached
the clearing where she'd stashed the supplies.

She touched her gyr to a halt, swung a leg up and over,
came down running to catch hold of the other gyr's halter and
pull him to a stop. Aleytys's face was flushed. There was
enough light coming into the clearing from the stars and the
setting moon to show her that. Her eyes were drifting about

restlessly as if she didn't understand anything she was seeing. Shadith slapped her on the thigh near the arrowshaft but she didn't show any awareness of either the slap or the jiggling of the point within the flesh. Shadith frowned and chewed on her lip, then lifted her head. "Harskari," she shouted. "Help me. Ride her off this beast and get her flat."

The silence stretched out. Aleytys's body sat unmoving. Shadith fumed at Harskari's extreme reluctance to embody herself. She jigged from foot to foot trying to think of something else to do, frustrated because she couldn't think of anything. The body she had now was smaller, lighter, weaker than Aleytys; if she tried to shift Aleytys off that gyr she'd drop her and god knows how bad those ceramic points would chew her up inside.

Aleytys's head turned. Her lips moved. "Blankets."

Shadith cursed her flitter-headed stupidity, ran at the tree and went up it double time. She tossed the blanket roll from the crotch, then went down again in a barely controlled fall.

Aleytys's body was standing by the gyr, clinging to the saddlepad. The diadem was chiming softly about the wet hair, its ghost image waking highlights from the darkness of the damp red. Her face was stiff as a wax mask, Harskari obviously refusing to do more than she must.

Shadith whipped the roll open, discarded one blanket and spread the other over the littered earth.

Harskari staggered a few steps, dropped Aleytys's body onto its knees in the middle of the blanket. Aleytys's head turned. "Work the points through, Shadith, they're tanged, you can't pull them out. And you'll have to do it, she can't." The mouth moved without sound, the tongue fluttered along the upper lip, then Harskari drove the voice on. "Push them through, I'll guide you so you don't chew things up too much. Not the one in the shoulder, you'll have to cut that out. Bone in the way." Aleytys's eyes drooped shut and the body began to slump; a moment later it straightened, the effort of that straightening visible in face and neck. "Need bandages, antiseptic powder. Hurry. Her strength drains rapidly. Yes, you'd better hurry."

With a sobbing curse Shadith was away again, up the tree and down in a scrambling rush, carrying the saddlebags and

the belt. Hurry. Hurry. Hurry. The word beat in her brain.
She shuddered as she thought about what would happen if
Aleytys died, her fear as great as her grief. Kin and kind.
Dead and gone. Alone. Bereft of Aleytys, of Harskari, yes,
of Harskari too, if Aleytys went. Alone.

Aleytys's body was still on its knees but slumped like a
sun-softened wax figure. Shadith dropped her armload and
went for water.

The next half hour was not something she wanted to remember but the job was finally done, the points and shafts
cast aside, the wounds bandaged, even the grisly hole in
Aleytys's shoulder. Aleytys lay on her stomach on the bloody
blanket, strips of bandage circling her body, the white already
vanishing as blood soaked through. Shadith sucked air through
her teeth, laid her hand against the sweaty forehead. "Fever.
Damn. Lee, can you hear me?" She bent until her ear was
close to Aleytys's mouth, straightened. "Nothing. What do I
do now?" She watched Aleytys shudder with a sudden chill.
"Fire. Get you warm. Cha? I wish I knew if that'd help or
hurt. Lee!" She listened again but there was no answer, no
sign either Aleytys or Harskari heard her.

She rubbed wearily at her eyes, looked around for the
discarded blanket, shook the leaves and debris off it and
wrapped it about Aleytys. Even through the blanket she could
feel the waves of shuddering passing through the battered
body. She touched Aleytys's face again. Hot. The wrong
kind of heat. Aleytys's breathing was raspy and uneven, each
breath a struggle. Shadith dragged her hand across her mouth,
looked up. The sky was paling. Dawn was close, might bring
searchers from the island. She didn't like to think of that. She
touched Aleytys. "Oh god, I have to make a fire." She
gazed blindly about the clearing, not really seeing the trees
and brush. "Lead them right to us. I have to fix that."

She jumped to her feet, swayed a little as her head swam
with weariness, then dashed about collecting wood, rushing
over every few minutes to check on Aleytys. She scraped out
a fire hole, making dirt and litter fly, stabbed four branches
into the earth and tied the tips together, draped one of the
blankets over them and tied it in place, leaving the side
toward Aleytys open. Cheered a little without thinking about

it by the brisk physical activity, she began whistling through
her teeth as she built the fire in the hole and set cha water to
heat.

When the fire was burning steadily she took hold of the
end of the blanket Aleytys lay on and hauled her closer to the
heat, watching anxiously, hoping that the necessarily rough
ride wouldn't do too much damage. Aleytys moaned and
moved her head.

"Lee," Shadith cried; she scrambled on hands and knees
until she was looking down at Aleytys's face, the side of it
she could see, the visible eye half-open, no sign at all she
heard the cry, no sign she knew where or who she was.
Shadith touched her shoulder, felt wetness under her hand.
Blood was seeping through the blanket that covered the
wounded shoulder. She pulled the blanket away. The bandages had slipped; the pad was bright with fresh blood.
"There isn't much more, you didn't bring a lot, oh god, what
do I do when these run out?" She lifted the soaked pad and
tossed it at the fire, scowled at the blood welling up from the
wound. "Lee, oh Lee," she whispered as she pressed new
pads over the three wounds, tied them in place with the old
straps, frayed and bloody though they were. "How do I reach
you? I don't know what more to do."

The fire hissed as the water boiled over. When she took the
lid off to drop in the cha, it clattered against the pot. Her
hand was shaking. She threw in a handful of cha leaves and
fumbled the lid back on, lifted the pot from the fire and set it
to steep close beside Aleytys so that bit of heat could be
added to the rest. She drew her legs up, wrapped her arms
around them and rested her head on her knees. Behind her
she could hear the gyr moving about, nipping at the tender
tips of new green on the brush, at a greater distance the
twitter of birds, the soft soughing of the wind through the
treetops, tentative rustles in the grass as small rodents woke
up. She was tired. So tired. In spite of her desperate anxiety
she nearly slept, had to force herself to raise her head when
she'd given the cha more than enough time to steep. She
forced her aching body to move, to search out a mug. She
half-filled it with the strong almost black liquid, gulped it
down, burning her tongue but gaining a spurt of energy from

the heat and the stimulant in the drink. She poured more cha
in the mug and frowned down at Aleytys. She didn't want to
move her again, but there was no way she could drink lying
on her stomach. Shadith set the mug down, pulled the covering blanket away and eased Aleytys onto her back as gently
as she could. Aleytys moaned with each movement. Shadith
sweated, chewed on her lip. Again, as gently as she could,
she lifted Aleytys, an arm about her shoulders just above the
gouge where she'd cut free the arrow point. She raised the
cup, held it to the slackly open lips and tilted a little of the
hot liquid into the mouth. After a long tense moment, she
relaxed just a little as she felt the throat working. Aleytys had
swallowed the cha. Shadith trembled, swallowed a lump in
her throat, blinked away tears that blurred her vision. Little
by little she got the cha down Aleytys, then laid her back on
the blanket. The awful shuddering had stopped, even the
fever seemed not so consuming when she touched Aleytys's
face.

Shadith sat on her heels, both hands wrapped about the
refilled mug, savoring the warmth that was heating the worst
aches out of her own body. She emptied the mug with hasty
gulps, set it aside and bent over Aleytys.

"Lee," she said. "Listen to me." She touched Aleytys's
face, turned the head so Aleytys's eyes would see her if they
opened. She waited. No reaction. "All right," she said. "We
try something else. Harskari." She made the name sharp,
demanding. She called again, louder, when there was no
response. She slapped the face, pulled the hair. No response.
She sat back on her heels, starting to grow frightened again.
I've got to reach her somehow, she thought, before she
bleeds herself empty. Somehow. How?

As if in answer a hawk cried in the distance, her hawk that
she'd forgotten for so long. She rubbed at the nape of her
neck, turned her head to one side then the other. *Mindrider?*
she thought, then shook her head, the wooden beads clacking
loudly in the hush. "Mindrider?" she said aloud, as if by
saying it aloud she could convince herself it would work. She
closed her eyes. Slowly, very carefully, she tried reaching
into the fever-ridden mind of the woman before her. She
didn't know what she was doing, though she knew that brain

well enough, having used it for herself when Aleytys permitted. Permitted, that was the problem. She had no permission now, not for what she was doing. She told herself she wasn't trying to take over the body, not this time, only to reach some spark of consciousness. She didn't like this, it felt creepy, it felt like she was voluntarily giving up her hard-won freedom, re-entering the trap of the diadem. She shivered and fought herself and continued to probe. *Aleytys. Lee. Hear me. Wake up, Lee. Heal yourself before it's too late. Harskari, come out, help her, help us.*

On and on this went, this wandering in blackness, in nothingness, calling out futilely in blackness, in nothingness. She began to feel tenuous, disoriented, she began to doubt she'd ever find her way back into her own body, it was new, yes, but it was hers. Yet she went on. *Aleytys. Lee. Hear me. Gather what strength you can find. Try, Lee, please, please try. Hear me. You're dying, Lee, you're bleeding to death. You're fever-filled and poisoned and torn up and you have to wake enough to heal yourself. Hear me, try. . . .*

And finally, oh finally, Harskari was there, dimly, weakly, but there, chanting something, chanting strength into herself, Shadith could neither truly hear nor understand what she was chanting but the fog and fever haze began to thin and finally, oh finally, Aleytys was there, dimly, distantly, oh weak so very weak, but there.

And Shadith began trying to find her way back, a maze, a desert, a featureless land, but the tiny tug grew stronger and she fled toward herself and found herself and fitted back into herself with a tidal relief that left her weak and trembling.

And she opened her eyes and she looked down at Aleytys.

The face she saw was no longer vacant but grimly scowling. The hands she saw were clenched into fists. The body was taut, straining.

Slowly the strain lessened. The face lost its hectic flush.

Carefully Shadith turned back the blanket and lifted the pad over the high shoulder wound so she could see that bloody gouge. No more oozing blood. The hole was filled and the new skin that was thickening over it was brightly pink. As she watched, the pink began to fade to the cream-gold of healthy skin.

Shadith closed her eyes, her head buzzing with weariness and relief. She settled on her heels to wait, poured herself another mug of cha. It was lukewarm, strong enough to float a rock, acid enough to tan her insides, but she drank it down with pleasure, laughed when cha leaves stuck to her tongue and her front teeth, spat them from her tongue and rubbed them off her teeth; she felt like singing but sat in vibrating silence, she felt like dancing, but stayed where she was, too comfortable to move, and she watched Aleytys heal herself, replacing lost flesh, replacing lost blood, washing away the last corroding taint of poison.

Sometime later, when the fire was dead and tree shadows were black bars slicing across the clearing, Aleytys sat up and began stripping away the pads and gauze straps, dropping them in an untidy pile. She wrinkled her nose at the clutter, grinned at Shadith. "Thanks." Scratching absently at a smear of blood on her side, she nodded at the cha pot. "Any water left but that?"

"Some." Shadith yawned, blinked. "Want it heated?"

"I'd love it heated but I'll take it cold." She grimaced. "Can't say I like it here this side of the mountains. Sooner we make the pass the easier I'm going to be."

"Uh-huh." Shadith nodded, heard the clack of her hairbeads and scowled. "Use your comb? I've put up with these long enough."

13

About an hour past noon the ancient road finally flattened as they reached the winding saddle of the pass. Shadith was dozing as she rode, lulled by the easy rocking gait of her gyr and the pleasant warmth of the sun. Her gyr stopped suddenly, jarring her awake.

Aleytys had stopped; she sat her gyr facing a slant of rock that was still smooth and intact except for a little erosion near the top that let trickles of coarse dirt trail down the slope. She turned her head. "Look, Shadi." She pointed.

"What?" Shadith scrubbed at her eyes, rode closer.

"Old fox. He got past." Aleytys smiled at a mark neatly chiseled into the rock.

V

ROLLING TO THE OCEAN AND
COLLECTING MORE THAN MOSS

1

Shadith yawned. Her lids drooped so low over her eyes almost none of the chocolate showed. She rode comfortably slumped, left foot in the stirrup, right leg crooked before her across the rolling muscles of the gyr's shoulders. Her hair was an explosion of brown-gold fuzz about her thin young face. In a revulsion against all things zel, she'd torn the beads from her hair, combed out the profusion of braids, each drag of the comb a bit of barely controlled anger. She would have torn off and thrown away every stitch she wore if she'd had even a rag to cover her, but since she did not fancy riding in a blanket, she let prudence rule her rage. "I think I'd kill for a hot shower, shampoo and clean clothes," she said, watching enviously as Aleytys got dressed.

Aleytys glanced over her shoulder. The black paving climbed in lazy loops behind them, vanishing finally behind a bulge on the mountain. The hawk flew above them in long graceful curves. What wind there was blew against their faces, a soft tickle laden with green smells and the aroma of damp soil, damp rock. Of larger beasts, ruminants or predators, there was no sign, though now and then she heard small secret rustles in some bits of grass. For an instant she looked through the hawk's eyes, but even to these the road behind was empty, and the mountain on either side of the road. She shrugged off her uneasiness and turned to watch Shadith. Somehow in the past few days, especially the traumatic hours of last night, Shadith seemed to have altered muscle and bone, growing closer to the mind image she had of her. Or was it the play of expression, the combination of gesture and overall body language that had changed? *Or am I simply getting used to her,* she wondered. *She does look different now. The hair? I don't know. What does it matter?* She twisted around to gaze once again at the slopes and the road.

A shadow had followed them across the mountain. A shadow of a shadow—so faint she only knew its feel, a fugitive itch in her back hair. Eyes and her other senses told her there was nothing there, common sense and experience told her there was nothing there—except perhaps a phantom born of her overheated imagination.

"What's the matter, Lee? We got lice?"

Aleytys straightened. Shadith was watching her, no longer sleepy, body taut, eyes sparkling, a fierce half-grin on her face. Aleytys chuckled. "Down, girl. I don't know," she went on more soberly. "Got a feeling I can't trap. I never see anything, hawk never sees anything. Ghost." She shivered, curved her hand around the back of her head. "But the itch won't go away."

Shadith wiggled her body, slumped again. "If that's all it is, then forget it." She yawned. "Stand guard-turns when we camp, that's all. When do we camp? Sun's low. No river for fishing so we'll need game. Flour's almost gone, dried stuff too. Better keep it for. . . ." She broke off, the last word swallowed by another yawn. "For emergencies."

Aleytys twisted around and watched their elongated shadows dancing on the slope behind them, diffused vague shadows as fuzzy as the shape of the sun glowing behind the thickening layer of clouds, black and heavy with water, shreds blowing past above them, a blanket over the unseen lowlands ahead. Even in the past few minutes the air moving against them had picked up a damper feel. "Going to rain."

Shadith lifted her head, her nose twitching as she sniffed the air. "Uh-huh, maybe not tonight, maybe tomorrow."

"Maybe. You awake enough to fly the hawk and find us a campsite, preferably with water?"

Shadith snorted. "Don't get above yourself, mama. I'm no child."

"Sorry." She ran her eyes over the slight body. "I keep forgetting."

"Hunh!" Shadith grinned at her, then set herself to ride the hawk.

2

Midmorning the next day, a gray and glowering day, they came round a curve and found a long and sinuous valley laid out before them, both ends vanishing in dull gray haze, the ghosts of mountains on the far side, topless, smothered in clouds. A river, slate gray, taking its color from the lowering sky, snaked along the valley floor, dark splotches snugged in its curves. Walled cities. The nearest of these had a patchwork of fields fanning out from it, people at work in them, bits of dark moving between the rows. Beyond that, like dapples of textured shade, more fields, north and south. Peaceful. But the cities and their surrounding fields were as isolated as any of the settlements ringing the Plain on the far side of the mountains, no visible roads except the ancient ones that still webbed the land, evidence of a different pattern of living, no boats on the river, its whole length empty of traffic.

Closer, between them and the valley floor, was a richly bluegreen patch of forest, a rough oval, the long axis parallel to the line of the mountains. It sat across the road like a hairy amoeba. Aleytys twisted around and touched the left saddlebag but changed her mind about wrestling with it. She straightened. "Shadi, get me that book, will you? It's easier for you."

Shadith backed her gyr and dug around in the bag until she found the extract of Esgard's notes. As she passed the book to Aleytys, she flicked a hand at the river and its cuddled settlements. "Them?"

"And that." Aleytys nodded at the forest. "Since the road goes through it."

ESGARD'S NOTES:

Dryad forest. Not much to say about this, except that
Fasstang is emphatic about going through it fast. I can't get
any idea what the danger is, only that it exists. Can't go
round. South, there's a marsh, not exactly a Blight, but
close enough. North, bands of mutant outcasts from the
cities. Kill anything that moves, sometimes for eating,
sometimes for fun of it. Tossed out of the cities because
they're too ugly or too maimed to be useful. Soon as they
reach their fourth year. City rulers call themselves righ-
teous and moral and will not abandon infants to die, but
they are practical and don't want an overabundance of
hungry and angry ferals hanging about. The fourth year
seems an acceptable compromise between morality and
practicality. Not many of the ejected manage to stay alive.
Those that do become very good at surviving if not much
else. Go past the cities with some prudence. Don't stop. If
you somehow manage to irritate the city indigenes, they'll
swarm out after you but if you can leave them behind, they
won't persist. According to what Fasstang and others have
told me, they don't like to go far from their homegrounds.
Satellite cameras seem to confirm this. Go warily.

"Comforting." Shading her eyes, Shadith leaned forward
and peered down at the forest. "Looks peaceful enough."
She settled back, passed a hand over her hair. " 'Ware the
joker."

Aleytys shook her head. "Cross your fingers, Shadi, and
hope that's not quite so prophetic as the last time you said
it." She shoved her gyr's nose away from her knee, tapped
her heels against his sides and started him along the road that
looped through rambling switchbacks down the face of the
mountain into the dreamy peaceful valley so far below them.

The trees were immense. Even before the two riders got
close, the dome-shaped crowns blotted out a large portion of
the sky. On the fringes of the forest small trees and brush
grew in a tangled brake of exuberant complexity. They wove
together into a tunnel arching over the road. Small tendrils
like feelers dropped from the roof, naked except for a few
trembling leaves at the tip. Heavy, thick silence slowly filled

with innumerable subtly hostile whispers radiated from the brake. Aleytys pulled her mount to a stop, eyed the murmuring blackness with considerable distaste.

Shadith ran a hand through her curls. "Why don't we just take a chance with the mutants?"

Aleytys rubbed her nose. "You might have a point."

Both gyr were nervous, sidling about, backing away from the tunnel as much as Aleytys and Shadith would allow. Her mouth set in a grim line, Aleytys fingered her thigh where Shadith had shoved the point through. Her hand was unsteady, fingers trembling. She glanced at Shadith, looked away again. "I'm not ready to face power minds yet."

"Esgard didn't say they had those."

Aleytys shrugged, said nothing. Her fingers still moving up and down over the vanished wound as if she felt it even through the soft brown suede of her trousers, she stared at the tunnel's mouth. The darkness gradually lightened. She could see open space at the other end filled with a deep twilight and a glimpse of the massive boles of the giant trees. "It's not that long," she whispered. "Once we're through. . . ." She tilted her head sharply back and stared up at the silent giants looming over them. Abruptly she was no longer worried. She laughed, kicked her heels into the gyr's sides and urged him forward.

The dangling shoots trembled about her, the soft leaves caressed her; the whispers had changed moments ago, calming her, calling her, a sweet enticing song. She broke out of the tunnel into a world of tranquil majesty, of dreamy beauty. Beams of light delicately greened, dotted with gold motes, broke through the canopy and streamed in a static dance about the dark silent trunks, touching here and there the lacy white skirts about their bases, thickly interwoven air-roots shaped into wide-based cones.

Esgard's warning a tiny spot of alarm at the back of her mind, Aleytys kept the gyr to a quick trot along the crackled black paving, but the wonder of the forest was slowly overwhelming that reservation. The trunks rose straight and sheer sixty meters before the first branches arched out from them. And these branches rose higher, leaping across the wide empty spaces between the trees, growing into each other to create a lacework groining whose highest peak might be eighty meters above her.

The song grew sweeter and a little louder, a cooing hum that was as pleasant and enticing as the sharp green scent of the trees.

Aleytys lets her gyr slow to a walk. She breathes in the beauty and serenity around her. She is vaguely curious about the strange song but not alarmed by it. She turns to Shadith, smiles at her, but says nothing, unwilling to break the peace.

The song grows louder and more insistent, though still of a loveliness and tranquility to wring tears from a stone. It threads through flesh, bone, brain until body and mind are thrumming with it. Aleytys hears Shadith begin to sing with it, a wordless rise and fall of the clear young voice.

Small brown-green figures slip from the great trees as if they dwell like spirits within them; they are translucent like tinted glass, cast in the moulds of sexless little girls about a meter high. First one appears and moves silently along the side of the road, then another and another and many more, melting out of the shadows, tiny naked figures moving with boneless grace, fine greenish hair fluttering about narrow shoulders, waifs with glowing green-gold eyes and tiny mouths pursed to shape the croon that is filling the space around them. The simple melody has gained complexity, added chords to the linear progression of the song, more lovely, more heartbreaking than before. They crowd around her, they crowd around Shadith; before she realizes what is happening the gyori amble to a stop and stand with hanging heads, dazed into stillness by the song.

Undisturbed for the moment, she watches with delight the elfin faces as the dryades dance in their circle about her and about her until she begins to feel dizzy. Of course, she thinks. Dryad forest. How can it be anything else.

But even as she vibrates to their song and to the beauty around her, a vague uneasiness begins to scratch at the velvet overlay they have woven for her.

Shadith has surrendered wholly to the dryades' spell. She slides down from her gyr and joins the circle dance, hand clinging to hand, echoing the wordless song with her own song. She dances off with them as the two circles split, the greater numbers of the small creatures remaining about Aleytys. Aleytys watches them drift away, uneasiness growing pricklier under the cream and velvet.

The dryades dancing about Aleytys intensify their croon, beating at her resistance, a touch of impatience roughing their surfaces. Up to now she has let herself surrender to the song, because of its seductive charm, because of its serenity. She is weary to death of all the crises waiting for her decisions, all the questions rubbing at her. She feels a great relief at being able to set all these aside, at least for a moment. She is so tired of pushing herself to do what she ought rather than what she wanted.

But the pressure the dryad song is putting on her is becoming an attack, not a seduction any longer. She looks around, suddenly alert, and sees Shadith has vanished. "Harskari," she calls, alarmed by this, the harsh cry shattering for an instant the numbing drain of the dryad song. Her shields snap tight, she snatches at the ties of her metal-shod staff, tucks it under her arm as she kicks her gyr into motion.

Or tries to. He stands without moving; even a sharp jab at his mind cannot reach him. Out of the corner of her eye she catches a flicker of movement, twists around. Two dryades are mounted now on Shadith's gyr, others have hold of the rein and are starting to lead him away. There is a sudden small pain like a bite. She twists to look at the back of her upper arm. A bit of fluff sits on the skin just below the cuff of her short sleeve. She plucks it away. There is a tiny black thorn in the center. Holding the fluff in her fingers she stares at the dryades who stare back, waiting. She smiles at them, a broad mirthless smile. "No," she says. "Not this time."

She *reaches*, she flashes out the poison, burns it out of her blood. She *reaches* again, drawing gulps of power into herself. It is easier now—as if the struggle with the Zel had opened pathways blocked before. The diadem chimes, flickering about her head; she cannot see it but sees its reflection in dryad eyes, hears its phantom song. The power churns in her. Distantly she feels more pricks but she ignores them until she is ready, then with a shrug and a flick of the power, the poison is burned away. She points a finger. Gold fire so

searing bright the dryades moan with fear gathers about that
hand, runs in drips about it like molten metal. She jabs the
finger at the nearest tree. Fire leaps from her hand in a long
hot blade; she slashes the fireblade against that tree; a dryad
screams with pain as the blade bites through bark into the
living wood. The tree screams silently. She closes her hand
into a fist. The blade vanishes among the moans and curse
sounds from the dryades. She turns her hand palm up, un-
folds her fingers. A flame dances on her palm. Her eyes
on the shuddering creatures, she curls her arm about the bladed
staff, hugs it close to her side, snaps the fingers of her left
hand, re-absorbing the flame. "I don't know if you understand me," she says, speaking slowly and very clearly, using
the zel tongue, willing them to understand her. "I want my
friend back." She touches herself over her heart. "I want."
She points to the empty saddle pad on the other gyr the
dryades have abandoned. "My friend." She snaps her fingers,
the flame leaps high. "I want her back or I will burn this
forest about your ears." She points a flame-gloved hand,
swings it round in a circle. The dryades shrink back, whining
with fear. She closes her fist about the fire, then makes the
blade again and bites deep into another tree. "Where?" The
word rings under the canopy like the clash of sword on
sword.

The dryades melt away from her, they don't seem to grasp
what she is saying. They are filled with a rage they are too
afraid to vent on her. Two of them are whining and squealing
with pain, long burns cutting across their stained glass torsos.
She swings a leg up and over, slides off. She stands a
moment looking around, then stalks away from the gyr. She
burns a tree, hears/feels the yelping of the dryad. "My
friend," she cries. She strides on, starts to burn a fourth tree,
hesitates, cannot quite bring herself to do it. She stops by one
of the root-cones, re-absorbs the fire, attacks the fragile-
looking roots with the butt of her staff. A smell wafts up to
her, the sickly sweet smell of old death. Her staff rebounds
from the resilient roots. Snarling, she whips the staff around
and slashes at the roots with the bladed end. Bleeding a
viscous reddish fluid, the roots spread away before her, like
curtains pulled aside. The battered frightened tree is shudder-

ing and swaying, that massive, somber giant swaying back and forth as if caught in a high wind. A dryad is huddling against the curve of the trunk, staring at her, radiating pain/fear/rage, with fear the greatest of the three. The ground within is littered with bones, she does not think they are dryad bones, too big, wrong shape, do the dryad's even have bones? Several withered and rotting bodies are more or less intact, enmeshed in flimsy cocoons of hair-fine white roots hanging down from the air root cone. Biting her lip to hold back nausea, not breathing, Aleytys moves closer. Mutants, she thinks. Young, not much bigger than the dryad. She backs out, hand pressed hard against her mouth, sick, shaking, cold with fear. Somewhere in this maze Shadith—she refuses to think about that. She backs farther, turns. There are eyes watching her, she can feel them, but no dryades linger in view. "Give me my friend," she screams. "You want me to burn you all to ash?" The words fall dead in the silence. She swings the staff high over her head. "Burn and cut. And you can't touch me."

She doesn't want to do this, the threat alone makes her as sick as the smell of the rotting bodies. The dryades are only acting out of their natures. She suspects they are animal rather than human, acting from instinct rather than intelligence. They might once have been human, but that is so long ago there is little vestige of it except perhaps in the shape. They don't understand what she wants of them, that is becoming clearer with everything she does to them.

She stalks to another tree, attacks the air-root cone with the staff blade. It opens. Another dryad. More bones. More bodies. No Shadith. She backs out, moves to the next tree, trying to follow the line Shadith was taking the last time she saw her. She is drowning in fear and pain. To lift the shaft and slash at the roots one more time is almost more than she can endure, but she can't endure, either, the image of Shadith being sucked dry, rotting inside a cocoon of fine white roots.

A dryad appears suddenly before her, trembling, almost opaque with terror, a second comes with equal reluctance to join it. They wait for her, hand in hand like frightened children. She aches for their agony but cannot let it stop her.

The first beckons, the pair begin to back away. Warily she follows.

A root cone opens before her.

Shadith is curled up, her back pressed against the trunk, white roots already beginning to curl about her. The roots are hastily retreating. Aleytys drives the two dryades in before her, she does not trust them. They slip round either side of the trunk and hide in the darkness beyond. Aleytys forgets them, flings the staff beyond the circle of the roots and kneels beside Shadith; she wants to burn away the sucking roots, but only for a moment. Forgetting them, she lifts Shadith, stands with her, backs out and turns to see the two gyori waiting for them. Shadith is bleeding from hundreds of tiny wounds but she is alive. She is not conscious, but she is alive.

Eyes watch as she ties Shadith's body across the saddle pad. Hate, anger, fear smother her, swirl around her, the trees are hating her creaking and groaning with that hate. She turns and dips to pick up the staff, has to force herself to move against waves of hate and rejection. The closest tree seems hysterical as she comes near, quiets when she turns away. She ties the staff in place and swings up onto the saddle pad. She rides close to Shadith's gyr, snatches up the dangling rein and starts along the road.

Behind her a shrill keening rose, blasted at her, the trees were swaying, creaking, groaning, the dryades were shrieking, high whining sounds that drilled into her. They were pushing her out, willing her to leave faster. She was no longer raging, only saddened because there was no malice in any of what happened, only hunger and instinct. *Maybe they've learned something*, she thought. *Maybe the next few through will have an easier time*. She thought about the shadow and chuckled at the irony. "Cleared its way, if it's there at all."

Trying to ignore the hate throbbing behind her like the thuds of a massive drum, she pulled the gyori to a halt and frowned at the tunnel through the westernbrake. It was alive with the same hate, the dangling withes snapping so viciously they tore off the tiny leaves at their tips. Twisting on the saddlepad, she glared back at the trees. "All right, you," she yelled, "You want me out of here, then you ease off."

Nothing changed. She didn't really expect it would. Weary, annoyed, she summoned fire to her hand—and was a little startled at how easy this had become—used the fireblade to shear through the brush, saplings and thorn vine until the blackened surface cleared her head by at least a meter and was a meter wider than the width of the pavement. She clenched her fist, but kept the fire burning around it, liquid red-gold flowing round and round it as she thrust it high over her head.

She rode through the quieted tunnel, unhurried, ignoring as best she could the silent roars of pain and rage that thumped against her, but she sighed with relief when she emerged into gray daylight.

Beyond the forest the road cut across a short stretch of rocky barren soil then rode the arches of an ancient bridge across the river. Not about to trust that bridge without giving it a good look, she turned off the road and went north along the bank until she could look back and see those arches. Dropping the reins to groundhitch both gyori, she dismounted and walked to the edge, jumped back as dirt crumbled under her feet.

The river had eaten deep into frangible whitish earth, the banks falling away in soft vertical wrinkles, small bluffs a few meters high. She licked her lips, swallowed painfully, dehydrated from the effort in the forest. Canteen and waterbag were empty, dry camp last night, a pot of cha for her and Shadith, the rest for the gyori. She jerked her eyes from the water and scowled at the bridge. The spare graceful arches seemed intact enough, constructed of some smooth gray-white composite rather like metacrete with, apparently, some of its stability and strength. She looked over her shoulder at Shadith, then at the forest before her. Sturdy enough. I hope. She frowned at the bridge. There were sets of wavery lines on the composite, dried mud and moss, highwater marks. Flood and drought and flood again and it's still there. No point in staying here all day. She looked at the sun, a fuzzy round barely visible through the clouds. Just past noon. Not much time lost after all. Cupping both hands about her eyes, she gazed across the river at the land waiting her and Shadith.

Brush. Brown and gray. Dull. Even the mist of new green

was dull. Wasteland. She sent a probe out as far as she could reach, swept it in an arc across the brush. A life system complex and vigorous, small lives and slightly larger, small and slightly larger heat sources, touches of fire against her face, but nothing as large as a man within that arc. *All right*, she thought. She swallowed again, then turned from the tempting but out of reach water and walked back to the gyori.

She touched Shadith's face. Fever. Lifted an eyelid. Still out. She smoothed gentle fingers over the tangled mop of brown-gold hair, tested the artery under the angle of the jaw. The pulse beat strongly. With a rather guilty smile, she patted the face, aware that it was a relief not having to talk to the girl, argue with her, accommodate to her. She turned away, caught hold of the reins of both gyori and swung up onto her mount, frowned a last time at Shadith, then clucked the gyr into a fast walk.

On the bridge the paving was worn and spotted with small holes, pieces of the railing had crumbled away here and there but the understructure was steady as the earth itself. In the middle of the river, she glanced north where there was a wide bend, wondered how many of those bends before it reached the next walled city, glanced up at the lowering sky wondering how long the threatening rain would hold off. And realized suddenly that the hawk was nowhere about. She reached out, searching for him, but he was gone out of her range. Shadith isn't going to like this. Must have happened when the dryades knocked her cold. He's been fidgeting this side of the mountains. Cut loose. All he needed.

On the far side of the bridge she stopped the gyori and frowned at the road curving gradually north until it was lost in the brush. "Water first." She kicked her heels into the gyr's sides and started him along the riverbank, hunting a place where she could get Shadith, herself and both gyori down to the water.

3

Late afternoon. The bridge gone from sight. The brush stretching on and on. The forest only a smudge on the horizon. The bluff finally began shelving back, its slope gradually gentling until she reached a wrinkled incline she thought she might manage. The gyori seemed sure-footed beasts, their split black hooves could find ample purchase in that chalky soil. Would it hold them without crumbling? The slope was easy enough that she thought it might. She looped the rein up into the halter so Shadith's gyr wouldn't stumble over it, then started cautiously down.

The river was shallow for several strides out, the white soil gleaming through the clear cold liquid and patches of grass that leaned with the current.

The gyori snorted with pleasure and waded into the water until they stood hock-deep, the weed tickling past them, then started sucking greedily at it. Aleytys laughed. Balancing precariously on the pad, she pulled off one boot, then the other—couldn't afford to let them get soaked and stiffen on her, the last pair she had and no way of replacing them. Twisting around, she examined the bank, tossed one of the boots at a weathered fold a little way up it. It caught and settled with a dusting of chalk settling on and around it. She moved her shoulders, swung the other boot and loosed it, nodded with satisfaction when it thudded just above the first. She crooked a leg, rolled the soft suede up above the knee, grabbed at the saddle pad and switched legs. The river droned past. The gyr slurped contentedly, more slowly now that the edge was off his thirst. Now and then the wind up above brushed grit over the rim, sending it in scattered small avalanches down the slope, grains cascading into a dancing patter and fading again.

Aleytys slid off the saddlepad, a small cry startled out of her as the cold water closed about her legs. She shivered and stood still until she'd got used to it, then dug in her saddlebag until she found her mug. She dipped up some water, swallowed a mouthful and waited. No fuss in her body. "Must be clean enough." She scratched her gyr along his neck, laughed as he pushed a dripping muzzle against her side. "Go back to drinking, you." She gulped down the rest of the water, eyes closed with pleasure as the cold clean liquid slid down her parched throat. She filled the mug again, drank more slowly, sighed, wiped her mouth, then tucked the mug back into the saddlebag. The gyori were beginning to tear up mouthfuls of watergrass and crunch them down. The sight made her remember her hunger a bit too vividly with all that water sloshing around in her. One more bit and we both can eat, she thought.

She waded around behind her gyr and stopped beside Shadith, flattened her hand against the girl's forehead. No change, far as she could tell. She unroped the body and carried it to the bank, stretched Shadith out close to the water. With the river's drone and gurgling descants in her ears, she set her hands on Shadith and *reached*.

The fever yielded quickly, the small festering wounds cleared and closed, the poison was washed out and its corrosion repaired—and Shadith sighed, blinked up at Aleytys. She lifted an arm, frowned, moved it stiffly and touched Aleytys's hand. "Lee? What. . . ."

Aleytys sat back on her heels. "Your little friends, they tried to feed you to a tree."

"What?" Shadith tried to sit up. "God, I'm whipped."

"Wait a minute. Lie down will you." Aleytys flattened her hand on the girl's shoulder, fed energy into her, a short burst, took her hand away and let the tap dissolve. "That better?"

"Some." Shadith pushed up, slapped at herself, sending out small puffs of white dust. "I'm hungry, I think. Thirsty for sure." She jabbed her thumb at the river. "That water safe?"

"Uh-huh. Cold too."

"Good. And a bath after." She plucked at her tunic, slapped at the leggings. "These're starting to grow on me."

4

They threaded through clumps of brush; the rising wind out of the north that tossed the brush about slanted across them, cold and drear. The rain still held off. They rode south and west, cutting through the wasteland to regain the ancient road.

For the first dozen minutes they rode in silence, then Shadith scanned the sky, a startled look on her face. "Where's the hawk?"

"Other side of the mountains by now." Aleytys spoke more calmly than she felt, kept her eyes fixed on the boiling clouds. She was tired and cold in spite of the rest by the river while they fished and recovered from the strain of the passage through the forest and she didn't feel able to cope with Shadith's irritation.

"You sent him away?" Shadith's brows drew together, her body seemed to pull in on itself.

"Stop scratching, bantam. Of course I did no such thing. He was gone when we came out of the forest. The dryades broke the link between you when they added you to the larder. He was happy enough to leave. You know he wanted back with his mate."

Shadith rode in gloomy silence scowling at the bobbing head of her gyr. "I suppose," she muttered after a while.

More silence between them. They rode along the bank of a gully, watching it gradually narrow, jumped their gyori over it, turned southwest again.

"Lee."

"What is it?"

"I've got to have a change of clothes."

Aleytys waved a hand at the scrabbly growth around them. "Take your pick."

"No. You know what I mean."

"Right. I just don't know what to do about it."

Shadith stretched, reaching her arms as high as she could, her body undulating with the roll of the gyr. She yawned, gave a vigorous wiggle of her torso as she dropped her arms. "Jump someone when we pass the cities."

"That's a great idea."

"Well, we could leave one of your silver bits. Should mean a lot here, there being very little free metal."

"Or nothing at all, there being very little free metal. Damn." Aleytys stretched her back, glared past the gyr's head at the broad gully ahead of them, just too wide and deep to try jumping. "Blasted hawk. We could really use him now to save us the bother." She stood in the stirrups and gazed along the irregular crack. A heavy cold raindrop broke over her nose. She wiped the back of her hand over the wet. "You know, Shadi, I keep feeling we'd have been ahead if we'd spent the day in camp."

Shadith giggled. "Way things are going, yah."

A few more drops splashed down but stopped at that first minor flurry. The wind blew in heavy gusts, smelling of damp and pollen and something dead somewhere not too far away. Shadith began shivering. After a few minutes she broke out her blanket and wrapped it around her. She followed Aleytys around a stand of whipping briers. "How far is that road?"

Aleytys shrugged. "Probably not too far. I don't know."

"Raining now and we need to hunt. You think we should camp there? On the road I mean. Anybody's liable to come on us. Why don't we stop now?"

Aleytys shook her head. "I don't want. . . ." The wind took her words and cast them away and she didn't bother finishing the sentence. Though Shadith continued grousing, she stopped listening. Something was touching her, neither rain nor wind, soft brushing touches. She shivered, then caught her lip between her teeth, closed her hand tight about the saddle pad as pain arrowed through her, sudden sharp pain. Then it wasn't pain but a desperate agony. It stopped. Began again. Stopped. Began. As if a man, a projective empath, were being beaten not too far away, slowly, steadily, the beater taking time to rest between blows. Her stomach churned. She turned her head slowly, swept the probe across the creaking shuddering brush. The wind howled in her ears, the grains of coarse dirt skipped across the earth, rattling through the brush, noisier than raindrops, slapping against leaves. Hair in her face. Shadith riding close, touching her arm. "What is it?" Five bright burning heat sources, four triumphing, one shooting out those shafts of pain, piercing her until she shook with it, couldn't shut it out. She had to do something, something to stop it. "Lee!" Shadith was tugging at her arm. She turned, stared at the girl without really seeing her. Burning. She clutched at her groin. Burning. Oy-ay Madar, it hurts.

She wrenched herself loose from the hold of the tormented man, bent over, hands gripping the pad, shuddering with the effort. The victim, whoever he was, had to be a projector, his attackers must be protected or natural non-receivers. She felt cool fingers; at the same time several drops of rain broke apart on her face. She looked around.

Shadith's face was drawn with anxiety. "What's happening?"

Aleytys brushed aside another jab of pain, saw Shadith wince. "You feel it?"

"Something." Shadith hugged her arms across her chest. "Let's go. Get away. Leave it behind."

Aleytys pulled away from her hand, startled by a reaction she hadn't expected. She continued to look at Shadith, saying nothing.

"Oh, all right, Lee, but I'm sick of. . . ." She clamped her lips shut and looked away.

Aleytys nudged her mount into a slow walk, questing ahead of her for the heat sources, holding herself as aloof as she could from the empath's uncontrolled projections, watching warily for a change in the auras of the tormenters, a warning that they'd heard or seen something that alerted them to the presence of strangers.

As they got closer, the blasts from the tormented man grew more demanding, as if he knew she was there, as if he'd fished for her and yanked on her now to set the hook. Hooked Shadith as well; the girl was shivering in convulsive waves, aware of what was happening, a sullen resentment growing in her. But the compulsion had her now.

More rain, blown against them by the wind. The five heat sources were close now, though she couldn't hear them, not even the screams of the victim. Thunder rolled across the valley; lightning walked ahead of it. More rain, still no steady fall, only flurries driven flat before the rushing wind.

She pulled her gyr to a halt. Dropped the rein to ground him. Slipped from the saddle. Unlashed the staff. Dropped onto her stomach. Pulled the staff with her as she crept forward, twisting through the brush, the small sounds of her passage covered by the thunder, the wind and the rain.

Hidden by a screen of brush, she looked into a round clearing. Four outcasts were shifting about a shallow pit at the center of the clearing. As soon as she saw them, she shuddered and her eyes slid away without her willing it to the pit and the captive staked out on the flat bottom, wrists and ankles tied with smooth thongs to bits of brush stem pounded into the earth. Beside him a small fire was steaming to blackness as the coals succumbed to the rain. A small man, naked, spread out, parts of him charred, other parts smeared with blood. She closed her hand tight about the staff and forced herself to examine the others.

The four . . . creatures? . . . men? were busy cutting brush and carrying it back to the cleared ground, beating clump into clump, building it into a crude shelter from wind and rain. Men by courtesy only in that they shared the common shape. A shape eaten away, distorted, until only the ghost of the pattern remained. In spite of herself Aleytys found she could not watch them for more than a few minutes at a time. This world still had its pustules—the Blights, the rotten marshlands where corruption leaked in slow eddies. What she saw before her were the pustules of the race that had reduced itself to tiny cells that even now were not proof against the consequences of their ancestral murder sprees. Thrown from the city because their fathers could not bear to look upon them, these were scapegoats for the ugliness of spirit that had set going the process that made them.

Shadith crawled up beside her, peered through the screen of twigs and leaves. Aleytys heard the breath catch in her throat, touched her on the shoulder.

The creatures—outcasts—were chuckling, grunting, gobbling incomprehensible syllables, obviously pleased with themselves and waiting with excited anticipation for the full force of the storm, each of them glancing repeatedly at the staked-out man. One caught hold of a scraggly throat ornamented with gray spongy masses, probably external gills, thrown out by a body that thereafter forgot what they were for, then he jabbed at the captive with a two-fingered thumbless hand. A flurry of rain spattered on the outcast, waking him to cackling, convulsing laughter; he beat on himself and repeatedly pantomimed a gasping for breath. Gurgling. Drowning.

Aleytys swallowed. Shadith's hand closed hard about her arm, her eyes were wide, questioning. Aleytys nodded. Slow inexorable drowning. The creatures in their shelter watching. Enjoying.

The victim was a little man, might have been a boy except

for a lined, ravaged face older than the earth, a face that popped out of the gloom with each flicker of lightning. He was naked, blood smeared over plummy bruises, mouth swollen, eyes swollen almost shut, battered, moaning, tugging feebly at the thongs, wrists and ankles raw, purple, swollen.

Shadith moved close to Aleytys, whispered in her ear, "Bow." She began wriggling back, moving with limber ease, the storm too loud for her to bother with much caution in her movements except to keep her head down. The wind tossed the brush over Aleytys's head, made it creak, groan, shudder, though its thick small leaves caught the pattering rain and kept her reasonably dry. Lightning cracked suddenly, so close it blanked out the scene. She snapped her eyes shut. As soon as she blinked away the purple blotches, she saw that the pit was already beginning to fill. The little man was yelling, twisting against the thongs; he understood now, if he hadn't before, what would happen to him. Water splashed about him. He blasted out silent yells of pain and rage, demanding, yes, demanding help. She struggled to blank him out, moved, without thinking, with such violence the brush about her rattled loudly enough to be heard over the storm.

The outcasts snatched up spears and came loping raggedly across the clearing toward her.

She lunged up out of the brush. An outcast hurled his spear at her. She knocked it aside with the staff and ran at him, moving far faster than these maimed grotesques could manage, circling around to come at him before the others could close on her. She feinted at his diaphragm with the blunt end of the staff, twisted it up as he dodged and tried to run backward, caught him on the side of his tiny ball-shaped head. She twisted away from the spear points as the other three closed on her, circled warily, holding the staff at its balance point, the clack-clack of staff against spear so rhythmic and continuous it was like a peculiar music, seductive because her feet found the rhythm and if she let them, they'd take her into predictable patterns. She was wary of the points too, they made too free with poison on this world.

A shaft whistled from the brush, missed one of the outcasts by a few inches; he howled and swung about, his spear coming up and back for the throw. A second arrow caught him in the shoulder; he went to his knees, foam spattering from a rubbery working mouth. Aleytys slammed her staff against a spear, knocking it from the hand of the startled creature, slid her hands down the staff and punched the metal-shod butt into its belly with a force that knocked it against the last of the creatures, jumped over the writhing bodies and kicked that one in the head. He stopped his mewling and went limp. Aleytys straightened, the staff dropping with a muted clunk against the beaten earth, turned to face Shadith, her hands brushing repeatedly against each other. "You'd better collect the arrows."

Shadith raised her brows. "What's got into you?" With a soft grunt she unstrung the bow, wiped her arm across her streaming face, though the rain wet it again immediately. She coiled the bowstring and slipped it into a pocket in her leggings.

Aleytys shrugged. She looked at her hands, rubbed thumbs across fingers. "I don't know. Don't fuss. Do what I told you. Get the arrows." With a quick impatient movement of her hand, she turned away and knelt beside the two creatures. Again she rubbed thumb across fingers, then forced her hand to touch the thing. Fighting with nausea, she slid her fingers over the cold wet skin, feeling for any life left in the creature. Over the nubbin of an ear, the skull gave under her fingers with a grating sound that was more tactile than audible. Thunder rumbled around her, the wind blew rain against her, the brush creaked; somewhere not too far away something long dead tainted the wind. She touched the other. The long knobby head moved too easily, rolling away under her fingers. Dead. "Too easy," she muttered. "As if they didn't. . . ." On her knees she moved to the others. The one skewered in the shoulder was cold and dead, not even much blood had come from the wound, only a few short worms of red. The arrow was in place. *I told her. . . .* Still on her knees she whipped around to blast Shadith, an unreasonable fury suddenly possessing her. The heat drained out of her when she saw Shadith kneeling beside the man, sawing at the thongs that held his wrist to the stake. *I forgot about him,* she thought, *stupid, stupid.* The water was already above his ears, the knife was splashing through it, sawing at the thongs. The little man's face was still, he radiated wariness as well as pleading, his hook well sunk in Shadith if she read right. She watched them, listened to Shadith crooning to him in interlingue like a mother to a small and naughty boy. She shook her head and turned back to the corpse.

Sickened by it, sickened by her reaction to it, she began cutting into the soapy flesh intending to extract the arrow intact. She drew back, pressed her fist against her mouth and fought to still the knotting of her stomach, not sure she could force herself to continue cutting into the creature's corpse. Creature. She sat on her heels and stared through the rain at the dark heaving line of brush. Creature. The mind plays subtle games with words without the will's consent or knowledge. Creature. As well say beast. *Man*, she thought. "Man," she said aloud. She bent her stubborn neck and looked more closely at the body. "Woman," she whispered, closed her eyes. Somehow it was worse that the thing . . . the body . . . was female. "Tool-user, language maker," she whispered. "I won't let myself. . . ." She let the words go, forced down revulsion, pity, shame, and went briskly to work, cutting free the arrowhead.

She got it out, swished it through the deepening water by her legs. When she lifted it she saw why so trivial a wound had killed the woman. (She stumbled over the word in her head but said it firmly enough.) The point gleamed milky white in the gloom, the poison-steeped fibers behind it like black barbed wire. A zel arrow. She got heavily to her feet and walked over to Shadith. The collecting rain sloshed about her boots. She looked down, remembering her care to keep them dry, shrugged off what couldn't be helped, glared at the arrow and held it carefully before her.

Shadith looked around, raised her brows at the arrow. "What did you expect?" She sat unconcerned in the water, the little man's head on her knee, rain running down her face, plastering the exuberant curls close to her narrow head, her chocolate eyes wide and defiant. "Forget that thing, Lee. He needs you." She smiled down at the little man, absently patting his shoulder. Aleytys circled round his feet, knelt beside him, grimacing as cold water rewet her trousers.

His bruised swollen mouth moved, a wince more than a
smile. He had stubbly red-brown eyelashes, thick like fur,
soft short red-brown hair darkened by the rain. His ears were
large, pointed, but not excessively so. His eyes were swollen,
slits in puffy darkening flesh. His expression changed, he
lifted his hand, tried to speak.

"Hush-hush," she murmured, pushing his head gently
onto Shadith's knee. He yielded with some reluctance, opened
his battered bloodshot eyes a little wider, then began project-
ing warmth, friendliness, trust. His lips moved, soundlessly
at first, then produced blurred mushy words. "Who . . . are
. . . you?"

Interlingue. Aleytys raised her brows, then brushed away
his attempt to set his hook in her. "Never mind that now,"
she said, and *reached*.

5

The shelter had brush walls, chunks of brush crushed together
until they were reasonably watertight, the groundsheet lashed
over the top. Aleytys sat beside a small fire built in a shallow
depression burning away the poison fibers, digging the points
of the zel arrows into the earth then passing them again
through the fire to burn off the last vestiges of the poison.
Shadith was out hunting, working off her annoyance at the
scolding she got for using that poison.

He watched her as he worked, amused, wide blue eyes in a
crumpled net of laugh-wrinkles. The Eload ven-myda Wakille.
Free trader, he said. Sometime smuggler, she thought. Age
uncertain. Vigor definite. Cunning probable. They had recovered his gyori, Shadith had, and picked up as much of his
gear, supplies, tradegoods and acquisitions as they could
find, though the outcasts had trampled, torn, and flung about
a good deal of his things in an orgy of destruction that had
overtaken them. For no discernible reason, he said. Frightened the stiffening out of his bones, he said. She didn't think
so then, watching him as he pulled on trousers and tunic
much the worse for spear-points. And she didn't think so now
as he sat, busy with needle and thread, making quick neat
repairs in the tunic, his hands clever as his round face.

"They let you into the cities?" She dealt with the last of the points, moved about on her knees, adding wood to the fire, digging out the pot for cha, filling it from the waterbag and setting it to heat on the three-legged stand contrived from soaked green brushwood.

"Not inside." He snipped the thread, ran his thumb over the repair. "No. But the news gets round when I show up and anyone interested eventually shows outside. Chancy." He rolled a knot in the thread and felt for another rent. "They get bored with what you've got to show. . . ." he grinned, rubbed the hand holding the needle across his throat. "Or you show too much and they get greedy." A flicker of long slim fingers. "Takes patience and craft, my lioness, but once you get them used to you, there's a comfortable profit in it."

Aleytys chuckled. "Doesn't hurt if you're a projective empath."

"Doesn't hurt." He ran a hand over the red-brown plush on his head. "You trading?"

She drew her legs up, rested her arms on her knees. "No. No competition, Eload Wakille."

"I rejoice, my lioness." His voice was rich, caressing, an instrument of some power, especially when delicately underlined with his talent.

"Hands off, Wakille, before I get irritated."

"So, sweet lioness."

"That's the third time you called me cat. Should I be flattered or angry?"

"Ever watch a Haberdee lioness stalking? No? Too bad. You might know what I mean. Great golden beast pacing through dry dusty grass, powerful muscles sliding and shifting under her skin. Formidable and beautiful and terrifying."

"Poetic, but not terribly applicable."

"You can't see yourself."

"Clever, aren't you, little man."

"Um, I think, yes." He worked in silence for a moment, setting the last stitches to close the rent, then looked up, his face going quiet, his eyes wide and serious. "I owe you."

"Right." She said it with some satisfaction, tapped lightly on her knee as she watched his mobile but unrevealing face.

No clues there that he hadn't put there. "We could have ignored you, just ridden past."

"Um." He lifted his brows, thick red plush hyphens tilting into an inverted vee, clipped the thread, knotted it, brows down now in his concentration on what he was doing, shifted the tunic to a new hole. "So what are you doing here?" The brows went up again. "If I may ask?"

"Tourists," she said cheerfully. "My friend and I."

He snorted. "Not likely."

"It's all the answer you'll get."

"Thought it might be." He reached behind him and brought out the note extract, lobbed it to her. She caught it, anger flaring in her that he carefully refrained from trying to soothe away. "When you went out for wood," he said. He smoothed his thumbnail along an invisible moustache, his wide mouth curled up at the corners. "A trader without a nose is poor and maybe dead."

She set the book beside her. "So?"

"You'll find it." He said that with such certainty she had to smile. "So, I think I'll come with you."

"Why?"

"For what I can pick up." He snapped the thread, tucked the needle through a fold in his trousers, pulled the tunic over his hand, searching for other tears. "Dama Fortuna throws your way, you're a fool to let it pass."

"Throws hunger, thirst, discomfort, even death."

"But you can't know what it means, can you."

"You don't gamble."

"Eh-lioness, what else can a poor trader do?"

"Not without a solid edge on your side.

"True, but then. . . ." His eyes twinkled at her from their nests of laugh wrinkles, his grin bared small neat teeth. "But then I have an edge on you, don't I. A Wolff Hunter. *The* Wolff Hunter, I might say." He laughed, a rumbling bumble almost a basso giggle. "While back, I happened past Helvetia; friend of mine got me into the hearing room."

"Goggle-eyed fools, the lot of you." Aleytys sniffed. "None of your business, any of that."

"Interesting, you have to admit. Besides you never can tell when a bit of stray fact will prove useful. Look at us, now.

How much more confident it makes me to know Aleytys the Hunter is around to save my hide when circumstances dictate.''

"Looks to me I made a large mistake saving it this afternoon. Perhaps I won't repeat that mistake.''

"Ah.'' He smirked at her, shook his head. "You couldn't do that, now could you, lioness.''

"Don't keep calling me that. You know my name.''

"Despina Aleytys.''

Aleytys lifted the lid on the pot, dropped it back. Not boiling yet. She shifted until she was sitting on her heels, tilted her head and gazed at the groundsheet stretched drumtight above them, the few drops of rain tapping out an irregular rhythm on the taut surface. The greater part of the storm had passed to the east not long after they finished setting up the camp. She frowned, swept a probe over the wasteland outside, touched nothing. That worried her. Shadith had been gone over an hour, not too long for a hunt in these conditions, but worrying all the same. She glanced at the trader. He was folding the tunic with small, neat movements that made her smile. "Have you ever crossed the ocean?''

He looked up, startled. "No point to it, Hunter. No shipping either. And the markets on this continent aren't that close to being worked out.''

"Better rethink coming with us.'' The fire hissed as boiling water forced the lid to one side. She snatched the pot off the stand and dumped in a handful of cha leaves, set it aside to steep, picked up the book, flipped through the pages, found what she wanted and began to read aloud.

ESGARD'S NOTES:

The ocean has a number of strong, broad, multi-stranded currents. The one you should be interested in, my follower, sweeps along the western edge of the ocean, splits into two sections, one of which dissipates in turbulence among the ice floes in the far north. The other flows south along the coast of the Yastroo continent, turns west along the equator. (Strongest and speediest here from my observations, thank whatever gods or devils there be, because that's where the speed is most welcome.) Completes the circle somewhere

under the belly bulge of the second continent. Floating
islands ride the current, taking just over a year to complete
the circuit, shore to shore and back. By the way, all the
oceans have these islands, even the west wind drift around
the bottom of the world and several islands seem to—what?
—transfer their loyalty from one current to another, if you,
my follower, will allow the anthropomorphism. Fortunately,
that happens far more often in the southern hemisphere than
in the north so unless you are blessed with an excess of
ill-luck, it isn't likely to happen to you. However, since the
danger does exist, I record it here. Some of the islands are
small—a stunted tree or two, an apron of weed, a bit of
brush. Others are very large, slow and stable. Their trees
act as sails, their mass lets them ride out the storms without
breaking up or capsizing.

The ancient road leads to a finger of land protruding
from the west coast. A series of sandbanks go out from it,
almost touching the fringes of the current. Now and then,
several times a year, these banks will trap one of the larger
islands. It breaks loose after a week, a day, sometimes only
an hour depending on the tide and the wind. The larger
ones grind loose most quickly, especially if a following
wind combines with large waves kicked up by a storm out
at sea and a flood tide. I have tracked these islands for
several years now. Since the currents aren't single but
braidings of many strands, the courses of the islands are
impossible to predict, though the majority of the larger
ones seem to hit the sandbanks near the end of the winter—
the increased speed and velocity of the storms, I suppose.
One of the elements that determined my departure date.
With Fasstang and his men we'll need a good sturdy mount
to carry us and weather the storms. You who follow, be
sure to bring along a still of some sort. Water will be the
biggest problem you face. The islands have extensive skirts
of seaweed. Dried, it makes a passable fodder for the riding
beasts. And, I understand, a good enough flavoring for fish
stew. Also bring something to pass the time away; the
fastest speed you'll make is five or six knots. There will be
an abundant assortment of crustaceans and small fish living
in the weed, so food will be no problem, monotonous but

nourishing enough. The life in the oceans was nearly destroyed during the hot war but mutation and time have begun to fill the empty niches and being left alone by the indigenes hasn't hurt. If you forget the still you could build a catch basin. Depending upon the season, you could catch enough rain to survive. I wouldn't try depending on it any season, though. And be prepared to wait. Don't take the first island that lodges in the sand unless it is at least half a kilometer long. Less than that a storm could flop over, or wash over, neither of which is very good for lengthy survival.

Three days through the unchanging waste, riding warily along the ancient road, rising early, stopping to hunt before sundown, calm, uneventful. Eload Wakille earning his way with a thousand tales of downfalls and sudden reversals and cunning tricks inexplicably gone wrong. He was an entertaining companion and Shadith succumbed to his charm, her surrender helped along by the subtle touches of his talent. Aleytys never caught him at it, he was a bit too clever for her, but she suspected him. She was sure of only one thing. He hadn't told her his real reason for attaching himself to them. Already, though, Aleytys found his constant presence an irritation. She and Shadith had to watch their tongues or tell him more than they wanted about themselves, things they'd rather no one knew. They could and did chat easily and pleasantly, but kept to impersonal subjects.

On the third day as the sun poked up over the mountains, they broke camp and rode yawning and sleepy onto the ancient road. Their shadows, grotesquely elongated, jerked and flirted on the pavement ahead of them; droplets of dew on the brush twinkled in another kind of dance, hidden and revealed and hidden again by their progress along the road. All traces of the storm had vanished. The sky was cloudless and in the strengthening light of the sun, the shadows had sharp edges and even distant objects had a clarity of form, a solidity in their thingness that made them oddly less real—as if such solidity and clarity existed only in dream landscapes. On the horizon, dark against the pallor of the coast range, lay a walled city. Distant as it was, Aleytys could see the sharp outlines of the corner towers and a few roofpeaks behind the wall.

The road curved very gradually northward, nudging around to meet the skittishly advancing and retreating river. The city before them was the last one they would pass, the only one they'd come close to according to the map in her belt. The road touched the river again beyond it, then went up into the mountains, crossed a lowish pass and went down to a mild unspectacular coastal plain, neither salt marsh nor sea cliffs, just grass and sand fading into sea.

From a vague blotch against the pale blues and greens of the folded hills, the walls grew solider and higher. And less threatening. They were a cobbled together conglomeration of mud and stone and anonymous chunks of ancient things, scraggly with grass and weeds growing here and there like patches of hair on a mangy dog. A mud dauber's nest plunked down in the gentle curve of the river. The ancient road cut through the cultivated fields; according to the map they could go around the fields, thread through the brush and take the road again beyond them. It was the prudent thing but suddenly she didn't want to do it. She felt relaxed, filled with a lazy well-being; reluctance was a wall before her, an invisible resilient wall, shutting off the possibility of going around. She glanced at Shadith. The girl was slumped, her slim utterly relaxed body moving as one with the gentle roll and dip of the pacing gyr. She pulled up her own mount, waved Shadith on when the girl looked lazily around, then drew in close to Eload Wakille.

"You traded with those?" She nodded at the mudpile ahead.

"Some."

"Hostile?"

"Now and then. Depends."

"Think we need to go around?"

"You don't want to."

She eyed the bland rubbery face, smiled. "Feeling lazy."

"Um." He twisted around. The sun was still sitting on the mountain peaks, a narrowing streak of red on either side of the squat red circle. He shifted back, frowned at the walls ahead rising over the thick brown brush. "Half-hour, more, getting there. Fields will be filling with the miserable clots the families half starve and work to death. They don't count. Won't lift their heads more'n a minute from their work. Afraid of being culled. Thrown to the outcasts. A few overseers. Um. Could raise a fuss, those. Probably won't. They used to me coming through. Mostly alone. Hadn't got this far this trip, not yet. You're women, you and the young 'un up there—though how you turned a zel friendly beats me.'' He sighed with exaggerated disappointment when she declined the ploy. "Figure you're entertainment I brought along. Um. 'F we stopped, I'd get an offer or two for you." She snorted and he chuckled, the low rumbling giggle that continued to amuse her whenever she heard it. "Not my idea, lioness."

"Don't call me that." She kicked her gyr into a quicker gait and rejoined Shadith.

There was a ragged fence of jammed brush and crude stakes around the cultivated fields. At the road that barrier was reduced to a few dry branches scattered over the pavement, a stake broken into shards.

Aleytys stopped her gyr in the opening, the others stopped with her; she could feel them watching her though neither spoke. She moved her shoulders impatiently as she scanned the planted land. There were people on their knees in some sections, gray bundles humped along the rows of plants like ragged beetles. A man sat on a high stool placed in the center of the nearest field, slumped, half-asleep, a strung bow swinging from a hook screwed into one of the stool's legs, a whip coiled on the same hook. More like him sat in other parts of the enclosure. In the distance a worker walked a waterwheel around. The clack-swish of the leather buckets and water came clearly to her. The broad high wall of the city was deserted except for a few small birds flying into and out of holes in the mud and the patches of grass and weeds that shifted a little in the sluggishly moving air. The morning was very quiet, cool and dew-wet, crisp and filled with distant sounds, soft and murmuring. The scattered overseers were silent. The nearest of these snorted, woke himself, sat up, saw her, but he said nothing, did nothing, just sat staring lumpishly at her. He lifted a hand and ran it over an unshaven face; she could hear the rasp of his hand against the stubble.

With a brisk nod of her head, she clucked the gyr into an easy walk and started across the fields.

Her lips tightened as she got a closer look at the folk bent over, grubbing among the plants, but she got a grip on her anger and tried to keep from seeing the desolation about her. There was nothing she could do, nothing to change their miserable lives or help them in any way. She could destroy but not create, destruction took seconds, creation could take years. She could free these serfs easily enough, but free them to what? To a quick death, eaten or tormented by the outcasts. To slow starvation and death from exposure. And she'd learned a little more about people—ordinary people who needed familiar things about them and would fight and claw to keep a hold on these until the last hope was gone, ordinary people who were suspicious of promises or even proof of a better life, suspicious of strangers, generous and loyal to their own kind, a solid block against the intrusion of outsiders. There was nothing she could do to make their lives better. All the power she controlled, all the skills the years had taught her meant nothing here. Time and energy and hope, that's what they needed and she was not willing to spend any of those to help them. *Mountain girl, you've finally learned your limits*, she thought. *Look away. Refuse to see.* She looked away from them, turned to gaze thoughtfully at Eload Wakille. *The one hope*, she thought and smiled to herself. Him and others like him. He wasn't enough by himself, but there had to be other traders working these people for the profit in it. Maybe they could catch the fever from the traders, these shut-ins, maybe they would start up some trade for themselves, city with city. Her smile vanished. No. Not yet, anyway. If the social structure in that mudheap is what I think, the ones on top will sense, if not fully understand, what opening up would mean to them. Still, there were others close to the top that might take the chance. She smiled again, a tight curving of her lips. Angels and pinheads again. You're making towers out of nothing. No data. Or not enough.

The silence held behind her. No alarums, no shouts, no missiles coming at them. She relaxed still more as she reached the narrow gap in the brush fence where the road left the fields.

The gyori began to snort and sidle about, shaking their heads, twitching their ears as if gnats bit at them. Then something small and agile and brown darted from the gap, scrambling along, using the bulk of the gyori to shield it from the view of the nearest overseers.

There was a shout from the fields, but Aleytys didn't turn or stop. Instead she bent down and offered a hand to the child running beside the gyr's front legs. When she got no response to her offer, she frowned, called softly, "Let me help you."

The child glanced up. Aleytys stifled an exclamation. The small pointed face had no eyes, just shallow indentations over the high cheekbones. *Born without eyes*, Aleytys thought. His thin lips were pursed and pulsing, the large mobile ears shifting about, their pointed tips in constant movement.

"Take my hand," Aleytys said, anchoring her left about the saddle pad, moving her right in a slow flutter she hoped the little boy could perceive.

The boy's mouth stretched briefly into a broad grin, then went back to its pulsing flutter. Two small hands closed tight on hers, the small body leaped with her lift and was quickly settled in front of her on the gyr's back. He had understood either the gesture or the words or both.

"There goes my trade route," Wakille said.

Aleytys scowled at him. "Too bad," she said. She touched the narrow shoulder resting against her ribs. Up close the child's skin was covered by a soft short pelt, a pale beige dappled with faintly darker splotches. He twisted his head around and up at her touch, curiosity written in the spare lines of his face. "What's your name, child?" she said, hoping he did indeed understand the words, it would make things a lot easier.

"Linfyar, Mistress."

Aleytys damped her startle reaction at the extraordinary music in the boy's voice; he did understand, that was all that was important now. "That's a pretty name."

He continued to "watch" her with his whistles, indifferent to her praise. "Take me with you?" Small hands closed painfully tight on her arm. "I sing for you."

"Don't you think you'd be better off with your family?

You might be angry with them now, but sure as sure, you'll miss them come the night.''

''If I go back, Bigman, he cut off my feet. Besides, I got no family.''

''You're young for that.''

''Old enough for gelding to keep m' voice.'' Linfyar spoke with a grim matter-of-fact lack of emphasis that was more convincing than any angry protest.

''That why you ran?''

''That and Ol' Kus. He like boys. Me Mam, she die a week ago. Long time she was Bigman's cook, so she get to keep me.'' The boy's ears fluttered, then he leaned back against her, warm and soft and small, his head between her breasts, the tangle of brown-gold curls fluttering against the russet of her suede tunic. ''She die a' somethin, don' know what. Bigman, he been having me sing for him long time too. Now he tell me, he sell me to Ol' Kus who going to cut me, keep the voice from changin. We kradj, we know more'n big folk they think. Lots stories about Ol' Kus and things he do. Me Mam, she wouldna like any of that, no, nor me, so I figure better to get 'way, outcast they eat me maybe, but that over fast, the cuttin, it for always.'' Aleytys could feel the slight body tremble against her, then the tiny boy sighed with pleasure and moved with a twisting motion against her as if he wanted to be sure he could feel her there holding him. ''They guardin me after Bigman tol' me, he not softhead. But Klian, she new cook, me mam's blood kin, she bring the guards hot drinks when she dare, comes back close to nightend when drink makes them sleep. She aks me I want stay or cut out 'n I say o hes, cut out, 'n she give me this to wear.'' He patted the coarsely woven shorts and sleeveless top dyed a dull brown. '' 'N she put me with the field kradj who bound out to pull weeds. They don' say nothin, they don' care nothin but do they work and eat somethin if they can sneak it 'n watch out for they overseer whip. So I sneak out with them and when overseer not lookin. . . .'' He grinned then and bounced a little on the saddle pad, feeling quite at home now and secure, something that told her a lot about his short life. Women must have always been kind to him, all women, not just his mother. He had a quick acceptance of kindness, a sort of expectation that the world would be good to him. Even the troubles ahead of him hadn't struck deep; with the help of one of his protecting women, he'd got away from that and was sure now that he was safe, sure of her.

"Not looking," she said. "How do you know that?"

"I know, I do." Linfyar gave a soft gurgling laugh. "I feel when they look, be like bugs crawling on the place they lookin at." the thin shoulders moved in a little ripple. "Then you all come 'n I get out 'n go with you." He relaxed against her again with a little contented sigh.

"Linfyar . . ." she started, then fell silent as the small face turned up to her, the lips fluttering in those silent pulses of sound that drew her face for him. "We go into strange lands, Linfyar, there's always danger in that. Isn't there anyone anywhere you can stay with?"

"No, Mistress. Take me, I sing for you."

She felt the small body gather itself and hastily touched the boy's cheek. "Not now, Linfy. We're too close to the city yet." She looked over her shoulder. There was no sign of pursuit so she relaxed again. Shadith was scowling and Eload Wakille looked sour, but she didn't care about them, Linfyar was a way to salvage some of the self-respect she'd felt slipping away from her.

"We're running a damn conducted tour," Shadith said. Then she shook herself like a horse getting rid of flies, smiled reluctantly. "I suppose we really couldn't leave him to the outcasts." She rode closer, ran her eyes over the boy. Aleytys could feel his breath slowing. He was close to being asleep. "Asleep," Shadith said. "He knows he's found himself a home."

"Shadi."

"Never mind, Lee. I understand." Shadith looked from the small fur-child to Aleytys's face and back. "Me, I never had any kids. Just as well, considering."

"That's enough, Shadi."

"More than enough, I think," Shadith said cheerfully, not at all oppressed by Aleytys's stern tone.

They rode in silence after that, the boy slumbering in Aleytys's arms. The extraordinary clarity of the air vanished with the rising of the wind and the stirring up of a haze of dust and pollen over the everpresent brush and the yellowing grass. On the right the river hushed briefly beside them before turning north. The land began rising toward the mountains, more grass now than brush, long grass whispering in the wind.

Linfyar stirred, yawned, sat up and turned his head from side to side, his lips fluttering rapidly as he scanned the rippling hillsides on either side of the road. Aleytys watched, curious about just what it was the eyeless child perceived. What a strange world he must live in, she thought. She swept a swift probe over the hillsides, but the quiet emptiness on the surface was echoed by the hidden quiet. Small-lives in large numbers and variety pattered about, nosing out grubs, picking crawlers off leaves and grassblades, munching on tender greens, sucking juice from plants or other animals, grubbing up roots and tubers of all kinds, a web of busy life invisible and vigorous and non-threatening. The boy turned his head up and smiled at her, the broad angelic smile that turned her insides to mush even as she realized it was something he cultivated, part of his survival game. "I'm hungry, Mistress," he said, pathos lightly touched into the lovely voice.

Aleytys glanced at the sun. "Not time to stop yet, Linfyar. When did you eat last?"

"Klian she give me a bit bread fore sunup. That be long long time since." His silvery voice was coaxing, teasing, setting a lilt into the words that made them almost a song.

"Hang on." She ran her fingers over the pockets of her belt, found the pocket where she'd stashed a trail bar. "Here." She touched the boy's arm, put the trailbar in his hand. "Take the skin off before you eat this. It's sweet, but eat it slow. Slow, Linfy, or you'll give yourself a bellyache."

He giggled, sighed with pleasure, settled back against her, gnawing at the small sticky square with little murmurs of delight as the sweetness of the dried fruit touched his tongue.

6

The stream sang down the mountainside, sank into a culvert that passed under the road and let it cut its way downhill to the river. A small fire hissed in its firehole. Overhead a few

insects whirred and clicked, a tree-nesting amphibian chirped
its two-note nightsong at measured intervals. Aleytys sat
apart from the others, cradling a cooling mug of cha between
her palms, leaning against the knotted and twisted trunk of a
small tree much like the willows that favored riverbanks on
the world where she was born. Long supple withes with
heart-shaped leaves paired along them swept back and forth
before her face, paper-thin leaves that fluttered at the end of
long stems and whispered thinly at each breath of air. She
took a sip of the cha and smiled at the three by the fire.

Eload Wakille was over his snit—almost over it. He sat
across the fire from Linfyar and Shadith, watching them with
a speculative look he kept shielded most of the time behind a
mug of cha. He took repeated small sips and kept his light
eyes on them.

Shadith was back to her old habit of collecting songs. Her
earlier irritation forgotten, she'd focused on the boy—who
was delighted at the attention and intensely proud of his skill.
Songs rippled out of him in an easy silver flood. His boy
soprano was clear and sweet and astonishingly powerful.
When she first heard the volume of sound he was producing,
Aleytys grew uneasy, afraid of who that voice might be
reaching; she swept a probe around, stretching as far as she
could reach but she touched neither malevolence nor intelligence, certainly nothing large or hungry enough to threaten
them, so she relaxed, settled back against the willow trunk
and watched the play unfold through the tips of the long thin
branches.

Shadith quickly slowed the boy's outpouring and demanded
he teach her his songs. They squabbled cheerfully over them.
The boy yielded to her at first with automatic charm. Gradually,
though, he began to respond to Shadith's quite different
expectations and argued fiercely with her, sometimes, Aleytys
thought, for the sheer joy of being contrary. Aleytys watched
them with affection and some amusement. Shadith who in
spite of her centuries had never matured, ancient precocious
child in a child's body at long last, reverting to adolescence
with an exuberance that wore Aleytys out just watching it.
And Linfyar, another ancient child, wise beyond his years in
the darker sides of human nature. She smiled again, wonder-

ing just what she was loosing on the world, took a sip of the
cha. It was almost cold now, but its faintly bitter taste felt
clean and refreshing in her mouth.

Shadith and Linfyar were singing a duet, a raunchy song
about the exceedingly improbable adventures and misadven-
tures of a fully functioning hermaphrodite.

Harskari's eyes opened, their brilliant amber grown disturb-
ingly dim. Her voice when she spoke was remote, flat, as if
she were only partly there, as if she struggled against that
remoteness and was present now as part of that struggle.
"Many of their songs seem to be about mutants," she said.

Aleytys nodded. "Yes. Especially the . . . um . . . less
respectable ones."

"No doubt mutants both terrify and fascinate them. An
escape from a rigid class structure, but a horrible one."

"Rigid class structure?" Aleytys wasn't especially interested in this speculation, having bored herself with similar
ones earlier in the day, but she was worried about Harskari so
she provided verbal encouragement.

"The other most frequent sort of song is the one celebrat-
ing the tragedy of star-crossed lovers. A kradj daughter and a
ruling son. Always a tear-jerk ending. I presume it's the few
on top who the boy sang his songs for. They can feel noble in
their pity and safe in their mastery."

Aleytys sipped at the cha. Harskari was looking ragged
about the edges, (she smiled to herself—an illusion showing
strain was an absurdity). But as she thought about it, she
wondered if her brain was interpreting subliminal clues and
presenting her with the result. "You're acerbic tonight," she
said.

Harskari made a shapeless small sound that held compressed impatience, disgruntlement, weariness and general
malaise. "Too many times," she said. "I've seen them too
many times, these static societies. And I've seen the carnage
when they explode from self-generated pressures."

"You think the cities on the river are primed to explode?"

Another sound, something like the clicking of teeth together.
"I'm saying nothing of the sort. I don't know enough to
predict anything."

"But . . ." Aleytys broke off as the amber eyes snapped

shut. *Ragged around the edges in more ways than one*, she thought. She gulped at the cha, her pleasant mood shattered. One thing more she had to worry about. *What am I going to do with that child?* she thought, too disturbed by Harskari's fraying to think about that anymore. Shadith was teaching the boy a fast bouncy whistle-song. She narrowed her eyes as she watched Wakille staring at Shadith and Linfyar. That's an agent's glint if ever I saw one. She grimaced. More than one of the breed had been sniffing around her since the first time on Helvetia, the glint of gold shining in their organs of sight; whatever species they belonged to, the glint was the same. Damn, she thought. She dropped her head back against the knotty trunk and closed her eyes. It was a solution of a sort, not so bad a life, he'd be sure to keep the boy in good health. But she couldn't convince herself. The boy ran to escape the knife, ran in spite of what seemed insuperable difficulties. Eyeless. Sheltered. Tiny child. If his chances of surviving his escape here were so limited, what would they be in a high-tech, heavily populated world? If his new masters decided to take the same measure to protect that voice, how would he run there?

She opened her eyes and watched the trio at the fire. The boy was chattering with Wakille, teasing him, flirting with him. That was the only way to describe the teasing approach and retreat, the flutter of hands, the flatter of the boy's words. She could tell Wakille knew what was happening, could also see him beginning to succumb to it. The boy broke off his courting at that point, having the instinctive wisdom to avoid pushing too hard. She finished the cha, feeling tired and a little amused. No use worrying about that imp. No matter how hard he landed, he'd find his feet, long as there were people about—especially women—he'd find himself an advocate, make himself a safe nest. As he was doing now. What was he? Six? Seven? Older? Prepubescent according to him. Whatever that meant.

The boy got to his feet and sauntered out of the firelight. Humming a soft tune he curled up on a blanket and pulled part of it over him, wriggled about a bit and went still, already asleep.

Aleytys stood, ducked through the dangling withes, strolled over to the fire. "We'll split the watch three ways. How do you want to work this?"

7

Wakille shook her awake. "Quiet," he said. "Something's hanging about, but not threatening. Don't know what it is. Curious mix of emotions. Stays on the edge of my reach."

Aleytys sat up, drew a hand across her eyes. "What next."

"If you will take on strays. . . ."

"You objecting?"

"Ah. That's a question."

She snorted. "Get some sleep. We'll be off early."

Much later, near dawn, she prowled about the camp, looking down a moment on each of the sleepers, resisting a strong urge to tuck a thin arm under the blanket as she hovered over Linfyar. She turned her back on him and moved out from the shade of the scrubby trees to stand looking down at the road, a black scar startling against the pallor of the sun-bleached grass, the light gray of the scattered patches of bush drained of color by the moonlight. Once again she felt the presence hovering behind them, the thing Wakille had noted. The feel was familiar enough. The follower, of course. She'd missed him or her or it awhile, after the forest, hadn't thought of . . . well, call it her, since more than likely it was one of the zel, hadn't thought of her for days. Still coming, still hanging on. As Wakille said, the mix of emotions seemed strange. She could only catch whiffs of these like faded perfumes, but she thought she smelled anger and fear, desolation and doubt and finally uncertainty. A deep eroding uncertainty that distressed her when she touched it, yet she went back to it again and again, like someone with a rotting tooth, exploring the aching hole over and over with his tongue. The ghost of a ghost, that following zel. Not theatening but there. A bother.

There was a faint glow in the east. Time to wake the others.

They reached the pass at noon. Aleytys saw Esgard's sign cut in a rock wall, met Shadith's eyes, smiled her relief. They nodded, but said nothing and continued placidly on. Aleytys slanted a glance at Wakille. He was grinning at her, fully aware of what that sign meant. Blasted snoop. Linfyar rode with him this morning, back at his coquetting, pulling stories out of the trader, though pulling wasn't precisely the right word. Wakille's stories were part of his trading craft, a way to ingratiate himself with those he needed. In a way he and that imp were much alike, the imp doing by instinct what years of experience had taught the man.

All that day they rode undisturbed, even the small black biters that had swarmed about them and the gyori vanished once they started down from the pass. The slope of the road was gentle, the wind blew mild with the sweetness of summer light on it. The sky was overcast, a high thin layer of clouds that was enough to blank out shadows while leaving the air about them with an underwater clarity, all colors darkened a little until they glowed with the unreality of a color photograph.

A little after nooning Shadith took the boy up with her and threw off the brooding that had kept her silent and rather melancholy during the morning. She began playing up to his teasing, joining him in whistle songs he'd learned from her the night before, questioning him about life in the city he called Courou, learning new songs, their voices making a pleasure in the undisturbed beauty of the mountain slopes.

When the sun was low in the west, dissolving into the mists that clung to the treetops, they reached the coastal plain. It was open and parklike, grassy, with widely scattered trees and groves of trees that dripped musically with condensation from the mists caught in their crowns. Except for the muted sounds of the breeze, of the gyori hooves, the muttered exchanges between Shadith and Linfyar, the parkland was eerily silent.

A herd of slender brindled beasts moved out of a small grove beside the road; flicking drops of water off large hairy ears, twin jasper horns turning gracefully down in perfect moon arcs beside each elegant elongated face, the herd turned as one to watch the riders coming toward them. Calm, unafraid, vaguely curious, they continued to watch until Aleytys was less than a dozen meters off, then they moved off across the road, disappearing behind another grove.

Aleytys touched her bowstave, took her hand away. Somehow it was impossible to disrupt that serenity. She met Shadith's eyes. The girl stared, then laughed, the ripple of sound oddly shocking in the stillness. She lifted Linfyar off the pad in front of her, passed him to Wakille, then she kicked her gyr into a trot and went after the herd.

"A lioness with a plushy heart." Eload Wakille twinkled at her over the matted curls of the sleepy boy. He was being charming again, she didn't quite see why.

She gazed thoughtfully at him for a long moment, but made no comment, then looked around at the sodden turf beneath the trees and the covering of mist. "Not much downwood I can see, from here at least." She frowned at the dripping trees. "Making camp could be a problem." Balancing herself carefully, she straightened her legs, stood in the stirrups. With a grunt of satisfaction she settled back onto the saddle pad, pointed ahead and to the side. "There are some bare humps over there. Out of the wet, I'd say." She rambled on aloud as she left the road and rode toward the mounds. "Nice of them, whoever they are, providing campsites. Wonder what the catch is. On this world there has to be a catch. Shadith calls it the Joker in the Grass. Catch or not, I'm not sleeping in a slough. Look at that black muck. Weren't for the grass roots the gyori would be up to their knees in it. They don't like it either, liquid black muck squishing through their hooves, sogging their fur."

The mounds turned out to be hard-packed earth platforms with a splotch of black ash at one end. She rode her gyr up the slanting side onto the flat surface, slid down and turned to face Wakille who was sitting his gyr out on the grass, watching her. "I don't see any alternative, do you? Unless you want to sleep wet."

She turned back to her gyr and began stripping off the gear, starting when Linfyar appeared suddenly at her elbow and took the blanket roll from her. She looked over her shoulder. Wakille was leading his mount to the center of the mound.

He dropped the single rein and beckoned to the boy, made a soft clicking sound as he realized the futility of the gesture.

"Eh-Linfy, come help me find dry wood if any such exists in this showerbath."

Linfyar dropped the blanket roll and ran eagerly to him. Aleytys started to protest, Madar knew what lurked out there, then she met Wakille's challenging, too-knowing gaze and bit back that protest. Linfyar wasn't hers, no matter how powerfully he aroused her possessiveness—the trait that had troubled her with Shadith not so long before and came back to haunt her now. Control. The boy in her hands. A need for a kind of loving that neither Grey nor Swartheld had ever, could ever supply. She watched the two of them walk away, small hand in slightly larger hand, the man not greatly taller than the child. She watched and fought with the urges that surged up out of some morass within and appalled her with their ferocity.

She went to work setting up the camp, testing the air, watching the clouds. It wasn't going to rain, she was sure enough of that but she converted the ground sheet into a tent with the collapsible poles that had been the stiffening ribs for her backpack. No rain, but the mist would certainly thicken and drop before the dawn, condensing on every available surface, promising damp, cold discomfort if they slept uncovered. It would be crowded, but possible; none of the other three were very large—though they ate enough. She thought ruefully of the supplies that were supposed to last her several months. *Never meant to feed two let alone four. We live off the land from now on,* she thought. *And hope it proves generous enough so we don't have to cut too drastically into the amount of ground we cover each day. This is madness, really.* She started rummaging among the packs for the cha pot. Jumping off the edge of the world. At least the Eload had his own supply of cha. A while before we run out of that. As for the rest. . . . She sighed.

8

By noon the sun had burned the mist away and the upper level winds had torn the covering clouds to rags. Down where they rode there was little sign of that wind, only a continuation of the profound stillness they'd experienced the

day before. The sea was close enough to smell. There was a
briny tang to the voluptuous silky air that nudged so gently
and intermittently at them. Linfyar was riding with Shadith
and the two of them were laughing and singing and filling the
stillness with exuberant noise.

Abruptly the boy stopped singing and leaned forward, his
ears swinging out, quivering with the intensity of his
concentration.

"What is it?" Shadith said, a bite in her voice.

For a moment he didn't answer. There was wonder in his
voice when he spoke. "Music. Funny music."

"Funny to laugh or funny scary?"

"Scary." He wriggled closer against her, his ears folding
closed and snugging back against his head. Aleytys rode over
to the pair, touched the boy's arm, her fingers barely denting
the brown plush. He was trembling but at her touch he
quieted and his ears unfurled a little.

"Don't fuss, imp," she said. She stroked her fingers along
the fur that clung so close to bone and muscle, crooning the
words as she spoke. "I won't let anything hurt you. None of
us will let anything hurt you. We can handle it, I promise you
we can."

His mouth unpursed into a tiny smile.

Shadith chuckled. "Believe it, Linfy. You haven't seen
Lee working, but I have."

He sighed and relaxed against Shadith's narrow torso. "It
feel bad, it doon't like us."

"Well, Linfy, with your warning maybe we can change his
mind."

Linfyar said nothing but radiated an intense skepticism.

Aleytys laughed. "We'll do our best. Shadi, you and the
Eload stay back, you hear?" She didn't wait for an answer
but clucked her gyr into a quick trot, stabbing probes out to
the front and the sides, pushing as far as she could, flicking
them out like a frog's sticky tongue. She touched things like
gossamer burrs, harsh and poisonous but without substance.
Something touched her then, something that ill-wished her.
She heard the boy cry out. Rage flushed through her. She
urged her gyr faster, leaving the others farther behind. A
dozen long gyr strides and she heard wisps of the music

Linfyar had proclaimed, eery wavering sounds that plucked at her nerves, brushed past her, winning more moans from the boy. She screamed out her rage and clawed furiously at the burrs with her mind fingers, clubbed at those shapeless malevolences.

The music got stubbornly louder. Her strikes accomplished nothing. Each resistance melted away the moment she touched it. She ground her teeth together, pulled the gyr back to an easy lope. Foolish to run him into the ground chasing will o' the wisps.

The music was still louder. More than music. The boy felt it first, the other thing. It crept into her and maddened her. The gyr beneath her began to hump his back irritably and curl his limber neck around so he could nip at her knees. The new irritation was oddly a relief, something she could counter easily enough. She smoothed away the induced rage, returned the beast to his usual placid amiability. And smoothed out her own jags at the same time.

And heard a faltering in the music.

"Ah." She brushed aside the renewed attack on mind and body and projected instead friendliness, serenity and inter- rogation—not a probe but a broad-fronted warm glow.

She brought the gyr to a stop and waited for the others to come up with her, sending out warm pulses as she waited.

Wakille had Shadith's bow strung, arrows ready. Shadith followed, worriedly trying to comfort Linfyar who huddled against her, shaking as with a chill. The merchant stopped beside Aleytys, peaked his furry brows. "Smothering them with sweetness?"

"If it works, eh-Eload."

"Does it?"

"Startles the hell out of them," she said, her laugh almost a giggle. "Give me a hand? You're a stronger projector than I am." She ran her thumb thoughtfully along her jaw line. "Fact, you could do it while I weave a shield around us." Tapped her thumb on the end of her nose. "Do it better than me, I'm sure. More practice."

"Sheathe the claws, lioness." He grinned at her, flicked up a brow, then melded his projections with hers. He took her crude mixture and modified it, modulated it, weaving in hints of laughter, a pinch of acerbity, a thread of determination and other subtle messages that contributed to the taste of the whole, a bouquet-garni of emotion. She laughed aloud at the wonder of what he'd done, then began her own weaving, blocking out all but the few disconnected trills that were reaching them. The boy was still wincing and uneasy but his fear was gone; he was sitting up, turning his head from side to side, vibrating with interest and excitement.

They began moving forward to a slow walk, advancing steadily, evincing a determination to proceed whatever waited for them.

Short agile figures came out of the shadows under the trees, slight, naked or almost so. Unarmed or so they seemed. Pale hair like dandelion fluff caught the brilliant sunlight and shimmered with it. Weaving in and out of shadow, like shadows themselves, gleaming like smoky amber in the sunlight. They kept a constant distance from the intruders and their mounts. In the stillness of that bright day, their movements were soundless, as if they were images rather than living beings.

The road curved about one of the larger groves. Two waited, standing hand in hand in the center of the road, seeming identical in their androgynous beauty, slim and brown with beaten bark cloth tucked about their loins, their dandelion manes pale as moonlight standing out from narrow delicate faces. A second look showed them male and female, a slight difference in outline, width of shoulder, width of hip, the shallow curves of the girl's breasts. The boy held a syrinx casually, the aggregation of pipes dark against the pale bark cloth. The girl held a gourd against her thigh, its nubbly gold and orange a bright splotch of color on the pale fawn skin.

Aleytys halted her gyr. She exchanged a measuring gaze with the pair, glanced at Wakille, brows raised. A slight but emphatic shake of his head. He knew nothing of these folk. And Esgard's journal said nothing about them.

She draped the rein across her thighs, sat with her hands laid lightly over it. "I greet you, brother-sister," she said.

The girl gazed into the boy's eyes, then turned to face Aleytys; the tip of her tongue, pale and colorless, slipped round her parted lips. Finally she spoke. "Am bli'idu-tes binlau-bilau laki-laki harroumindarou."

Aleytys sighed, pressed a hand across her eyes as the translator worked. When the pain passed, she looked up. The boy-girl and the girl-boy waited, faint lines marring the smooth flesh between their perfect brows as if they felt along with her the stabs of pain as the faculty within her reached out and swallowed their language. Indigestion of the brain, she thought and smiled, then lost the smile as she belatedly understood what the words meant: *You took life from the brother in fur, you drinkers of blood.*

Aleytys dropped her hand. "The life was taken in need, not play, Two-are-One. The least of the herd, not the best."

"Go away," the pair said, speaking so closely together it was difficult to separate the voices—voices as alike as the narrow delicate faces.

"That is not possible," Aleytys said slowly, calmly, backing her words with an implacable determination. "We will not stay here longer than we need, but that long we *will* stay. Since it appears to distress you, we will refrain from hunting your brothers-in-fur. As long as there is sufficient provided by the land and the sea." She lifted a hand, let it fall. "We cannot promise to starve to suit your scruples."

Yellow-brown eyes watched her, unblinking, humorless, unresponsive. "Go away." The girl spoke alone, the boy nodding, his spiky hair fluttering about his face. He lifted the syrinx, pressed it against his flat cheek, ready to his mouth but not playing yet.

"No," Aleytys said. She waited.

Two sets of small white teeth bit on lush lower lips; the lines between two pairs of winged brows deepened in each young face. The gourd shifted, rattled faintly. The syrinx rasped softly against the boy's cheek. He shifted it suddenly to his lips and blew a cascade of notes.

Aleytys waited for him to go on, but he moved the syrinx from lips to cheek and stared at her. Stalemate, she thought. What happens now? She glanced at the Eload Wakille, but there was nothing to read in his bland trader's face. We wait, she thought. We wait.

Linfyar made a rude impatient sound. She looked around.

He was bored, she saw, by the words he didn't understand and troubled by currents of emotion he apprehended but also did not understand. In that hive he was born into he grew up unused to silences; he was always humming or murmuring or snapping his fingers or tapping them on handy surfaces, making his own sound to fill quiet times when he was awake. She thought of shushing him, but changed her mind and let him fuss however he wanted.

The sun beat down on the Two-are-One and was caught in brown glass flesh and played around the shadows of bone and organ hung inside like fossils in dark amber. They stood utterly still, their eyes unblinking, their fine hair spikes raying out from their heads. Then the girl blinked once. Then the boy blinked once.

Linfyar's mouth fluttered as he sent out his pulses. Suddenly he laughed, a ripple of silver sound, dimly echoed—to Aleytys's astonishment—by the pair. He began a lilting wordless song, full of gaity and bounce.

The immobile pair dissolved from their heiratic stance, laughing and echoing the boy's song. Then they were dancing, the male picking up the song on his syrinx, the female shaking her gourd as she spun round in her sudden joy, wheeling round and round, a sinuous sensuous teasing playing dance around the similarly sinuous sensuous dance of the male. Aleytys relaxed, not quite sure why it had happened, but pleased to have the danger leached from the scene. Linfyar wriggled energetically, trying to get down from the saddle pad. Aleytys nodded to Shadith and she let the boy go.

He ran between Aleytys and Wakille; still singing, he circled round the Two-are-One, fascinated by them, though what he perceived of them was something to wonder about later when it was certain that the danger had passed. She watched Linfyar charming them and laughed silently at herself. And I was worried about him, she thought. A shadow brushed at the back of her mind and she shivered. The follower again. Still there. I wonder how these folk will react to the zel. She slid off her gyr and walked to meet the Two-are-One and the silent groups of men coming from the groves to stand and watch the dance with a wonder and a wariness that matched hers.

9

Aleytys sat on the tip of the sand finger, watching an empty ocean with growing impatience. Two months. Two nothing months. Shadith was out on the ocean with a party of fishers, intrigued by the fish-singers that called the schools to the nets. Having picked up enough of the language from her (he had a talent for languages, something most useful in his business), Wakille was busy with the elders of this odd people, coaxing supplies out of them, supplies and their secrets if he could, all this paid for in advance by the entertainments the four of them had provided, Linfyar and Shadith singing, Wakille with his tales, and sometimes Aleytys who did minor magics when Harskari consented to break her silence and take over.

The old one was increasingly less reluctant about accepting Aleytys's willingness to share her body—as if she slowly and somewhat awkwardly was preparing herself for an independent existence, slowly and awkwardly because (or so Aleytys thought) even after Swartheld's sudden, almost accidental embodiment, even after Aleytys's fervent promise to find bodies for her and Shadith, she hadn't really grasped the truth of her coming freedom, nor was she ready to accept it. She was afraid but fighting that fear now, having come to terms with a reality that said in another year or two—or maybe even tomorrow—she would be torn from the womb of the diadem and thrust into the body of a stranger.

Behind her Aleytys heard a steady thudding punctuated by the voices and laughter from a gather of Ekansu women. The trees most common on the gentle plain bore twice each year a thick crop of nuts. The women gathered these and boiled them repeatedly in sea-brine until the acids and impurities had been leached away, then set them in the sun to dry. Now they were grinding those nuts into a pale beige flour that made a tasty chewy bread that took a long time to go stale. She looked out across the blinding blue ocean. Near the horizon a few white clouds puffed south. They were deceptively solid, might have been one of the islands, but she had been fooled too many times to be taken in now. Funny how little she knew about these folk. One night and a day had taught her far more about the zel; of course there were always Esgard's notes to add to her own experience.

Linfyar was playing with the Ekansu children. She could hear his singing now and then in an eddy of the sea breeze, sometimes other voices laughing or melding with his. She stretched, yawned.

The Ekansu seemed scarcely advanced enough to be called tribal. A collection of elders had an unspecified moral force on the actions and attitudes of the younger folk, but she didn't see how it worked, or any of the principles behind their decisions. The role of the Two-are-One was even more enigmatic. No one spoke of them. For several days a friendly young woman followed Aleytys about like a puppy, fascinated by her hair; she would sidle up and sneak her hand out to touch the hair, draw it back, then, if Aleytys showed no disposition to deny her, she would stroke the gleaming mass a few times, then draw back again. When Aleytys put tentative questions about the Two-are-One to this child-woman, she reacted oddly. It was as if she simply did not hear the words. She continued to smile, no strain or other awareness visible to Aleytys's eyes or other sensors. It was as if Aleytys hadn't spoken the words at all, as if she'd only dreamed the question. After the same thing had happened with several others, she sighed and gave up. More than once the Two-are-One came wandering along the shore when Aleytys and some Ekansu were there. No Ekansu took any notice of them. On their first appearance Linfyar had scampered to them, chattering in a mixture of tongues. The pair drifted away from him as if blown like thistle-down before the wind of his exuberance. He quieted, bewildered and confused by the lack of response; with a deep sad sigh, he trudged back and curled up against Eload Wakille.

Despite the gift he shared with Shadith, Linfyar was most powerfully attracted to Wakille. Linfyar had been drifting, lost, needing some pole of stability. The strength in Aleytys was inaccessible, he'd tried manipulating her and was resigned to failure. And Shadith had no desire to let herself be adopted. She was good enough for a fair-weather friend, but he seemed to realize that she would dump him the moment he became too much of a burden. In Wakille he found a core of strength and a vulnerability he could exploit. Eload Wakille fought against the gradual in-creeping of the boy—Aleytys and Shadith had watched the play unfold with some amusement and concern, something to help pass the interminable days of the waiting time—but in the end he succumbed, camouflaging his surrender by telling himself that he'd caught a valuable asset in the boy and that might have been partly true, but it was nothing like the whole truth. Fighting and kicking all the way, he gradually began to accept a relationship that was an odd combination of repressed sexuality and friendship and need and a growing reluctant affection.

Day merged with day, one like the next. Ekansu wandered into the strangers' camp, wandered out again with as little fuss. The female Ekansu tended to linger close to them far longer than the males, as if the strangers' presence served to crystallize their fluid existence. Sitting in chatty circles weaving baskets from thin strips of wood split from saplings or twisting net cords from the fibers in the inner skins of bark stripped from those same saplings, they spoke to each other, their words indirect questions of Aleytys and Shadith, Wakille or Linfyar. Often they sang rhythmic repetitive worksongs; sometimes the songs drew in the Two-are-One who breathed into the syrinx and shook the gourd and were gently disregarded.

And the gyori grew fat and sleek on the lush grass and frisked with the small four-legged fur brothers and were reveling in the attention they got from the few Ekansu children who ventured near the shore.

A darkness melted into the white clouds flowing toward land from the northeast. Storm, she thought, and looked away. Linfyar flowed like water, changing effortlessly to match each of them, a son to fill her empty arms, a companion and song-source for Shadith, for Wakille, what? Part lover, part son, part daughter, part merchandise. The thought distressed her. He was a child now, filled with vigor and joy in life and his chameleon quality was enchanting. But as an adult? She'd met a few men who lived on their charm and found them rather sorry sorts of folk, losers in important ways no matter how successful they seemed to others. She sighed, brushed the tips of her fingers lightly across the front of her tunic and flicked them several times as if brushing away something unpleasant.

The darkness in the north was larger and less vague and it clung stubbornly to the sea, didn't rise and scud south like the yeasty white clouds. She frowned at it. Dark and slow. "Well," she said. "If so, it's time."

She got to her feet and ran along the sandspit, through the dunes, then up the grassy slopes to the camp. Wakille was puttering about baskets of leached nuts and dried fish and tubers and the fish-bladders full of nut flour and the multitude of other things he'd twisted out of the Ekansu elders. He looked up as she came trotting along the worn path from the sea. "Island?"

"Might be." She stopped by the meager pile of their own possessions, dug out the pocketed belt, ran it though her hands until she found the pocket she wanted. She thrust her thumbnail under the snap and jerked the flap loose, swearing as she tore a jag into the nail. She shook the pocket over her hand, caught the parts of the skeletal telescope. "A closer look will tell. Anyway, it's hours off still." She flipped the belt back over the bags and went trotting back along the path.

It was an island. A large one. The kind Esgard recommended. Now if it just came in far enough to get stuck. Even with the scope she could only make out the jagged tops of stubby trees, the low dark mass of the land.

A touch on her arm. Wakille stood beside her. "May I?" His eyes laughed at her a little, admitted his impatience, his mouth was pursed into a wrinkled knot.

"Right," she said. The relief at her coming release from stagnation was making her giddy. She watched him a moment as he adjusted the crude scope to his eye, then dropped to the ground beside him, pulled her legs up and draped her arms over them, the bubbled fringe of the retreating tide teasing at her toes. The Ekansu lived tranquil unbusy lives, quietly attuned to the rhythms of season and growth. They were a cheerful people and even the most ancient had elegance of bone, a certain fragile beauty. They had to be more complex than they seemed, there were hints of subterranean things

they held so privately they never spoke of them even among
themselves. And they bored her. In spite of the subtle puzzles
they presented, they bored her. She bored herself right now.
Much longer in this eventless tranquility and she would start
screaming.

Wakille dropped to the sand beside her, handed her the
scope. "Looks like what we need."

"Madar be blessed. Another month and. . . ." She laughed
and shook her head. "I don't seem to thrive in tranquility.
Head told me once if my troubles stopped I'd die of boredom.
I didn't believe her. Then."

"Um. Restful, but not much profit in them."

Aleytys frowned at the sighing salt water a few inches
farther from her sandy bare toes. "They're certainly a surprise after the hostility inland."

"Um. Not many children."

"Keeping numbers down, I suppose."

He pursed his mouth. "You think that's all?"

"I don't know." She rubbed at her nose. "Probably not.
No." The word was a long sigh. "Dying out."

"Pity in a way."

"Yes. A pity."

10

They sat their gyori at the point of the finger, bags and
baskets roped high on the packer and high behind each rider,
nuts and nut flour, dried fish, tubers, rolls of cording, a small
net, flattened fish bladders for holding caught water, rolls of
skin from the fatfish, a huge placid creature much prized by
the Ekansu who made boats from the tough skin, fish meal
from the flesh, ink from a gall gland, various implements
from the bones, medicines and dyes from other parts. Aleytys
passed her hand over her hair as she watched the monster
island rock closer. Huge, silent, unstoppable, mass on the
move that would grind down before it anything that stood in
its way. It had slowed almost to a stop but wasn't quite there
yet. A long way out from the land, too big, too much below
the water surface to let it come in much closer. How did that

ever manage to float itself? She rubbed at the back of her neck. The follower had circled wide around them and the Ekansu, shuttling back and forth in a wide arc, running before something, Two-are-One perhaps, or others, but not retreating, hanging about, refusing to go away. Sometimes she thought she heard the hate music again, but Ekansu, both male and female, showed no sign they knew anything odd was happening. She was back there now, watching, that stubborn zel, a gnat too small to see, too agile to swat. Aleytys glanced at Shadith. Shadith laughed. "Have to give up soon, our shadow." She waved her hand at the island. "If that thing bothers to stop for us."

"Mm." Aleytys looked once more over her shoulder, past Wakille who was having some difficulty keeping hold of the boy who was so excited he couldn't sit still. She spared him a brief smile, then focused on the base of the sand finger.

A number of Ekansu were gathered there, watching silently, a few children, a few elders, a number of the ageless adults, the bright morning sun turning their translucent flesh into crystallized honey. They stirred, broke apart to form an open aisle and the Two-are-One came walking through and stood hand in hand watching them. Just watching, faces blank as far as she could tell.

Aleytys swung around when she heard a shrieking groan. The island shuddered and screamed and jammed to a stop just beyond the point of the spit, about a kilometer out, a precarious stop. The rear end continued to sway as it ground noisily against the sandy bottom. "Well," she said. She nodded to Shadith and Wakille. "Time to go."

The land sloped so gradually that even half a kilometer out the water was brushing against the bottoms of the rope stirrups. Ripples occasionally broke over their feet. But it dropped off with startling suddenness when there were a dozen meters left between them and the weed fringes. The gyori complained but swam the last stretch, paddling strongly, heads held high, whining their fear and dislike of the salt water.

As Aleytys set her gyr at the tangle of roots and weed near the point of the island, she heard shouts behind her, gyr-hoots, and a war scream. She got her mount onto solid ground, slipped off his back and slapped his rear, sending him at a cautious trot into the trees. She set her back against a tree and frowned at the land.

A zel. Crouched low on the back of a gyr, charging up the finger and into the water, the gyr running full out, whining and roaring and fighting against the control of its rider. Tranjit. Head shaved a while ago, a new growth of brindled hair hiding the painted design on the skull, dirty white robes hitched high on reedy legs. Juli. She sighed.

"Lee," Shadith was at her side, bow strung and ready. "Let me. . . ."

"No." Aleytys rubbed her face. "No. She's a baby, Shadi, can't you see it? No older than you."

"You know her?"

"I know her. A zel. One of my guards." She moved her shoulders, straightened her back. "I'll wait for her here, Shadi. Go and help Wakille set up camp. Feel that wind? You can smell the rain. I can handle this one."

"If you're sure. . . ."

Aleytys raised a brow. Shadith grinned and rode on, trampling the bracken and the spindly saplings clinging to the ungenerous edge of the island. Before she entered the shadow under the trees, she turned again, scowling. "Watch yourself, Lee."

"Not 'ware the joker?"

"Bad precedent. Don't let her on board, Lee. Like cuddling a viper."

"I hear you."

"Huh. You hear but you don't listen. Never mind. I go. And you do what you have to." She plunged into the shadow. Aleytys heard the crashing sounds of her progress through the underbrush gradually diminishing.

The zel reached the island and drove the weary gyr up the treacherous footing of the tangled roots and tough weed. She stopped her mount in front of Aleytys and sat there breathing hard, her dark eyes hating, her mouth pressed into a tight line.

"Juli," Aleytys said. "Tranjit Juli."

The zel gulped in air, clamped her mouth shut again.

"Go home, Tranjit Juli, there's nothing for you here."

Juli glared at her, brought her stick down sharply on the

gyr's bleeding rump and drove him into a stumbling run into the trees.

Worried, Aleytys followed her, running along the trampled path through the bracken.

In a smallish clearing at the base of one of the hills in the middle of the island where a large old tree had fallen victim to the shaking of a summer storm, she found Wakille standing by the tangle of branches, Linfyar huddled close to him disturbed by the storm of emotion in the clearing, Shadith caught in the middle of stripping gear from one of the gyori, all of them staring at the shouting zel.

As Aleytys came from under the trees, Juli went quiet and stiff. Before she could say anything, the zel tumbled off her mount and ran to Shadith, arms outstretched. When she was almost touching the silent, unresponsive girl, she faltered, stopped, stood staring, her arms dropping slowly to her sides. "Maslil," she whispered. "Laska. . . ." She reached out again, closed her hand into a fist and drew it back in slow jerks until it rested against her stomach. She was still a moment, then she wheeled to face Aleytys. "You . . ." she whispered, her voice hoarse, breaking. She swallowed. "Let her go, take your demon from her, let her go or. . . ,"

"Or what, child?" Aleytys sighed. "Juli, listen. You don't understand anything." She pushed the hair out of her eyes. "Forget what was, it doesn't exist any more. Your laska is dead. And not by my hand or hers. Her organs scrambled, her skull broken." She spoke the words with brutal clarity, meaning to shock the young zel out of her hysteria. "Shadith," she said. "Come here. Wakille, untwitch your nose and keep on what you're doing. That rain's coming soon enough. We'll be back to help once we settle this problem." She ignored his not-quite-audible grumble and scowled at Shadith who was staring with much unfriendliness at the imploring zel.

Shadith circled round the zel and marched pugnaciously to Aleytys's side.

Aleytys touched her arm. "Go back to the edge," she said. "We'll follow." She waited a moment until Shadith vanished under the trees, then said, "Tranjit Juli, come, listen. Know what happened. Be comforted. There was nothing you could do then, there is nothing you can do now. Come." She kept on talking as she started away from the clearing, her voice soothing, making sense more or less, repeating herself, the sound a fragile rope linking the two of them, her and the zel, and the zel followed.

At the island's edge Aleytys settled on a root, Shadith by her shoulder. The zel stood slumped in the broken path until a sudden lurch of the island sent her stumbling onto her knees. The wind was rising and the cottony cloud puffs were thickening, lowering, getting darker. The swing of the island's rear grew more exaggertated, the groaning and creaking grew louder, the island inching along, grinding against the sandy bottom. The current was powerful enough in conjunction with the strengthening wind to drive it along the path it had taken before, the path that was the same but never exactly the same as the thousand times it had come this way before.

Juli crouched on the trampled bracken, her dark tragic eyes shifting slowly between Shadith and Aleytys, back and forth and back and forth, an automatic swing with little awareness or volition behind it.

Aleytys sighed, glanced at the shore. The sandspit was already several meters behind the island. A few Ekansu women lingered on the sand, watching. The Two-are-One had vanished, the elders were gone on their way, sinking back into the leisurely rhythms of the day-to-day Ekansu life, the way things were before the strangers intruded.

She faced the zel. "Tranjit Juli," she said softly. "Believe me, if you can. Shadith is no demon. I did nothing at all to your laska. Before I touched her she was dead, completely dead, killed by a man from the settlement north of you when your gather-band ambushed a band of theirs. If it helps any, that man is dead, the zel cut his throat."

Juli looked up but didn't look at Aleytys. "Maslil," she whispered. "Please remember. Please. We pledged to death and beyond the year of your testing. Can't you remember? When you flew the hawk the first time and they burned the sign in your flesh, I held your hand and ate your pain so you wouldn't shame yourself. Please remember. You held me down when I drank the slika-sovis for my passage dream.

And we pledged . . . we pledged . . ." Still on her knees, she crept closer to Shadith.

Aleytys felt tension coiling tighter and tighter in the zel; she got to her feet and stepped between her and Shadith, knowing as she did so that the act might precipitate the attack she wanted to prevent. "Go home, child," she said.

The zel uncoiled, leaping so fast she caught Aleytys off balance and knocked her flat. She fell awkwardly, lay sprawled over the bracken, the zel's knife hard against her throat. "Run, Maslil," Juli shrieked. "Get away. I'll hold this thing. You!" She glared down at Aleytys. "Let her go."

Shadith stepped over some roots and crunched through the bracken and came without hurry or fuss to stand beside the zel. She bent down, touched Juli's shoulder. The zel trembled. Aleytys saw her eyes shift, the tendons in her neck strain, then reluctantly, slowly, against her will, the zel turned her head and gazed up at Shadith.

Moving with smooth sudden violence, Shadith slid her arm about the girl's neck and wrenched her up and back, flinging her away from Aleytys. Whirling, Shadith pounced on Juli again, twisted the knife from her loosened grip, then leaped back to stand beside Aleytys. "You all right?"

Aleytys got to her feet, touched her throat and grimaced at the film of blood on her fingers.

Juli lay trembling and beaten on the trail, staring in anguish at Shadith. Her mouth opened, trembled, clamped shut as the island shuddered and ground a few meters farther. The wind overhead deepened its note to a growl and the rear of the island swished back and forth with a twisting surging motion, throwing Aleytys and Shadith off their feet. The zel said something but the words were lost in the noise of the island and the gathering storm. Juli spoke again, almost shouting, "Why?"

Shadith shook her head, the brown tangle of curls whipped about by the wind, blown back from her high round forehead. She got back on her feet, balanced precariously for a minute until the island settled for a while, then stomped across the short distance between her and the zel. She reached down, caught firm hold of Juli's hand, though the young zel tried to wrench herself free, and dragged her up onto her feet. "Look, zel,'' she said, refusing to use the name even though she knew it. "Your laska is dead. How many times do we have to tell you? Get it through that hard head. Maslil is dead, dead, dead, dead. You hear me? The body is mine now. Think of me as a demon if you must, though believe me I've got nothing to do with gods or magic or any foolishness like that, but get it through your head, there's nothing left of Maslil and there's nothing at all we had to do with that." She stepped away. "Get your gyr and go back to your people. Aleytys told you the truth. There's nothing for you here."

The zel bit her lip, wheeled, ran stumbling into the trees.

Aleytys sighed. "Compli. . . ." The island lurched violently, squirted forward, caught momentarily, then slid smoothly away from the shore. There was a sense of movement now, a gentle rocking, the hiss and slap of the sea against the edge near them. When Aleytys found her feet and looked back, the shore was rapidly retreating, empty, and touched with the gloom of the advancing storm.

Shadith came and stood at her shoulder. "Stuck with our little viper, it seems." She looked up. "Appropriately gloomy."

"You're the soul of compassion."

"Hunh. Better she faced facts and went home. Too late now. How much you bet she can't swim."

Aleytys shook her head. "No bet. Come on." She looked up. "We've got work to do before that breaks."

VI

OCEAN PASSAGE

day 1

The storm passed rapidly behind as the powerful following wind rocked the island back to the center of the current which sucked it in and took it south.

Aleytys and the other three worked at setting up a shelter of fair size, using four trees at the edge of the small clearing for corner posts, cutting the straightest saplings they could find and driving the sharpened ends into the soil. As the strongest of the four, Aleytys did the driving, Wakille cut and fetched the saplings for her, sliced the ends to points, Shadith and Linfyar took smaller branches and wove them horizontally between the verticals. The work was slow and tedious, they only had the knives and the single hatchet to work with, but they were going to sleep wet until they finished the shelter, the ground sheet being needed to protect the food.

They stopped working a little after noon, ate bread baked by the Ekansu women, drank some cha, started tubers roasting for supper, fish stew simmering with some greens Wakille found when he was looking for more saplings, set the still producing water for supper's cha. There was enough water caught in the hollows, water from the storm, to keep the gyori from thirst for a few days so they didn't bother worrying about the beasts.

By nightfall they'd finished three walls and half the fourth, Shadith and Linfyar still weaving as Aleytys built up the fire and Wakille went prospecting for shellfish. When everything was ready, she looked at the others, frowned, then went to the edge of the clearing and called the zel, but the girl stayed hidden in shadow and would not come though Aleytys called her several times.

day 2

They finished the walls of the shelter, leaving a low narrow opening for a doorway, then began arguing about what would serve as a roof. Wakille listened a moment, went off and came back with the roll of fishskins he'd eased out of the Ekansu, each skin taller than he was, enough to cover half a boat's skeleton. He produced a clay pot of the glue the Ekansu used to waterproof the boats and set it on the remnants of the breakfast fire to heat. Shadith groaned as a powerfully nasty smell began rising from the pot, but Linfyar was enchanted by it, he twittered about the fire, sniffing with delight at the rank odor. Shadith eyed him with some trepidation. "Keep yourself away from that, Linfy, or you'll be sorry." He ignored her after flashing her a grin. She snorted and went to help Wakille unroll the stiff skins.

Aleytys left them squabbling cheerfully about how to set up the roof and support it. Worried about the young zel, she swept the island with a probe, searching for her. She touched nothing definite, frowned, then remembered how elusive the follower had been. There and not there. As if the zel had thrown a shell about herself so tight only the faintest smell of her got out.

She started to track the ghost, then frowned again and turned back, dug out one of the flat round loaves the Ekansu had baked for them, then she wove through the tree-tangle, the grass and thick bracken, following the ghost traces of the zel as she'd follow wisps of smoke to find a fire, working her way gradually toward the nose of the island.

The zel was sitting close to the water, legs drawn up, arms wrapped about them, hands clutching forearms, chin on knees, a package, all ends drawn into the knot of flesh and bone, eyes fixed on the water rolling past her feet. Since they rode

the current and were moving at nearly the same speed as the
water, there was no bow wave, only a touch of turbulence
that came more from the thick school of silver fish shimmering in the water before the broad blunt snout of the island.

"Juli," Aleytys said. The fish were leaping in shining
arcs, myriads of them flickering in the air a fingerlength
above the long dark rolls of water; the continuous plopping of
their bodies, the soughing of the wind, these noises were loud
enough that Aleytys thought at first the zel hadn't heard her.
She worked herself out on the roots beside the girl and squatted beside her, touched her arm. "Zel Juli, I brought you
some bread. You have to be hungry."

The flesh under Aleytys's fingers was cold and unresponsive.
The zel would not acknowledge her, but Aleytys felt a quick-
ening in her. She had to be half-starved; her body reacted to
the bread Aleytys offered her though her will rejected it.
Some of the stiffness went out of her. Her mouth opened a
little and her tongue touched lips that trembled before she
clamped her mouth shut again.

"There's water in rain pools," Aleytys continued, separating the words and speaking as clearly as she could to make
herself heard over the noise. She set the round loaf on the
roots just behind the zel, far enough away so she'd have to
move to reach it and couldn't simply fling it into the sea in a
fit of petulance. She'd come here with the intention of taking
the zel back with her, by force if needed, but now she thought
it would be better to leave the girl on her own. No emergency,
not yet. Let hunger, thirst and exposure operate a while
longer, let the girl convince herself to join them, coercion
would only stiffen her resistance. I'll send Linfyar with food
tomorrow, she thought, felt suddenly very very old and wondered if she'd ever suffered so intensely the minor tragedies
of her own life—well, losing a lover to death and, I suppose,
worse than death, isn't that minor—conveniently forgetting
her own stubbornness and the rage that had churned so furiously in her and so complicated her already complicated life
the years before she finally ran.

After a short silence, she got to her feet. "There's water
and hot food when you want them. You're welcome to join
us whenever you feel like it." She looked at the rigid set of

back and head. How they do suffer. As she started for camp, she remembered what the child had endured and still must endure and was briefly ashamed of herself. It was so easy to make fun of an unsophisticated inarticulate youngster, to point out with quick clever logic how foolish she was, how much of her pain she created herself, but the pain was real and not of her making. *Not of mine either, not really, just the perverse malevolence of chance.* She smiled, shook her head at the roll of the words. Suddenly she thought of that moment when Stavver told her that mad Maissa had sold her and gone off with her baby. She stopped walking, closed her hands into fists until her nails cut into her palms. For a moment, a moment only, she was that girl again and the loss was as raw and new as it had been those ten years before. Only a moment, then she straightened her back, lifted her head, anger at the zel flashing through her (the zel who was somehow mixed with Linfyar in her mind), anger for waking memories she'd prefer to leave undisturbed.

When she stepped back into the clearing, Shadith was chasing Linfyar away from the steaming glue pot. He danced before her, avoiding her sweeping grabs, skipping over obstacles as if he had a ring of eyes about his head instead of none at all, giggling in between his pulsing whistles. Shadith saw her and stopped running, stood glaring at the boy. "Lee," she said, exasperation sharpening her voice. "Tell this hardhead that we'll have to shave him naked if he gets stuck up with that stuff." She drew her forearm energetically across her sweaty face. A sharp call, rather panicky, from Wakille. "Oh shit." She trotted around behind the shelter. "Look, I told you that wouldn't work, here let me. . . ." Her voice dropped until it was too muffled for the words to be more than staccato noises rising and falling and bumping into each other with the lower growl of the man interrupting the rush here and there. Aleytys snapped her fingers. "Come here, imp."

Linfyar canted his head, his ears moving like moth wings as he thought over what she said; then he whistled a fragment of song and ran to her.

Aleytys stood gazing down at him a moment and then she laughed and reached out to rumple his mop of curls, but didn't touch him. His face hadn't changed but she stopped her hand. "You don't like that."

He sighed, an exaggerated puff of air, an exaggerated lifting and dropping of his narrow shoulders.

She took a step back. "Linfy . . ." she started.

He smiled up at her, a three-cornered angelic smile.

Aleytys gazed at him in silence, opened her mouth, shut it again. He was a child, a sensitive intelligent child, but not ready to understand what she'd meant to say. He'd have to learn for himself that he didn't have to flatter and manipulate them. "That glue is hot, Linfy. And it won't come off once it's on you. Do you want to burn yourself? Do you want to look like one of those mocker crabs your Ekansu friends showed you, all stuck up with dirt and leaves and bits of junk? If you do, then go right ahead and make an idiot of yourself." She frowned, smiled at a sudden thought. "I could use your help if you feel like doing something hard. Will you?"

The grin on the small face broadened, the ears twitched eagerly. "Oh yes, mistress," he said. He put out a small hand. "Please, what is it?"

Aleytys took the hand in hers, felt a surge of pleasure as the bird-light, feather-soft fingers quivered in hers. "You remember the girl who came on the island after us?"

Linfyar nodded. "Sad and mad," he said.

"Right. Well. She's just lost someone, like you lost your mother, and she's feeling upset. You know, Linfy. She's hating herself and the whole world. She won't listen to me, but maybe you can persuade her to come for supper and comfort her a little. It won't be easy. She doesn't want to be comforted. But talk to her, see what you can do. If she won't let you help, she won't, so don't feel bad. We'll just have to give her more time. Will you try?"

Linfyar nodded, no longer grinning, but radiating real pleasure in being given so serious a task. He loosed his hand. "If she won't come, can I take food to her?"

"I'd appreciate that, Linfyar." She watched him run into the woods, his whistles a ghost echo in her ears. I wonder if that was smart or stupid, she thought. Have to wait and see.

Linfyar led the zel to the fire that night. She sat in the

shadows but ate the fish stew and bread he brought her, drank a cup full of hot cha. Though she never looked directly at Shadith, she continually stole peeks at her as if she couldn't keep her eyes away from the thing that pained her. With an instinctive tact that both impressed and oppressed the watching Aleytys, the boy left Juli alone most of the time, coming back at intervals, though, to touch her lightly and let her know he was still there and hadn't forgotten her.

Shadith was uneasy but refused to give in to her vague guilts. She did not look at Juli but chattered brightly with Wakille, giggled at his sallies, listened with apparent delight to the stories he told. Later she and Linfyar sang, blending at times, contesting at others, a song contest not meant to be taken seriously. Sometime in the middle of this Juli slipped away.

day 3

The shelter finished, they began digging holding ponds for gyori—and for bathwater. Aleytys left Wakille and Shadith working on the ponds and went hunting for the zel.

Juli was back at the nose of the island staring at the heaving water, the silver arcs of the fish. Aleytys stood beside her a moment, looking at the endlessly rolling blue ahead, the land line lost in clinging morning mist. There didn't seem to be much change in it, the little she could see, but then they hadn't come that far south. She'd checked their position as best she could last evening, would check again this night for a more accurate estimate of their speed. When she located them on the map she was appalled by the distance they had yet to cover. Only thirty kilometers a day so far, according to her rough estimate. Nine hundred kilometers south before they even began to turn west, another two thousand, more, across the ocean. A hundred days, give or take a few, if their progress continued constant, something she didn't expect. According to Esgard the speed of the current could vary considerably, depending on a lot of things.

She heard a few birds crying overhead, watched them plummeting from the sky to snag and carry off the little fish.

She shut her hands into fists. Slow, slow interminably slow.
Interminable impossible quest. "Over!" she shouted suddenly,
then felt foolish, protesting so vehemently what couldn't be
helped. She looked down at the old-young face of the zel,
then settled herself beside her.

The roots were damp and slick and springy, with a tendency to shift with the roll of the island and prod into the
tenderer parts of the sitter's anatomy. It is disconcerting to be
immersed in a vast brooding philosophical dissertation with
oneself and find oneself suddenly goosed by an intruding
root. She giggled, shifted herself. "You'd be surprised," she
said, looking out over the ocean. "You'd be surprised how
quickly you forget what home is like. The place where you
were born and grew up, I mean. Now me, just look at me, I
sit here muttering—well, shouting—curses at the air because
this damn island moves slower than a gyr can walk. I should
know better; time was, the fastest thing I knew was a horse, I
should find adjusting easy enough. I think it's having nothing
much to do but wait. Wait and watch the slow days creep
past. I don't think I'm very good at waiting. Then there's
knowing if things were just a pinch different, if I had a
skimmer, I'd already have the coordinates I need and be
scooting back to Wolff, done with this blasted world. I've got
a ship, young Juli, hanging up there with skimmers in her
belly powered and ready to fly. If I knew what my cousins
seem to know, I'd rebuild one of the skimmers so it'd come
when I whistled. Like Maissa's ship, the one Stavver turned
up with a while back. Wonder what he did with her and how
he got round the ship's safeguards. Probably never know, he
can't be liking me much now, not that he ever did even when
we were lovers. Maybe when I come up with my dear mother
I can get a few modifications out of her. I'd prefer a full
re-doing of my ship. Trouble is no one knows anything about
what Vrithian's really like. I can't get an idea of what to
expect, so how can I plan anything? I met one Vryhh who
said he was kin to me, but what's that? Kell. If they're all
like him . . . but how can I tell? How many Vrya are there?
Who makes beds for them, cooks, all that? Robots? Slaves?
Wouldn't put it past Kell to keep slaves, the others, I don't
know. Could be there's no more than a dozen, could be

there's not even standing room left. There's the Vryhh who fixed Maissa's ship for her. Mischief, a debt, a whim, what? Turning that madwoman loose on the universe, that'd appeal to Kell. I keep talking about him, Phahh! wash my mouth out. You don't understand a word of this, do you. Where was I? Ah. I did have something to say before I started maundering. If you'll just stop fighting it, time will begin healing your grief. You'll get used to being alone; it's not easy, I wouldn't lie to you and say it is, you wouldn't believe me anyway. You should have let us go, Juli. You should have grieved with your sisters and let us go. Think about it. I'll see you home again if you wish it. Somehow. My word on it, child. Though, dammit, it may take another year's trek to get back where I started. Madar grant there's some way out of that. Bad enough to have to spend all this time reaching the place, retracing the same miserable steps is too much, not even the little bit of excitement about what comes next to lighten the boredom.''

She went on talking, rambling on and on about nothing much, hoping that time and habit would soften the young zel's resolute hostility. As she kept her soft unassuming voice flowing, she probed very lightly at the zel's mind, drew back almost as soon as she touched it, disturbed by a darkness and pain beyond anything she'd ever felt even at the several nadirs in her life. I can cure the body, she thought, but not the soul. Wakille most likely could operate on her; no, he wouldn't touch this, nothing in it for him. In a way she regretted her lack of skill—for the girl's sake, that is, not for her own, she had enough moral dilemmas to resolve without adding another. Brittle, she thought, she won't bend, just break. That zel culture, rigid, fossilized. She's young, though. Maybe she's still flexible enough to survive this. Damn. Too bad she had to see Shadith in her lover's body. Ground's shaking under her. Funny, it's almost the opposite of what happened when Swartheld came out. My friend, my lover, in another body. Hard to see him behind that strange face. What are we going to do with her? I don't want the responsibility for her on the other side. I wish she'd go home. That's the best place for her. Madar, I'm starting to feel like the boy with the magic goose who collected himself a parade of followers, each one stuck to the one ahead and bound to follow wherever he went. That old tale had a happy ending, for the boy, at least, I don't remember what happened to the others. She's uneasy, unhappy with me here. And stubborn. Determined to keep on suffering.

Aleytys sighed and got to her feet. For a moment she stood gazing out over the sparkling blue swells, then swung around and went to take her turn digging the ponds.

day 4

The zel wandered about on the periphery of their activities, watching as they hauled in long fronds of seaweed and gathered the crustaceans growing on the stems, watching when they cast the net out beyond the nose of the island to haul in a catch of the little silver fish. She made Shadith nervous. She hung around like a bad conscience, grating on the girl's nerves, a constant reminder that she had in a sense stolen the body she wore. Shadith grew irritable and avoided the sad girl as much as she could. Linfyar worked hard to break down Juli's resistance and make her feel welcome in the group. In optimistic moments Aleytys let herself hope the boy would finally succeed. He did get her to come to meals, he surprised a smile out of her now and then, though these were always brief and reluctant. As Aleytys watched, keeping her distance to make the boy's task easier, she began to feel a lightening of the gloom in the young zel and thought she saw her starting to accept Shadith as Shadith and not the person she kept trying to make her be.

But with this lightening and this acceptance came rage, a rage the zel turned on Aleytys and Shadith, but most of all on herself. She was refusing to let herself heal.

day 5

Black storm clouds hung in the northeast, creeping gradually closer as the day passed by, but there was no smell of rain in the air despite the pummeling of the wind. They spent most of the day building a smoking rack for fish and a drying rack for weed, then a wattle screen to keep the wind from attacking the fire. In the evening when they sat around that fire, the wind noisy about them, Wakille looked up from the net he was mending. He kept his hands busy as he talked, the firelight shifting in and out of the crevices of his face. "A long way from here and a long time ago in a place where trees are as big around as this island and the rivers are sometimes wide as seas, there lived an old man (Yes Linfy, older than me, older by a lot) who had several fine sons. He was a thief, his sons were thieves, his father and his father's brothers were thieves and his grandfather and so on back longer than anyone could remember. Now, when the old man got too old to climb in and out of windows or leap on travelers going from town to town, he and his sons followed the family tradition and turned to swindling. (Another kind of thief, Linfy, someone who uses words to steal. Take that grin off your face, Hunter; me, I'm just an honest trader trying to make a living.) He and his little band came into a rivertown one day and settled there for a while, looking about for a mark.

"In that rivertown there lived a merchant who bought and sold anything he could find a profit in. That was his legal trade. Under the counter. (That means, Linfy, that no one in power was supposed to know about it, yes, like the men who brew beer in Courou.) Under the counter he was a moneylender; that was against the laws of that place; no one was supposed to charge interest on money lent. (Interest has another meaning, Linfy, when it's used like that. It's a kind of rent men pay to use other men's money. Money? Don't ask me to explain that, child. Just figure, in other places it's something men want a lot of and will do most anything to get.) He was a mean man and a rather stupid man, but since most of them owed him money, they kept telling him he was the cleverest of men and laughing at his jokes until he began to believe that he'd never been wrong in his life.

"It didn't take the old man long to find this out, so one day he walked into the merchant's shop with an embroidered fan he said was his mother's and some other bits and pieces he said he had to sell to pay his rent. (Yes, Linfy, the old man was about to play his tricks on the merchant.) He came in off the street and crossed to the counter, a frousty bumbling old sort, half senile and more than half blind, with a mild and helpless face like he wouldn't harm the peskiest fly and couldn't think up a lie to save his life. He put the things on the counter and began haggling with the merchant about what he could get for them. After about a minute of this, a young man came into the shop and walked over to him. The young stranger greeted him most courteously, handed him a letter and a package, saying 'your son in Luktanara' (that's another rivertown, Linfy), 'honored sir, knew I was bound upon the river with my father's boats and gave me this to carry to you. I was on my way to your house when I happened to see you in here.' He bowed to the old man, bowed to the merchant, circled round some other customers in the shop and vanished into the street outside.

"The old man opened the letter, held it close to the end of his nose, shut one eye, then the other, then shook his head and handed the letter to the merchant, saying, 'I left my glasses home not knowing I would need them. Would you be so kind as to read this to me.'

"The merchant read the letter aloud, most of it complaints about the son's wife and the pranks of his eldest child who was a very naughty little boy and in the end it said, 'Honored father, as a name day gift, knowing you like such things, I send you this small carving of a sleeping jyag. (That's a little beast, Linfy, that hunts and eats vermin, rather like the cedi you know.) An old man who looked like a tree-root gave it to me for some fish. It's a nice copy of an Ogaretz. (Ogaretz, Linfy was an artist whose carvings men value like your Bigman valued your voice.) May the seven Great ones rain blessings on you this nameday.'

"The old man opened the packet and took out the carving. He looked at the other things he was selling, looked at the carving and sighed. 'Let me see it,' the merchant said. 'It might be worth a little something to me.' So the old man handed it over.

"The merchant weighed it in his hand. It was as heavy as jewelwood, it was the color of jewelwood, it was as smooth and shiny as jewelwood. And Ogaretz was said to be a little old man as tough and wrinkled as a root. And Ogaretz was the only man who knew where to find jewelwood and how to work it. And on the bottom of the little carving he found the sign Ogaretz made on all his work; the merchant had seen a piece or two of it but had never been able to afford to deal in it. Stupid old man, he was thinking, stupid son, why should I tell either of them. (Yes, Linfy, he was going to cheat the old man. That's what swindlers count on. You got to watch yourself in this universe, anyone will do you if he thinks he can get away with it.) The old man dithered and dithered, yes and no about the carving, put in, take out and each time he changed his mind, the merchant offered him more money, but never even a taste of what he should have offered if the carving was what he thought it was. Then finally, the old man sighed again and said, 'Ah it is such a sadness, but life is like that, a poor man cannot afford sentimentality. Not when the rent is due and the belly says feed me.' So the merchant counted out the coin, a lot more than he'd thought he'd pay, and the old man left with his sack of money.

"As soon as he had tottered out, a customer standing near the counter started to snicker (like this, Linfy, he-he-he) and said, 'Looks to me like you been took, mister. That old man he's been a swindler for years, but I was afraid to say anything while he was in here, that young bully who brought him the things, he breaks legs if you get in his way.'

"Frowning like a thunder cloud about to rain on the world, the merchant took a knife and scraped at the base of the carving and found a plug of lead to make it weigh so heavy and found that the color was stain, that what he had wasn't jewelwood but common ollawood. (Worth about as much there, Linfy, as a pat of gyr dung here.) He clamped hold on the customer, sent his clerk for an official of the city and together the three of them, they went through the city toward the Dimgal gate, one of the three gates in the citywall where the customer said the old man lived. (I didn't say the city had walls? Well, it does, so be quiet.) And close to the gate they saw the old man sitting with some others in an open-face wine shop, drinking and laughing. 'There he is,' the customer said. 'You grab him, I'm going.' And he slid off into the crowd and no one ever saw him again. The merchant elbowed his way through the drinkers and grabbed the old man by the collar of his shirt. 'Arrest him,' he told the official. 'You crook,' he shouted at the old man, 'you sold me a fake carving for good coin.' He shoved the statue's base under the old man's nose.

" 'I never said it was anything but a copy,' the old man said. He spread out the receipt the merchant had given him, beckoned to the official. 'Look,' he said. 'Doesn't it say there a copy of an Ogaretz? I haven't got my glasses, you read it.' And the official did and the paper did say a copy of an Ogaretz. And the old man took the paper and shook it under the nose of the merchant. 'Copy, see. And if you thought it was real, why didn't you say something. You trying to cheat a blind old man?'

"And the merchant looked about him and saw the anger in the faces of the men collected there and looked into the official's face and saw the suspicion there and he drag-tailed it out of the shop. And the story spread through all the city so in the end he had to leave and start over in another place."

Linfyar clapped his hands, giggling with appreciation of the old man's game. Aleytys smiled. "A story with a moral of sorts." She folded the trousers she was brushing and trying to clean, set her hands flat on them. "I remember something a hiiri maid told me once, when I was a slave on Irsud. Once in the dawn time before the hyonteinim (No, Linfy, I'm not going to keep interrupting the story to answer your questions, you'll pick up most of what you need if you listen hard enough and use your head. You can ask me later anything you really want to know.) Where was I, oh yes, before the hyonteinim made a sadness where there was joy, a prison where once all things went free, there was a man with seven daughters and no sons. Now, you don't know the hiiri so you don't know what a terrible thing it was to have seven daughters and not a single son, no son to hold his face at the tulkoda, no son to care for him in his old age, no son to sing him into the blessed land when he died. So he mourned his fate and cursed his wife, but he loved his daughters, loved them all and the youngest most of all. He took her with him everywhere, taught her how to hunt and track, how to read the winds and signs, everything a son should know, forgetting completely at times she wasn't a son. Each daughter was more beautiful than the last, the eldest could sing to charm the birds from the air, the second danced more supply and seductively than a lumikaer, the third knew all the herbs to cure and flavor; each of them had a gift, even the youngest who knew the language of beasts. Even so, even with the beauty and the gifts, it was hard for him to find them husbands. They were daughters of a mother who bore only daughters. But one by one he did it, by hard work and stripping himself of his possessions, he did it, one by one, until only the youngest was left. Sadly, he was too poor to find a dowry for her, so poor he ate the scraps from the tables of his clan-brothers.

"Now that you know him, let's go back awhile. When the youngest, whose name was Takti-Persilli, was only four, a great worm crept out of the darkness and made himself a nest at Makemaha pools, one of the best waters of the desert plain, and before spring had used up two moons, the worm had swallowed a double hand of man and beasts. There was no choice for the hiiri clans, they had to use the pools, so they tried staking out a six of herkala, their small striped cattle, a double six of kayrilli, fast little beasts with long white hair, but the worm had a taste of manflesh now and would not be appeased. One night all the witchmen dreamed and all the dreams said this, the worm will withdraw a time from the pools if they fed it tender girlflesh or boyflesh, ten years to fourteen, no older and no younger. So it came about that each time a clan drew near the Makemaha pools a drawing was made and a daughter of the clan was taken into the grove that grew around the pools and tied there to a tree and left there for the worm to eat. For ten years this was how it was, for ten years each hiiri clan lost a daughter to the worm. When the time came again for Persilli's clan to approach the pools, Takti-Persilli went to her father and said, 'Dear Father, you have stripped yourself of goods for my sisters until you depend on the charity of the clan for your sustenance. I am only a daughter. I cannot hold your face in the tulkoda, I cannot care for you in your old age, I cannot sing you into the blessed land, what am I but a drain on you? What does it matter if my life finishes sooner than it might? Let me win honor for you the only way I can. Let me take the clan burden on my shoulders and go to meet the worm freely and with laughter instead of tears.' But her father loved her too dearly to let her do this. So she said to him, 'You have taught me hunting, Father, you have taught me well. Let me speak to the dog Kaermelka, give me your skinning knife, give me six balls of fat kneaded with honey about sharpened sticks bound with gut and let me go to face the worm.' And he said, 'My daughter, my son.' And he embraced her and he said, 'Come back with honor, my son.' And he took her to the headman and said, 'My daughter is fourteen and wishes to face the worm for the clan.'

"They led her off with crowns and song, with flowers woven into her long fine hair, dressed in fine white leather beaded and fringed, the fringes swaying gracefully about her slim young body, her eyes bright and laughing, a spring in her step. Others of the clan marveled at her and marveled at her father who stood proud and straight as a tent pole, beaming at his daughter. Then he went back to his tent and loosed the dog Kaermelka with the skinning knife and the sack of fatballs tied to his harness.

"The clan brothers tied her to the tree like all the others were tied and she did not object; they wrapped the rope twice about her wrists and twice about the wrapping and tied it and took the other end and tied it about the tree, then they went quickly away, not quite running, and it was very quiet under the trees, quiet and cool, but the stink of the worm was heavy in the air. She looked at the braided leather about her wrists and she lifted her head and waited for the drums to begin, the drums that called the worm and she waited for the dog called Kaermelka to come to her as she'd told him to do. But the stink of the worm was strong and strong and she began to be a little afraid, so she stood herself straighter and she stared with anger at the tangle of thornbush and at the round black hole where the worm would come for her.

"The dog Kaermelka came trotting into the tree-shadow and he stopped before her, growling low at the stink of the worm. And she cut herself free of the tree and she cut her wrists free of the rope and she piled the balls of fat and honey in a little heap twice her body length from the hole and she moved back and sank onto her knees another two body lengths from the pile of fatballs. And she sent the dog Kaermelka to the downwind side of the hole. And then the drums began their beat. And she smiled and knelt with her head high, laughter in her eyes. And she waited.

"And the dog Kaermelka crouched in the shadows laughing a dog's red laugh. And he waited.

"The worm came out. His head was longer than Kaermelka, even with his curling tail stretched straight, and his eyes were black mirrors bigger than both Persilli's fists. And he opened his red mouth and his red tongue came out and tasted the air, tasted the fat and honey piled there ready for him. He came gliding out, dry and glistening, gaudy red and black and yellow, poison dripping from his fangs, he came out of his hole, careless and fat with easy living, he came sliding out of his hole and gulped down the fatballs and gulped down with them the sharpened and springy twigs tied together that Persilli had set in them to avenge her death if death was her fortune under the trees.

"Takti-Persilli smiled. She signaled to Kaermelka and Kaermelka crouched low in shadow, his brown and black and white melting with the light and shadow and he crept on his belly silent, silent toward the worm.

"The worm raised his great head and opened his great mouth and tasted the presence of Persilli and came undulating toward her, the shimmer of light through the trees dancing on his scales. And she signaled again to Kaermelka and the dog Kaermelka leaped at the worm's soft underthroat and set his teeth in the worm's flesh and began grinding inward. And Persilli threw herself onto the worm and rode his neck and drove the skinning knife into the hard black eye and ground it round and round and deeper and deeper and the dog Kaermelka held on though the worm battered him against tree and ground and the girl Persilli held on though the worm battered her against tree and ground, and the dog Kaermelka ground his teeth deeper and deeper into the worm's neck and the girl Persilli ground the knife deeper and deeper into the worm's eye and finally the worm lay down and died.

"Takti-Persilli cut the skin from him and Kaermelka gorged himself on the flesh of him.

"In the worm's nest Takti-Persilli found the skulls of all

the girls who'd gone before her and she sighed over them.
'With a little courage and a little thought,' she said to the
skulls, 'you would not have come to this case. I sigh for you,
but not for the men who sent you.'

''She walked back to the camp singing, the wormskin roll
on her shoulder and the dog Kaermelka prancing by her side,
his belly bulging but his spirits high, knowing as all good
hunting dogs seem to know that the day was good and he'd
done a great thing. She marched into the camp and she
dropped the wormskin roll by the headman's tent and she
stood waiting.

''And the headman came out and looked at what lay at his
feet and looked at the blood smeared over Persilli, blood from
head to toes, but none of it hers, and he looked at the dog
Kaermelka grinning beside her and he bowed his head in
honor of her courage and her skill.

''And the clan sought to honor her; they named her son to
her father, and all the other clans paid her great honor. She
wed no man, but cared for her father until he died and she
lived to a great age herself, honored by her clan and by all the
hiiri that lived. This is a womansong passed from mother to
daughter so it will not be forgotten.''

Linfyar clapped his hands, caught up in the cadences of the
story and the triumph of the girl in the story. Shadith chuckled and Wakille looked amused and rather too knowing.

Shadith glanced at Juli who had come in closer to the fire
during the last two stories. ''I've got a story too,'' Shadith
said. ''A long time ago before any of you were born, on a
world a long long way from here, a poor young man left his
father's farm to seek his fortune. Handsome he was like all
such poor young men in stories like these, charming, of
course, and not quite as smart as he thought he was. He
walked along the road, red dust floating as high as his knees,
whistling and enjoying the bright spring day, expecting the
road to turn gold under his feet and the pebbles turn to
diamonds. They didn't, of course, but the weather continued
fine and the farm wives along the way continued kind, so he
had a roof over his head each night even if only a barn, and
sufficient food to keep his belly off his backbone and his eyes

bright enough to fascinate the wives and daughters who helped him on his way.

"But fortune proved more elusive than he expected. Spring passed and he was still on the road. There were holes in his boots and holes rubbed into his dreams.

"One day toward the end of summer he was walking beside a river that wound through a series of small hilly valleys. The mornings were growing chill though the days kept hot and golden still. He'd come a long way since morning, across one unfriendly valley and into another no less unwelcoming. The folk up here were clannish and hostile to strangers especially one whose height and golden beauty— that still survived in spite of all his troubles—made them feel squat and dark and mean. If women and girls looked wistfully after him they didn't let their menfolk catch them at it and they offered him not even the coldest charity, not at all the bounty that he'd found in the lowlands. He was tired and hot and his feet hurt. The riverbank was grassy here, with a gentle slope down to water flowing round a wide lazy bend, slow enough on the inner curve to breed patches of cattails and water lilies, cool and green in the shadow cast by ancient huge river oaks. He sat on the grass beside a clump of cattails and pulled off his boots, wiggled a finger through one of the larger holes, laughed, shook his head, set the boot down, rolled up his trousers and let his feet slide into the water. A smile born of pleasure more intense than any he could remember—at that moment anyway—spread over his hot tired face. He stretched out on the grass, used his hat as a fan for a moment, decided he didn't need to do that because there was a nice little breeze following the water, dropped it over his eyes and let the sounds of river and wind, the hum of bugs and heat, carry him into a deep drowse that was not quite sleep. He wasn't quite as stupid as some like to think big handsome blonds must be. There was a cold hungry night ahead if he didn't stir himself to find some sort of shelter. But right now he didn't want to move, he was feeling too good to move.

"Something started tickling his feet. It would brush past, then something like fingers would move up and down from heel to toes and back. The first time he thought it was grasses or maybe a fish. The second time his eyes popped open and he sat up. The third time, he jerked his feet from the water and stared down into eyes greener than the leaves dipping low overhead, set in a lovely pale face framed in fine wet green-gold hair. The watermaid's lush mouth pouted slightly, then widened into a teasing smile. He stared and stared into the green eyes, reading wonders in them he could not quite put into words even as he was watching them; he looked and looked and could not get enough of looking, seeing in the fathomless eyes the fulfillment of all the desires that drove him from his father's farm. He bent closer and closer, tee-tered on the verge of tumbling into the water, tumbling into the reaching arms of the watermaid.

"Behind him, up on the road, there came the creaking of wheels, the steady clop of hooves, the tinkle of a smallish bell, a wagon and team passing to the north where he wanted to go. He was distracted, swung round, swung back only to see a green and white flash as the maid darted away and was lost in the depths of the river. For just a moment he thought of leaping after her, but at that same moment, a girl started singing, a husky attractive voice, a familiar childhood song. He shook his head, snatched up hat and boots and ran up the slope.

"It was a vintner and his daughter making the rounds of the small mountain vineyards. I could go on and on about how the vintner offered him work and the vintner's daughter fell in love with him and wanted to marry him, about how he shucked his dreams and worked like twenty demons, to make his own chance for fortune, to forget the things he saw in the watermaid's eyes, how he prospered, how he married the vintner's daughter, how he got first a son and then a daughter, how he became a happy and mostly contented man. And how, over and over, he dreamed about the watermaid and what he thought he saw in her eyes.

"Dressed in rich wool riding garb and a fine silk shirt and a pearl gray hat, mounted on a spirited black gelding, his hair still gold, his face still handsome, his body still strong and lean, with five years of hard work and prosperity and a good marriage surrounding him like a scented aura, he rode back down the chain of valleys to the river bend where once he'd drowsed an afternoon away. Men watched him, and he saw the envy in their eyes. Women watched him and he saw the beckoning in their eyes. But he left them behind without a twinge, he had everything he needed and wanted. And that too he'd left behind but not with any intent of abandoning it. No. There was just this teasing itch that had to be assuaged so he could go back and fully enjoy the good things that life had heaped on him.

"He dismounted, tied the horse's reins to a low hanging bough, walked down the slant and stared into the water. Stared a long time without seeing more than water-skaters dimpling the surface. After a while he sat down, pulled off his boots, set them carefully on the grass beside him, rolled up his trousers and slid his feet into the water. It was cold, far colder than he remembered, and he didn't like the thick black mud that oozed around his toes, or the rotten smell that rose from it. He'd forgotten too how his feet had burned and ached, making the mud a heaven those long years before. He lay back on the grass and waited. Bugs crawled on his face, dust was an aggravation in his nostrils and the grass blades pricked the back of his neck. He lay a long time, stiff and cold and uncomfortable. When he felt the rapid tickling that walked the soles of his feet, he sat up and gazed into the deep lustrous eyes of the watermaid. But they seemed shallow now, rather dull, somehow expressionless, even fishy, the pearly skin had tiny scale markings, not deforming but rather off-putting. He thought suddenly of his wife's faintly tanned face with the flush of rose on the cheeks and the light dusting of orange freckles on her nose and was suddenly and terribly homesick. He shook himself and refused to give up his dream, forced himself to look deeper into the maid's eyes, trying to ignore the burgeoning roll of fat under the delicate pointed chin, the smudge of mud along one cheek. Fighting, clawing to regain that long-ago dream, he fit himself finally into the boy he was and saw again the fugitive fluid promises in the green green gaze. Closer and closer he bent; pale arms reached up and closed around him, drew him down under the water.

"He drowned, of course. And the watermaid went serenely on doing what she'd always done. She hadn't cared when he got away before, she didn't care now that he'd whipped himself into succumbing to her. She did what she did because that was what waermaids did, she neither questioned nor accepted it, having neither the need nor the capacity to do either.''

When she finished there was a rather appalled silence. Juli stared at Shadith's unsmiling face. Slowly she crossed the circle of firelight until she stood in front of Shadith. She reached out, touched the faded brown outline of the hawk's head, then she wheeled and ran into the darkness under the trees.

Linfyar turned from one to the other, not understanding what was going on, disturbed by what he sensed in that clearing.

After a while, Aleytys cleared her throat. "Rather like using a sledgehammer on a gnat, don't you think?"

"And delicacy has been working so well?" Shadith sounded both defensive and combative. Moving with a slap-dash overflow of energy, she gathered a handful of plates and pots and flounced off toward the pool they used for washing up.

Late that night the storm broke over the island, making it rock much more than usual; the trees groaned, the roots groaned beneath them. The shelter held well enough, the glue-mixed mud turned the rain, even the heaviest spate when water came down more like a river falling over a cliff than simply rain. But the trees that were the cornerposts shifted about under pressure from the wind, opened small leaks that by morning and the passing of the storm had let in enough rain to make the four of them thoroughly uncomfortable. Not even Linfyar had been able to persuade the zel to take shelter with them.

Morning brought the sun and air so clean and cool and mild it ran like silk on the skin. Water droplets glittered everywhere, clinging to leaves, to blades of grass, to the tips of twigs, catching the sunlight and shooting it out again. The cisterns were full, overflowing, with clear clean water, the mud rapidly settling with the gentle rocking of the island as it wallowed along across the long swells the storm left behind. The gyori were grazing placidly on the grass in the little clearing, grass that seemed to grow as she watched.

Wakille busied himself inspecting the shelter, Linfyar pacing beside him, pulsing the walls with the gravity of an elder inspecting his wealth. He was very good at finding the tiny breaks. Shadith snatched up the hatchet and went whistling into the trees. Aleytys fidgeted about, nervous and uncertain, a hundred things for her to do; she began clearing away some of the debris blown down around the shelter. Of the hundred things this was the simplest, the least demanding. Lifting a limb heavy enough to try her strength, she hauled it to the recumbent trunk and heaved it up among the broken branches of the tree's crown, then went back to gather up those stones they'd searched out for the firehole. Rock was scarce on the island and to be cherished. She reassembled the firepit, annoyed to find one of the larger stones shattered into pea-sized gravel and a second split into three awkwardly shaped bits.

And as she worked, her thoughts reverted again and again to the young zel. Juli was not responding any more to Linfyar's charm. A dozen times Aleytys had felt her begin to soften, to respond, but the moment the zel realized what was happening, she wrenched herself away from them, her anger and hostility redoubled. Time, Aleytys thought, give her time. It's something we got plenty of. She surveyed the results of her effort at reconstruction with a dissatisfaction that had nothing to do with the neatly fitted circle of rocks. With an explosive sigh she got to her feet and plunged into the tangle the storm had whipped up under the trees. The ground was soggy with a tendency to slip unexpectedly under her feet if she put them down carelessly enough to tear through the frail webbing of bracken roots.

The island's snout was draped with puzzles of looped weeds, the dark green leaves wilting though the morning was cool and damp. Juli crouched on the roots, huddled in on herself until she was a damp miserable lump. Aleytys leaned against a tree watching her, frowning, bothered by what she sensed, a blackness gathered like a fog around her, a fog of carefully maintained despair. That wasn't exactly right either, yet it was true that Juli stoked her despair regularly and kept it billowing about her.

Aleytys pushed away from the tree and moved quietly to stand beside Juli. "You all right?" She pitched her voice

high enough to cut through the noises around her. Once out
of the shelter of the trees the gusting wind blew so strongly
and so uncertainly that she found standing difficult. She
dropped beside Juli, sat like her, arms wrapped about her
drawn-up legs, huddling in on herself against the chill of the
wind-driven spray that broke against the side of the island and
struck stinging against them. She looked anxiously at Juli.
The young zel sat with apparent stolid indifference to the
battering, but Aleytys saw her shiver with each gust of the
wind. Juli ignored these periodic shakings as she ignored
Aleytys. In one of the sudden short lulls, her breathing
sounded hoarse and labored. There was a hectic flush on her
thin cheeks, a bright enough flush to glow through the worn
spots in her disintegrating face paint. Aleytys hesitated, knowing only too well how frantically the zel would react if she
touched her, then her anxiety took a firmer hold. She rose
onto her knees, found a fast balance on the springy roots,
caught the zel by the arm, laid her free hand against the girl's
face. She sucked in a breath. "You're burning up." She was
suddenly angry. As the zel began struggling against the hold,
she jerked the girl to her feet and dragged her back to the
comparative shelter of the trees, talking at her though she
knew it was futile, the zel was refusing to listen. "Fool,
idiotic young fool, what do you think you're doing, making
yourself sick, making yourself . . . ah . . . sorehead. . . ."
     The zel was fighting her now, kicking, clawing, mindless
as a frightened beast. Aleytys trapped her arms and tried to
soothe her, finally pushed her onto her face, arms twisted up
behind her back. She straddled the child, held her down.
"I'm going to fix that fever, Juli," she said to the back of the
girl's head. "You think you want to die. I won't let you.
Foolishness." She sat, holding the girl pinned with her weight;
she broke a hand free, caught hold of the inch-long stubble
growing through the paint on the delicate skull and turned the
zel's head so she could breathe and wouldn't choke on the
mulch and mud. She continued talking in between the convulsive surges of the frail body under her. "This ruins any slight
chance I have of reaching you, doesn't it, though why should
I ask you? I don't have to ask you, you've made it plain
enough. But I can't let you die." The last word came out like

a sob; Aleytys closed her eyes, breathed deeply a few moments. "I can't let you die," she whispered. "Young fool, grow up, damn you." Stupid, she told herself, trying to talk to someone when she doesn't want to listen. "You can't get away, child. I'm stronger. You see?" The struggles did not stop though they grew feebler as Juli's strength ebbed. She was gasping raggedly now, liquid bubbling in each breath. Aleytys held her a few moments longer until she stopped fighting and started sobbing, each breath a struggle that shook her whole body.

Aleytys touched her cheek again, but Juli jerked her head away as far as she could, though she didn't interrupt the steady rhythm of her tearing sobs. Aleytys sighed. She loosed the zel's wrists and pressed both her hands flat on the zel's narrow back, closed her eyes and *reached*. Juli shrieked as the healing force poured into her, or rather, she tried to shriek but the sound got caught in her throat and bubbled out in a hoarse whisper.

The healing was finished quickly. Feeling like a beater of babies, Aleytys got stiffly to her feet and stood gazing down at the fragile sprawled figure, the sodden white cloth clinging to the too-thin body with its limbs like sticks. Honey hair striped with black was growing again on the shaved skull; the damp had coiled the inch-long stubble into tight curls so she seemed shaved again, the irregular black lines like an indecisive design running through the dark honey of the blond ground. She lay without moving. Aleytys sighed. "Your fever is gone for the moment," she said quietly. "You came close to drowning in your own juices. Do you have any idea how miserable a death that would be?" She sighed again. "If you would only listen. . . . I can't reach you, can I." She hesitated a moment longer, then walked away. Before the trees closed around her she looked back a last time. The zel hadn't moved.

day 10

The days settled into routine, busy enough with the drudgery of staying alive, but monotonously the same, hauling in strands of the seaweed, plucking off crustaceans for stewing, hanging the weed to dry for the gyori, netting the small fish that schooled ahead of the island, repairing the nets, cooking, running the still, going over their gear, cleaning it, cleaning themselves in a bathtub contrived from one of Wakille's fishskins and a framework of branches, doing a dozen niggling little tasks that took time and patience to complete. Juli drifted around in her cloud of gloom, wary of Aleytys, still unable to stop watching Shadith. For several days after Aleytys had forced healing on her, she followed Shadith around, trying to talk to her, rambling on and on, disconnectedly, in a husky murmur that swallowed a good many of the words. Followed Shadith and murmured at her until Shadith refused to take it anymore and rounded on her, temper flaring, shouted at her half the length of the island, yelling she was sick of the zel's stupidity, that the zel should accept fact and leave her alone, get it through her hard head, her laska was gone, gone, gone, and there was no way Shadith was going to let herself be chorused into taking her place. The zel fled before the storm of the raging voice and vanished for the rest of the day.

day 14

The next several days after Shadith's onslaught, Juli hung around the camp's edge, a shadow under the trees, never coming into the open; though she would take the food and drink that Linfyar brought her, no one else could get near her; she fled into the trees at the slightest sign anyone was coming toward her. Aleytys watched her, fretting and helpless. With Harskari nervous and irritable in her head, with Shadith impatient with her and angry at the whole situation, with Linfyar increasingly reluctant to waste his time coaxing the zel to eat, with Wakille watching the passing play, not bothering to hide his amusement, Aleytys began to feel as if she had ants crawling about just under her skin.

Day piled on day. The island rocked steadily along through the alternations of sun and moon under an empty sky, the air about them still and hot, hotter and stiller the farther south they went. Aleytys sat with the map spread over her lap looking at the marks on it, each day's progress, fourteen marks now. Thirty to thirty-five kilometers a day. Nearly five hundred kilometers of the passage behind them, more than two thousand left. Somewhere below her she could hear Shadith and Linfyar whistling to each other. She folded the map and went down the gentle slope of the hillside and back to the camp to put the map away. She found Wakille puttering about the pile of supplies, fussing at something, humming to himself; he looked up when she came into the clearing, raised one of his furry brows, but said nothing and went back to what he was doing. She snapped the map back into the belt pocket, stood and looked around. No sign of Juli anywhere. "Seen the zel this morning?"

"No." He dropped into a squat beside one of his packs. "Not since yesterday."

Aleytys swept a probe across the island, but felt nothing, not even the ghost of a presence. She ran a hand through her hair and looked about the clearing. A few coals glimmered in the heap above the baking pit where tubers and fish were cooking slowly under the embers. She moved her shoulders. Make things worse, she thought. Always make things worse by sticking my nose in. She walked quickly into the trees heading for the island's snout where Juli usually parked herself, walked faster and faster until she was almost running.

She burst from the trees, stumbled to a stop, swallowed. There was no one there. The briny smell was clean and strong in her nostrils. Out in the distance ahead of the island a large fish arched from the water, splashed noisily back. A pair of sea birds fought over a bit of fish, dropping it in turn, snatching it up again in turn, the chunk disintegrating as they clawed at it. Aleytys rubbed at an eyebrow, then cupped her hands about her mouth and yelled Juli's name, then listened. Though she didn't expect any sort of answer, she hoped to startle a reaction out of the zel. Straining, she felt nothing, heard nothing but the sounds of wind, water, fish, birds.

A cold knot in her stomach, she began to search the woods, moving slowly back along the island, leaving no bit of space unexamined. She moved past Shadith and Linfyar busy with the gyori, playing with them, brushing knots out of the short manes and the stiff hairs on the tail flaps, working at the beasts until they were groaning with pleasure. Shadith called out to her, but she was too involved in her search to do more than nod at her in passing and ignore her questions. Across and across, walking every inch of the island, a kilometer and a half long, about a third of that wide, across and across, up the sides of the hills, down the long trailing tail until she stood looking out over the bright blue swells of the ocean, at the pale blue line of the coast. Close enough to swim, she thought, trying to convince herself of that. Close enough, she whispered to herself. She stared at the thick stroke of blue for a long moment then shook her head and turned to walk back to the clearing.

Shadith left the gyori and Linfyar and came after her. Walking beside her, she said, "What's wrong, Lee?"

Wearily Aleytys brushed at her face, drew her hand back over her hair. "She went into the water. Must have been sometime last night. So useless."

Shadith made a small brushing motion with a hand. "Took long enough to make up her mind."

"Shadi!"

"So? You did what you could. We all did." Shadith turned away, took a few steps, looked over her shoulder. "Wallow in it if you want; me, I'm going to relax with that sour sister off my back." She clasped her hands behind her and strolled off with exaggerated nonchalance, beginning a whistle song that Linfyar took up, Shadith's defiance waking an echo in him. He added overtones that converted song into the equivalent of sight, took Shadith's hand, interrupted the whistles with a rapid rippling giggle.

Aleytys watched them, her depression deepening. "Ay-Madar." She walked the length of the island slowly, circling round the clearing because she didn't want Wakille's eyes on her, didn't want to have to answer his questions. Unconsciously aping Shadith she clasped her hands behind her and trudged through the trees. "Harskari," she said. "Talk to me. Tell me not to be a fool like I tried to tell Juli. Tell me there was never anything I could do, she was as she was."

She settled herself on the roots at the island's front end, the spray pricking at her. The day was beginning to go gray; ravelings of cloud slid by overhead and the rain smell mingled with the briny stink of the shore. "Harskari?"

The amber eyes opened but Aleytys felt little lessening of her solitude. Harskari was very reluctantly present. "What is it, Aleytys?"

"I lost Juli."

"You?"

"Oh, I suppose Shadith's as responsible as any, I don't know. I did my best to help the child. There's nothing more I could have done, at least nothing I can think of. I didn't even like her, not really. So why do I feel so rotten?"

Harskari blinked. "You don't know much about yourself, do you."

"I thought I did. Before this stinking world. I thought I knew who and what I was. But . . . but, you know, in the NewCity ruins, you know what happened. And after that . . . I thought it was a game. A kind of game. I thought I, ah you know, the need that keeps surprising me. And this. Look at me."

Harskari said nothing but her presence was comforting in spite of her protracted silence. After a while there was an eerie noiseless sigh echoing in Aleytys's head. "Why?" Harskari said, her voice very soft. "Why. How often have you failed the last few years, Lee? How often when it really mattered?"

Aleytys blinked at the graying swells, wiped the spray from her face and thought about it, flipped through memories of the years since leaving Jaydugar. "You need to ask? Sharl. My son. Again and again." She closed her eyes. "Funny. That's about it. Out of the things that really mattered. About it." The words dragged as she sought the reason Harskari asked that particular question, then her eyes opened wide. "You think I saw Juli as a surrogate for Sharl?" She moved her shoulders, disturbed by the thought, about to deny it with passionate certainty, stopped before she spoke, brushed her hand across her face. "I don't know." She was beginning to feel slowed down, tired, very very tired, as if something strung taut inside her had broken and let everything else go limp. She yawned, moved about on the springy roots, yawned again. "Failed. You mean more than Sharl?"

The amber eyes blinked.

Aleytys went on. "Sharl's more than enough, don't you

think? The rest—I was just doing my job, never mind I was
forced into those Hunts, a job I'm good at and I suppose,
well yes, one I do enjoy. Nothing earthshaking about that.''

"But you won every time. In other words, daughter, you've
had control of your life and its circumstances to a degree that
would wake envy in most people, no don't interrupt. The
games you've played you've won and even the Cazarit Hunt
you played on your own terms, not theirs. More on your own
terms than even Head knows. Right? Never mind. Success is
addictive. You're suffering withdrawal.''

Aleytys snorted. "Jokes yet. You're a big help.''

"I try.'' The words were devoid of energy as if what little
interest the old one had in Aleytys, her problems, and the
whole situation had drained away. Without saying anything
further, she closed her eyes with a finality that forbade any
more disturbances.

Aleytys watched the darkening swells a little longer, then
got wearily to her feet and walked back toward the camp.

day 30

The coast was beginning to recede. Juli was a distant
memory, not even a ghost—except for a few wryly sad
memories that came back at inconvenient times, especially
when Aleytys woke late at night and was unable to get back
to sleep.

On the thirtieth night after they'd left Yastroo's continent,
Aleytys left her blankets and wandered about, the island
rocking gently beneath her, the swells slapping quietly and
continually against the shoreline. They were near the equator
now and beginning the curve that would carry them across the
widest part of the ocean to the smaller continent. A hot
breathless night, the full moon directly overhead hanging so
low, shining so brightly you could read by it; she went back
to the clearing, hunted around until she found the small black
book and took it to the island's nose, the one place she could
find with even the slightest breeze. She settled herself on the
roots and ruffled through the pages. The NewCity ruins. The
Blights. The list of the indigene settlements about the Plain,

their habits and perils, a sketch of cultures she might touch on. The dryad wood and the cities on the plain, the outcasts, nothing about the Ekansu, the islands and their habits. Having this slim black volume had given her something of the same confidence her mother's letter had given her, something to hold onto, not real, not necessary, like a nice teddy bear to cuddle against. She laughed at herself a little, then turned to the last passage and read it again.

ESGARD'S NOTES:

Follower, if you've caught yourself a proper island, then you are on the edge of the known. The satellite maps, limited as they are, will have to do for the rest of the journey. Depending on the season and chance, the ocean passage can take from ninety to a hundred fifty days. During the summer and fall there are some horrendous storms that could break up the island, perhaps capsize it, leaving you to tread water a thousand miles from anything. Cheered up enough? No telling where you'll hit land, I never did figure that out. The islands nose against the belly of the coast there, tapping into land several times. Avoid the swamps if you can, even if it means a lot of extra days. All the pictures of those swamps I've teased out of the satellite cameras have shown me just how deadly they are; makes the dryad forest look like a playground—you probably know more about that now than I do if you followed me through it. It's difficult to advise you, my follower, so use your own judgment. I've circled the area I'll be heading for on the map I'm going to leave with this book. Follow me there. I'll start leaving my signs again, sooner or later you'll come across them. I've watched for you, Follower, I think I know who you'll be. You'll come after me and you'll find me and you'll get your answer then. I wish you good fortune, Follower, and not too many disastrous surprises.

KENTON ESGARD X_E

Aleytys closed the book, looked at it a moment, then with a sudden irritation, flung it into the moon-silvered swells sliding past the island.

She moved restlessly on the roots, then sat staring at the calm beauty of the ocean. Off to the right some great sea beast broached and breathed sending a plume of steam several meters into the air, shimmering silver against the blackness of sky and water. She rubbed absently at her breasts, missing Grey abominably at that moment, needing him with an ache that began in her loins and spread up through her body. She stretched, shifted on the roots, clasped her hands behind her head. Wakille knew what was bothering her, damn him, that empathy of his that she couldn't seem to block, and he'd managed to convey with a subtle tact that was an insult in itself that he'd be more than willing to help relieve her tension. She couldn't be too angry with him, not when she was giving off signals like a pulsar. Well, it would pass, a week and she'd be calmer, wanting Grey and Swartheld with mostly mind not body, an itch that was easier to deal with, at least more private, even with a powerful empath about. I'm not going to sleep any more tonight, that's sure. She pulled her legs up, wrapped her arms about them and sat as relaxed as she could, staring at the water ahead.

day 35

The island rocked on through long swells into daily thunderstorms that fell straight down like showerbaths and uncertain winds that niggled at them and teased the island into swooping zigzags, wobbling from one side of the many stranded stream to the other, its foresting and three small hills providing surfaces for the winds to push against.

Five days out from the coast the rains stopped and they began to nuzzle through bits of broken island and islets without mass enough to plow undisturbed through the swirl of conflicting forces crossing the flow of the current. Sometimes being on even an island the size of the one they rode was like trying to ride a worm with the hiccups and a warped sense of direction. What was worse as far as Aleytys was concerned, their forward progress slowed to near nothing.

Linfyar was perversely delighted with the instability of the earth beneath his feet. At first Aleytys was troubled about him, wondering how he was going to manage the uncertain footing, whether his other senses, whatever they were, would be confused by what was happening and trick him into danger. She followed him about for a few hours after a storm that left swollen waves and erratic winds that pitched the island about energetically enough to make her worry about his safety. But he was sure-footed as a squirrel and twice as energetic. He danced up one side of the middle hill and down the other, wound through the trees, racing over the island from end to end as if he burned with an energy that wouldn't let him rest a moment.

Shadith sat crosslegged on the grass lazily making half a dozen small mice-like rodents dance on tiny hind legs for her. Linfyar trotted past her without noticing the dancing beasts, perhaps they were too small for his senses. Or, even if he did notice them, it was only as small warm presences scurrying about Shadith's feet.

Aleytys dropped beside her. "Ay-Madar," she breathed. "I've never felt so antique."

Shadith giggled. She caught up one of the soft furry mouselets and let the others scamper away. She sat holding the small brown ball of fur in the palm of one hand and scratched delicately behind tiny translucent pink ears. The mouselet stretched out flat on her palm, a look of bliss on its furry face.

"Maybe you shouldn't get too friendly. We may have to eat them," Aleytys said. "Not that I think I could."

"Me either. I'll stick with fish." Shadith sighed. "When we get off this wallow I'll never *touch* another fish."

Aleytys chuckled, nodded.

Linfyar came trotting past again, showing no sign of running down. He warbled an ascending trill at Shadith, giggled happily as she inverted the trill and played a few changes on the notes. The island gave a sudden wild lurch. Aleytys fell over, caught herself with her hands, but the boy danced with the lurch; ears twitching with delight, trailing a burst of giggles behind him, he vanished under the trees.

Shadith straightened, set the mouselet down and let it scurry off. "Linfy's flying."

"Tell me about it. I've spent the past hour trailing him to

be sure he could cope with this." She patted the shifting earth.

"I keep forgetting he can't see."

"I know. Me too. Whatever he does, it's efficient enough."

"Bat blips." Shadith yawned and lay back on the grass, staring up at a sky empty of clouds. "Does the sky look a bit odd to you?"

Aleytys stretched out beside her. "More than sonar, I think. Odd? How odd?"

"Kind of fuzzy. Not clouds but like a very thin layer of dirty glass between us and it."

"Mmm. Air's tricky sometimes. Ever wonder what this world must be like for Linfy?"

"Sometimes. Lee. . . ."

"Umm?"

"Storm's coming, I think."

"Because of the way the sky looks?" Aleytys pulled her tunic up and scratched idly at her stomach. "Hot and sticky. Maybe a little rain would cool us off a bit."

Shadith moved uneasily, lifted her arms and spread her fingers between her and the sky. "I've seen skies like this before, particularly once. Ever ridden out a hurricane?"

"No, but I've read about them. You think one's heading for us?"

"Read." Shadith lowered her arms. "Reading's no good." She blinked slowly, yawned again, shivered. "I got that feel, Lee. The smell. The hush. The swells long and sleek, no whitecaps, air heavy, thick. Clouds should be whipping in soon. And my premonition's jumping. There's a heller coming, Lee."

Aleytys scratched some more, then laced her hands behind her head. "This isn't the land, might blow us about some, but we can ride the top."

"Maybe. I still say you don't have the faintest notion what's coming at us."

"And you never saw Jaydugar in the winter." Aleytys turned her head, eyed the slender eager face. "And you've got a story to tell."

"Fool! Hunh, I got a notion not to."

"Not much of a notion." Aleytys chuckled. "All right, if

you want to be coaxed—got nothing else to do. Please, pretty please.''

"That's what you call coaxing?" She rubbed at her nose, closed her eyes. "Long time ago there was a world called Yag, frontier world, just cut loose from mama and feeling its oats. One thing and another, I was grounded there, couldn't get off for near four years. I rambled about, doing this and that and after a couple years ended up on the south coast of the best developed of the nine continents, singing for my supper etc. in a port tavern a couple steps above a dump. Late summer when I got there was hot and dirty and the air was so thick you chewed it instead of breathing it. Hadn't rained for a month or more which was not usual according to the types I talked to. The weather almost beat out women and money as a topic of conversation. The folk who ran the country were getting worried. They had planes and satellites searching the ocean but there were no storms heading for Merzit, that was the port's official name though some of the others I heard were a lot more descriptive though not printable in any moderately repressive society and that one wasn't moderate in much, certainly not in its official attitude toward morality, or what they called morality. The folk I was in with lived in the cracks of things, rats living in twilight and night, sleeping mostly during the day, liable to be hassled any time by the police or the church enforcers. Those who could carried getting-off money hid somewhere on them, sometimes several stashes according to how times were going, and everyone knew the police or enforcers you could pay and those who used the knot on you if you tried it, when to run like hell and when to weasel and when to crawl. Something you picked up through your skin by living there. Though I was a newcomer, I'd been in places like that before, or close enough that I could make the right moves, well, keep from making an idiot of myself while I learned them. If I hadn't been flat broke at the time, I wouldn't have stopped there. I could've shipped out just about any time if I wanted to go as shipwhore, but that wasn't a choice that appealed much to me and I thought I'd take my chances earning a stake. Seemed to me that with all their security, the rich quarter here was easy enough for some little tools I happened to have with me. Meantime, I was singing to keep my belly off my backbone. Don't poke me, I like that phrase, it says what I mean.

"Well, I was starting to get a bit of a name for singing after working a month or so and I was circling about just about decided on the house I was going for, when the weather started getting really weird and folk started getting edgy, then the weathermen started giving warnings of a storm out on the ocean heading our way. And what you know, the important types cleaned out their homes and took off like someone goosed them. The rest of us went about best we could, those that could got their kids out or took off themselves, those that couldn't spent most their time fiddling about with the shacks they called home, not that there was much they could do but ride the storm out and hope. Me, I was too dumb to know what the fuss was about, I'd never seen a hurricane. I'd heard about them, but I'd never tried sitting in the middle of one. So I wasn't that worried; I figured I'd get myself into one of those fortress houses the rich were abandoning so recklessly and spend the storm time in comfort and in a leisurely prospecting of the place, maybe pick up enough to finance my way offworld. I was beginning to get a bit fidgety. There was this church enforcer developing a thing for me, I could see it in his little squinty eyes and the way he kept hanging about whether I was singing or down in the market looking for fresh fruit or a bit of meat for my supper. Long gaunt man, hollow cheeks, mouth that looked as friendly as a snapper's beak, wore a tight-fitting cap, going bald, I think. Shows you, ugly as warmed over dogshit and vain as any Adonis. He was looking me over before he made his move. If he finally decides I'm good enough for him, I spread my legs for him or I end up in the workhouse with them doing what they called correction on me and if I don't keep my mouth shut about what he tried, what'd happen to me then was something you don't talk about to anyone with a weak stomach. I began hoping the storm would hurry here before he got set and then I thought maybe he was hurrying himself because the storm was coming. I got ready to go to ground fast.

"The reports kept saying it's a paper monster, poorly organized, low windspeeds and all that, but the bums that nested under the wharves and in doorways, they were all vanishing, walking out of town, the barman told me. He was a good sort, liked me but no problem there since he had himself a steady boyfriend. He knew all the rules to staying alive, though he didn't always follow the one about not trusting anyone and keeping himself to himself, he just couldn't do that, and it was going to kill him one of these days and he knew it but he couldn't help liking people and going out of his way to help them. He spotted the enforcer hanging about and warned me what could happen when I still thought it was some kind of sick creep I could brush off and forget. He said the vanishing bums meant this was going to be a killer. Their brains were rotted so they couldn't think, but they been there so long they knew by feel when a storm was going to hit and when they cleared out it was time to duck your head and pray. I nodded and thanked him as if I understood but I really didn't and I think he knew that but there was a limit to what he could do.

"Well, next day I scrounged some drugs I knew about from a dealer and made myself really sick and came and told my boss I just couldn't go on that night, that I was going to have to hole up a while and get over whatever it was. He took one look at me, I looked like death on the hoof I think, backed off and told me to get the hell out and not come back till I kicked the thing. When I left the place, I saw the enforcer coming. For me, I suspect. I made sure he got a good look at miserable suffering me. I was sneezing and dripping and my eyes red and my hair a mess and reeking of this gunk I rubbed on my chest and he looked like he'd got a whiff of something rotten. I was a mess and he wasn't wanting any part of me now. The look on his face made me feel a lot better though the stuff in me was just getting worked up; I had a hard time not grinning at him.

"I had this little battery radio in the hole I lived in and I turned it on soon's I got there and this announcer was having fits. Seems like the storm had taken a sudden hook and sort of pulled itself together and was heading right for us. Up to a few hours ago they thought it'd hit land a ways up the coast and we'd get the fringes but nothing more. Now it was heading right for us and the wind speeds were up, the eye was tightening, getting smaller by the minute. They were

starting to call it a killer and they were saying the roads out
were clogged with people trying to get away and there was a
hefty panic going on and they were evacuating the evacuation
centers because it looked like even these places weren't going
to be safe and anyone with any sense was getting out while
there was time. There was still about a few hours before the
thing came on land. It was so quiet outside you could almost
hear the fear around you. High up, the clouds were coming
in, there was still no rain, but there was this feel to the air as
if you couldn't get enough of it when you breathed so you
opened your mouth and bit off big chunks and were panting
and that was enough to scare anyone. I was starting to feel
that making myself sick right now was not the great idea I'd
thought it was.

"The rain began just before nightfall and the stillness
broke and that made things a little better, but I could feel that
whole damn city waiting. Then the folk at the radio station
were calming down a bit. A little after sunset the storm took
another jag and everyone started breathing again, at least
here, down the coast the panic was beginning since the storm
had completely reversed direction and was going back the
way it came. I lay in the dark listening to the mosquito buzz
of that radio and believe me I was breathing easier and not
only because the effect of the drugs was passing off. I could
hear my neighbors starting to talk, to call to one another
outside. Usually this part of the city was noisy enough you
had to be clubbed to sleep, but up to now you'd have thought
it was a city of the dead.

"A couple hours later when I was getting dressed for my
bit of burgling, I heard a long warbling shriek from outside. I
turned the radio on again. It said the storm had wobbled like
it was moving in circles. No one, not even those who'd
watched the weather for a lifetime knew where the thing
would finally come ashore, but folk were again believing the
worst. I heard doors slam, most of the tenants in this rickety
pile, from what they were yelling at each other, going to try
getting out of town or at least to the safest of the shelters and
if the respectable types wouldn't let them in they were going
to rush the doors and get themselves in if they were killed for

it which some of them might be, but that was better than trying to face that monster.

"I figured tonight was the best night for hitting the rich quarter and it was just as well to have some money before the enforcer got back on form, something to bribe one of the fruitboat captains who sometimes came to the tavern when they were in port. It didn't seem like I could get out legally, there were too many laws I didn't know about that could be twisted to keep me if anyone with some pull wanted to keep me. I could have gone overland, worse come to worst, but that mean traveling hard and sleeping cold and I liked my comfort. I'd have to stay off the paved roads. There were police checkpoints every dozen kilometers. Those in power in this miserable hole of a country liked to keep their populations in place. There are always ways, you know there are, to get around those kind of rules, but they're hard and grubby and dangerous. A lot easier shipping out. I was a fool ever to go there, I knew what the place was like, but there was a fiddler I wanted to listen to and talk with, and some others who had a new sort of music that I could only get snatches of outside, so I had to stick my nose in. The fiddler, he was dead by the time I got to Merzin, they said he hanged himself one night when the jimjams got too bad, but I did pick up some songs, worth the trouble they cost me, I suppose. Yeah, worth the trouble, music to tear the heart and laugh at the tearing and curse the strong and curse the weak and mock all that men dream of while sorrowing for the sorrows of the world. Sing you a couple sometime when I'm in the mood, you'll see what I mean.

"The rain was coming down like someone opened a faucet somewhere when I went out the door, and starting to blow, though the wind hadn't made up its mind yet where it was going to blow from. I cleaned out the things I cared about in the room, left some clothes and things, a pot or two I'd bought, but I could always get more clothes if I had to. I had my tool belt wrapped round my middle and the darter down my leg, what money I had left stuffed in the toe of my boot. I got into my coat and hesitated whether to take the radio or not, but it had a bonephone I could stick on my head and wouldn't make any noise. I was beginning to get a bit worried by this time, though I still didn't think any storm could beat some of the wars I'd near got killed in. I stuck the radio and the bonephone in my coat pocket, looked around the room. There were a couple carvings and a tapestry I'd have liked to keep, maybe I could come back for them, but right now I didn't want the weight about me.

"By the time I got to the security fence I was soaked and feeling like I was being beaten by clubs, the rain was coming down that hard. The current in the fence was enough to kill an ox and there were guards supposed to be walking the wall top, but thanks to the rain they weren't, no one came by while I was busy bypassing that current; it was hard to see, rain kept getting in my eyes, making my hands clumsy, two-three times I was sure I'd muffed it, but luck or skill got me through that part, then I had the inner wall to deal with, three meters high and topped with broken glass, more wires and outcurving spikes. They liked their privacy, these power-types, or maybe they knew a little about how us poor rats felt about them. You want to play with tigers, tease and torment them, better be damn sure you got a good fence between you and them. This I'll say for them, they had themselves one dandy fence. I was in good shape, though, had myself a ladder of memory plastic that wouldn't trigger the sensors, though I suspected some of those were shorting out because of the rain, and the guards anyway wouldn't pay too much attention to blips unless I got blatant. I was up and over that wall a lot faster than I got through the wires. The thing was two meters thick and solid. Take a tank equipped with penetrator rockets to get through it. Anyway I was in and slipping along with my darter out. They turned loose killer cats whenever they left the place empty, or so rumor said. I didn't see any that night, so I don't know if it was true. Being cats, maybe they had enough sense to be under something where they could keep dry and warm. I was very much in the mood for dry and warm myself by the time I was halfway up the little hill they'd built for themselves inside the wall. Me, I was aiming for the king house, the highest of them all.

I got in easy enough, they put their trust mostly in the walls and the outer ring of security. Found a safe in the basement, behind some racks of wine. Took awhile to puzzle the lock out, but I won't be tedious about that, just say I got it open in ways the maker never dreamed of; why not brag a little, I'm good, I'm damn good. The satisfaction I got out of emptying the thing almost paid me back for my trouble by itself, I was grinning like a fool thinking about the look on his exaltedness's piggy face when he opened the safe once he got back from where he was hiding. I figured that'd be a few days after the storm, he wouldn't want to have to look at battered and bedamned riffraff or smell the stink of backed-up sewers or whatever. I stuffed all I could manage into the shoulderbag I'd brought along for that, made a pile and burned the rest of the papers and paper money and stocks and whatever. Then I started futzing about the place, seeing what there was to see. Nobody there, not even a servant, I suppose he wouldn't let the servants stay, they might steal a bottle of his wine or maybe piss in his personal toilet or something horrendous like that. I was thinking pretty seriously about trashing the place while I was there, soon's I was finished looking around. I went up and up until I was looking out one of the highest of the windows, looking out over the port a long way down from there. I was looking out that window when the storm hit. My god, you never felt anything like the power of that wind, it tore into the city and when I say tore, I mean just that. And the water climbed up out of the harbor and came ramming inland and nothing, I mean nothing, stood before it, and it came on and on and the first of the tornadoes set down and came roaring up the hill toward me. Talk about paralyzed, I couldn't have moved if someone jabbed me with a hyped-up cattle prod. That big black funnel like death itself came roaring up the hill right at me. It came through that fence and that wall like the wall was tissue paper, turned a few houses into kindling so easy I couldn't breathe. I think I left handprints in the stone on that windowsill. It missed the kinghouse, went past not more than a hair away. There were more of the monsters all around, I could see them around me, see them eating through the city down below. And that was just the beginning. I stayed by the window until I was so much into the power and noise and grandeur of that storm, I wasn't thinking about myself at all, I was riding a high like none I've ever had before or since, yelling and laughing and beating on the stone. It seemed to go on forever, but when the eye moved over us, I came to myself enough to know I had to get the hell out of there. The night turned still and very quiet. I could see stars for the first time and the moon was coming out from behind shredded clouds. And that was only half the storm. Lee, it flattened that city and Merzin wasn't any half-assed back-water burg, it was a major port with tons of material passing in and out, over a hundred thousand living there. I don't know how many were killed. A lot of bodies got washed out to sea when the water pulled back, most of them us rats who nobody would miss much. When I finally got out of the house, there was a rusty old coast freighter sitting perfectly upright across the wall, driven through that two meters of reinforced concrete. Far as I could see there wasn't a building left whole anywhere.

I sat out the second half of the storm in the cellar of the kinghouse, praying to all the gods I could remember that the house wouldn't fall down on me. I could hear it tearing apart even over the noise of the storm. It was a toss-up for me whether I went outside or into the cellar, which would be better—blown away and drowned or trapped down by the rifled safe just waiting for pigface to get back. I tossed a coin, heads outside, tails the cellar, came out tails so there I was, hoping my luck would hold. It did. The second wing of the storm turned the house into a pile of rubble, but didn't quite block my way out.

"I got out of Merzin with a bunch of looters on a boat they picked up somewhere when the police and enforcers came swarming back once the storm fizzled out inland. Had to knock manners into some heads, but that's another story. Anyway, Lee, if that storm coming hits us full on, we've got about as much chance surviving as a worm in front of a stampede. First thing, I think you should get a look at it so we'll know for sure just how bad off we are, then see if there's maybe something you could do about it. We've got some time yet. The back of my head's twitchy but not twanging."

Aleytys lay looking up at the clear blue sky, feeling the island rocking beneath her. She turned her head. Shadith's eyes were closed, she seemed to be half asleep as if she'd abruptly forgotten the urgency that had driven her a minute before. "Good story," she said. "Where's Wakille?"

Shadith's nose twitched, she sucked in a breath, let it out in a groaning yawn.

"Well, if it's too wearying. . . ."

"Sarcasm doesn't become you, Lee. He's fishing off the back of the island somewhere, you should've seen him when you were chasing Linfy about." She yawned again. "I suppose he's still there. I really think you should go take a look at that storm."

Aleytys dragged her hands down her face. "How? There isn't a bird in sight."

"Ever thought of riding a fish?"

"No. Too many gone into my belly to make that a comfortable thought."

"Right. Maybe I shouldn't've said fish. What I meant was something bigger, good eyes, fairly complex brain. Whale or something like that."

"Mmm." Aleytys smiled, stretched, her body moving slowly on the grass. "I hate to admit it, Shadi, but that's a good idea." She rolled onto her stomach, rested her forehead on her forearms, then lifted her head again. "Keep them off me."

She went deep deep and out, searching for eyes and brain complex enough to make a mount for her. Deep and away, touch a myriad life-fires that were not enough, not right, too small, too limited, bundles of ganglions not brains, eyes that saw so little they seemed useless to their owners except perhaps some sight was better than no-sight. What was the world like for Linfyar?

Group mind, if mind it could be called, group feel, group feed, schools of fish or tiny things like single cells of a vast amorphous entity. The ocean teemed with life; where niches had been emptied a thousand years before, where radiation from the sun passing through the shattered ozone layer slaughtered whole species, new species had evolved to fill the emptiness or old species still lingering had changed or expanded their options. The water seethed with these small fires and slightly larger ones, but none was what she needed. She saw nothing, only sensed them. Is this what other-life is for Linfyar? How strange. She kept on searching, her mind pushed by touch not sight and it was far more confusing, far more uncertain than the sharp certainties of sight. It came to her then how much she depended on her eyes and the information they provided. Perhaps in some way that was why the first thing she saw of the diadem's indweller-captives was their eyes, her unthinking response in symbol to the importance of sight to her. Or perhaps it was nothing of the kind. She heard herself, chuckled at the thought and was almost jerked back into her body. But she wasn't ready to surrender yet and pushed herself to continue the search. On and on, out and out, deep and shallow—until she suddenly sensed purpose.

It was a fire that was hotter than all the rest, drifting close to the shifting boundary between air and sea; she felt its idle adjustment to the bounce of the water, a kind of pleasure it took in the motion of its grand body. It felt a little like the tars she once knew, the semi-intelligent beast that in his way taught her how to heal, or rather, taught her that she could heal. She remembered (comfortable now, floating with the creature here) that time and her reluctance to leave the magnificent predator who had befriended her and saved her life and more than life for her. She wondered for a moment if he still remembered her, then remembered for herself how brief his life would be, five winters at most, fifteen years standard, and probably less. He was adult, already passed his first winter when she came across him, he'd be dead now, certainly dead after twelve years, his body food for worms, his skull perhaps a trophy on a hunter's wall, though this, she thought, was less than likely, he was a shrewd creature, a beast of purpose and even a little wisdom if that word could be stretched to fit his deep and wide awareness of the animal and vegetable life around him and how he must fit into it. Sadness filled her, tears dripped from the eyes of her body, a friend forgotten in the many twists of her life. It seemed to her it was a betrayal to forget so thoroughly one to whom she owed so much, with whom she shared so strong an affinity. This sea beast sunning just beneath the surface had something of the same feral grace and strength of purpose, something of the same possibility in him, something of the same curiosity, the beginning of self-awareness. She came close and linked lightly with the creature.

Legs rippling, lifting and falling. Arms. Legs. The sensations are the same, arms or legs. Data coming in. Controlled flood of sensation. Legs/arms weaving about each other, brushing against each other. Data. Pressure. Change. Orientation. Color. Shape. Taste. And infinity of taste subtly differing, continually evaluated. Sense of repleteness, of lethargy, of vast contentment.

It seemed a strange combination of squid and whale, stretched its length a half dozen meters below the heaving surface of the ocean, its forest of tentacles moving with the shifting. Whale-squid. It was drifting . . . no, he was drifting with the current, trailing lazily behind the island. She had the impression of vastness but it was hard to evaluate size, the creature didn't think of himself this way. If he thought at all. She got the impression of a sleepy, rather amiable predator, amiable now because his stomach was full and the water was warm about him, taking him where he wanted to go without any effort on his part. He had a large complex brain; it needed to be large to cope with the amount of information his multiplex sensors fed into it, needed its size to accommodate the switching mechanisms that ran his huge body. Aleytys no longer doubted he was huge, the sense of mass she got from the whid? squale? She grinned to herself. Call it a squale, The sense of mass she got from the squale couldn't be that far off actuality. One part of the brain was continually busy, a kind of automatic control and computer, receiving and evaluating sense data, while another part of the brain dozed—one might even say snored—through the mild uneventful morning. Aleytys took her time getting to know the feel of that brain. She had to ride the squale well enough not to endanger him. She giggled softly again at the word *squale,* a little distracted by her enjoyment.

The squale came dreaming past the island as she stirred it cautiously to putting forth a bit of effort, that effortless effort doubling the speed he was making without waking the slumbering part of his brain. The squale came dreaming past the island, incurious and unhungry, a combination of attitudes always occurring together, Aleytys thought, smiling, and as she drifted with him she pried open one great eyelid and saw the tangle of roots dangling below the mass above her. The squale moved on, his head coming out of the island's shadow before the feathery ends of his idly beating arms came into it. Longer than the island, over a kilometer and a half long. Aleytys felt awe-stricken and somewhat disconcerted to find her estimates of the great mass of the squale erring on the low side. Nearly two kilometers long, eyes as big as her own head, bright intelligent eyes that saw in color, saw in the sharp detail common to most predators wherever they hunted.

Cautiously she began to increase her control on the brain.

Shadith pushed up off the grass, some mites on the stalks were climbing off the blades and onto her, into ticklish creases in her body of which she seemed to have an oversupply. She slapped at herself, ran her hands vigorously through her hair, wincing as she ran into knots, clawing from the tight bouncy curls a rain of small twigs, bits of leaf and other debris she'd acquired. "Having a body is greatly over-rated," she muttered. Her hair felt stiff and greasy. No wonder I pick up so much junk. Time I washed you. "Yukk," she said. She looked up at the textured sky with its accumulating strands of clouds, then across at Aleytys's twitching body. "Wonder what that means?" She sat on the fallen trunk, pulled her legs up, draped her arms over her knees and frowned at the stubby trees thick around the little clearing, not really seeing them. Tie down the gyori, she thought, keep them from being washed away, something to do, something to melt a little of the ice packed under her ribs. Fear. Helplessness. Colder, she smiled, colder than a Jaydugar winter. It would hit them or it would miss them or it would brush them, that thing rolling down on them, that juggernaut. There was nothing she could do. There was probably nothing Aleytys could do. Power. It was laughable if you didn't think too hard about it. Aleytys controlled enormous power and used it sometimes wisely, sometimes not. Enormous power when compared to the strengths of even the strongest of bodies and like a blunt-nosed needle against the sword of that storm. She knew it was a monster, her body vibrated with its emanations. If it hit the island direct-on, the island would flip over or break up or become so water-logged it ceased to float. Maybe it would blow them closer to the coast, maybe even into the coast. Head on, brush, miss. No way to know until Aleytys surfaced. Don't know if I want to know. What could I do if it was coming right at us? But knowing might be better than this gut-twisting uncertainty. Maybe. Maybe not. Maybe. Maybe not. He loves me, he loves me not. Oh god. There won't be a wall of water out here, just a swell that goes up and up and up. And the winds. No tornadoes, that's over land. What do they call them out here? Waterspouts? I've never seen a waterspout. Is it as bad as a tornado? Or do hurricanes birth them before they're close to land? I thought I knew so much, hunh! More than Aleytys anyway. I concentrated on surviving the things, not learning about them. Stupid. Stupid. What good's hindsight now? Still, I suppose it's better to act like we're going to make it, get things tied down. Tied to what? Trees, I suppose. She kicked with her heel at the trunk she was sitting on. Trees go down, but they're the best we got. They go, everything goes. Us too. Lifelines. The hills might help a little. God. What are we going to do about the imp? He's not going to take to being tied down. Poor kid, he's never going to understand what's coming at us. I bet he's never seen anything worse than a blizzard, maybe nothing worse than a summer thunderstorm. Seen? Well, heard. Aleytys giggled suddenly and Shadith turned to stare at her. "What the hell?" She got to her feet and nudged Aleytys with her toe, but got no response. "Hurry it up, Lee," she said, knowing that Aleytys couldn't hear her. "I'm getting antsy." She watched a moment longer then trotted to the shelter.

The glue-earth mixture plastered on the woven twigs had hardened into a tough, resilient substance that gave a hair when she kicked it but as far as she could tell was as strong at least as any of the trees. *Might last awhile*, she thought. There were other trees around, close enough to lend them some protection and even if the wind uprooted them, they were too close to crash down on the shelter, their branches would catch in other branches. *We'll be safe enough. Unless the whole island goes. That happens, a few crashing trees won't matter a spit in the ocean.* She giggled, then shivered

as she remembered the freighter driven through the wall.
When she came round to the front of the shelter, Wakille
stood beside Aleytys, a dripping string of fish in one hand,
his pole in the other. She was twitching again, making soft
sounds that were a lot like sighs of pleasure, embarrassingly
so, Shadith thought. She scowled at the little man, cleared
her throat.

Wakille looked around. "What's going on?"

"Lee's gone swimming. Never mind her. Dump those
runts." She jabbed a finger at the fish. "We got a problem."

"Linfyar?" Wakille dropped the fish, stepped over Aleytys's
legs and came toward Shadith.

"Hold it." She straightened her arm, interposed a hand
between him and her. "Calm down. Nothing to do with the
imp. He's running about somewhere, chasing his tail, I don't
know." She chewed on her lower lip. "You ever been
through a hurricane?"

"Ah." He straightened, swung around, clasped his hands
behind him and began examining the sky and the herringbone
clouds that were beginning to take over the blue. "Blow
coming?" He answered himself. "Long swells. That sky."
He sniffed at the air. "Uh-huh." He swung back around.
"I've seen a blow or two, here and there. Now and then.
What about this one? Coming at us?" He scratched at an
eyebrow. "At us or by us?"

"Lee's taking a look. I think it's awhile yet before things
start kicking up."

"They're tricky." He looked down at Aleytys. "She doesn't
look bothered about much."

Shadith shrugged. "Whatever. We better get started roping
things down."

A pulse rippled along the powerful black body. Aleytys
smiled. Never—even when she blew the Tikh'asfour to dust
and radiation—never, ever, had she had such a feeling of
power. The squale hummed with pleasure as she stroked his
brain, she swore he was purring or was it singing? She
nudged him out of the stream and sent him straight to meet
the storm. Despite his great size he was young, not at his
prime even yet, and he liked to play and his body was a

delight to him, so he was easy enough to send into a race against nothing but his own strength.

He dropped lower, tasting the water until he found a layer he liked where he was clear of the surface turbulence and went flashing along, brushing the edges of the current, going faster and faster until he was far outpacing it, driving through the water with powerful snaps of the mighty arms, faster and faster until Aleytys was gasping and clinging to the brain, too numb to do more than cling and exult in that speed and the violence of his passage, then he was flashing up, arcing through the air, expelling the air in his lungs, sucking in fresh, arcing down again, plunging down and down, going down and down endlessly and then he was curving up again, up until he was back at his chosen depth, flicking along beside the stream, singing now, low creaking basso songs, singing for sure, throwing out to the ocean and everything in it the magnificence of himself. He was king of everything in range of his voice and he knew it and he reveled in it and he made sure the rest of the world knew it. Aleytys cheered, caught up in that overweening joy.

The water grew turbulent. The squale dropped lower, then lower again. He was getting restive. And hungry. That bulk took a lot of feeding. Aleytys sighed and put away her pleasure. Business now. Too bad. She drove her reluctant mount around and around the turbulence, estimating time and using his length to measure how broad it was, how fast it was traveling, what direction it was going. Two hundred kilometers from ripple to ripple, the squale going his own length once a minute roughly. She ducked him under and up into the eye so he could breath and she could get a look at what was happening on the surface. Out of the water his vision was less acute but still good enough to give her details of wind and clouds and surging water, the feel of the monster, how it was organized, what seemed to be driving it, enough to show her the books had not exaggerated and neither had Shadith. The only thing even remotely comforting was the direction of the storm. The eye was north of the current and traveling just a hair north of east, so it and the strongest of the winds would pass them by, but even the fringes were enough to turn her hair white. She expanded her senses, trying to grasp more of the storm, but it was like trying to close her hand about a shadow and the power in it rasped at her nerves.

The squale was buckling under her hold, losing his temper with this gnat pricking at him. She held him until she had as much as she could grasp, then let him flop over and go deep. Before she left him, she tickled him back to his pleasure in himself until he was drifting lazily through the calm and friendly deep, sniffing about for food to fill his demanding belly. With a last affectionate touch, she floated loose then snapped back into her own body.

Little, weak, ineffectual, clumsy, she sat up, ruefully comparing her present form to the one she'd just put off. It was not a cheerful thought, nor was the information she had to report.

day 37

They huddled together in the shelter, Linfyar shaking with terror, all his senses overwhelmed by the clamor outside, blind now as he'd never been before, blind as the others were in the blackness inside the groaning walls. He climbed into Aleytys's lap and pressed against her shuddering and near hysterical. The trees outside groaned and creaked and even over that noise and the noise of the wind and the noise of the sea, she could hear crashes and explosions as tree after tree broke and tore apart. The shelter made its own noises, a continual creaking and thrumming, the wind breaking past the trees to slam against the walls and pluck at the roof. And the island twisted, rolled, bucked beneath them, beneath Aleytys, rain hammered at them. And the storm roared, most of all it roared, engulfing them; they drowned in noise, the small personal sounds of living utterly lost so that Aleytys had now and then to touch herself to reassure herself about her reality, to convince herself she hadn't melted away and become one with the storm.

And it went on and on—endlessly—until it seemed impossible that anything could sustain that level of violence. On and on and on. Morning came, a subtle graying of the blackness inside the shelter. Aleytys held Linfyar in her lap, his small soft body lying hot against hers. She cupped her hand over his curls and held his head against her breasts, slid her other hand up and down the narrow back, soothing him, whispering comfort he couldn't possibly hear though he was relaxed now, limp, heavy, hot against her, his ears pinched tight against the clamor of the storm. He was asleep, deeply, profoundly asleep, insulated by that sleep from the things that terrified him. And her leg was asleep. She didn't want to move it and disturb Linfyar, but the niggling little pain was rapidly growing unbearable. She straightened her leg, the splash and brush of the movement lost even to her ears in the storm noise, clenched and unclenched her toes, tightened and loosened the muscles until the tingling numbness went away. Linfyar moved and grumbled a few shapeless sounds; she heard those. Mother's ears, she thought, smiled, but the pull of her face told her it was more a grimace than a smile. She eased Linfyar onto her other shoulder, rubbed at her back, wriggled about in the mud sloshing under her. It seemed to her the noise around her was growing louder, the roaring of wind and water against them almost but not quite swallowing the tearing and crashing of trees, the corner-post trees straining, rocking, roots shifting through the sodden earth, churning it to mush. The beaten earth floor, now awash with water, sloppy with mud, dropped away sickeningly under her, then slammed up again in an irregular alternation impossible to anticipate or adjust to. Drop them slam, roll, slide, throwing her against the wall, throwing her at the others.

About midday she knew the battering was going to be too much, the island was melting away beneath them.

With Linfyar still sleeping heavily, retreating into that sleep from the danger and noise that overwhelmed him, Aleytys began probing through the island, her mind-touch feeling the particles of soil grown slippery, sliding one against the other, more and more loosely as time passed. The island's edges were already beginning to let go, crumb by crumb sliding into the churning salt water.

Aleytys trembled as the island trembled. Wait. All she could do was wait and hope. No. Something. There had to be something. . . .

Linfyar murmured a sleepy protest, his whimper warning

her that she was squeezing him too tightly, that there was a danger of hurting him if she got too deeply involved in whatever it was she had to do. "Shadith," she called, but the sound was lost in the storm noise. She cleared her throat, tried again louder. "Shadith!"

"What?"

"Take Linfy."

"Huh?"

"Take Linfy. I've got to do something." As she began freeing herself from Linfyar's clinging fingers, she felt a searing mixture of emotions escape from Wakille—anger and a touch of fear, but most of all a raging helpless jealousy—leaking from behind his shield as if he was too driven by them to keep from exposing himself. Linfyar was the focus of the emotion. The boy had turned to her, not him; for self-preservation, survival, he'd turned to her because he knew she was the strongest of the three adults and thus most able to protect him from the horrors around him. Wakille had to be as aware of that as she was but he couldn't seem to help himself, however irrational the reaction might seem to this very rational man who knew only too well how to exploit the emotions of others and how best to insure his own would never make him vulnerable. Yet he was and knew it and couldn't hate the boy for doing that to him so he had to hate Aleytys, turn on her the anger, jealousy, hatred stirring in him. She grimaced in the gray darkness, knowing she'd watch him always from now on, never turn her back on him. "Shadith, here."

"Right." Shadith took the boy, settled him in her lap, patted him, soothing his sleepy protests. "What are you going to do?"

"Don't know." Aleytys continued her exploration of the island. Trees, bracken, seaweed, fragments of earth were breaking away in increasing numbers, roots ripping through the softened earth; the whole surface of the island was mushing, starting to slip.

Got to get rid of that water, she told herself yet there was no way she could think of to suck up that disastrous soaking that was continuing as the rain continued to fall. She tried to build a screen that would shunt wind and water away from the island. Each time she tried it, her efforts crumpled before the power of the storm which howled on, ignoring her, indifferent to her needs and her struggles. She thought of it as a beast, a great immensely powerful beast too big to notice her and her puny stabs into its substance.

Everything she tried failed and that failure stirred up emotions she tried to put aside but could not. Failure. Emotions without name, without shape, a raw surge of something like pain, there was surely pain in it, but more than that. Rage, yes, there was rage in it. Frustration. A boiling mess pouring out of the corners and crannies of body and mind. She trembled—no, nothing so gentle as a tremble, she shook with it until her bones threatened to rattle out of her flesh. Her teeth clattered, her breathing was hoarse and uncertain, the storm noise somehow blocked. She saw things in the dark, not her companions, not the faces from the diadem. Kell, his bony face like a handsome skull, his red hair lank and lusterless. He sneered at her. The face twisted, dissolved, reformed. A woman. A face she'd never seen that she could remember. Remember? "Mother," she shrieked. The face she'd never been able to remember even in her dreams. Rage exploded in her, rage more powerful than the storm, rage focused on that face; she wanted to tear it, to burn it, burn it to ash. She was burning, wreathed in fire. She could see nothing but that smiling mocking face, hear nothing but the roar of rage in her ears. She was going to explode, that face, that face. . . . Chimes struck through the noise in her head. They felt familiar, she should know them. Chimes. Wavery light bathed the forms of the others, flickered along the walls of the shelter. She saw their faces. Shadith, eyes wide, mouth open. Wakille, closed in, brooding, eyes fixed on her with a dark calculation in them. The pulses of the fire consumed her, he shuddered, put his hands out, she knew she was striking through his shields and he was burning with her. She opened her mouth to scream but silence came out; she stretched her mouth until her eyes were forced shut by the bunching of her facial muscles, a long terrible silent scream. And always the face, the smiling mocking beautiful face hanging before her, indifferent to her, looking through her.

Harskari came from her retreat, hovered beside the rage

and fought against it, then took hold of it and used it to power
a shunt that turned the winds away from the island, a canted
shield that caught the rain and kept it from the burdened soil.
And somehow—though she powered it, watched what was
happening, Aleytys didn't know how it was happening—the
old one got a suction going that pulled water from the soil
and spat it into the sea, set a force going that sent the grains
of earth locking into each other, tightening up, solidifying.

Aleytys held herself very still and let Harskari use her body
and work with that sure knowledge and skill she could never
stop envying; she let the old one shape the power she provided and with that felt a growing calm in herself that began
to match the growing calm outside. They still ran against a
high sea, salt water crashing over them and trees torn loose
still groaned with the whipsawing of the island as current
fought with wind, but the air around them was quiet and the
island was stabilizing slowly to a steady roll and pitch—and
Harskari had drained away all the rage-heat from Aleytys and
was pulling hard on the power from the symbolic black river
source. Cool and reasoning again, not just feeling, Aleytys
expanded the tap into her powerflow; with the calm gray skill
of an accountant, debit, credit, debit, credit, no magic left in
it, the conduits she controlled blasted wider by that trauma a
moment ago, an eon ago, she supplied all that Haskari needed
from her, on and on, holding the shunt, holding the shield,
doing things she could not have done only a day before.

Until the island emerged from the storm, until the island
was rocking along placidly, climbing the long swells, sliding
down again, a steady rise and fall soothing as a rocking
cradle and the world around them was quiet, serene, now and
then a gentle rustling of leaves overhead, the snorting of the
gyori, hungry and wanting loose—until they were out of the
pounding, she held the shunt, she held the shield, and the
diadem glowed and sang its four-note song into the hush
within the shelter. Harskari sighed finally and went away,
letting shunt and shield collapse, Aleytys sighed and fell back
against the shelter wall, the diadem was gone, the light gone,
the song silent.

She felt burnt-out, gray-ash; she arched her back, rubbed
hard along her spine. Her face ached from that endless silent

scream. She tried to swallow, it was painful, her mouth was dry and stiff. She coughed, her hand covering her mouth, winced with the cough as muscles in her back and arm protested.

Wakille and Shadith were staring at her, Shadith worried, Wakille disturbed and cautious. He was frightened of her now, she sensed that in passing without even trying (it startled her—not the knowledge itself but the ease with which she acquired it). Covered over by the fear there were other things to bother her, greed and a sly calculation focused on her. She didn't like that and didn't bother to hide her dislike as she scowled at him.

Linfyar was awake, his ears fluttering, his pointed small face screwed into a puzzled frown.

Shadith patted his shoulder absently. "For a moment," she said, "I thought you were going to cremate yourself and us with you."

Aleytys slowly unbent her legs and stretched them out in front of her, fitting her feet between Shadith and Wakille. She eased over and began massaging her knees. "A confusion," she said. "I don't want to talk about it." She closed her eyes. "If you want to go outside, it should be safe enough. Turn the gyori loose and see what cleaning up we have to do. I'm beat." She rested her head against the wattle-wall, sighed. "I'll be out in a while.

Shadith watched her a moment, chewing on her lip as she often did when she was worried, then she dumped Linfyar hastily and without ceremony on Wakille and began working at the rope holding the doorflap shut. The water leaking in had swelled the knots and the jerking of the wind had jammed them tight. Shadith broke a thumbnail, cursed, her voice shrill with frustration; she took the pale zel blade she wore at her waist and slashed the ropes apart, shoved the flap aside and scrambled out on hands and knees.

Aleytys heard her shout of exultation and release, heard her start kicking through the storm debris, singing at the top of her powerful young voice. She smiled, feeling the girl's spirit expanding as she threw off the cramps of body and soul knotted into her by confinement in that small crowded shelter, by having to face a sudden and rather ignominious loss of the new life she saw before her; the extent of what she'd endured all the long night and the longer morning could be measured by the violence of that release.

Linfyar was whining and unhappy, roused to wakefulness by Shadith's rough handling, plucking and scratching at the mud that matted his short fur. Wakille was soothing him and shooting uneasy glances at Aleytys.

"Take him outside," she said. "There's a little wind, that's all."

Wakille nodded, said nothing. He shoved the boy through the doorhole and crawled out after him, leaving the flap partially pushed aside. The light coming in the triangular opening illuminated with cruel clarity the sloppy trampled muck and her muddy feet, her soaked and muddy trousers. She rubbed at her temples, leaving streaks of mud on her face, knowing that but not able to raise the energy to care. Her head was throbbing, her eyes were watering, she felt like death warmed over and the thought of moving, made her stomach lurch, but everything in her rebelled at spending a moment more in this hole. She eased onto her knees, crawled slowly, painfully, into the sunlight.

day 39

The morning dawned clear and calm, the sky a radiant blue, the waves still higher than normal but beginning to subside. After breakfast Aleytys left the others working desultorily at the clean-up, cutting away the branches of downed trees, stacking them for firewood, Wakille starting to work on a floor for the shelter, using the hatchet to cut flat sides on some of the larger branches. She climbed to her favorite retreat, the grassy nob on top of the center hill, settled herself on the sun-warmed grass, yawned and stretched, and stared blankly into the blinding blue. "Harskari." She waited. Nothing. "Harskari!"

The amber eyes blinked slowly open. A sense of yawning, then Harskari spoke, her voice drowsy and unwelcoming. "What do you want?"

"I need to talk about what happened."

"We've had this conversation before." The voice dragged a little; the eyes narrowed to yellow slits. "Why go over it again?"

"How could there be so much anger in me and I not know it?"

Harskari said nothing; her eyes continued to gaze beyond Aleytys at something she alone saw. She was waiting. Obviously and irritatingly waiting for Aleytys to talk herself out and let her go.

"I'm frightened," Aleytys said, refusing to let the old one retreat, demanding that she be present to listen if for nothing else. "What if I explode like that and try to kill her. My mother." Her voice faltered, her mouth was suddenly dry.

"What did you expect? What do you want me to say? It's yours, you deal with it. Transform it. Control it. You're not a child, stop acting like one. Surely you understand you must order yourself before you confront your mother? I know you understand you'll have to fight for your place on Vrithian. Whatever you feel about her, Shareem has seen you honed and moulded for that task. You owe her that if nothing else. You know the disciplines that lead to self-knowledge and you've avoided using them, finding a thousand excuses for not disturbing your comfort. You've got no choice now and you've got time. Use it."

Aleytys closed her hands into fists. "Seen me honed? No! She's got nothing to do with what I am now except for the genes she gave me." She pressed her lips hard together, swallowed, closed her eyes, started organizing her breathing to calm herself. She broke off after a moment and started again, broke off and started again, broke off and stared down at shaking hands. "You're right about one thing. I'm in no shape to take on Vrithian."

With something like a silent sniff of disgust, the amber eyes snapped shut and she knew no amount of shouting would get Harskari back again, not soon anyway.

Aleytys gazed out over the bright blue swells that merged indistinguishably with the bright blue sky. The sun was warm on her back. A gentle breeze teased at her hair, ruffled along the curve of her forearm. The sky was empty, the sea was empty. Somewhere below and behind her Linfyar was whis-

tling bits of song which Shadith would take up and vary back
at him. The calm about her mocked her lack of calm.

For the rest of the day and the days that followed, she sat
on her hilltop wrestling with the uglier aspects of her nature,
with hatred and resentment and self-loathing. With need and
fear and anger. Memories of love offered and rejected, the
times when she was hurting and helpless, the times when the
other children taunted her about her mother, what they called
her mother, what they called her, having to face the truth of
some of what they said, that her mother had left her, abandoned her. Carrying Sharl curled in the curve of her arm.
Sharl, nursing with such determined energy. Sharl, whom she
loved with all the agony of her own need for love. Her need
for love.

She hugged her arms across her breasts and stared unseeing
at a sky newly streaked with red, the day gone without her
noting it. Need for love, fear of rejection. What if she looks
at me like Kell did? Despises me? Anger. Why not come for
me once she made her way home? She rubbed at her forehead,
remembering Grey and how he kept her from exploding in a
frenzy of destruction when she came back from seeing her
son, when Vajd denied her and forced her to leave the child
behind.

Yet when she looked more deeply into herself, into what
she was then, she realized suddenly that Grey was able to
stop her only because, in spite of her very real pain, there
was more than a little relief behind the grief. Ambivalent to
the end, she thought. I ached for him and I knew he'd be a
drag on me. She blinked at the brilliant display thrown up by
the setting sun, drew in a long breath and held it until her
head roared then let it out slowly. "I am Shareem," she said.
"She's me. The same. Ay-Madar. The same." She rubbed
hard down her face. "I knew it, that was part of the rage. As
angry at myself as I was at her."

day 42

As the sky darkened, Shadith climbed the hill with a pot of
fish stew in one hand, a pot of cha dangling from the other,
both held carefully away from her thighs. She set them on the

grass by Aleytys and stood gazing down at her. "You looking better."

Aleytys moved her shoulders, twisted about on her buttocks.
"I've been spring-cleaning my head. Not much fun, but I
think I've about reached bottom."

"Just as well. Wakille's starting to pet me a bit much, not
long till he wants to work on my head, I'm afraid. Nothing I
can't handle so far, but it's irritating. I've had to slap him
down some. I think he'd behave himself better if you were
around. You and Harskari, you near scared him honest when
you fixed the storm."

Aleytys stretched, straightened out her legs, worked her
knees. "In the morning I'll have a talk with him. Unless it's
urgent."

"He just needs reminding." Shadith blushed, startling
Aleytys. "This body's virgin," she said. "Be damned if I'm
gonna be forced by the first horny bastard who gets an urge."
She looked fierce, then laughed. "But I mean it."

"Bring your blankets up here if you want. You won't
disturb me if you don't talk."

"Thanks, I think I'll do that."

Aleytys watched her run down the slope and into the trees,
felt a sudden burst of jealousy that she ridiculed at first then
forced herself to face. No more hiding. Can't afford it. When
we get back to Wolff, she'll be going off with Swartheld. My
love. My other love. Her mouth worked. A problem resolved
without any act of mine. She closed her eyes, stretched, laced
her fingers at the back of her head. I want them both. No way
I can keep them both without hurting too many people. What
about me? Swartheld and Shadith. It hurts. Madar, it hurts.
Come to terms with it, Lee. Maybe it won't happen. Maybe
they've known each other too well too long. If it happens, it
happens. Make up your mind, Lee, face it. You are not going
to leave Grey and go off with Swartheld. You know it.
Swartheld knows it. Grey's probably the only one not sure of
it. Time. It'll pass and we'll drift away from each other,
Swartheld, Shadith, Harskari and me. We've been too close
too long and need some distance now. Madar grant we don't
lose each other entirely. It could happen. I don't want it to

happen. I need them, all of them. Shadith and Swartheld.
And Harskari when she gets out.

She moved restlessly on the grass. There was that familiar
ache in her loins, her nipples were tender, her breasts swollen.
This too, dammit. Her hands moved restlessly over her thighs,
her breasts, combed through the hair she'd let hang free about
her face. She folded her arms again, hugged them tight
against her. Shadith, damn you, she thought, her mouth
twitching into a wry half-smile. Talking about horny bastards.
You're no help, girl. She sighed, picked up the spoon and
began on the fish stew.

day 43

She stirred, looked around. Shadith lay close by, wrapped
in her blanket and sleeping heavily as if she hadn't been
getting enough rest. Why did I let him leech onto us? He'd
have followed anyway, but I didn't have to let him get close.
I'll skin him if he bothers her anymore. She got to her feet.
The moon was long set and the night was so quiet each breath
was like a shout. She was tired, very tired, but there was a
final slough she had to drain, the self-loathing that lay beneath the worst of her fears. Say the words and pull their
sting. She sank down onto the grass, ran her hands back and
forth along her thighs, worked her mouth, this was the worst
of all the things she'd dug for and she was very reluctant to
begin.

"I am a freak," she whispered. Something to frighten
babies with. Thing. Thing. That's how I see myself. Ugly.
Nothing about me anyone could like let alone love. A grotesque.
I buy people with my skills and my power but I hide from
them. If they really knew me, they'd despise me, hate me,
kick me away from them. So I play my tricks. Clown. Puppy
wagging her tail, begging to be noticed just a little, whining.
If I face Shareem, she'll see all this. Kell saw it. Mud. She'll
turn her back on the thing she birthed.

Said like that, brought into the light instead of festering
unspoken, she saw the distortion in that view of herself, and
seeing it found the pain greatly diminished. Against all the

rejections of her past—her cousins and half-siblings, her lovers, her son—put against those was her pleasure and pride in what she'd accomplished the past few years, a sense that she was doing things worth doing and doing them well. Roots put down into Wolff, her ship, house, horses, the job. Then there was Grey. Just Grey, loving her, needing her, that was real, it had to be. And Shadith. She looked down at the girl, sleeping curled up on her side, a small fist pressed against her mouth, felt a surge of affection for her. And Harskari, when she settled down again. And Head, Canyli Heldeen. A real friend. A woman who demanded respect, who gave respect where it was earned, gave herself fully and freely to her friends, once her friendship was earned. And Swartheld, old bear, old dear.

She stared up into the star clusters that lit the ocean and the island with a cold white light, twisted her torso hard to the right, then hard left to get some life into her spine. It felt like a solid spike of chalk and about as fragile. Off to her right there was a touch of faint pink near the horizon. Sun coming up, she thought. What day? She counted on her fingers. Forty-three. Over a third of the way, if the storm hadn't blown them too far behind. She swung around so she was sitting with her back to the sleeping Shadith, facing the dawn, very weary but finally content. There were questions still to be answered, but that could wait now. She yawned, snapped her blanket out, rolled up in it and went to sleep.

The days rocked tranquilly on, hot, sticky, monotonous, one fading into the next, the same faces, the same food, the same trees and grass and soil. To avoid bickering and bitter feuds, Aleytys, Shadith, Wakille and Linfyar took to separating after meals and keeping as far apart as they could in the limited area of the island. They marked out small territories and snarled at anyone who set foot on them without being invited. Linfyar developed a habit of malicious tricks that gave vent to the resentment once suppressed beneath his charm; he stopped being a puppy and became a pest. He got very good at directing his whistles so they turned into something like weapons, knocking birds out of the sky, killing mouselets whenever he felt like it. He stayed away from Aleytys, except

for a whistle now and then that went through and through her
until her head felt like her brain was shaking itself to pieces,
usually after she'd punished him for some thoughtless or
hurtful bit of mischief.

One day he drove the gyori into frantic flight, kicking and
squealing, the length of the island and almost into the sea
before Aleytys got close enough to singe his fur and soothe
the frantic beasts. She chased him through the trees until she
cornered him, then turned him over her knee and gave him a
few hearty whacks on the buttocks to reinforce the scold she
planned to give him. She set him on his feet, scowled at him.
"Don't move, imp. Now tell me a gyr hurt you, bit you
maybe, stepped on your foot?"

Linfyar hung his head and looked miserable.

"Makes you feel big, does it? Strong? Important? That you
can hurt them and not get hurt yourself? That's fun, right?
Now, let me tell you something, Linfyar. I'm going to make
sure every time you hurt something, you feel exactly what it
feels. Uh-huh. That's not so much fun, is it. You understand
what I'm talking about?"

He sniveled pitifully, his small body slumped, his ears
rolled shut and folded tight against his skull. After a short
while, he nodded.

Aleytys eyed him skeptically. "Well, we'll see. Now,
imp, go and get some dried weed for the gyori and sing them
calmer. They're going to be your responsibility from now on.
Brush them, keep the burrs out of their coats, make them
forget what you've been doing to them, make them like
you." She frowned at the huddled small figure. "It'll be
something to keep you out of mischief, maybe teach you . . .
never mind. Scoot, imp. You've got work to do."

Shadith retreated into a solitary brood, surfacing for meals,
complaining about having nothing to write on, disappearing
back into the trees and going on with whatever she did to pass
the time.

Wakille slept a lot.

Aleytys spent hours running, exercising until her body
trembled with weariness, then sat sunk in meditation, going
over the events of her life, beginning to find a symmetry in
them. The trek across Ibex was a kind of recapitulation of the

trek across Jaydugar. This slow and seemingly tranquil progress across a water ocean was very like her long slow trek across the ocean of grass, the Great Green, with the medwey herd. *Sweating, hot, dusty, heavily pregnant, she walked beside the animals and rejoiced in the smooth sliding of her muscles and the strength flowing in her body. Underfoot the springy grass pressed up against the thinning leather of her moccasins, living grass pressing up from the source of life, the flesh and bones of the world.* On the water ocean she was older and presumably wiser, separated by too much knowledge and experience from such elemental sources of strength and comfort. A loss, one she faintly mourned. Other similarities. Tarnsian, holding her captive until she escaped and finally killed him. Centai zel holding her until she escaped and finally killed—or helped kill—Juli. The downed Romanchi trader, a spot of high-tech on a low tech world. Sil Evareen—a high-tech city that might or might not exist on this world that had regressed to the stone age. The same and not the same, echoes not identities, but there to look at, there to wonder at when there was nothing else to do.

day 104

About two hours after dawn the island ground to a jarring halt. Ignoring the excited exclamations from the others, Aleytys ran for the middle hill, the highest point on the island, but when she reached the summit, she saw nothing on either side but water rolling slowly, heavily north, breaking now and then into foam as the strengthening south wind blew the tops off the waves. No sign of land, not even the deadly swamps. The island rocked and twitched under her, battling against the hold of the bottom.

"Too far out. Ever figure how much water we draw?"

Aleytys turned. Shadith stood beside and slightly behind her, hands pressed flat against her head, keeping the wind-whipped curls from stinging into mouth and eyes. Her chocolate eyes were over-bright. There was a flush darkening her tanned cheeks. "I loathe this damn island," Shadith said suddenly. "And this worn-out, useless world. All this. . . ."

She flung out a hand with an excess of drama and awkwardness that was oddly unlike her, glared at the heaving water rolling for the horizon, then turned and walked down the hill, a stiff-legged stalk that seemed to spurn the ground under her feet.

day 105

Morning brought high tide and a wild heaving thunderstorm that kicked the island loose and shoved it farther along the coast. Rain refilled the holding ponds and washed away a lot of friction between the four of them. They were all nervous, irritable, with a floating sense of expectation that made settling to any task close to impossible.

Aleytys boiled water, pot by slow pot, and poured it into the fishskin tub, washed herself, her hair and her underclothing, then stood guard while Shadith did the same. Later, she sat on the hilltop, her long wet hair spread out to catch the sun, not-thinking as fiercely as she could, concentrating instead on the feel of the sun on her body, the play of the warm wind in her hair. At the moment she didn't care what was happening with Shadith or Linfyar (though she could hear them yelling at each other down below) or what Wakille was up to. She forced her wandering attention back to the caress of wind and sun, to the briny tang of air fresh and clean from blowing over the water instead of the land. Flies began buzzing about her, crawled in the sweat-drippings that ran down her back and arms and face, their tickling feet a nuisance that kept her in a constant twitch until she wound up the fire in her hand and used a tiny blade of fire to zap the pests. They sizzled when she got them, charred fly corpses falling like rain to the grass about her, the necessity turning quickly into a game of sorts. She went after the flies with the concentration she'd give a battle for her life. She got two at once and laughed with triumph. But the supply of flies finally ran out, there was a limited number of them riding from the land on the legs of seabirds.

She got to her feet and stood gazing north. No closer to land even now. Esgard said we should bump several times. I don't know. I'd hate to ride this island into eternity. She hunted through her clothes, found her comb and began running it through the long hair, teasing at the few knots, taking a minor pleasure in the rake of the comb's teeth across her scalp. When she finished, she held up the translucent underthings, let the wind blow through them. Dry and warm and clean. She dressed, left the sun-caressed hilltop and went down the easy slope to the camp, her bare feet taking pleasure in the feel of the grass under them, not spurning it as Shadith's feet had done.

day 109

The island nudged a sandbar, ground to a momentary halt, broke free, shuddered on for a short time, bounced off another sandbar, rocked ponderously onward, a blind mole bumbling toward something it didn't know what. Back on her hilltop, waiting for some clue about what she should do, she felt like screaming with frustration. The island had slowed until it was hardly moving, its momentum stolen by the bottom and the tides, its mass too great to be swept up to speed by the current, however powerful it was.

The sky burned from blue to a curious dirty copper that in turn altered the ocean's tint, turning its blue to a muddy green. The odd-colored water went heavy and oily, the air turned heavy and hotter than before with a burnt smell/taste. The wind dropped until the air seemed to hug the contours of the island without moving. The island slid heavily on with no sign of faltering or even hesitation. Sounds were muted and few. Aleytys stood on the hill summit, turning round and round, probing out over the sea, searching blindly for some sort of explanation. Her hair crackled with electricity.

Linfyar came rushing up the slope, his ears pinned tight against his skull. His lips pursed now and then for one of his guide whistles.

He stumbled to an awkward stop beside her, panting and excited. "Shadith," he called, jumping from foot to foot, clinging to the hem of Aleytys's tunic. "Shadith, she say git everything packed, git the gyori saddled. She say something coming. She say you better come down and talk to her. She say hurry, hurry, she got one powerful damn itch.''

Down on the flat, the air was even more oppressive. Leaves hung without a shiver. She saw two gyori trotting through the clearing, sluggishly avoiding Shadith's lunges, ignoring the cursing Wakille. Aleytys stood staring, then shut her mouth. She marched into the clearing and began gathering the thousand bits of gear tucked into odd corners of the shelter and the clearing. Frantic was the word for Shadith. Chasing those beasts. When all she had to do was stand in the clearing and summon them. Proof of the intensity and awfulness of the premonition. Now what?

A gyr came trotting past her. Aleytys stopped it with a snap of her fingers that sent gold fire sizzling before its dainty black nose. Shadith broke panting from the trees, gaped at the gyr standing still, head down, eyes rolling, saliva dripping from its mouth. She turned wide terrified eyes on Aleytys, white showing stark against the chocolate, sweat sitting in droplets on her burnt-gold skin.

"Shadith." Aleytys spoke as calmly as she could. "Hawk-rider," she said and smiled, the word a gentle reminder. "Stand and call them. That way you won't wear them out and yourself with them."

Shadith stood frozen. Then seemed to collapse all over from stone to limber resilent flesh. She grinned, tossed her head, her curls bounding like springs suddenly unleashed.

"Yes mama," she said, then giggled and sauntered out of the shadow into the odd light in the little clearing. The light seemed to collapse on her, around her, haloing her head, her limbs, moving when she moved, power danced around her unnoticed as she sank with childish, awkward grace into a heap of arms and legs on the grass, the glow moving with her, only just a fraction of a second later, an eerie afterimage. Wondering if what she saw was there or only in her mind, Aleytys got a rope and tethered the gyr to a tree, tethered each of the other four as Shadith called them in. Then she went to sit in front of the girl.

"What's coming?" she asked.

The fear returned momentarily to the chocolate eyes, sweat oozed again from the smooth dark forehead, for a moment of panic the body was stone again, then a sigh escaped from her. "Tsunami," she said. "Tidal wave. There was an explosion of some kind south of here. Volcano, I think. I get the feel of intense heat, immense violence, suddenly focused then released. Heat and violence like you wouldn't believe, like half the world blown away, ka-boom. I don't think it's quite that bad, maybe almost. Spewed out dust and steam. Wind brought the dust north. That's why the sky's that color. Tsunami coming at us, driven by that. Surge of water out there. Wall of water a dozen meters high when it hits the shallows." She shivered. "When it hits, it will drive us into the shallows and roar over us, either capsizing the island or tearing off everything above ground and battering the rest to bits against the bottom."

"How long? Both senses, Shadi. How much time do we have before the wave hits, how broad is the wave front? And could we possibly outdistance it?"

Shadith's face took on a distant, listening look, then it twisted into a grimace of frustration. "I don't know." She pounded with slow heavy anger on her thighs. "I don't know. It's huge. It crushes me when I think about it. I can't breathe when I think about it. I feel like I'm shut in a room with no door and the ceiling is moving down to crush me and the walls are moving in to crush me." She shuddered. "Huge and unstoppable and unstopping. It's far enough off yet, I can still bear the pressure, but it's fast. It's coming fast." She looked up at the sun. "I think . . . I think it comes with the dark. We got to be off this hunk of garbage by then. I suppose you might survive even this, Lee, but the rest of us, we won't. Not if we stay here."

Shading her eyes with her hand, Aleytys looked up, chewed on her lower lip. "Six hours till dark. Around that." She rubbed at her eyes. "And we have to get off soon as possible so we can get some way inland. Right. You hunt up Wakille and set him and Linfyar to packing the gyori. Keep the packs light, we're going to have to move fast and through difficult going. Essentials only, but I don't need to tell you that." She got to her feet. "I'll hunt me some eyes and take a look along the coast, see if I can spot a place to land."

*   *   *

Barrier islands like dunes pushed up by the sea, long and
narrow with pale green saw-edged grasses bent in low arcs,
weighed down by the clinging salt crystals that turned the
pale green almost white. Patches of scraggly brush. And
birds. Thousands of birds large and small, hundreds of species existing in noisy comity. Beyond the islands, beyond a
half-kilometer more of sea, winding fingers of salt water
thrust bluely into the dark thick marsh growth. More birds
and a multitude of life in the salt swamp, healthy vigorous
life, not so deadly as Esgard had suggested, but bad enough.
The swamp was stinking, humid, full of death, full of life
preying on life, but the aura of disease and decay and distortion that hung over the blights and the sloughs of the Plain
was pleasantly absent here. As the mottled gray and white
seabird swooped low over the tree tops, she frowned at what
she saw. No way they could make any time going through
that mess. She sent the bird winging west along the coast,
hoping to find better footing. For about a half hour the bird
flew on following the coast, then Aleytys caught a glimpse of
something a little north of west and some kilometers inland
from the sea—dark towers, several of them, with sharply
squared corners.

The tree-swamp turned to grass-marsh with patches of still,
scummy water, teeming with things that slithered in and out
of sight in the flicker of the bird's eye, a web of life as busy
and deadly as that among the trees.

In the center of a vast ruined city stood rows of tall
buildings, windows in bands about their spare unadorned
sides. For a moment they seemed intact, then the bird was in
among them and the illusion evaporated. They were shells. A
number of the windows gaped empty, birds flying in and out
of them, some had fragments only of their glass, the shards
melting like sugar under the wear of the ages, more than she
expected had their glass intact, glaring out over the waste
about them like blind black glittering eyes. The veneer attached to the rough base was crumbling and falling away;
there were fragments of it cradled in the leaf clusters of the
thick vines that crawled up the sides of the great structures,
other bits falling into the still, black water that filled the
spaces between the towers. Here and there slabs of veneer not

quite broken away flapped in the wind, creaked and crackled until they too were ready to fall. Down near the water, near the base of those towers, the walls were smeared with oozing mosses and slime molds, higher up they were pocked with layered fungi and scabby lichens. Smaller structures, more broken and littered and overgrown than the towers, rayed out from them in serial clusters that still held a battered memory of their ancient organization. The city spread for kilometers in all directions, even on the far side of the river, crossed and recrossed by elevated roadways that were cracked and littered with the debris of the ages since they were last used, but many of them seemed far more intact than the best of the buildings, ready—after a little sweeping—for traffic to use them again. Rather like the ancient bridges on the other continent.

She sent the bird turning and turning over the city, looking for other forms of life, looking for some remnant however slight of the folk that had once lived in that city, or some life form large enough to threaten them when they passed through it, but saw nothing more than shadows that vanished as soon as the bird turned toward them. Shadows in her imagination perhaps, born of the lingering horror she felt whenever she thought about what the people of this world had done to themselves.

The ruins sat like a patch of rot in the bend of a river that flowed south in broad lazy sweeps, a huge river that looked as if it drained most of the continent. One of the raised roadways that crossed the city went along the river, a causeway now, raised on thick pillars that lifted it less than a double handspan above the flickering needle points of the salt-grass. In places it was overgrown with weed and lichen and tangles of bramble vines, littered with bones and shells and dead leaves and mud and rotting carcasses, shapeless in decay. Aleytys began to breathe a bit easier as the bird flew south along the river. If it just went all the way to the coast, that causeway was going to save them.

Then the bird was swooping out over the river's broad mouth, the silted fresh water creating a wide fan of pale green in the darker green of the ocean. She sent the bird spiraling higher until she could see the island, a dark spot on the dingy

sea, a speck against the copper sky, lumbering with ponder-
ous inevitability in a wide curve as the current got set to
swoop along the delta and pass out beyond the countering
current from the river mouth. She tried to estimate the distance the island would have to travel before it got within
reaching distance of the causeway, but only got confused.
She turned the bird loose and snapped back into herself.

The day hurried on. Late in the afternoon the island lodged
for the third time against a sandbar. The wind blew relent-
lessly out of the south, too loud to speak over. Great clouds
of birds rode the air over them as the island shuddered to
what might be its final halt. The final halt certainly for the
four of them.

   Standing on the springy roots at the island's nose, Aleytys
watched the water retreating past her, as if the onrolling
tsunami was sucking it up to add to its substance. It's only a
normal low tide, she told herself, but she didn't believe it.
The water was retreating but the shore was still out of sight,
too far away for her to see anything but discolored water.

   She stripped off her outer clothing, rolled the boots inside
pants and tunic and tied them to her saddlepad. Then she
turned to the others. Shadith in her zel leathers and loincloth,
the leggings rolled around sandals and tucked away in saddle
bags, her chocolate eyes shining as they had not for too many
days, eyes focused not on Aleytys but beyond her on the
heaving water. Wakille the uncertain, grown more uncertain
and more certainly dangerous in the long silent days just past.
He made her uneasy and she couldn't hide that from him.
There was something stranger about him than she'd seen
before, as if the slow wearing away of the days had taken off
one by one the layers of concealment he'd plastered about
himself, decade by decade of his wandering ill-regulated life;
as urbanity and civilized habit thinned away something was
starting to peer out of his eyes, something that frightened her.
She looked quickly away. Linfyar was perched on Juli's
mount, ears glowing pink and translucent, stretched to their
utmost, moving restlessly about, tasting all the sounds; he was
as excited as Shadith, at the same time afraid of the empty
unknowns ahead of him, tired of this island and reluctant to

leave it. He was smiling again, about to burst into chatter given the slightest encouragement, back to working his charm to keep his place with them. Aleytys sighed, pulled her hand across her face. "It shallows fast," she yelled, raising her voice over the whine of the wind. "First kilometer or so we'll have to swim. Wakille, you and Linfyar, if you have trouble with your mounts, yell for Shadith or me. Linfy, you hear me, don't wait till you're really in trouble to yell for help. Tide's going out, that'll be against us, but the gyori are strong enough to fight that. Keep close as you can. Soon's we hit the causeway, we don't stop for anything, head inland top speed we can make, each of us make top speed he can and let the others take care of themselves. I'm not going to waste breath talking later. Any questions?" She looked from face to face, sucked in a long breath, exploded it out. "Right. Let's do it." She swung around, slapped her gyr on the rump and followed him into the water.

The swells were long and heavy, just too close together for a whole number of completed strokes; the water dropped beneath her in mid-stroke and she found herself kicking head-on into the rising wave ahead of her. The waves kept plucking at her, burying her with their tops as they turned over on her. Blasted world, she thought. Damn all oceans. Why haven't I ever learned how to swim in ocean waves?

Then the gyr was plunging past her, his feet gaining purchase on the swiftly shallowing bottom. She caught hold of the saddle pad and let him pull her along until he splashed up onto one of the long skinny barrier islands. She looked over her shoulder to see the others close behind her, caught the gyr's rein and began trotting along the length of the island. There was a deep channel between this island and the next; the tide was pulling more strongly now and she had to fight the sucking that threatened to take her back out, but she thrashed her way onto the sand and kept on trotting.

She kept looking out to sea, she couldn't help it, not knowing what she should expect to see, seeing nothing but the disturbed water and the darkening copper sky, the bloody stain from the setting sun moving out and out from the west. Island to island she ran, fighting across the narrow channels between them, the others behind her, grimly following. Until

the delta curved out before her, flat and pale, a wide stretch
of sand. She set the gyr at the shallow water and ran beside
him, the water never coming above her waist. When she
reached the shore, she stopped the gyr, swung onto the saddle
pad, drew her legs up and raised herself until she stood
balanced on the beast's back. The salt-grass swamp stretched
out before her in unbroken pale green, bending gracefully
before the huffing south wind, the sky was filled with flocks
of birds that swirled thickly up, darted in dark angry zags
across the blue, swooping down to settle momentarily, only
to flare up again, a visible expression of the uneasiness that
worked in her, an uneasiness that grew out of the world's
waiting for the thing coming, the wave that hung over them
all.

Finally she saw a long flat streak—the causeway railing—
and breathed a sigh of relief. She dropped back to the
saddlepad, glanced over her shoulder, her eyes moving quickly
from face to face, then she swung about again, kicked the gyr
into an easy lope. The wind was worse, hammering inland; it
smelled of heat and melting copper, a poisonous, unpleasant
stink laid over the briny fishy smell of the shore. The gyr's
hooves cut into the wet hard-packed sand and kicked up
heavy spurts.

At one time the shore must have poked much farther out
into the ocean, or there was an island out somewhere beyond
the mouth of the river; there had to be some reason for
building the causeway, but that reason was gone now, the
causeway broke off a few meters into the water, the concrete
side rails broken, the reinforcing rods twisted and rusted
away to fragile ghosts that the wind was already tearing loose
and the wave to come would finish.

She kicked the reluctant gyr into the turbulent water and
circled round the broken railing, the gyr putting his split
hooves down with exaggerated care, shaking his head, his
moans lost in the shock of the wind and the crashing of the
water. He jerked his head about, spray driven into his face,
snorted his disgust.

When they'd turned the end of the causeway, she clucked
to him; he tensed, settled low, then leaped, the powerful hind
legs uncoiling to drive him up onto the flaking concrete with

rags of old black paving still clinging to it. Momentum and the wind carried him several strides after he landed. She heard Shadith's whoop and kept him moving to make more room for her, held him to a stiff-legged walk though he fought her and wanted to run. She looked over her shoulder. Shadith and Linfyar, side by side, popped up onto the pavement and rode toward her. As soon as they were a few steps in, Wakille came up, the pack gyr following without need for guidance. She looked beyond him. There was a low dark line on the horizon and a near subsonic rumble underlying the scream of wind, the crash and groan of the water. Shivering, she let the gyr out until he was moving in a reaching lope, hoping she wasn't overestimating his strength.

The light was slowly dying from a sky turned a muddy sorrel in the west, a bloody purple overhead. The murky uncertain light made judgment of the surface a haphazard thing of guesses and hopes. She rode as lightly as she could, balancing her weight to make it easier for the gyr. He was tiring. She was the heaviest of them all and when she looked back after a few moments, she could see the other gyori being held in to keep them behind her. She scowled, waved her arm. No use trying to shout, no voice could break through that roar. *Come on*, she thought at them, *go by, fools, don't wait*. She waved again, putting more energy and urgency in the sweep of her arm, pulled her gyr out of the lope into a jolting trot, waved again, relaxed a little when Wakille and Linfyar went past, the packer following nose to tail. Shadith rode stride for stride with Aleytys, shaped slow words with her lips and body. —Why? What are you doing?—

Aleytys leaned down, stroked her hand over the laboring shoulder of her weary gyr, straightened and mouthed some words to Shadith.—He's tiring.— She shaped the words slowly, carefully, saw Shadith frown. —I can try fixing that, but you go ahead.— Shadith glanced over her shoulder, shuddered, then looked despair at Aleytys. —Go.— Aleytys stabbed her hand urgently toward the other riders. Finally, shaking her head, Shadith loosed the rein a bit and took off after them.

Aleytys looked back, the dark line was thicker and blacker. She urged the groaning beast faster, *reached* and began to feed energy into him, washing away the poisons of fatigue, replenishing the energy he'd expended, feeding the power carefully; she could start him burning away muscle tissue and tear him apart with excess force if she didn't keep the inflow balanced. She focused all her will on him, got into the rhythm of the feed and relaxed a little, then she couldn't keep from looking over her shoulder. The line was huge and black and getting higher and coming faster and faster. She could see it moving now, coming like a great broad ram, she couldn't even see the sides, it filled the horizon on both sides of her. "Ay-madar," she gasped. She wrenched her eyes from the wave and turned herself to look ahead at the causeway.

The other riders were dark fuzzy shapes in the sunset murk. She thought she saw Shadith looking back at her. In case it was so, she waved a hand at her. Or maybe Shadith was looking at the wave.

On and on. Nightmare. They were forced to go slower as the sun sank below the horizon. The gloom made footing treacherous, along with slippery moss, broken paving, the gaps here and there, the patches of stinging brambles, the razor-edged shells. Nightmare. Fleeing at a walk, sandpaper on the nerves. On and on. Galloping over the few patches that the starblaze showed comparatively free of traps, walking again, forcing the reluctant beasts through thick patches of bramble, on and on, until the whole world seemed to shake and the noise was a thousand hammers beating on them, a noise so pervasive it was around them as solid as the air slamming against them. Letting the gyr run on his own, she looked back.

The great wall was broken, filled with glassy green-gray spaces interrupted with veins of foam, broken against the land, broken into huge boulder-sized fragments, but coming on, sweeping on in its broken might, unstoppable and terrible. Their flight was hopeless, no way were they going to outrun the monster, but they kept riding, every meter gained a meter more of hope.

On and on, drowning in noise, gyori staggering with weariness and the uncertain footing, then the water was at their heels about to crash into them.

And Harskari was out, the diadem was shrieking with the drain of power and Harskari was holding them all safe in a bubble of something. And the shell she wove about them, a flickering glimmering gold sphere, that sphere rode the turbulent water. On and on, slowing gradually as the water finally began to slow and fall away. And the slide back began, faster and faster the water went back to the sea bottom, the elaborate dance of the tsunami slowing and slowing, falling away.

With a last burst of power, Harskari shifted the sphere back over the causeway, then it popped! and Harskari was blown out like a candle flame and Aleytys was shivering convulsively with a weakness that left her with no grip in her arms or legs, with a mind that flittered about like the bits of light from a glitter ball turning in some cheap and gawdy palace of the dance. Her mount stumbled as the bubble dropped him into the foot or more of water still on the causeway. With neither mind nor strength enough to cling, she let the lurch dislodge her. She was falling. Falling into darkness. She didn't hear the splash as she splatted face down into the filthy water. She didn't feel the cold stinging brine that closed over her.

VII

ON THE ROAD TO SIL EVAREEN— AT LAST

1

Shadith had no time to catch her breath. When the bubble collapsed; dumping them into the last weak surge of the tsunami, she was too busy holding onto screaming gyori threatening to bolt in blind panic, maybe taking them off the causeway into the river, drowning them all. Dimly she heard Wakille cursing as he jerked at the rein of his packer, in a panic himself at the thought of losing everything that might help them survive the hardships ahead, heard him muttering resentfully about being stripped of his possessions, cursing Aleytys, blaming her for his losses, never himself, never his decision to tag along when he wasn't wanted; she seethed with resentment as she fought to hold onto six slippery rebelling minds. Controlling all six was beyond her, but she rotated her hold rapidly from one to the other, clamping them in place long enough for the panic to run down. They were placid, amiable creatures in ordinary circumstances and as the circumstances around them became more ordinary, they quieted rapidly.

She was too busy to see Aleytys fall, but when she heard a double splash she looked around. Linfyar had dumped himself off his mount and was squatting in the water holding Aleytys's head up against his shoulder. He couldn't turn her over, he hadn't strength enough for that, but his hands were locked in her hair and he was holding her head out of the water. Shadith finished with the gyori, then slid down and splashed over to him, scowling, wondering why Wakille hadn't done anything to save Aleytys; he had to know how dependent they all were on her strength and her talents; besides, she'd saved his life back there when the outcasts had staked him out to drown, now he was letting her drown. Gratitude, she fumed, that's all it's worth. He sat on his gyr, watching with a detached faint interest that made her want to kick him. "What do you think you're doing?" she yelled at him, then knelt beside Linfyar and pressed trembling fingers beneath the clean line of Aleytys's jaw, let out the breath she hadn't known she was holding when she felt the strong steady throb. She smiled at Linfyar, never mind he couldn't see it, knew the smile was in her voice when she spoke. "Good job, Linfy. She owes you her life." She felt the pleasure and pride in his laugh, enjoyed for a moment her own relief, then looked ruefully at the long slim body clad still in the translucent—now transparent—undershirt and pants. Slim but too heavy for her and Linfyar to get back on the gyr. She eased the body over, brushed the sodden red hair off the face. It had gone slack, the mouth hung open, the skin had lost its golden velour look and even in this darkness had a chalky pallor that frightened her.

She looked around. Wakille sat watching them, his face lost in the murk except for an occasional gleam of eye-white. "What are you doing? Get over here and help us, trader."

He sat without moving for what seemed to Shadith an eternity, then swung stiffly down and splashed through the receding water, stopped behind her. "Is she dead?"

"Fool! Would I bother if she was." Relief that she wasn't made Shadith's voice louder and harsher than she intended. "Help us get her on that gyr. Belly down, I suppose it'll have to be. Well?"

"You take her legs, leave me the head and shoulders," he said amiably enough.

Together they fought the limp awkward burden up and over the saddlepad. Shadith frowned. Aleytys looked both uncomfortable and precarious hanging that way. It couldn't be good for her. But when Wakille came with a length of rope to tie

her hands and feet, she rejected that with considerable passion.
He shrugged and went to his gyr, mounted with some
difficulty—they were all close to the limits of their strength—
and waited, his body shouting his refusal to take any responsibility for this expedition. It said *if I weren't too tired right
now, I'd abandon the lot of you to your probably miserable
fate*. Shadith glared at his back then calmed down. You're
imagining things, she told herself.

Linfyar stood beside her, shivering, his soft fur clumped
and matted by the damp. ''Can you ride by yourself, Linfy,
or do you want to come up with me?''

Hesitantly Linfyar held out his hand. The thin trembling
fingers were hot and frail against Shadith's palm. She touched
his face. Fever, she thought, another thing on my head.
Resenting all the pulls that demanded she take responsibility
for them, resenting Aleytys for being unconscious when she
was needed, resenting Wakille for making problems he had
no business making, she swung Linfyar up onto her gyr,
mounted behind him. She saw Wakille gazing at her, his face
a pale round in the dark. The buzz of the insects was loud and
constant, clouds of them hovered about the gyori and the
riders, settled in every opening, crawled on every available
surface. It was almost too much. But there was no one else,
so she gritted her teeth, straightened her back and looked
around. The dust cloud from the distant eruption dimmed and
reddened the starlight, the moon wasn't up yet, so there was
little she could see. The water was still receding, running out
between the holes of the railing. Snakes, she thought, sure to
be snakes. God knows what else is crawling around up here.
''Wakille.''

He said nothing. She felt him resisting her, paying her
back for times on the island when she'd told him to keep his
hands to himself, for the time he caught her bathing and she
had to knee her way free of him, for the time she'd lost her
temper and told Aleytys about his pestering and what happened to him then. She held back the words that waited to
snap off her tongue. Right now she needed him, no matter
how intensely she resented that need.

''Ride point,'' she said, ordering him, not asking him
because she knew he'd take pleasure in denying her even if it

hurt him too. "Ware snakes and other jokers. And keep us clear of traps."

For a moment she thought he was going to refuse after all. "How far?" he said finally.

"Till you find a place we can camp without getting eaten alive or overgrown with fungus. How the hell do I know how far?"

"What about her?"

"Either she wakes or she doesn't. The camp's the thing. We got no choice, trader. No place for us round here." She waved with irritation at the bugs swarming about her head. "Let's get out of this, huh?"

Wakille swung around, started his gyr forward at a walk.

On and on, slowly and painfully, Wakille warning them when there were problems ahead, sweeping snakes and other crawlers out of their path with Aleytys's metal-shod staff. He'd produced that from somewhere, startling Shadith who thought they'd left it on the island as excess weight. The moon came up after an hour of fumbling through darkness thick enough to cut and helped a little to light the way, a full moon, bloody with the dust across its face.

The city ruin was a blur ahead of them, outlines gradually sharpening until the towers loomed dark and eerie above them. The causeway began to slant upward. The gyr Shadith rode groaned and stumbled and stood with its head hanging. She sighed and slid from the saddlepad, feeling not much better off herself. She hesitated, then patted Linfyar's thigh and told him to stay on. Ahead, Wakille dismounted also and started leading his gyr.

They went up slowly, clumsily, the gyori reluctant but still moving, inch by inch they went up that long grade that was only one in eight but in their present condition almost too much for them. Broken buildings were scabs on the left of the road and on the right of the road and the stench was strangling. Shadith could hear small indeterminate sounds, creaking noises, heavy splashes as they curved deeper and deeper into the city and the towers began interfering with the sweep of the wind. The gyori shuffled on, Shadith shuffled on, tense and aware that even a ghost would be too much for her to contend with now. A shred of ectoplasm—her lips twitched into a grimace that tried to be a smile—even a flick of nothing like that would knock her flat.

On and on, one hour crawled past, then another as they finally crawled out past the dead towers of the dead city's center and into the ruins of small houses and other structures beyond. The land was rising to meet the road and a few of the houses on the slope were almost intact but Wakille didn't stop and Shadith didn't bother asking him why. She was as reluctant as he to face whatever made the vines sway in the windows of those dwellings. Then they were out of the city. There were grass, trees, bushes growing thickly, crowding in on the road ahead of them. Shadith saw those trees with intense relief and a weakness in the knees that made her wonder if she could manage to reach that inviting patch of moonlit grass just before the grove began. The end in sight undermined her grim concentration on continuing to walk and made continuing ten times the struggle it had been before.

But she did reach it and saw with pleasure that the grass was heavy with dew. This meant no hauling water for the gyori, the dew was enough for them to get by on until morning. Indeed morning couldn't be that far off though the precise amount of time it had taken to come from the coast to this point seemed wholly beyond her ability to calculate. It felt like a week, must have been several hours. She found herself stumbling the last few steps beside an impatient gyr, going over and over this as if this was the only important thing left in the world. The gyr bumped into her as he stepped clumsily off the roadway and began ripping up great chunks of that dewy succulent grass.

She pulled her hands hard down her face, rubbed at her eyes, stared at the grass and tried to find the last bit of strength in a body that threatened to fold under her.

She went to the gyr with Aleytys still draped across his back, cupped her hand along the side of Aleytys's face, lifted the heavy head, the sweat-sticky hair dropping to curl about her wrist. She stared at it a moment. '*A bracelet of bright hair about the bone,*' she thought, blinked. *Where did that come from? Oh god, my brain's mush.* She let the head fall back went round behind the gyr and wrapped her arms about Aleytys's hips, pulled her off the gyr with a desperate lurching tug, fell with her onto the grass. The dew struck cold into her. She coughed. *I hope Aleytys can cure the common cold,* she thought and giggled, the giggle breaking into another cough. She pushed Aleytys off her and went to help Wakille unroll the groundsheet.

When they had Aleytys wrapped in a blanket and Linfyar tucked up next to her, Shadith straightened and stood rubbing at her back. "We should stand watch," she said slowly. "No telling what's out there wanting to eat us." She smiled wearily at him. "At the moment I wouldn't care much if something did try to eat me. You?"

Wakille yawned and didn't bother covering the gape. He swung his blanket around him. "Me? I'm going to sleep a week. Mangxi's twenty demons stomp any fool who tries waking me." He went to his knees, fussed a bit with the blanket, rolled about until he was satisfied, then went still. A moment later Shadith heard a soft snore.

She untied the strap to her blanket roll, snapped the blanket out, hesitated. She turned in a slow circle. To the south, the city was a dark blotch outlined against the dimmed blaze of the stars. To the east there were more trees, here and there among them glimmers of white, ruins of fancy houses, she thought, riverfront property. *It doesn't seem to change world to world, well, not domed cities, but on oxygen worlds like this whatever the species, the privileged have the air and the sunlight and the riverview.* She flipped the blanket about, knowing she'd make the same choice if she wanted to settle anywhere and had the money for it. *Which I certainly don't have. Never been this broke I can remember.* She grinned. *Except the day I was born. About the same thing, I suppose. I think I'd better settle on Wolff if anywhere. Has its problems, but it'll never have too many people and the ones it's got are too bloodyminded to admit anyone could be better than them. I wonder if Lee will settle there. She's got a nesting look about her. Not me. Wonder what the lifespan is on this body.* She smiled and turned a little more. *Thick trees to the north. Forests on this world seem to have nasty secrets, wonder if this is the same. I should be sleeping. I'm too tired to sleep. Can't find the stop-switch.* She walked past the grazing gyori to the shallow bluff and stood looking down at the great river.

Two-three kilometers wide. *Hope we don't have to try cross-ing that. No way, unless some natives are running a ferry.* She stretched, yawned. It was getting cold. *Heading into winter. Front must be passing through. Rain? No clouds, not yet anyway. Could be it's going to stay clear a while.* She shivered. *Lee, you better wake in the morning. My throat feels like something with a lot of teeth and claws died there. And Linfyar . . . I hope you're with us tomorrow, healer. Besides, Wakille's getting snarky again. Thank god, he's such a little creep. Strong though. Lot stronger than this body. Hey, Shadi, it's your body now, get used to that. And take care of it. You're stuck with it.* A corner of her mouth curled up as she thought of the body she'd really like to have. Aleytys's. But that was impossible and she might as well be satisfied with the one she had, she'd asked for it, no, de-manded it. Time to forget what was and get on with what is. She stretched out on the plastic, the blanket tucked around her, beginning to relax as she grew warmer. Her last thought was about Swartheld and joining him once she got back to Wolff.

2

Shadith woke with a feeling of urgency, great danger, lay very still in the blanket's warmth holding her breathing steady. Cautiously she opened her eyes.

Wakille was bending over Aleytys, his hands about her throat.

With a surge of desperate energy dredged up from she didn't know where, she was on her feet the blanket dropping away, launching a kick that tumbled him away from the inert body he crouched over. Then she was standing between him and Aleytys, the zel knife in her hand gleaming like ivory in the long light of the early sun. His eyes on the knife, Wakille got carefully to his feet, stood without moving, the dappled leaf-shade playing over his face as the morning breeze stirred the branches over his head. When he spoke, his voice melded oddly with the wind until it seemed the wind not he spoke the words.

"You saw her back there," it said. "You saw the diadem.
The RMoahl diadem, little savage. You've got no idea what
wealth that means. Off this cursed world and living high the
rest of your life, everything you ever wanted, everything you
ever could want. And power. Who are you, little savage?
What are you? So what if she saved your life. You aren't
lovers, I'd know that. There's some tie between you, I don't
know what it is, but think. Friends and lovers, little savage,
they're easy enough to find out there if you've got wealth
enough. Don't be a fool and let a splendor out of your life.
Whatever you owe her, you've repaid her a dozen times over.
Look at her, she's worse than dead in this state, a vegetable,
not a person; help me release her from that. . . ."

The voice went on and on, searching out her weaknesses,
but that was the least part of what he was doing. She felt
warm touches in her mind, touches that gently and steadily
leached away her anger, or rather turned that anger from him
onto Aleytys, touches that searched out and enhanced the
resentments she already felt—and was ashamed of—and tickled away that shame. Wakille, the trader, working at his top,
seducing her as much with his mind manipulations as with his
words, which were after all just the paint on the surface,
partially there as a distraction from what he was doing in her
head, not from any great hope he could talk her around,
though he might think he could do that too since he was
ignorant of some very important details about her relationship
with Aleytys. And he was succeeding to some extent, distracting her from her focus on him into thinking about that
relationship, the years of give and take, of generosity given
and regiven, of learning to hold Aleytys dear, very dear. She
wondered if Harskari had known that passionate consuming
commitment to Swartheld and herself and thought perhaps
she had. Perhaps it was a necessary thing for those prisoners
of the diadem to be able to love the bearer, necessary in order
to endure the intimacy of the connection. We've all been
lucky, she thought, one after the other, in the bearers the
diadem found. She blinked and looked at him. No, she told
herself. No.

Without thinking about it, without giving him any warning,
she collapsed and lay on the clean smelling grass, her fore-

head resting on a forearm, her head tucked into the curl of that arm, her other hand pressed against her ear as if she could no longer bear to listen to his words. He came closer. She could hear the scrape of his boots on the tough plastic as he walked around her and stood beside Aleytys. He kept talking, the same soft smooth tones, kept pressing at her—but now she ignored both the words and the attempted manipulation of her mind, gathered her talent and drove into Aleytys's body, the body she knew better than the one she wore now. She settled into that mind, stifling her doubts about the right she had to do this, took hold in that body. The body came onto its feet with a surge of strength and potency that startled Shadith as much as it terrified Wakille.

She looked through Aleytys's eyes and saw Wakille leap back, eyes wide, mouth open in a silent scream, terror turning the round face ugly. Too frightened to use his talent to read what was happening, Wakille ran full out to the gyori and vanished among them, reappearing a moment later on the strongest of the beasts, already saddled with bulging saddlebags. Ready for flight before he started on Aleytys. Once he got the diadem off her, he wasn't about to encumber himself with a girl and a blind boy, he was going to abandon them with the corpse. She watched him flee into the forest, too bound in Aleytys's body to stop him. And she didn't dare release it, not until she could be sure he wasn't coming back.

When she could no longer hear the sound of the gyr's hooves she closed Aleytys's eyes but kept her body standing for a moment until she was sure of what she was doing, then she sat the body down and with a continuation of that movement, laid her on her back. Shadith sat up, rubbed at her temples. A lot harder than riding bird brains and prodding them a bit now and then, doing this from the outside. She leaned over, her face inches from Aleytys's. "Harskari," she shouted. "Move it, old witch. Chase her out. Dammit I need her help." She swallowed, rubbed at her throat. Her voice was disappearing fast. "Linfy is sick and I don't feel so bright myself." Her croak trailed off as Aleytys lay like a corpse. Linfyar, she thought. She reached over Aleytys and turned back the blanket. He was very still, shrunken, pitiful. For an instant she thought he was dead. She bent lower and heard the soft scrape of his breath. She felt weak with relief. She touched his cheek. Hot. The fever still burned in him. He looked miserable, his soft fur matted, roughed, his breathing hoarse and painful. Tiny fragile creature. She pulled the corner of the blanket over him, then sat on her heels, contemplating the inert body stretched out before her. No use trying to slap or shake her awake, not if a little strangling had no effect. "I swore I wouldn't. . . . Twice in one day. Hell, Lee." She shut her eyes and invaded the brain again, shouting as she moved about in it, prodding and jerking at every nerve she ran across until she felt a sudden blast of presence. She jerked away.

Aleytys sat up. "Ay-Madar, Shadi. What the hell did you think you were doing?"

"Waking you up. I did, didn't I?"

"That you did." Aleytys moved her shoulders, frowned and touched her throat. "What happened?"

"The wave hit us. You remember that?" Shadith swallowed, smiled at Aleytys as she too rubbed at her throat. When Aleytys nodded, she went on, speaking slowly, hoarsely. "You and Harskari, you dumped us on the causeway and you crashed. Bugs driving us crazy, wet all around, we couldn't stay there. Linfy was feverish and I didn't feel so good either. You think your throat's bad." She grimaced. "Listen to me croak."

Aleytys nodded. "I'll take care of that if you want." She looked around. "You said Linfy was sick. Where is he?"

"That lump beside you. He's not so good but alive, just asleep."

Aleytys touched her throat. "I don't feel sick, just sore."

"You really don't know?"

"Know what?"

"Diadem put on some show, like the other time. And Wakille's a man who knows a treasure when he sees one. Woke awhile ago and he was doing his best to strangle you. He had to figure this was his best chance for a killing—in both senses of the word. You dead, no more a danger to him, he gets back at you for all the times you put him down, the diadem drops off into his hands—you know, I'd bet anything he knew about it all along and came with us on the off-chance he'd get a hack at it—then he rides off and leaves us, me and Linfyar, to get on how we can. But I woke a bit too soon, good ol' premonition kicking me out of my nice comfortable sleep. I take my turn kicking him off you, then he starts selling me on helping him do you. He's something, could sell teeth to a tyrannosaur. When he was playing me, I started not knowing up from down, so I jumped into you—I know I swore I wouldn't do that, I don't like it, but this was an emergency if there ever was one—I jumped into you and got you up on your feet fast. And he took off like twenty devils were biting at him." She shook her head. "Took all I had to keep you on your feet." She frowned. "He's not going to give up, bet you."

"I know." Aleytys closed her eyes, yawned, ran her hand through her hair. "I'm drained, Shadi. Don't know if I could raise enough oomph to light a match." She pushed the hair off her face. "All right. Suppose you check what our little friend has left us while I see what I can do with the imp." She went over onto hands and knees, turned round until she was looking down on Linfyar, straightened until she was sitting on her heels. As Shadith went off to look for the saddlebags and the rest of the gear, Aleytys was turning back the blanket.

When Shadith came back with her meager gleanings, Linfyar was sitting up and turning his head about, his ears quivering, his lips quivering as he probed about him.

Aleytys lay on her back, staring up at the cloudless sky, hands laced behind her head. She looked tired and depressed. Shadith wondered what she was thinking but didn't really want to know, right now anyway, she had enough with her own problems. She dumped her armload on the plastic. "This is about it."

Aleytys turned her head, then pushed reluctantly up until she was sitting cross-legged, shoulders slumped. She yawned. "Looks like he pretty well cleaned us out."

"Looks like." Shadith dropped beside Aleytys and began picking through the odds and ends discarded by Wakille when he'd stuffed his own saddlebags. A few lengths of cord, three pots, a moldy slab of dried fish, a ripped bladder of nut flour. "He took both bows, the staff—yeah, I know, but he brought it with him, don't ask me why. All the arrows. The last of the trailbars. All the cha we had left, worms eat his mean little soul.''

"We still have this." Aleytys groped among the blankets and came up with the pocketed belt, slapped it down beside Shadith. "He had it off me, but I suppose you scared him into forgetting it.''

"Mistress." Linfyar's voice was sweet and coaxing. "I'm hungry.''

Shadith started; she'd forgotten him in her irritation at Wakille. No longer anger, just a feeling she'd like to swat him as she would a pesky fly. She swung around, smiled at the boy. "Aren't we all. Tell you what, Linfy. See if you can stun us a couple birds for breakfast.''

Aleytys made a quick little sound that was a bitten-off protest, but said only, "Stay away from the river, imp. You fall in that, neither of us could fetch you out.''

They watched him trot off. Aleytys rubbed at her forehead. "Seen any of Esgard's signs?''

"Not likely, is it.'' Shadith tossed the slab of moldy fish into the shade under the trees and began packing the things she thought worth keeping into a pair of saddlebags. "Got the hatchet too, damn him. We're really going to miss that.'' She looked around. "He get off with your knife?''

Aleytys yawned. "Um. No. Still in its sheath.''

"That's a help." She chuckled. "Means you get to hunt up wood to cook the birds Linfy's going to bring us.'' She ran her thumb along the split in the bladder. "Needle and thread?''

Aleytys yawned again. "I can't remember ever being this tired.'' She scooped up the belt and began pulling it through her fingers until she found the pocket she wanted. "Here.'' She held out the miniature sewing kit, then went back to fiddling idly with the belt.

Shadith opened the kit and began poking the end of a thread at a needle's eye. "Damn. Ah. Got it.'' She cut off the thread, twisted a knot into the end and began repairing the rip in the bladder. "Where do we go from here?'' Her hands went still a moment as she looked over her shoulder at Aleytys.

Aleytys had a map unfolded, resting it on her thighs.
"Follow this road north. Feel around," she said absently.
"Look for Esgard's signs." She slapped the map back into its
folds, tossed the small square at Shadith, then stretched out
on the groundsheet, hands under her head again. "Esgard
drew a circle around the headwaters of this river. Way north
of here, takes in some thousands of hectares." She patted a
yawn. "Where he said he was headed." She stopped talking,
lay breathing deeply, halfway on to sleeping.

Shadith cleared her throat. "Before you get too comfortable,
we need wood. It's your knife."

"Mmmm."

"And you better stir your head a little and keep watch for
Wakille. He took both bows, remember."

"Mmmm. I don't feel like moving."

"I notice."

"Hah." Groaning and moving with exaggerated care, Aleytys
got to her feet. She stood a moment beside Shadith, turning
in a slow circle, a slight frown pulling her brows together.
Then she shook herself out of her reverie, scooped up the belt
and slapped it around her middle. As she worked the buckles,
she said, "Linfy's coming. He went overboard a bit, got half
a dozen birds. You're right, time I got busy."

3

They followed the road which followed the river north,
riding through huge ancient riveroaks and smaller more anonymous trees, low-lying brambles that rioted through clearings
and encroached on the road until at times the gyori were
doing a twisty dance, picking through the tangle of thorny
shoots. Where the sun reached the brambles, they were thick
with small sweet bluish-red berries, a very welcome supple-
ment to their diet of fish and birds and small mammals.

They started late and stopped early, forced to live off the
land. Linfyar grew very good at stunning the beasts that seem
to litter the ground under the trees, small furries of assorted
kinds that roasted up well enough on the improvised spits
they had to use. Though there was no pressure from hunger

or even time, Aleytys quickly began feeling uneasy and her spirits remained low most of the time during the ride. It was the emptiness of the land that bothered her. Emptiness in fullness. There was much life here, healthy life with little of the lingering contamination of the other continent. But man in any of his forms was missing. They rode through what could pass for virgin wilderness—except for the road they followed and the others that split off from it. It felt strange and unnatural to her, but insensibly she began to relax her vigilance. All of them began to ride through the land as if it belonged to them, even Shadith, though she fussed over the possibility of Wakille waiting in ambush somewhere ahead. She mind-rode birds at intervals the first two days, sending them circling low over the road ahead, then back along it, searching for the little man. But she saw nothing of him and worried at that, trying to figure out where he'd gone and why she couldn't get a smell of him. By the afternoon of the third day she wasn't bothering anymore. She settled into the tranquility of the land, relaxing into that sense of the emptiness around them that gave them at least the illusion of security.

Wakille had vanished into the distance, too frightened to come near them. Apparently too frightened. Aleytys felt an itch between her shoulderblades that told her not to believe it, but it was hard to remember the danger as the tranquil days cycled past, unchanging except for the growing chill in the mornings and the smell of autumn in the air. Whenever she thought of him, though, she was troubled. Up to this point Wolff had protected her, Wolff and before that her disappearance into the vastness of space. She was too well known to do that now. It seemed to her Wakille was only the first she'd have to watch for now, there'd be more after the diadem, tougher than Wakille would ever think of being. She pressed her lips together, scowling at the flicking ears of her gyr. Vrithian. Her refuge? She laughed aloud but wouldn't explain when Shadith asked her what was funny. Refuge. Everything she'd learned so far about the Vrya made Vrithian look like the kind of refuge a spider offered a fly. They went after things like the diadem, her Vryhh kindred. And they'd be the worst she'd ever have to face if she was right about them, fighting her with her own weapons. She probed tentatively for Harskari, but found no sign of her and gave that up for the moment.

On the fourteenth day the trees thinned, there were wide stretches of open grass and patches of bald ground showing pale through the litter of old leaves. About mid-afternoon Aleytys pulled her gyr to a stop and looked down a steep crannied bluff into a river winding in from the east to join the one they were following. At one time there must have been a bridge here, but it was so long gone there wasn't a trace of it left. She scowled at the wide expanse of water. Not a chance of fording it. It was nearly as wide and powerful as the river it joined.

Aleytys slid off her gyr and went to stand at the edge of the bluff. "Far as we go this way," she said.

"Looks like." Shadith dismounted and stood beside her.

Linfyar said nothing. He cared little which way they went. He was happy with this life and as long as they were around to scare away the demons of the night and the devils of the day, he was content. Aleytys looked at him and smiled. He was turning out better than she'd expected, taking earnest and proud care of the gyori, taking intense but unvoiced pride in his role of hunter and provider. The fretful cruelty of the island had vanished as if it had never existed.

"What now?"

"Turn east until we can get across. Then slog back." She pulled the belt around, flipped open a pocket and took out the map. As she shook it open, she said, "I was hoping for some kind of bridge."

"Way the luck falls." Shadith slid off her mount, came to lean against Aleytys's arm and look down at the map. "What's that?" She scratched lightly at a dark line crossing the river some distance inland. "Looks to me like that's your bridge."

"Mmm." Aleytys frowned at the map. "Five or six hours' ride, at least. We've got time to make it by sundown if it's till there. Better get started." She looked around at the grazing gyori. "Where's Linfy?"

Shadith went back along the road a few steps. "Gone hunting, I suppose. I don't see him or his gyr."

"He worries me when he goes off like that, he's still a baby, Shadi."

"Yah, Mama. Don't let your maternal habits get out of hand. I've seen that glint in your eye when you look at me. I know I'm only a few years older than him."

"A few millennia." Aleytys slapped the map back into its folds. "All right. I know what you mean. Damn, that's a whole day lost."

"Well, no one here's in all that much of a hurry. Though to say true, I'll be glad to get off this world. I'm tired of it. Wonder what Swartheld's doing now. Hope he left some way for me to get in touch with him."

Aleytys looked sharply at her, then shoved the map back into its pocket with unnecessary force and had trouble snapping the flap down. "We'll worry about that when we get finished here." She looked at the sun again, a gesture since she didn't really see it. "We need all the time we can get. Find the brat, will you?"

"Why not." Shadith swung up onto the saddlepad, settled herself, smoothed her hand back over her hair; it had grown half an inch and the curls were looser and heavier. "You're going to have to deal with that sometime, you know. Never mind. I'm going since you're in a mood." She kicked her mount into a trot and vanished quickly into the trees. Aleytys heard her alternating between whistle talk and shouts for Linfyar to get back to them.

She sat down on the grass and looked out over the river to the forest beyond, tall dark trees like the ones behind her. The wind was blocked by a thick stand of brush, the sun was hot on her face. She stretched out on her stomach listening to Shadith's whistles and the low pleasant hum around her. Shadith was right, she had to wipe out that possessiveness or she'd wreck everything. She drifted into a drowsy half-sleep, fragmentary images passing through her mind, drifted in a sort of timeless trance—until the brush shadow moved across her face and she realized suddenly that too much time had passed and the only things she heard now were the forest sounds.

She rolled over and pushed up, sat rubbing at her temples, glanced at the sun, her eyes widening as she saw at least an hour had passed since Shadith had gone hunting for Linfyar. She jumped to her feet and stabbed a probe into the forest.

Touched a large life form. A gyr. Close. Her own mount.
She probed farther. Nothing. Driven by an impulse she didn't
stop to examine, she kicked off her boots and started walking
slowly back along the road, her feet silent on the paving, the
sun that trickled through the canopy hot on her head and
shoulders, the shadow patterns of the wind-teased leaves
dancing in front of her. Still nothing. She stopped walking.
Linfyar would have gone off the road to hunt. No use going
any farther like this. Stretching her senses in a wide delicate
web, she went questing cautiously into the forest, sick with
the realization that she'd been criminally careless, that she'd
let the tranquil sameness of the days seduce her into a dream
of security. It was Wakille, she knew that without needing
more proof than the silence around her.

She eased up to one of the huge old trees, the acrid woody
smell of the bark sharp in her nostrils, usually a pleasant
enough odor but too strong now, distracting her. She crouched
in the space between swollen roots and tried to ignore the
ache under her ribs, swept the fragile probe carefully north to
south, moving out from the roadway, coming back to it as far
south as she could reach. Nothing. She rubbed at her forehead.
Wakille was strong. He was hiding them. But there had to be
a clue; they were the bait in his trap. She knew he felt her
searching; he was waiting for her to come on deeper into the
trees. She made the sweep again, slower this time. Again
nothing.

But at one place there seemed to her to be an excess of that
nothing, an absence of life fires that could be unnatural, like
locating a planet by watching the stars it occulted. Subtle bait
for a trap. She swept again. Still there, that emptiness. Heat
began to boil in her a growing anger that he dared attack her
companions, friends. She clamped down hard on it, as afraid
of it as she was afraid for Shadith. Harskari, she whispered
into the red darkness of her head. It's happening again. No
answer. She hadn't really expected one. She tightened her
shield. In that at least she was as strong as he was.

A shadow in shadows, she drifted toward the emptiness,
moving in a loose uneven spiral, zagging this way and that to
avoid the brambles and dead weeds, twigs and dry grasses
that littered the forest floor, anything that would make a

noise. Practice, much practice, hunting in the Wildlands with Grey, hunting with sling and stones so they had to get close without spooking their prey. A skill she was glad of now because the game she stalked was far more dangerous than any of Wolff's predators. And he knew she was coming.

She rounded her last arc, started closing on the silence. She could almost smell Wakille, as if he exuded a musk, a thick oily stench of danger. Still nothing. All that was imagination. Nothing. Nothing. Where is he, may his hair fall out and his tongue grow worms. Where is he? If he's hurt Shadith or Linfyar. . . . Rage threatened to erupt through her. She swayed to a stop and throttled it back, too distracting, too betraying.

Ahead, dust motes danced in fans of light coming between the great trees. A clearing of some kind. She moved on, ghosting in a wobbly circle round the clearing, searching the trees as she passed them. Nothing. As far as she could tell, no little man perched on a limb waiting to leap on her. She slipped on, keeping to the shadows, trying to avoid even the faintest whisper of a sound, knowing he could feel her, hoping he was unable to locate her very precisely. Ahead, a giant had toppled some years ago and was in the process of rotting back into the soil. She eased into the shadow of the great round of straggling roots and of the small tree growing among them. Keeping low she moved her head until she could see into the clearing.

She froze, clamped down the fury that threatened to erupt.

Shadith lay in a tumbled heap on the limp yellow grass, a trickle of blood dried beside her mouth. Linfyar crouched beside her, his head tied into a bag, his limbs bound tight against his body in a position that must have been increasingly painful as time passed. He was sitting very still. At first she didn't understand, then she saw the loop of rope about his neck. If he moved, he tightened that loop, strangling himself. She pressed a hand hard over mouth and nose, struggling to maintain her silence and control. With deep anxiety she watched the thick dry grass beside the girl's mouth. After a minute, she thought she saw the grass move. It might have been the wind, she couldn't tell, but there was a chance Shadith was still alive. And because there was that chance she had to walk into Wakille's trap. She stood and walked into the clearing.

A blow. Arrow in her side.

Despair, so intense she fell to her knees, her mouth open but her throat locked. No sound.

Terror. She shook, sick with terror. Couldn't see anything. Shadith and Linfyar forgotten. Wakille forgotten.

Fear and terror rolling over her like the tsunami, crushing her.

No resistance.

No use fighting.

Nothing.

A blow.

Pain and nausea.

An arrow in her back. Poison. Happened before hadn't it? Let it work. What's the use trying? Nothing was worth this pain, there was no escaping the pain of living, of being who she was, the freak, ugly, misfit, no one really wanted her, they all despised her, used her, threw her away when her usefulness was finished. Mud. Filthy half-breed nothing. Rotten mother, went off and abandoned your baby, whore, lie with anyone who'd lie hard enough to get round you, use you, throw you away. There's no refuge for you ever, no place, you have no place. There is no meaning to your life, you're nothing, the pattern of your life is not pattern only chaos and futility, only absurdity. You are nothing. Let it go. Let it go now, be at peace.

Despair melting her like wax.

And the rage she had fought to control tore through her and exploded out of her.

She was on her feet, burning, screaming.

The trees circling the clearing burned. Like torches steeped in resin they burned, a circle of fire.

A shriek. Agony. A burning screaming thing fell from a tree, rolled over and over, a frantic fire-squall, whirling about and about the clearing.

Face contorted, burning away from the bone, Wakille rushed at her. With the last of his strength he leaped at her, arms terrible in their strength closed about her and clung to her and the fire that ate his flesh passed into hers and she was eating herself.

She reveled in the pain, in the cleansing fire. For an instant only. Before it shocked loose the mountain girl in her, the sturdy practical woman that remained after the high flights had ashed and her lunges into ecstasy or despair had stabilized. She wanted to live. She *would* live.

And she came to herself, burning, a charred corpse locked to her body by its death-grip, the forest burning around her, grass and debris burning at her feet. Shadith and Linfyar burning.

With a croak of disgust and loathing, she tore Wakille from her and flung him away, called a deluge of her black water, washed the fire from her body, pulled the arrows from her, healed the jagged wounds. Breathing shallowly, the air searing throat and lungs, she stumbled to Linfyar. She cut him loose, jerked the bag off his head, cut away the gag. "Harskari," she gasped, "Get your thumb out and shield us."

A branch crashed behind her, its heat seared her. The grass was gone, fire had flashed it away and, fuel gone, had left char behind. Linfyar was crying and clutching at her, so frightened he didn't know what he was doing.

Shadith lay as she'd lain when Aleytys first saw her. Impatiently Aleytys tugged her hand free. Linfyar seized it again and tried to climb into her arms. Fear and need making her rougher than she thought, she shoved him away and dropped beside Shadith. Sick with worry and doubt, she touched the girl.

Life. Fluttering feebly under her hands. Like a sudden dash of ice water in the face, the relief steadied her. She forgot the chaos around her, forgot Linfyar, forgot Harskari, forgot everything but the fluttering life under her hands. She slid her fingers gently over the body, feeling for the injuries.

Cracked skull, blood clot pressing on the brain. Puncture wound high on the shoulder near the neck, badly lacerated flesh there, more blood distending the flesh. Burns and internal bleeding.

Aleytys flattened her hands on the body, *reached* and poured energy into the body, powering the flesh to repair itself, burning away the blood clogging the hollows under the bone, washing it out of the battered flesh, stimulating the marrow to replace what had been lost, pushing the broken bone of the skull into place and knitting the bits together.

Shadith's eyes opened. She blinked a few times. Aleytys sat back on her heels, noticing for the first time that the searing heat was gone. She could see trees like torches around the clearing but the air was cool around her. A tree leaned toward them, pressing down on an invisible barrier. In her head Harskari chuckled. "What are you going to do when I'm out, Lee?"

"Die, it looks like," Aleytys said. "Thanks, Mother."

Shadith sat up, looked around. "Well! What happened here?"

"You might say I was a trifle annoyed."

"You might at that. Where's Wakille, the little rat?"

"Roasted rat."

"Hunh. Can't say I'm sorry. Linfy?"

Aleytys looked around. "I forgot. He should be all right, but. . . ."

Linfyar was huddled as far as he could get from her still within the cool. She sighed. "Come here, Linfy," she said. He quivered but didn't move. "I'm sorry I shoved you away, little imp, but Shadith was near dying, do you understand? I couldn't deal with you then and I had no time to explain." She held out her hand. "Come. You hurt. Let me fix it." It wasn't the whole truth; she knew it and suspected he knew it as well. Shadith was far more important to her than he was. If it came to a choice between them, he was out. Slowly, reluctantly, he crept toward her, twitched sharply as she touched him.

She felt that and regretted it but there was little she could do about it and she wasn't even sure she much wanted to try. She *reached*, energized his body to heal itself, it only took a few minutes, then she took her hand away and got to her feet.

Shadith was standing, frowning at the fire that was beginning to sweep away from them, driven by the wind out of the west. She bared her teeth in a brief nervous grin. "Hope you never get that mad at me."

Aleytys shrugged, turned away. Over her shoulder she

said, "Let's get out of here." She scooped up Linfyar and began running toward the river road, ignoring the pain of cinders scorching her bare feet, appalled by the dead and smoking trees, the scattered fires still burning. Harskari held off the heat and smoke, pushed aside tongues of fire. The black stretched on and on, then there was grass and bramble and trees whose leaves were withered by heat but otherwise intact. She ran on until she reached the road, then stopped to hop from foot to foot as the surge of need left her and the pain came back.

With what felt like a sigh of weariness Harskari let the bubble collapse. Hot air slammed into Aleytys with a loud poof almost like a shout of laughter. Wakille's laughter. She set Linfyar down, stood on one foot and brushed debris off the bottom of the other, wincing at the sores in the tough surface. She sat down abruptly, feeling curiously weak, as if she had been feeding off her own reserves rather than reaching for the force she thought of as coming from outside, she only the conduit, the shaper. She sighed, closed her eyes, but her feet were too sore to ignore longer, so she *reached* again.

When she looked up, the sores patched over with new skin that would be tender for a time yet, she saw Shadith coming along the road, frowning. The girl stopped in front of her. "The gyori are gone," she said somberly. She dropped Aleytys's discarded boots on the grass beside her. "Thought you might want these. Not a smell of the beasts far as I could reach."

"Fire," Aleytys said. "Damn."

"Yah, running ahead of it, more'n likely. Kilometers on and getting farther by the minute. What do we do now?"

"Wakille!"

"Yah, I know, worms eat him." Shadith plopped down beside Aleytys. "What now?"

"Go on. Only now we walk. If there's nothing in Esgard's circle, we come back, find ourselves another island."

Shadith groaned. "Another three months, more, god knows how long, on a damn island scratching to stay alive."

"Just hope we do find Sil Evareen."

"More'n likely that's smoke and dream. And Esgard is bones and scum, growing grasses out of his eyes."

"Right now, way I feel, you're probably right. Ah, Shadi, why do I get us into messes like this?"

"Hah. Don't ask me. You wouldn't like the answer."

4

They walked east along the river, keeping as close to it as they could. The bank was the same sort of chalky bluff they knew from the days of riding along the river road. The heat from the fire was still intense. Now and then tongues of it licked at them, but for the most part the great expanse of it was ahead of them, speeding away from them driven by a heat-energized wind, leaving behind a smoldering smoking deadness. Aleytys plodded along the river bank, tired and depressed, sweating, filthy with ash and dust and debris from the whippy thickets of new growth going gold for the winter. The river bluff was far too steep to negotiate except when they needed water and in sections the growth was thick enough to force them into the cindery smolder. Linfyar whined and clung to Shadith, clung to Aleytys when Shadith rebelled. Her scratches stung and itched, her bones ached with a weariness she wasn't used to and couldn't throw off, and the forest kept burning, death and destruction, all her fault, her lack of control. Oddly it was far easier to deal with the dead men in her past than it was to think about the beasts out there, dying, hurt, or dangerously displaced. Madar be blessed, it was autumn and no helpless newborns had to be abandoned to the fire. She tromped along morosely, eyes on the ground, as miserable in mind as she was in body.

Shadith caught at her arm. "Lee. Look."

"At what?" She tilted her head, stared up at the smoke darkening the sky, rubbing absently at her upper arms as she finally managed to see what Shadith was trying to show her. The three of them stood in a grassy open space, ash drifting gently about them. And in the white-gray-black seethe above them a shimmering bubble hovered, twenty meters across, very faintly iridescent, as insubstantial as a dream, more so than some dreams that had plagued her. She wiped at the sweat and ash on her face, doing little good, only smearing it more, wiped her hand down along hip and thigh, leaving a smear of black on the worn brown suede, annoyed at having to face strangers when she was such a mess. She looked at her dirty hand, slanted a glance at Shadith. "Looks like I lit us a beacon."

Shadith nodded, then scowled resentfully at the bubble as it continued to hover and do nothing else, making no sign that it saw them. "I don't much like their manners. Not so friendly." She absently patted Linfyar, who had snuggled up close to her, his ears flickering, his mouth fluttering as he probed at the clouds, trying to find for himself what they were talking about.

Aleytys sighed. "I'm tired of this." She dropped to the grass, sat crosslegged, round-shouldered. Silently she called Harskari, saw the yellow eyes open slowly, wearily. "Be ready to screen us if they attack." Aloud she said, "Shut Linfyar up and sit."

Minutes passed. They sat without moving, without speaking, the three of them tired and apprehensive but most of all just numb. Aleytys would not look at the bubble. It might be the finish of the long trek, it might be nothing. It could open to them or leave when it was finished observing them. There was nothing she could do either way, nothing but sit and wait and watch the smoke eddy over the blackened forest.

The sphere was drifting lower, weightless and uncertain as a soap bubble, yet purposeful. It hovered before them not quite touching the rustling brambles that it crushed against the ground, hushing their rustle, freezing their small flutters. A square opened in its side, a bright insubstantial ramp extruded from the bottom of the square, flattening the grass close to where Aleytys sat.

A man stepped into the doorway, tall, spare, with a cut-glass beauty and fragility. Pale bloodless skin, smooth and nearly translucent. Pale bulging eyes, the green-gray-blue that lurks deep in clean ice. Short hair, white as spun glass. Elongated hands. Silvergray tunic and trousers that hung smooth as polished stone, giving little hint of the body beneath. His mouth was delicately curved, pale pinkish brown. He scarcely seemed to breathe, more not-there than present to all Aleytys's senses but sight. For a moment she wondered if this

was an android or a holo. She rested her hands on her knees
and sat silent, waiting and bracing herself for the ache in her
head when the man finally spoke.

For some time it seemed neither would speak first but
Aleytys was in no hurry and was willing to wait forever.
Shadith was fidgeting and Aleytys could feel her fighting to
hold her tongue. The man turned his pale gaze on the girl, put
pressure on her, but that merely stirred up Shadith's stubbornness and she set her lips and sat grimly silent, her narrow face
as unrevealing as she could make it.

Aleytys smiled.

The pale eyes returned to her. A long narrow hand lifted
and fell with a calculated grace. "Caran tethy dun-ta," he
said, with a casualness that she thought was intended to deny
the test of wills he had suddenly ended. "Thii tedhna lor-ta
kai?"

She kept her face still as the translator pain bounced about
inside her skull. "What are you, woman?" (The word he
used for female person the translator told her was a deroga-
tory term with overtones of intent to insult one into one's
proper place in the chain of being, somewhere down among
the animals.) "And what are you doing here?" None of the
insult was in the man's light tenor voice. She got to her feet
and stood looking up at him, throttling her irritation, thinking
no more about her battered filthy appearance. She smiled at
him, stirred out of weariness and lethargy, energized by his
unspoken disdain. A bitchy smile, she knew that. And she
enjoyed the flicker of resentment that tightened the lips of the
man, the first visible reaction she'd forced from him. "I
hunt," she said.

"Those?" He was looking at Shadith and Linfyar.

"Companions in the hunt."

"What do you hunt?"

Aleytys smiled but said nothing.

"That is your doing?" A graceful gesture that took in the
smoldering blackness spreading south from them.

"I was attacked."

"There is no one on these Plains but you and your . . .
companions." He hesitated on the last word and gave it a

twist that spoke of contempt for her and for them. "This land is preserved pure."

The corners of Aleytys's mouth twitched down into a quick wry grimace as she remembered the Centai Zel's determination to purge the other continent of all but their own kind, and she supposed a few breeding males though she couldn't even be sure of that. She stared at the man and wondered what kind of insanity had infected this world and driven the people to scourge themselves off its surface leaving only remnants behind, remnants that never increased because each devoted too much of its energies to destroying the others. She smoothed her face. "Perhaps so, I couldn't say; a man came with us but let his greed overcome his sense and attacked me." She turned her head, looked at the charred trees. "I was irritated." Then she wrinkled her nose and chided herself for turning that once-joke into fake, smug deprecation.

A muscle at the corner of the man's mouth twitched twice then smoothed away. "You hunt?" For the first time she noted a tremor in his voice and began to feel a bit better, more in control of the situation.

"I hunt a man called Kenton Esgard."

"You hunt a man here? I have said there are none here outside of ourselves."

"Sil Evareen is here and Kenton Esgard came here." She spoke without hesitation or any sign of her doubts. "I seek Esgard, thus Sil Evareen."

"Why?"

"Because I must. Why else? Look at me."

"Why must you?"

"That, goodman" (a word with connotations of amusement and faint slighting, not actually insulting but not far away), "is my business not yours."

The man stared down at her, protruberant eyes narrowing a little as his thin white brows drew together and a shallow vertical wrinkle appeared in his smooth forehead. He let moments slip by. Aleytys felt herself tightening with a tension she couldn't soothe away. Bastard, she thought. Her sense of controlling the situation began to slip away but she didn't speak or move or change the slight smile on her face or turn her gaze from him. She waited and hoped she looked as relaxed and confident as she wanted. "You have a name, woman?" (The same insulting word but there was more of a snap in the pleasant voice.)

"I have a name, man." She chose the counterpart to the word he chose to use for her, saw with considerable satisfaction the tightening of his lips, the reddening of that chiseled pale face. He took a step back from the opening and she began to regret turning her rancor loose—but he had to have a reason for asking her name. Esgard, she thought. "My name is Aleytys. Hunter of men and anything else that pays well enough."

He took a step forward, repositioned himself in the doorway. She suppressed a smile. Esgard for sure. The ice-colored eyes were fixed with a peculiar intensity on her. "Aleytys the half-Vryhh?"

"I see you do know Kenton Esgard." He wanted something of her, that was obvious enough, and as long as that was true she had an edge over him. "Aleytys daughter of Shareem of Vrithian," she said.

"We know Esgard. What do you know of Sil Evareen?"

"Know? Nothing. Snippets of legend and speculation." She spread her hands, smiled. "Notes Esgard left behind."

"What do you want of Sil Evareen?" There was a curious indifference in his voice now, as if his questions were a ritual, no more than that, as if he didn't care what her answers were but had to go through the motions.

"Nothing."

"Nothing?" Now there was skepticism in the light voice, a glint of interest in the pale eyes.

"You've got nothing I want, nothing but five minutes with Kenton Esgard." She put her hand out to her side. Shadith took it and moved to stand close by her, Linfyar pressed against her side. "I'm willing to ask politely, goodman, but I will have those minutes any way I can get them."

"That is a threat?"

"Certainly not. Merely a statement of intent." She looked at Shadith. The girl was scowling at the Evareener and trying to quiet Linfyar who was wriggling about, moving restlessly from foot to foot. She put her hand on Shadith's shoulder, heard a muttered word from her she preferred to ignore.

Harskari was watching too, her eyes open wide, shining with curiosity and amusement. She turned back to the man, wondering if she should prod him about his intentions but decided it was either not necessary or might produce the wrong results, so she simply stood waiting.

For several minutes there was a tense silence as the man did nothing but stand looking at her, then he turned his head and began looking at something inside the bubble.

A moment later Aleytys felt a subtle probing at her body, considered defending herself and the others. Again she did nothing. The probes were only seeking information, not threatening them. Whoever they were inside that bubble, they'd gain some information about her body, but resisting the probes would give them far more dangerous information about her capabilities. Perhaps they would think she couldn't do anything about them and relax a bit, a nice bonus for a little patience.

The man turned to her, insolence delicately concealed by a spurious courtesy. "To speak to Kenton Esgard, you must reach and enter Sil Evareen."

Aleytys raised a brow. "That's reasonably obvious, goodman."

"Your companions will wait for you here. We will return you, no need to concern yourself about that."

"No. Not the least need. My companions will remain with me."

"That is not possible."

"Then you'd best close up your pretty bubble and flit back home. We'll be along in our own time."

"There's no need for such intransigence, goodwoman; we will provide food, clothing and shelter for the child and the pet."

"There is no pet, only a small boy. You don't impress me much with that kind of ignorance, man, not to know the difference between an animal and a being." She let contempt slip into her voice and had the pleasure of seeing him flush again. "Good day, man." She turned her back on him.

The silence grew thick behind her. Shadith squeezed her hand and grinned at her. When she spoke, it was in the language of her own ancient people. "Getting under his skin and scratching, aren't you. Not that I mind, I don't think him and me will ever be soul-mates. What was that all about?''

"He wants to leave you here, says he'll bring me back. The first part I believe, the second I strongly doubt. There's a lot going on here I don't understand, Shadi. More I talk to him, more I think he's got some strong reason for wanting me. Far as he's concerned, the way he acts, I'm something on the level of a gyr compared to his exalted self, but he takes insult from me and comes back for more.''

"Like Wakille? The diadem?''

"Madar knows. I get the feeling Esgard's been talking fast and free. That doesn't sound like what we got from Hana. What you think?''

"Or what we got from Swartheld. Tricky man, hard to fool, not about to give anything away. Wonder what they did to him. You sure you want to take the chance?''

"If I had any choice. . . .'' She broke off as she heard her name called from behind, a new voice.

She turned, Shadith turning beside her, standing by her shoulder. A woman stood in the opening, at least she thought it was a woman, the same elongated form, the same short ice-white hair, the same rather bulging ice-colored eyes, the same cold chiseled beauty, but the line of hip and shoulder was slightly different and the very faint curve at the breast of the tunic suggested a subdued femaleness. This Evareener had more vigor, a sparkle of energy in her frozen eyes. "Viyn Aleytys," she said, her voice light, cool, melodious, an honorific now gracing the name the man had refused to use. "We did not realize you would feel so strongly about your friends." (Another change, Aleytys thought, companions to friends.) "If you will enter, we can carry you that long distance more easily than your feet could. It is your choice, of course. We wait.''

Aleytys looked at Shadith, switched languages and said, "She wants us to walk into her parlor.''

"Well, like you said before, we haven't much choice. I don't feel like walking another thousand miles if I don't have to. Old one awake?''

"Awake and watching.''

"You know, the thing I think I'm going to miss most is

that translator of yours. It's a bore having to wait for translations.''

"Hah. You never had the headaches.'' She turned back to the waiting woman, switched languages again and said, ''We thank you for the courtesy, Viynya.''

5

They followed the river until it narrowed to a thread of silver intermittently visible between trees thick on mountainsides, trees whose leaves were frost-turned garnet, plum, apricot, saffron and gold, followed it until it twisted high into the mountains and left the lowland forests behind, entering into a sparser, greener world of conifers. Finally they hovered over a circular lake that shone like a ruby mirror, reflecting the crimson of the setting sun. The valley around the lake was mostly meadow, a few trees, a bush or two, a small herd of ruminants placidly grazing at one end, nothing else visible. The sphere dropped, merged with the water, sank silently, swiftly to the muddy bottom, sank farther into the mud until mud closed over it, rocked bubble-light to a stop.

The male Evareener had kept himself out of sight the whole of the journey. Sulking, Aleytys thought. Aleytys and Shadith rode in the control room in padded egg-shaped seats, Linfyar on Shadith's lap, troubled and confused by this strange place. Shadith wouldn't let him sound his whistles; according to the Evareener woman they interfered with some of the instrumentation. He had his other special senses so he wasn't completely out of touch, but he was lost and uncertain and as a result clung frantically to her. The bubble-master had settled into a similar chair and apparently did nothing the whole trip but watch the passing scene in a great rectangular screen. Now and then Aleytys felt little tickling touches, not probes but some sort of connection the woman had with the machine.

When the dark frothy mud obscured the view through the screen, the bubble-master stood. "If you and your friends will follow, Viyn Aleytys, I will take you into Sil Evareen.''

6

What had looked to be a mountain was not, only a projection that hid the city. They walked from the glowing opaline tunnel into a garden touched with the crimson of the setting sun. A scented breeze, fresh, light, caressing, meandered around them. Looking around, Aleytys marveled, at first seeing only a profound beauty and perfection, then she felt an equally profound emptiness. She touched the trunk of a tree and felt cold metal. The trees and the other plants of the garden were sculptures of a sort, not living things, all of them made of metal with leaves of translucent light. The garden had the impossible clarity of objects in a super-realist painting, the stripped-down quality of something that had passed through the ordering mind of the artist. The farther into the garden she got, the more design she saw. It was a complex and subtle design but she felt weighed down by the deadness of it.

There were graceful crystalline structures rising here and there in the sculpture garden that the bubble-master told them were Evareener dwellings, but they saw no one until they reached the center of the garden and went into the largest of all the delicate structures. Their guide led them through singing crystal halls, following a spiral in toward the center. Others like her, male and female, came to stand in the mouths of side passages and stare silently at her, hunger glistening in their bulging eyes.

Shadith's fingers closed tight on her arm, nails biting into her flesh. "Premonition time," she murmured. "Not as bad as the wave, worse than a toothache." She said nothing more but walked beside Aleytys with the springy readiness of a tars in strange territory. Even Linfyar was alert, his whistles waking small songs in the crystal and metal around them.

Esgard lay in a crystal cocoon in a room like a cavern melted out of ice, a huge place with a real garden, a stream flowing gently through it, a carpet of lushly green grass, fresh bright smells of healthy flowers and plants, here and there, muting the glitter of the translucent walls, some primitive tapestries he must have brought with him, whose brilliance and uneven fibers should have sworn at the surroundings but didn't, provided instead a counteractant to the excessive polish of the place. He looked at her out of bright blue eyes, his overwhelming vigor giving Aleytys some intimation of why Hana was as she was. Crystal threads wound round and round his arms and legs and torso, only his head was free of them. He smiled with triumph and satisfaction. "Shareem's daughter," he said.

"I see you expected me." She moved her hand in an impatient gesture. "I came for the message."

"Been expecting you, yes," he said. "First time I heard about the Wolff Hunter Aleytys, I knew you'd turn up one day." He grinned at her, dominating her with his fierce enjoyment of this moment. "You sent that hard-faced scav, Quayle or whoever he was. That's who he said he was. Sent him to look me over."

"Yes," she said. "I sent him. How did you know?"

"Been getting transcripts off of Helvetia. You mentioned a man named Quayle in the hearing on the Haestavaada hunt."

"Transcripts off Helvetia. That isn't supposed to happen." She shook her head, sighed. "There goes one of the last of my illusions."

He winked at her, then raised both brows. "Why didn't you come yourself?"

"Busy. Well?"

"Oh no," he said. "Not so fast."

"Yes," she said. "What's the problem? I want to get out of here. Out of this." She waved a hand in a quick circle.

"It's very beautiful."

"So it is." She clasped her hands behind her. "I'd rather Wolff."

"What about Vrithian?"

She didn't respond, simply waited.

"Would you be so surprised," he said, "if I said those here would agree with you?"

"So let them leave."

"They can't, Aleytys half-Vryhh." He lingered over the last word; he was deliberately dropping hints, playing with her like a tars kitten with a mikmik in its claws. "They're bound to the machines that keep this place going. Can't leave it for longer than a few months or changes begin that are irreversible and they rot. Half Sil Evareen is deserted, you must have noticed that. Over the centuries a number of the Evareeners have used this as a means of escaping the endless boredom of their lives.''

''And you want that sort of existence?''·She gazed at the vividly alive face and eyes of the old man and couldn't believe it.

''Whatever it is,'' he said, ''it's better than dead.'' He went solemn a moment but he couldn't hold his face out of its grin and his bright blue eyes filled with a wild excitement that challenged and frightened her.

''I don't know,'' she said. She felt a tingling numbness in her fingertips, shook her hands. The past few moments she'd been feeling sluggish, finding it rather hard to think, but she'd put that down to the weariness that still clung to her. Now she looked up, angry and alert. ''What's happening?''

He laughed at her. ''You would come.''

''The message, old man. Tell me now.''

''Too late, little Vryhh, the city has you.''

''Oh no, old man. The message.'' The numbness was climbing her arms. She raised a hand, touched her face. It was like touching herself with a handful of twigs. Harskari, she whispered, guard a moment. ''The message,'' she repeated.

''Down the pipe,'' he said.

''What?''

''You mother said to send word the way I always did, but with a special key. We worked it out together, a one-time key no one else could use. Code this into the computer. The day, month and year of your birth in Jaydugari local numbers. Then this: Tennanthan scion four seven six five AL two seven nine ought ought dash one five. That will release access to a satellite transmitter and establish your identity at the same time. The satellite will send you on another leg, they're a cautious lot, your kin, half-Vryhh, that one'll pass you on to Shareem and you can say hello. Want me to repeat the key? No. Good. In case you're interested, that represents your mother's age on the day we set this up and the year, month and day of her birth in Vrithi years.''

''Would that unlock the Vryhh data?''

"Hana."

"How else would I be here."

"You don't know how right you are, Shareem's daughter. I do take care of my responsibilities, can't say I don't. I left the key with Hana."

"Ah." Anger surged through her but she blocked it quickly. This was no time to surrender to that mindless destruction so she tried to ignore what he'd just said. "Does it unlock the Vryhh data?"

"Of course not. I told you. One-time key. She knows that too. You tell Hana to be patient and wait. You might enjoy doing that, seeing what she's done to you. Be patient and wait. The Fund will take care of her."

"Hana hasn't much patience."

"Not much sense either."

"Enough to send me after you."

He cackled with glee at that. "Did, didn't she."

"You expected her to, didn't you?" The numbness was creeping farther up her arms and legs. She'd lost touch with them, didn't dare move without looking at them. Harskari, she subvocalized. Be watching. Soon as I'm sure I've got the key, we'll start shaking these twisters up some.

Harskari's answer had a distant echoing to it. "Don't wait too long."

Right. Aloud, she said, "You set her up, didn't you. To get me here. Why?"

The old man's eyes danced with glee. He was on fire with himself. "I've kept track of you since the Harewalk. Told you that. When I heard you had your ship, I began watching for you. That scav you sent, I called in a few debts and found out about him. You must have wiped his mind or something. He's changed, he has. Soon as I was sure he came from you, I sent word here I had the price they wanted."

"Price. Me."

"You." His eyes gleamed. "The Evareeners are sick of being tied to this place. But they hang onto life with a determination equal . . ." he bared his teeth in a mirthless smile ". . . equal to my own. I promised them a half-breed Vryhh to experiment on and here you are."

"Why not a full-Vryhh?"

"Now, Hunter, that would be very bad for business."

"And your promise to my mother?"

"You have the key. That's all I contracted to do. If you'd pushed Hana a bit more, you wouldn't be here now. A gamble, Hunter, but it paid off. It did, oh yes."

"How do I know you haven't lied about the key, crooked man?"

"I never break my given word, Shareem's daughter. Bad for business."

"The letter only."

"Of course. What else? It's expected."

"So. I have the key. Did you warn your skinny friends I might be a trifle hard to handle?"

"Oh yes. I translated the transcripts for them and we've been planning for you. Go ahead, Hunter, try your tricks."

Shadith gave a small sigh and collapsed at Aleytys's feet. Linfyar was already down, a small boneless heap.

Aleytys gazed steadily at Esgard. "One thing, my friend. They're hurt . . ." she nodded at the two on the floor, ". . . and I don't leave stone on stone." She was starting to breathe hard, the fury she'd learned so well on this world coiling up in her.

"That only matters if you can do it." He was watching her closely now, satisfaction like sweat on his face.

Aleytys threw her head back and shouted to the dull dead air, "Harskari, spin us free, Mother." Not caring that he heard, that they all heard. She forced lifeless arms out from her sides, closed her eyes and fought against the sticky cohesion of the damper field, searching for her power river, all the travails she'd passed through readying her for this moment.

The inhibitor surged on harder, clamped down on her. She gasped again and loosed the age until she was riding it like a surfer riding stormwaves, precariously in control still, drumming against the constraints of the fields around her as she had sought and over-ridden the constraints the zel witches had thrown about her. She found the pulse, rode with it, flowed with it through its irregularities, forced it against its timing; it whined and strained, driven by the great machines that powered the city—and they began to overheat, whining and

straining. She spent her power recklessly until she burst loose
from all constraints.

The diadem was singing on her head; Harskari slipped into
her body, began a contralto chant that pulsed with power.
Meshed with her Aleytys opened her conduits wide and gave
into the old one's hands a roaring flood of power. And the
diadem sang its clear lovely song and the crystal walls picked
up and amplified that song and began to stress and crack as it
vibrated in them. And the metal garden sang and vibrated and
shivered toward destruction.

Esgard is terrified.

The Evareeners rush about frantically. They try to attack
her. But the power is thrumming smoothly through the
Aleytys/Harskari meld. She is draining Sil Evareen's heart.
She can destroy it utterly and stand unscathed in the ruins.
She has forgotten Shadith and Linfyar isn't even dust in her
mind. She had the key and she is going to pull the city down.

Evareeners revolve about her, they can't reach her, they
beat futilely at her with weak hands. They try weapons only
to find their most powerful beams dissipated or blocked, the
weapons beginning to burn in their hands.

The bubble-master is there suddenly, in front of Aleytys
standing with her hands out before her, palms out, hands
empty and shaking a little. "Vijn Aleytys," she says.

Aleytys hears this dimly, her own name calling her. But
she is too wound up to pay much attention to anything but
what she is doing.

"VIJN ALEYTYS!" The words are as low and loud a
bellow as the bubble master can produce. "STOP. PLEASE
STOP. YOU ARE DESTROYING US. PLEASE. WE SUR-
RENDER. STOP. STOP."

Harskari/Aleytys powers down, Aleytys too caught up in
the heat and fury to want to stop, but overridden by Harskari.
Then they are both cool again, ashes in the mouth, weariness
in the bones. Harskari goes away and Aleytys is alone in her
body.

She was rather surprised to find Sil Evareen the Fabled
easier to overcome than the primitive Centai Zel. But perhaps
primitive was the wrong word, its demeaning and insulting
connotations having nothing to do with those women and

their honed skills and the power they controlled. Those Zel. They might just come close to achieving their Purpose. Given time. She shivered at the thought.

She blinked and looked into the harried faces around her, then at the treacherous and appalled Kenton Esgard, trapped in his cocoon, helpless to resist the anger of the Evareeners once she was gone. She looked down, saw Shadith on her knees, shaking her head, Linfyar starting to move arms and legs, then looked back at Esgard. She was beginning to feel sorry for him in spite of what he'd tried to do to her, she didn't quite know why, perhaps because he was so futile lying there, all his energy and intelligence useless to him. She bent and gave her hand to Linfyar, helped him stand, wondering what she was going to do with him. School. A trust fund maybe to give him security. She cupped her hand about his shoulder, grinned into his grin, finally looked up. "I'm not about to volunteer my brain and body for dissection," she said.

The bubble-master nodded. "Understood."

"However, I'll work a trade with you. You wanted to study my body, I don't want to spend another five months retracing my footsteps. Blood and some assorted cells for you people, a quick trip back to Yastroo for us. Enough genetic material for you to study, not enough for me to miss. That will give you something, if not all you sought."

"We do not leave this continent." The Evereener spoke slowly, rather tentatively, a look similar to Esgard's in her pale eyes.

"No bargaining," Aleytys said. "You picked up Esgard and laid his phony trail, don't try to tell me you didn't. You can easily drop the three of us outside the walls of Yastroo. Well?"

The Evareener looked around at the other faces so similar to hers, then she nodded. "Agreed."

7

Shadith stood watch when they took the blood and bits from Aleytys. She was deeply angry and told the bubble-master (in the harshest and most emphatic words the zel-tongue provided) that she thought Aleytys should have pulled the place down about their ears and rid this damned world of one of its worst plagues—so the Evareeners walked on tiptoe to avoid suspicion.

On the third day after their arrival Aleytys went to see Esgard again. She stood over him, pity strong in her, too tired of death and destruction, too weary in body and spirit to feel anger any longer—pity and a little fear, not of him but for herself. She'd thought about this aspect of longlife before but hadn't really understood how much some could covet it, how much they'd go through to achieve it. If the signs of aging didn't show on her soon, she'd have to figure a way to counterfeit them—if she wanted any kind of life on Wolff, any kind of life with Grey. After a long silence she said, "Want me to get you out of this or would you rather take your chances with the Evareeners?"

He looked tired but there was a glow in his eyes, not of life but of desperation. "I'll take my chances," he said.

"We're leaving in half an hour or so," she said. "If you change your mind, send for me."

"I won't."

"I didn't think so. But I had to to say it. Good-bye, crooked man."

"Good-bye, Shareem's daughter. Watch out for the Vrya. I may be crooked, but they're an endless knot."

She nodded, reached out and touched his cheek a moment. His desires were going to punish him for his treachery to her far more than she ever could.

"That is the real key," he said suddenly. "Don't doubt it, Aleytys."

"I don't, Esgard."

"And don't be too hard on Hana. She's what she is."

"I'm too tired to be hard on anyone."

He smiled briefly, closed his eyes, gave himself back to what the machines of Sil Evareen were doing to his body.

She shook her head and left.

8

It was odd to look down on land and water they'd traversed with so much sweat and pain and tedium, to see it passing behind them in an eyeblink, a heartbeat. Aleytys turned to the Evareener female whose name she'd never learned. "We had some gyori, our riding beasts. They ran before the fire with the gear still on. If you could find and strip it off them, I'd be grateful."

The Evareener nodded. "Certainly. That would be done in any case. We like to keep our beasts pure."

The floating islands were trundling in their complex circuits. Shadith looked down at them and sniffed, then explained to Linfyar what she was looking at. Aleytys thought she saw a dark form break water in a steaming leap, trailing a cluster of limbs that looked like threads from this height. She wondered a moment if it was her squale, felt a moment's nostalgia as they left it behind.

The trip had been planned to bring them outside the walls of Yastroo about three hours before dawn. Clouds hung low over the Plain, a thick dark pall that was heavy with snow not quite ready to fall. The bubble started down but hovered a moment in place when Aleytys put a hand on the Evareener's arm. "Wait," she said. She glanced at Shadith, at Linfyar sitting in her lap. "I don't know the limits of this carrier. Could you put us down inside the walls without triggering too many alarms?"

"No."

"Ah well, it was just a thought. Mmm. Do you have any kind of portable light source?"

Shadith chuckled. "Getting slow, Lee. I already thought of that." She held up a short length of crystal rod. As Aleytys watched, one end began to glow, then Shadith shut it off and tucked it away. "You'll have to get us in. I'll light the way."

"Get us in. Wakille went off with the com; could be a problem." She flexed her fingers, ran her thumb across their tips. "I don't think so, that wasn't a very complicated latch, just hope it isn't too heavy."

"If it is you'll just have to try something else."

The Evareener stood. "We are down. I must ask that you hurry." She looked at the blurred mass in the center of the screen, the walls of Yastroo. "I must not be seen."

The bubble was hovering a handspan above the yellowed grass outside the agrifence. They jumped from a narrow slit, knelt as the wind generated by the rapid retreat of the bubble blew debris against them. Aleytys stood, stretched. Linfyar was turning slowly, exploring his surroundings, a little startled by what he perceived around him, but re-invigorated by it; his resilience amazed and amused her. She watched him a moment, then called him and Shadith. "We'd better get started, we've got a way to go and I want you up in my ship before the morning's too old."

VIII

THE CIRCLE CLOSES

Aleytys sauntered down the tree-lined Promenade that cut through the free-trade sector of Yastroo Enclave, sauntered because she didn't have to hurry any longer. No more doubts, only a weary willingness to finish what she's started. Shadith and Linfyar waited above in the ship, safe from Hana's malice, if malice there was. Esgard's daughter wasn't going to be happy with the answers she had for her.

The morning had brought the snow so the lights were fighting cold gray gloom though the forcedome kept the streets clear. The wind that came through was chill and dank, whining along the empty Promenade, flapping the skirts of her black coat about the ankle folds of her soft black boots. She stopped before the door of Esgard House, straightened her back, brushed her hand across her face. No use dragging my feet, she thought, tapped the nameplate, waited for the door to open.

A couple of minutes later she stepped into the pleasant waiting room and found some things changed there. It still had green and blooming plants scattered about (not the same plants, the season had changed, but the effect was the same); its display niches still held small art objects, there were still bright tapestries like those that hung about Esgard's cocoon. But this morning the room hummed with voices; this morning the scattered nooks were filled with men and women of assorted races and species, drinking cha, kaffeh or other hot liquids from hand-glazed stoneware or elaborate, painted porcelain. Waiting. Talking casually. Turning to stare at her as she walked out to the center of the room and stood looking around. It made her nervous. She'd never liked folk staring at her, liked it even less after her double taste of treachery during the past months.

Hana came rushing from the office, two scowling men following her. They stood in the doorway, planted there as if to deny anyone access until their business with Esgard House was finished. Her blue-gray eyes glistening, her face alive with hope and anticipated satisfaction, she put her hand on Aleytys's arm, looked up at her, said, "I didn't know you were back. I didn't expect you for months yet."

More changes, Aleytys thought. *She's dumped a lot of her habits, Madar be blessed for that.* "I'm interrupting your dealing," she said.

"Oh no." Hana looked over her shoulder at the men in the doorway, a glimmer of her old mannerism in the movement, especially when she brought her head back around and smiled up past a fall of pale hair. "We had about agreed to disagree." There was a touch of acid in her soft voice. "If you'll wait a moment." She walked to the door, briskly and with very little dragging in her left leg. "Come back tomorrow," she told the men. "If you're interested in dealing at my prices. If not. . . ." She pushed the hair off her face. "There are other Houses."

The office hadn't changed that much, still small and comfortable, a pleasant combination of earth tones, its only furniture a few float chairs and a massive table set near a broad window meant to let natural light into the room on the days when that light was available. Today, handwoven terreverte drapes fell in soft folds across the glass. Hana led Aleytys to a float chair on one side of the table, took a chair on the other, sat tensely, her hands pressed flat on the polished wood. "You found him?"

"I found him," Aleytys said.

"Sil Evareen?"

"Exists, but it's no dream, more a nightmare." Aleytys tapped the top of the table with her thumbs, nodded at the door in the other wall. "I need to use the access."

Hana caught hold of herself. Her eyes dipped, her head

came down, the straight silken hair fell forward putting her face in shadow. "You can prove that you found him?"

"No games, Hana Esgard." Aleytys examined what she could see of the woman across the table from her. Her coloring was very like the Evareeners', but Hana was so much more vital than the best of them. More alive now than she'd been six months ago. Esgard's absence was good for his daughter. She smiled. He was going to have a hard fight on his hands if he tried to take the business back. If the Evareeners found what they needed in her blood and other bits. She watched Hana, surprised to feel so little anger at the woman who'd lied to her, fooled her, sent her on that long, destructive and useless trek; no anger at being misled, nothing but the need to finish this, to close out the circle. She went on, "I should be raging at you, but I'm too tired." Her mouth curled into a small sour smile. She could taste the sourness and didn't much like it—or herself at this point. It should have been comfortable not to have to fight down that rage, but she didn't feel comfortable, only numb. She passed her hand across her face. "That doesn't mean I'm going to trust you a hair more than I have to, or get less than I'm owed. Esgard told me he left the key with you and I believe him; he was enjoying himself too much when he told me not to be telling the truth. Then he gave me what I'd labored so uselessly to get." Again she passed her hand across her face. "I'm asking now, Hana Esgard. Access to the computer and the satellite link. In another minute I won't bother to ask."

Hana looked up, her face stiff with the effort she was making to control her need. "What did he tell you, what did he give you for me?"

Aleytys took hold of the table's edge and pushed, the float chair bobbing back and away. She stood. "Nothing," she said. "Except to tell you to be patient and wait."

"Nothing?" Hana's knuckles whitened as she clutched the chair arms; she jerked her head, tossing the fall of hair off her face, and stared up at Aleytys, her mouth thinning until it almost disappeared. "Nothing?" The word rose into a high squeak. "He promised. . . ." She broke off, looked away, down, her hair falling back to hide her face.

"Promised you the Vryhh data. If you sent me after him."

"No. No. If I could find him, if I was clever enough to find him." It was a little girl's voice now, her face was crumpling into a little girl's face. "He promised." She went still, breath hissing through her teeth, then she came surging up from the chair to stand bent over the table, a bird of prey. "You're lying. He told you. You're trying to punish me for sending you off. You're lying."

"Don't be a bigger fool than you were before. I was the price he paid for Sil Evareen. He told me. A half-Vryhh for them to experiment on. He used you to get me there, that's all. He tricked you and he tricked me and in the end he tricked himself, because he couldn't keep me, nor could they. Hana, I'm tired. I want off this world. You can let me into the access now or you can try blocking me. Make up your mind."

Hana pressed a shaking hand across her eyes, stood breathing deeply, her other hand clenched. After a minute, she shuddered, drew her hand down her face, looked up. "I haven't been very smart, have I." She didn't wait for an answer. "But I'm not completely stupid. Come." She crossed the room, flattened her hand on the palm plate, stepped aside as the door slid smoothly into the wall. "You know the protocol. Take as much time as you need."

Aleytys seated herself at the console, waited until the door slid shut with its usual lack of fuss or sound. She looked up at the screen, hesitated, feeling a little sick but mostly still numb, her head under pressure as if it was held between the jaws of a nutcracker, then she pressed her lips together, began entering the numbers and letters of the key.

The screen flickered. A face came into the center of it, a bluish metallic face, stripped to essentials, remote and passionless. Android. "Transfer in process," it said, stared at her for several more minutes, flicked away. Aleytys sucked in her breath. A woman's face there. In front of her. Not quite the one she saw in her mirror, but enough like it to make her uneasy. She couldn't quite believe it, she felt unreal. The woman spoke. "Aleytys." A rich contralto, rather like Harskari's voice when she was in a mellow mood. "So you made it to Ibex."

"Shareem," Aleytys said. There was no way she could say

mother to that woman. "Yes, I made it." The banality of the conversation troubled her, it seemed inappropriate, but what do you say to a total stranger even if once upon a time she bore you, suckled you? She waited for the rage, but nothing happened, perhaps she'd blown it all away, scattered it across the face of Ibex.

"I've heard some remarkable stories about you, Aleytys."

"They do get around. Don't believe all you hear."

"I never do. You've made a life for yourself. A good life?"

"On the whole, a good life."

Shareem rubbed at her nose. "I don't know what to say next, what to ask you," she said. "What do you want, Aleytys?"

"Vrithian," Aleytys said. "A choice. Mine." She hesitated, plunged on. "To know you. To know who, what I am."

Shareem's mouth curled into a half-smile, for a moment she looked down at something out of the range of the com, then she nodded. "I see. I'll come for you. I think that would be best."

"Not here. Wolff."

"Of course. Wolff. When?"

Aleytys rubbed at her nose, jerked her hand down, laughed shakily. "Three months standard. There are some loose ends I have to tie off."

"In three months then. You look tired."

Aleytys raised a brow. "Turning maternal? It doesn't suit you." She sighed and slumped in the chair. "I am tired. It's been a long haul."

"I suppose it has. Tell me about it when we meet. Take care." The screen went dark.

Aleytys sat without moving for some minutes. She had no strength in her, none at all. So that's my mother, she thought, but knew Shareem would never be mother to her. A friend perhaps, or an amiable acquaintance, if the meeting went well, an enemy perhaps, if the meeting went badly. That was all. When she felt a little surer of her knees, she got out of the chair and went into the office.

Hana was alone at the table. The drapes were drawn back. She sat with her arms folded, watching dead brown leaves blow across dead brown grass. When Aleytys came through the door, she swung the chair around and stood. "You got through?"

"Yes." Aleytys stopped walking and frowned at her. "Look, Hana, I don't know why I'm doing this, but I've got an idea. Shareem set the key up with Esgard's help. Starts off with my birth date, that you know. Finishes with Shareem's birth date, did you know? No, I thought not. Your father has a peculiar sense of humor, you must know what he's like. The entry code to the Vryhh data, you told me he changed that the day he left. Think of it. You and me, mother and daughter. How it would suit him to play that game with you, to base the code on you, knowing you'd probably never think of anything so simple. A gamble. Like his gamble with me."

Hana's mouth dropped open and Aleytys knew Esgard had won his gamble—up till now anyway. If he'd even made it. "It's only a possibility," she said. "A very slight possibility." Hana blinked, stared at Aleytys but didn't see her, then walked like a dreamer to the access door, palmed it open and went inside.

Aleytys watched her settle herself at the console, begin whispering to herself, her fingers rippling over the sensors. Obsession, she thought, rubbed at her nose, looked at her fingers and smiled. "We've all got them," she said aloud and walked out of the office. The waiting room was empty again, silent.

She passed through the silence, passed through into the street and walked along the Promenade, the wind blowing her coat back away from her legs, blowing her hair back away from her face. For years she'd dreamed of Vrithian, the place that was hers, shaped for her. Dreamed. It was the old impulse behind the magic tales of so many cultures—wish upon a star and get what you so earnestly desire, get it whole and ready, prepared for you, get it without effort. Ibex had, after all, given her something important, given her time to think and paradigms to guide that thinking. There are no magic places, there are only places you build for yourself with hard work and caring and commitment. But not autonomy. Autonomy she had now. Nothing could touch her unless she let it. Nothing is what she had unless she let things touch her.

She passed through the checkpoint onto Starstreet, busy, noisy, and raucous, even in the gray gloom of the snowfall. The noise blasted something loose in her and the numbness began to drain away, even the grayness lightened for her. She lengthened her stride, eager to get off this world and back to Wolff, eager to start her building.